T0137646

ALLIED FORCE: CHRONICLES

by Steve Calloway

Printed in United States of America.

ISBN: 978-1-4269-1777-6 (sc)
ISBN: 978-1-4269-1771-4 (hc)

Library of Congress Control Number: 2011908319

Trafford rev. 11/26/2012

www.trafford.com

North America & international
toll-free: 1 888 232 4444 (USA & Canada)
phone: 250 383 6864 ♦ fax: 812 355 4082

FALLOUT AT FARRAH'S

I T STARTED out as a much-anticipated and well-deserved vacation for two at the luxurious Farrah's Hotel and Casino, located on the bank of the Gila River in southeast Arizona. For the happy couple—Allied Force's number one man, Gatlin, and his number one girl, Blade—the vacation had been in the works for several months.

As the two arrived at the most extravagant hotel and casino in the land, turmoil and chaos were brewing in the desert. And it started within the mind of Tommy J's archenemy, Malakai. As the two heroes were checking into the hotel suite, Blade looked all around the lobby. With its open skylight roof some fifteen stories above her and its furnishings that looked like they'd come from ancient Greece, it was awesome. "It's the most beautiful place I've ever seen," she gasped. "It's perfect for fun and romance, just what I'm looking for, rest and relaxation. I can stand this for ten days, no problem. The problem may be getting me to leave.

"Oh look." She twirled in delight and pointed at the elegant-looking elevators settled in between two giant, beautiful, spiraling staircases. "I love it."

As Gatlin finished signing the couple in and getting their room keys, Blade continued to go on about the luxury hotel and casino. "Do you want to take the stairs instead of the elevator?" she asked. "That way, we can take in all the beauty and history of the place."

The bellhop was relieved to hear Gatlin say, "Let's take the elevator up to our room. Then when we return downstairs, we can take the stairs so that you can take pictures and look at all the beautiful sites. Deal?"

"Yes that's a deal," said Blade as they stepped into the elevator.

*   *   *

It just happened that Malakai was currently looking for some real estate in the United States. Malakai had been hiding and building up his own force to overtake Tommy J and Allied Force. Malakai's headquarters were currently located in South America.

Now that his team was complete and he felt that its forces were strong enough to take over Allied Force—and in doing so, take over the world—Malakai had turned his attention to the luxurious Farrah's Hotel and Casino. It was big enough to house all of his members and had an excellent security system and all the luxuries of a home. Most of all, it was located on American soil, across the country from Allied Force's base, which was located in South Carolina. It was perfect. Now all he had to do was take the hotel from the current owners, which shouldn't be a problem. The characters he was sending into the desert should be able to take over Farrah's by tonight.

The plan was in action. As soon as the people that Malakai had sent to the United States had taken the building, they could move their headquarters north. *It's just too easy*, Malakai thought to himself.

Malakai had handpicked his army for the job at hand. He'd selected each member for his or her size, strength, and individual special abilities. Among the handpicked army members was Psycho, a real modern-day mad scientist and the creator of all of Malakai's mutants. Also going would be Psycho's favorite creation to date—his robotic defender of himself, Ratchet.

Ratchet was Legion's equivalent to Gatlin, in metal form. Ratchet got his name from his upper body. It turned at the waist, rotating 360 degrees in just a few seconds so he never had his back to his enemy. His feet were unidirectional, which meant he could walk a distance in one direction, and, without having to turn himself completely around, he could go back in the other direction. All he had to do was turn his upper body 180 degrees and then head back the way that he came. In addition, Ratchet could travel upwards of 20 miles per hour. He was equipped with lasers located on each shoulder, a rocket launcher attached to his back and protruding over his shoulders and head that could rotate with his upper body 360 degrees in a split second, and 45mm cannons on each arm with unlimited ammunition—similar to Gatlin's, only of a bigger caliber. Gatlin's arm-mounted Gatling guns fired 30mm cannons. Ratchet had the capability of crushing a car like a soda can in just minutes. He came with a very large sticker price. But for Malakai money was no problem. Because of all this, Ratchet was Psycho's pride and joy.

Along with Psycho and Ratchet, Malakai was also sending Jackyl. He was an Australian fire-blowing, pyromaniac freak from the circus, as well as an unbelievable gymnast and acrobat. Jackyl walked with his protector, the enormous and very strong but not very bright part man, part gorilla known as Gorman.

Then there was Mite, an archery specialist from the Orient and quite a looker.

Also joining the group was Gage. Gage was a master of all arms. She was from Great Britain. She was also one of the most beautiful women on the planet. But she was quite nasty when she wanted to be. And she was Gatlin's ex-girlfriend—they had dated before she became an evil vixen.

Then there was Wrath. One of the world's ugliest beings—which was why he kept his face covered with a monk's cloak most of the time—Wrath possessed the ability to control the minds of the dead. Wrath dealt with lost souls from the spiritual world of the tortured. He could bring beings back from the dead, whether they had been dead for centuries or just minutes. And finally he had the ability of the haunting illusions such as loved one's dead in horrific ways, as well as different forms of gruesome death's that seem so real, it would cause people to get disoriented and lose their own concentration, not to mention actually scaring them to a point that they couldn't even function for periods of time, regardless how tough they are normally.

Grunge was a giant. He stood six foot nine and weighed 335 pounds. Grunge was made of a conglomeration of Psycho's bad experiments. He was very strong and could kill or maim very easily. He was very mellow and gentle, much like a modern-day Frankenstein—until he was injected with a serum of Psycho's. The serum enraged the beast, and Grunge would do whatever Psycho ordered him to do. Grunge had a very bad reputation that was extremely unfair because, without Psycho's orders, Grunge was a very gentle and peaceful being. His appearance, though, was horrific and terrifying.

Ram was made much the same way as Gorman had been, although Ram was half man and half ram. Ram was very powerful, and he could deliver one hell of a head butt. However, he was very smart. A loner, Ram traveled on his own. Unlike Gorman, Ram could speak. He came from the snow-capped mountains of Switzerland.

Hailing from Australia, a modern-day, real-life Catwoman, also joined the group. This viscous woman used speed and cunning, along with her various whips; assorted blades; and her very powerful, and very sharp, retractable claws. She also possessed the ability to climb just about anything in a matter of seconds. Believe it or not, more often than not, she landed on her feet. Like Gage she was extremely attractive. She was known as Mynx.

Last but not least was the very sick and heartless Nazi—a German officer well decorated for his wartime success during World War II. You're probably thinking that he must be old enough to be a grandfather. Well, you see, Nazi was killed in action toward the end of the war. He is a product of Wrath. Nazi is almost unkillable, or so Legion claims. This remains to be seen. Nazi had never met Allied Force.

That was the group of menace and mayhem that Malakai has chosen to take the hotel.

*　*　*

"I can't wait to run this casino into bankruptcy with my gambling knowledge and talents," Gatlin said.

"Don't even go there, sweetheart," Blade said with a smile. "You can't even win at solitaire."

"Well maybe not, but I won you over, didn't I?" boasted Gatlin.

"You didn't win me over. I thought you were cute and I felt sorry for your no-luck self," said Blade.

Blade and Gatlin had begun dating about six months after Gatlin found out that Gage, his lady at the time, for whom he had really strong feelings, was secretly, slowly working her way into Legion for Malakai. Legion paid her better, and she could hold a much higher position within the organization than she did in Allied Force. Gage was always all about money and power. What took the cake, so to speak, was when Gatlin found out that Gage had been giving Malakai information about Gatlin's armor and guns, as well as information about several other members of Allied Force.

Thus came Ratchet. His entire body was made of material similar to that of Gatlin's armor. The fact that Ratchet used Gatling guns as his primary weapons wasn't a coincidence.

What Gatlin didn't know was whether Ratchet's cannons heated up and overheated like Gatlin's tended to do.

Gage broke Gatlin's heart. However, Gage was still in love, or at least infatuated, with Gatlin. Malakai was using for bad the same things that Tommy J was using for good.

Tommy J gave Gatlin his body armor and guns. He invented them after Gatlin's parents were killed by a missile from Nazi—a hit ordered by Malakai eighteen years earlier. Gatlin's parents had been en route to Gatlin's football practice to pick him up.

*   *   *

Trevor (Gatlin) was just ten years old. The plan was the same as always—pick up Trevor from practice and then go by the sitter's and pick up his little brother, Chad (Nuke). Chad was only six years old at the time. Tommy J—being a friend of the family for years, as well as both Trevor and Chad's godfather—was also at practice that day. He had happened to have enough time to stop by and catch the end of practice. Unbeknownst to his parents, Trevor asked Tommy J if he wanted to take him home and stop off for ice cream. The two did that a lot.

Tommy J told Trevor that they would have to wait until his parents got there because there was no way to contact them. (Back then, there were no car phones or cell phones.) All the other boys' parents and the coaches were already gone. So Trevor and Tommy J played catch while they waited for Trevor's parents to arrive. Upon their arrival, Trevor would ask if they could go to the ice cream shop. Trevor had it all planned out. He knew that, if he didn't include his little brother, Chad, the chances for ice cream would decrease considerably. So Trevor would suggest that his mom and dad could go by and pick up Chad from the sitter's; then they could all meet Tommy J and himself at the ice cream shop.

In a few minutes, Trevor's parents arrived; Trevor took off running toward the car. Behind Trevor, Tommy J, still holding the football under one arm, walked toward the car as well. Young Trevor was about twenty yards away from the car. He could see his parents' faces. They were proud of Trevor and of Chad as well. The four were a very close and happy middle-income American family.

Then it happened—BOOM!

The car exploded—killing Trevor and Chad's parents instantly. The powerful blast sent young Trevor flying back. Trevor landed hard and very awkwardly on his hands and ribs, shattering both arms from the elbows down and crushing his chest.

Soon after he heard the blast, Tommy J saw the source of the terrible explosion. What appeared to be a German soldier in an old World War II fighter plane had fired the missile that Tommy J believed was intended for him, not Trevor and Chad's parents.

Many years later, Tommy J would learn the reason for the viscous attack on people who were both good and the parents of two very young and good boys. According to Malakai, the shot was a random shot, not intended to kill Tommy J but just to change his life forever.

It worked. From that day forward, Tommy J's life would never again be the same.

You see, Malakai and Tommy J were both young scientists at the same college. At sometime during their friendship, Malakai got in with the wrong crowd and began working with blood and DNA and some really out-of-this-world witchcraft and heavy devil worship stuff. Tommy J broke off the friendship and partnership, but Malakai needed Tommy J's knowledge and brilliance. When Malakai could no longer have that type of relationship with Tommy J, Malakai decided to branch out on his own. At the time Trevor's parents were killed, Tommy J hadn't seen or heard from Malakai in a couple of years.

When Tommy J's best friends in the world got married and had Trevor, they asked Tommy J to be the godfather of their new baby boy. Tommy J tearfully accepted. Tommy J did everything with Trevor and his baby brother, Chad. Tommy J was not just the boys' godfather. Thomas and Cathy Baron had appointed Tommy J. Trevor and Chad's legal guardian in the event that anything should happen to them. On that day, unfortunately, something had happened—something too horrific to put into words. Thus, Tommy J had become the new parent of Trevor and Chad.

Trevor stayed in the hospital for over four months. Upon his release, Tommy J took both him and young Chad home. Now a father figure to two young boys, Tommy J was unable to continue to attend classes at the college. Slowly, as the family of three adjusted to the situation, Tommy J began to pick his studies back up at home. The trio lived in the enormous and beautiful mansion that Tommy's parents had left to him, along with a seemingly endless amount of wealth, after their passing just a few months prior.

Tommy J began to home-school the boys. Trevor was unable to use his arms very well, even after numerous surgeries and therapy. Moreover, he was struggling to cope with the very sudden and horrific loss of his parents, as well as his arms, especially his hands and fingers. Trevor could no longer play football; he had been a very good linebacker and running back. It had been Trevor's dream to someday play in the NFL. Not only did the boy have excellent skills, he had a great work ethic, tremendous discipline, and always stayed in shape. Trevor was on his way to fulfilling his dream even at the tender age of ten.

Tommy J decided that he had to do something. And he did. He took night classes and eventually got his medical degree, specializing in surgery. He became a great surgeon, but not for the money or for area hospitals; he did it for one young boy—his godson. He combined his excellent surgical skill with his passion to give Trevor as much of his life back as he could and formed a plan.

After the surgery in Tommy J's basement hospital, Trevor regained some movement in both arms, and, hopefully, Trevor's chest wall would begin to heal itself with the bone grafts to young Trevor's chest and ribs. After six weeks of very intense physical therapy, Trevor began to show great improvement. His chest and ribs were getting stronger, as well as his arms and hands—although his fingers weren't improving on par. With the awesome workout that Trevor did three times a day, every day, sick or not, Trevor had literally made Tommy J tired just watching him.

One day, the phone rang when Tommy J and little Chad were outside playing. Trevor answered the phone; the caller asked for Tommy J. As Tommy J picked up the phone in the other room, Trevor overheard his godfather talking very hatefully and loudly, even threatening whoever it was on the phone. Upset, Trevor decided to listen to the rest of the conversation on the other phone.

Tommy J was talking to Malakai. As Trevor listened, Malakai told Tommy J that, when he found him, he would take both young boys from him permanently if he didn't give him the formulas or something like that so that Malakai could build an army of mutants and rule the world.

After the phone conversation, Trevor asked Tommy J about the man on the phone. "Was that the man who killed my parents and left me crippled and me and Chad parentless? Are you really going to kill him like you told him on the phone? Tommy J explained, "Killing is wrong, and the man on the phone is a mad man. I will stop him from hurting anyone anymore".

The years passed, and the boys got older, but the phone calls continued. Then Tommy J decided to take care of things in an entirely new manner.

Trevor was now fourteen and very buff and strong. His arms worked well, and his chest was a lot better and stronger; however, some of his fingers still didn't work well, although his hands did. Trevor graduated from high school at the age of fourteen. He hit the books as hard as he hit the weights, so that he could get them out of the way.

His little brother, now ten years old, began to work out with Trevor. The two become very close.

All the time, the threats continued.

Trevor told Tommy J, "I will revenge my parents' death, with or without you."

*   *   *

Now as strong as an ox, Trevor began training to become a police officer. With Tommy J's guidance, Trevor tried target practice with a pistol. Trevor is a great shot, but his fingers would only allow him to shoot just a couple of rounds at a time. Trevor knew that he would have to shoot longer than that to become a police officer.

Tommy J knew Trevor's determination, and he knew that his godson was strong, intelligent, street smart and as mature as any twenty-five-year-old person at just fourteen. Tommy J also knew that it could take a very long time for Trevor, if ever, to regain full functioning of his fingers. So Tommy J became more of a scientist and inventor, as well as a really great friend, than a parent, although he did a fine job at that as well. Tommy J told Trevor he would make his dream come true. He would invent a customized gun just for Trevor to shoot. All that Trevor had to do was pick out the gun he wanted to use and Tommy J would do the rest. Trevor, extremely excited, pulled out gun books and began researching the different types of guns that he might want to use. One evening, as Chad sat next to Trevor doing his homework, American history, Trevor continued his hunt for just the right gun for himself. Chad asked Trevor to help him with his homework. So Trevor took a break from the gun search. Chad was only ten years old, but like Trevor, he was using Tommy J's schooling method of getting it out of the way, so he could get on with his life.

Suddenly, Trevor yelled out loudly, "That's it; that's the gun! Why didn't I think of it sooner? With that gun, I can become a superhero. Right now, I'm too young to be a police officer. I think you have to be eighteen. That's four years away. Plus, I'd have to go to the police academy for probably two more years and maybe even longer. I'm ready now, Tommy J. You even said so."

"Calm down, boy," Tommy J replied. "Let me see what gun you have picked out. Besides, the idea was so that you could go and become a police officer, not a superhero," he added.

Trevor showed Tommy J the gun.

"Damn, boy. How do you expect me to find a Gatling? Not to mention rebuild and modify it so that it's light enough for you to carry around. Besides, the Gatling requires a strap of bullets. You can't just load it and carry it around. Another thing, all that friction makes the gun extremely hot. The idea was that I would modify a handgun that could be somehow strapped onto your forearms. Trevor, that gun would burn you badly and quickly—in just seconds. You could hardly be a superhero if your own gun kept burning you," said Tommy J.

"Oh, come on, Dad. You told me you would and could make me any gun that I wanted. This is the one. You also said that I could live as close to a normal life as anyone else. You told both Chad and me that we could be anything that we wanted to be, as long as we were willing to work at it. I'm willing to work for this. I need this gun," said Trevor. "Besides, I know that you can do it," he added. "You're the smartest man in the world. I can help you, because I want to be the second smartest man in the world. Come on; please, Dad?"

Tommy J melted—his acquiescence was a combination of hearing the boy call him dad, not once but twice, and listening to the boy. Trevor was right. He was the best kid, both very smart and responsible. Tommy J knew that he couldn't crush the boy's dreams—not after all the encouragement that Tommy J had given him in an effort to help him recover, not only from his terrible injuries but, at the same time, from the horrific loss of his own parents and the tragedy to which he had been an eye witness at such a young age. "Whether it's right or wrong, Trevor, if you dedicate yourself to helping your brother Chad, as well as to occasionally cooking breakfast, lunch, and dinner— well, you'll have to because I will be extremely busy on this project—I'll do it. Neither of you will see much of me. If I commit to this, you had better commit as well. Fair enough?" he told his godson.

"I'm already committed to this, Dad," Trevor said, giving Tommy J a hug. "Thanks so much. You have made my dreams come true. I love you, Dad."

"Hey, Trevor, can I have my book back please," Chad said, "so I can finish my homework? Then I can get a gun and be your sidekick, like Batman and Robin"

* * *

says Chad. About five months later, a plane crash over northern Russia killed over one hundred people.

Trevor once again answered the telephone.

"Hey, little man," the caller said, "do me a big favor."

Trevor, having no idea who was on the end of the line agreed.

"Tell Tommy J that I, Malakai, was responsible for the plane crash and that, if Tommy J doesn't give me what I want, there will be many more. I really enjoy killing people; I especially enjoyed killing your parents. If Tommy J doesn't hurry, more plane crashes, among other tragedies, are going to take place. Your little brother could be one," Malakai concluded.

Trevor wouldn't tell Tommy J about the phone call for a long time.

After the phone call and realizing that he had actually spoken to the one person who was responsible for the deaths of his parents, Trevor began to study the tactics of the Green Berets, the Navy SEALs, Army Delta Force, and the Marines Special Force Recon. Trevor gathered knowledge and began training to be them all, in one young man—a superhero.

Trevor didn't read comics because he didn't have any special powers and he couldn't fly. He was just a crippled boy who was going to become a superhero and save the world. If his little brother was serious about being his sidekick, well than Chad would have to get his diploma and then figure out what he was going to shoot or use as a weapon. Then they could save the world together.

Chad was ready with an answer to Trevor's question. "I want to blow stuff up, using all sorts of bombs and explosives," he said.

Trevor learned everything that he possibly could from books, movies, documentaries, and spy novels.

Trevor's birthday was just a couple of months away; he was going to turn fifteen. Now he started thinking that, since he couldn't fly, he would learn to drive. *What kind of superhero can I be if I can't get anywhere to save people?* he thought to himself.

Chad graduated from eighth grade in April, just as he turned eleven years old. He was now ready for high school books. Trevor gave Chad an express schooling, letting him learn enough but doing most of the work for Chad. By doing so, this gave Chad more time to study bombs and explosives.

Finally May rolled around and, with it, Trevor's birthday. For his birthday, Tommy J presented his godson with his only present, the present that Trevor wanted—his gun. Trevor saw the present and felt how heavy it was. An

I-know-what-this-is smile spread across Trevor's face. There it was—the gun of guns. His very own custom-made-to-fit-Trevor gun. Trevor pulled it out of the box and tried to figure out how to put it on and use it. Which side was the front and which was the back? Everything was complicated.

"Hold on, boy, before you try it on. Open the rest of your gifts," says Tommy J.

As the young Trevor—*the hero*—began to open his other gifts, he couldn't imagine what they could possibly be, as all he'd asked for was a gun.

The phone rang. Again two more planes had crashed—one in the United States and the other in the Atlantic Ocean.

"Yes, it was me and my people," Malakai told Tommy J. If you would look at the locations, you'll see that the first one that I told the boy about was over Russia and then the second one was in the Atlantic. The third was in your very home state of South Carolina. See, Tommy J, tragedy is coming your way if you don't cooperate. The next tragedy could be in your hometown, of maybe even your own backyard. If the plane crashes weren't enough, the next tragedy will, indeed, involve the boys.

"So you need to meet me for lunch tomorrow at the same café that we use to eat at in college. Bring the research. I won't be alone, so don't try anything. You better show up. I am watching the house. Have a nice day and tell the boy happy birthday for me, would you? Thanks. See you tomorrow." With that, Malakai hung up.

Tommy J returned to the party. He saw that Trevor had opened all of the packages and that the boy didn't understand what all of the items in them were.

"Dad, what is all this stuff?" Trevor asked. "Why do I have two guns and this steel shirt and these other pieces of steel? What is all of this? Is one of them Chad's or what?"

"Ha ha, you got a steel shirt for your birthday," laughed Chad.

"Shut up, Chad," Trevor told Chad.

"No it's all yours," Tommy cut in. "That isn't a steel shirt. That is your body armor. Come here. Let's strap it on."

"But why do I need all of this stuff just to shoot?" asked Trevor.

Tommy J tells him, "Well, boy, if you're going to be a superhero, you're going to need protection and power, so there they are. So come here and let's put you all together and see how it fits and if you can even move around well. If it's too heavy, then at least you can still shoot."

The body armor fit like a glove. The other two pieces of steel went on Trevor's forearms, and his guns were attached to them and not his arms in order to protect him from the intense heat that the guns produced. Plus, they looked really cool. When the guns weren't on his arms, he could use the plates of steel as a weapon, allowing him to deliver blows without hurting his arms. The body armor matched the plates for looks, and served as primary protection of his chest wall, which was, to this day getting stronger and stronger.

Tommy J strapped the guns on Trevor's arms without loading them. He just wanted to make sure that Trevor would be able to move his arms around as if they had nothing on them.

Trevor did just that, throwing his powerful arms around as if nothing was on them.

Tommy J then opened up each of the gun's ammunition housings and loaded them both up full. The guns were only nine inches long in total length. Each individual barrel rested two inches up from the wrists and hands. This way, the fired rounds wouldn't hit Trevor's wrists and hands. Each individual shell was only about the size of the tip of a ballpoint pen, which allowed maximum capacity in minimum space. The ammunition straps held about fifteen hundred rounds each but had the exact grain and grade as the 30mm cannon; only they were reduced in size. It was a $4 million plus gift.

Tommy J told the boys to go out back so that Trevor could try out his new superhero weapon. Tommy J also told the boys about the telephone call from Malakai, saying that he had no choice but to give Malakai what he wanted. He explained that, even though that it all sounded strange and unbelievable, with Malakai on the loose, everyone was in danger. They had no way of knowing how many followers Malakai had. Malakai was capable of inventing and creating weapons, machines, and even create people in the future. Tommy J went on to tell the boys that Malakai could, in fact, take over the world. And if Tommy J tried to warn someone about Malakai, well, nobody would believe him. He also knew that, if he did, he would be putting all three of their lives on the line.

"This is serious," Tommy J told the boys. "I will make both of you weapons, suits, and vehicles. I'll even get you some more people to join the group, and we can become the good guys."

It all sounded unbelievable to both Trevor and Chad.

"But if you are willing and want to do good for the world, as well as get rid of the bad and enforce the law of the new world, well then you could do that. But if you are scared—and being scared is a part of life; everyone gets scared—that's okay.

"However," Tommy J added before the boys could respond. "If you just want to be kids and grow up and be husbands and fathers, well that is just fine with me. I can go after Malakai with some other people that I know. And being a father is a pretty tough job in itself, but an extremely rewarding one. Fathers are heroes too, as well as mothers. So what do you think, boys—superheroes who are great and tough or father heroes who are great and tough?"

The boys didn't think very hard or that long. They gave Tommy J an answer that he wasn't expecting. "Dad, we want to be both," Trevor explained. "If you can do it, so can we." Chad nodded in agreement as his brother continued,

"You can train us with some of your friends and give Malakai the papers that he wants so that bad things will stop happening to innocent people. We will train long and hard, and we'll stop him before he even gets a chance to use the papers anyway.

"By the way," Trevor added, "the suit is awesome. Can I say something without getting in trouble?"

"Sure," answered Tommy J.

"I'm lookin' and feelin' pretty badass right now. So can I get a name, or should everyone just call me *badass*?"

Chad just laughed because Trevor had said a bad word, not once but twice.

"No, we will have to give you a name," Tommy J replied. "I've been working on it. If you weren't going to come up with a name, then I was going to suggest a name that suited a man with guns like that. How about, Gatlin?"

"Yeah Gatlin," Trevor replied enthusiastically. "That name is badass just like me. Just call me Gatlin from now on.

"But what can we call Chad?" asked young Gatlin.

"Well I've been kinda working on Chad's name also," Tommy J admitted. "I overheard the two of you saying that Chad wants to blow stuff up, and I have seen all the explosive books lying around. So tell me, Chad, what is the most powerful bomb in the world?"

"The most powerful bomb in the world would be the . . . uh . . . nuclear bomb," Chad replied.

"That's right. So if you're going to be the baddest bomb specialist in the world, how about we call you Nuke?" suggested Tommy J.

"Nuke, yeah that's a cool name. Nuke," said young Nuke.

The boys and Tommy J start training to become superheroes immediately.

That's how Gatlin became Gatlin, Nuke became Nuke, and Malakai became able to mutate people and animals to build his army known as Legion—and archenemy number one.

*   *   *

As Blade and Gatlin finished their room service dinner, they enjoyed some quality time together for a change. They didn't get much quality time with the busy schedules they had.

"I'm going to take a shower. We need to start getting ready for the show downstairs tonight," said Blade.

As Blade got in the shower, Gatlin got his clothes ready. Then he went out to the balcony to sit and look at the beautiful Arizona sunset. Really, he went out to smoke a cigar. Blade didn't like him to smoke. So he smoked on the balcony and awaited his turn in the shower.

*   *   *

Meanwhile, downstairs entering the hotel were Gage, Mynx, Mite, and Jackyl. Coming in shortly after them was Psycho. All appeared normal, not attracting attention. The mutants were in a cargo van parked just outside the front door of the hotel. The five troublemakers spread out and took their positions. Gage went into the casino. Mite stopped in the lobby, just left of the front desk and directly in front of the security doors. Mynx stopped at the entrance of the casino, next to two security guards and began to flirt, allowing her very low-cut top to hang even lower. Jackyl looked around the lobby and then moved toward the elevators and the stairs. Psycho, looking very businesslike, went to the front desk. All their people were in place inside the hotel.

Outside, Nazi and Ram worked their way around the building to end all communications to and from the hotel, as well as deactivate all security alarms and the hotel's cameras.

Back inside the hotel, Psycho gave Mite the nod to go as planned. Mite let both Jackyl and Mynx know. Mynx then let Gage know that it was a go.

Chaos erupted. Mite shot four of her poisonous darts and hit four security guards. The four men struggled for a couple of seconds, and then they were sleeping. Mynx, her retractable claws filled with the same poison put the two security officers she was flirting with to sleep as well. Gage, on her mark with her silencer-equipped guns as well as the same sleep agent as both Minx and Mite used had began to drop employees and guests in the casino. Psycho took out the front desk in the same manner. He then notified the van, via headset communications.

Gorman, Wrath, Grunge, and Ratchet secured the parking lot while Ram and Nazi entered the hotel through the kitchen. The van crew then entered the hotel and secured all the doors—nobody in, nobody out. Psycho, at the front desk, set up non-traceable communications with Malakai.

The rest of the group moved the hostages into the dining room. There was no escape route from the dining room, unless you passed through the front lobby, where Ratchet would be guarding once they get all the hostages transferred into the dining room. They supplied the dining room with food and water so that, when the hostages did come to, they could eat and drink; there were even bathrooms accessible, just off the dining area. It was a perfect holding cell for a couple hundred people. The group wasn't going to hurt the hostages; they were just holding them until everything and everyone was secure and Malakai could inform the authorities that the building now belonged to him—at which time he would use the hostages as collateral.

Psycho did get in contact with Malakai. "Malakai, we're in. The kitchen, lobby, casino, dining room, pool, and recreation area, as well as the parking lot, are secure. Six minutes; count seventeen security cops, thirty-one employees and eighteen guests in custody; ready to begin room sweeps with two-member teams. Will call back when totally secure. This place is so far out in the middle of nowhere, in the desert, it is perfect to set up shop. It will be ours in about an hour."

"All right, people, listen up." The group, except for Jackyl, gathered around Psycho.

Jackyl was guarding the stairway, the only way to get from floor to floor now that Nazi and Ram had fixed the elevators so that they would no longer operate. Jackyl would await his prey, and as guests came down the stairs, he would fill them with the sleeping agent. There was about a two-second delay in between the dart hitting the victim and the victim sleeping. Thus, there would be no screaming. The dining room and the casino, with the doors closed, became soundproof from the rest of the hotel.

"We'll break into two-member teams," Psycho told the group. "There are fifteen floors, and every two-member team will be responsible for getting the guests from their assigned floors transferred to the dining room. The teams are as follows: Mite and I will take floors 1, 6, and 11—oh damn, the first floor is already secure. We will be team number one. Team two is Mynx and Ram. You have floors 2, 7, and 12. Team three is Wrath and Grunge. You have floors 3, 8, and 13. Gage and Nazi will be team four. You have floors 4, 9, and 14. And finally, team five will be Jackyl and Gorman. You will, of course, get floors 5, 10, and 15. The honeymoon suites are on fifteen, according to the hotel legend. There are only two rooms because they are such large rooms. That is the special floor, according to this. Unless you want to go swimming or eat in the dining room, you never have to leave your room. And finally of course Ratchet will be guarding the first floor, stairway so that no guest's can escape if any get by any of you.

"Okay, let's get moving. It is now 6:20 p.m. If you aren't going to make it back by 7:30 p.m., you need to contact me. If I don't hear from you, you better be here by 7:30 sharp. We will get a chance to play when the building is secure. Hell it belongs to us. What are they going to do? Call the cops? Oooh, I am scared. Enough talk; get going now. Leave please," Psycho ordered.

*   *   *

Blade finished up in the shower and was drying her hair. Excitedly, she called to Gatlin, "Its 6:53. You need to get up and in the shower. Damn, sweetheart, you were taking a nap. Are you tired?"

"No. I just got relaxed watching the sunset. No, I'm not tired. I got my second wind. I am ready to wine and dine and, more importantly, gamble," said Gatlin.

"Okay, well hurry up. I'm going to finish unpacking and put my makeup on," said Blade.

*   *   *

Downstairs, Legion was finishing their room sweeps. Gage and Nazi finished the fourteenth floor as Jackyl and Gorman began to climb one more flight of stairs to the fifteenth and final floor of the sweep.

As Jackyl and Gorman reached the fifteenth floor, it was 7:03 p.m. Jackyl called Psycho. "We are now on the fifteenth floor. We will, hopefully be down no later than 7:30 p.m. but that is a lot of climbing."

Jackyl then turned to Gorman. "In order to make this faster, we'll each take a room up here. You take 1501, and I'll go to the other end of the hallway and do 1502."

Gorman appeared to understand Jackyl. He watched Jackyl walk down the long hallway, just to make sure that Jackyl got there okay. Then Gorman kicked down the door of room 1501, causing the door to look like it had been made from particle board.

Now it was Jackyl's turn. He first tried the knob. "Damn, they are always locked," he said to himself, not noticing one of the bellhops returning from the roof from his break. "I am so tired of this shit." He looked down the hallway and saw that Gorman was still inside 1501. So Jackyl decided to knock on the door of 1502.

*   *   *

Blade got up from her vanity. She had just finished putting on her makeup and was wearing her sweat pants shorts and a cut-off T-shirt. She really didn't want to answer the door looking like this, but why should she care? Her man was in the shower singing "Born to Be Wild."

Blade opens the door. To her surprise, there stood Jackyl. For a split second, the two just looked at one another. Blade knew that one of her belts was sitting next to the door. (Blade wore many belts when she was in full gear. Each held several different blades, knives, stars, and a sword. Thus, she was called "Blade.")

From the belt, Blade drew a knife and hurled it at Jackyl, hitting him in the shoulder. Jackyl screamed out like a little girl with a scraped knee and fell against the wall behind him.

Hearing the scream from down the hall, Gorman recognizes that it had come from Jackyl. Gorman exited room 1501 and ran down the long hallway, bursting through the dividing doors in the middle of the hallway. Gorman's massive strides shook the floor as he moved, causing plants and pictures to fall to the floor and leaving a path of destruction behind him.

Jackyl, caught by total surprise, reached for his flame blower. Before he could grab it, he felt another sharp pain in his abdomen. Blade had hit him with another of her knives, followed by *BAMM*! Blade kicked Jackyl in the face. She then did a 360-degree turn and, *BAMM*! She kicked Jackyl in the face again, all the while calling out for Gatlin. But Gatlin was still in the shower, and he heard nothing.

During the struggle with Jackyl, Blade's room door closed behind her. She reached to her belt, feeling for her "Death Sword." She heard and felt the thumping of Gorman coming down the hallway toward her before she saw him. And then Blade did not only see, but she could hear, the rage of the untamed beast. As of this moment, Blade was number one on Gorman's hit list. Knowing that she didn't have her full arsenal with her or her room key and that Gatlin was still in the shower singing and couldn't hear her calls, Blade had to make a decision. She could use up precious time and energy finishing off Jackyl or take on the raging beast, knowing that she didn't have enough weapons or strength. So Blade took the third option. She ran for her life, hoping the beast, Gorman, would stop to help his dear friend, Jackyl, rather than give chase to her.

* * *

Not really sure what had happened to his little friend, Gorman picked Jackyl up and looked into his eyes. Then he gave a horrific roar, as he carried Jackyl back downstairs. He knew that he had to get Jackyl some help, but he didn't know how to get the others to understand that Blade was in the building.

Gatlin, hearing Gorman's roar, turned the shower off. He called out to Blade, but there was no answer. As Gatlin looked around the room, he noticed that Blade's outfit that she was going to wear tonight was still on the bed, and her room key was on top of the television. More importantly, one of her belts was missing, along with her Death Sword.

Gatlin knew immediately that something was wrong. Blade wouldn't have left without telling him. Gatlin got dressed; strapped on his armor, his guns, and his attitude; and opened the door to the hall. The first thing that Gatlin noticed was the blood on the floor and the wall. Then he noticed one of Blade's knives lying in the blood. He looked down the hallway and saw all the destruction. It looked like someone had driven a tank down the hallway. Then his mind began to wonder about what had happened. Where was Blade? Was this her blood or someone else's? Why had she left? It just wasn't adding up.

As Gatlin turned to follow the blood trail that led down the hallway, he heard a noise, coming from behind him at the bottom of the stairs that led to the roof. Gatlin raised his mighty guns and looked at the corner.

"Hold on! Don't shoot! I just work here!" a very frightened voice explained.

"Who the hell are you, punk?" asked Gatlin.

"I'm Chris. I mean, my name is Chris, sir. Please don't kill me. I'm just a bellhop," said the very scared Chris.

"What in the hell are you doin' in the corner hiding behind a plastic tree?" asked Gatlin.

"I was coming down from the roof from my break when I saw this lady beating the shit out of this little, funny-looking dude. She called out a name several times. I believe she was saying, Gatlin, but I can't be for sure of it. Then, as she was kicking the shit out of this little dude, this huge, pissed-off-looking monkey dude came running down the hallway, roaring and yelling. The lady then turned and ran down the stairway. The monkey dude looked at her for a second and then picked up the little guy, roared a couple more times, and then turned and headed back down the hallway that way. Then I lost sight of them. I guess they went down the other stairway, but I don't know for sure.

"I was going to try and catch the lady and take her to the security office so she could get some help. Then you came out, and I freaked out again because—well, look at you—you're huge with guns on your arms. Are you the good guys? I mean you and that lady? Because I don't know. But those other two guys were pretty scary-looking. They looked like bad guys," Chris concluded.

"Yeah, Chris, we are that good guys. I'm Gatlin. The lady is my girlfriend. Her name is Blade. We are members of an elite group of people known as Allied Force. The two bad guys that you saw are bad news. I'll bet you anything they're not alone. Those sorts only run in packs. I'd also bet that the phones don't work and that, right now, the hotel belongs to them and their friends.

"Now they will soon know that Blade is here, and it probably won't take them long to figure out that she is here with me. Then they will come looking for us. Do you have any place that you can go?" Gatlin asked.

"Just back to work, but if the bad guys run the hotel, I'm sure that I don't have a job and I have been replaced. I don't think that I want to go down there," said Chris.

"Okay, Chris, you stay here or on the roof, if you feel safer there. I'm gonna find Blade. I have to find out how many of them are here. Stay out of sight and don't make a sound. Most of all, stay out of the rooms." Gatlin dropped the hallway phone back into its nook. "Yup, the phones are dead," he said.

"I can do that, sir," said Chris.

"I hopefully won't be long. I'll be back for you in a little while, so take cover and be quiet," ordered Gatlin.

Chris headed back toward his hiding place on the roof, as Gatlin headed down the stairway that Blade had taken earlier.

* * *

As Blade made her way around the hotel, she wondered if Gatlin was all right and whether Jackyl and Gorman were still upstairs.

When should I go back to the room? she wondered. *Gatlin better be all right.* Blade prayed that Gatlin was fine. Then she worked her way down the hallway of the thirteenth floor planning to get back to the fifteenth floor the opposite way, just in case Jackyl and Gorman had followed her down the same staircase.

She saw Wrath and Grunge walking down the hallway toward her. Blade quickly stepped back into the stairway. As she began to back up, she heard voices above her. The voices were those of Gage and Nazi. Soon after, Blade began to hear more voices coming from below her.

She was surrounded. *Oh where is Gatlin?* Blade thought to herself, as she strapped on her belt. On it, she carried another set of her blades, leaving six knives, eight throwing stars, and her Death Sword. Blade had no choice and nowhere to go. She hunkers down on the staircase between floors thirteen and fourteen, with knives in hand and her fingers crossed, all the time hoping that God would answer her prayer—that Gatlin was ok and that he would show up and end this nightmare that she was now living.

The voices that Blade heard below her now were those of Mynx and Ram. It sounds like they were going to walk right up the stairs that she was hiding under. *If they walk up these stairs, they are going to see me plain as day* Blade thought. So she moved back into the shadows of the corner under the stairs. Just as she was moving back, she heard footsteps coming down the hallway. She knew they belonged to Wrath and Grunge. Blade hoped that, if she doesn't make a noise, the two would walk down the stairs in front of her with their backs to her. That was a lot better than the other two below her coming up the stairs; they would probably be able to see her even though she'd moved to the corner.

What in the hell are they doing here? Blade wondered. *Why are there so many of them?"* Blade had seen or heard eight of the Legion team already—two of them much closer than she would have wanted. Then she thought, *how much longer do I have before the rest of them know that I am in the hotel?* She would then become the hunted—with very limited ammunition and cover. *Where is Gatlin?* Blade asked herself once again.

She thought about trying to stop Gorman and Jackyl before they reached the others, but where were they now? How was she supposed to stop Gorman with such limited ammunition and still no Gatlin? But the odds were tempting; two against one was better than at least eight against one.

Nevertheless, Blade decides to leave Gorman and Jackyl alone. *What if they got Gatlin when he was in the shower?* she wondered. *Or what if he goes out and they are waiting for him?*

But since she hadn't heard his guns, chances were Gatlin was still around and probably looking for her. So Blade decided to go back up the way she'd come down. Maybe she would find Gatlin? If not, she'd eventually have to face Gorman and Jackyl anyway. So back up the stairs Blade went.

Blade worked her way up the stairs toward her room. Gage and Nazi were coming down. As Gage turned the corner to go down the stairs, Blade stood at the top of the same stairway. When Gage turned the corner, the two lovely ladies were face to face. As a reflex, Blade punched Gage in the nose. Gage fell back a step. Nazi drew his weapon down on Blade.

"No!" Gage shrieked. "Let me handle this little bitch my way. This is personal." Jumping to her feet, Gage faced Blade. "Is that the best that you can do?" she snarled. "I guess Gatlin hasn't taught you shit about how to take care of yourself." She dropkicked Blade directly under the chin.

Blade fell back onto the stairway. Gage jumped on her, planting her knew against Blade's throat, and began punching Blade in the face again and again.

Blade reached and grabbed a blade from her belt and stabbed Gage under the arm, in the upper ribs. Blade then grabbed Gage's beautiful, jet-black hair and pulled Gage's head over to the side and delivered two rapid blows, punching Gage in the face and the side of the head. Then still holding her opponent's hair, Blade actually pulled Gage off of her by her hair. She jumped to her feet.

As Gage was getting back to her feet, she reached for her gun. "You damn bitch," she snarled. "You pulled my hair. Now you're going to pay."

As Gage pulled her gun on Blade, Blade kicked Gage in the face. Gage fell back and dropped her gun. Nazi pulled the hammer back on his weapon. Blade, hearing this, turned and slung a throwing star, nailing Nazi in the forehead, and immediately did a jumping, spinning heal kick, causing the star to drive deeper into his forehead and knocking Nazi to the ground. His weapon dropped beside him.

Blade once again turned her attention back to Gage. She ran at the black-haired vixen and kicked her in the ribs—four, five, and six times. Gage fell to her belly. Blade straddled her back. Grabbing her hair once again, she pounded her face into the hotel floor three, four, five, times.

While this is going on, Nazi managed to get back to his feet, remove the star from his forehead, and pick up his pistol. He raises it once again to fire on Blade, but Blade was totally unaware, as she continued to pound Gage's face into the floor repeatedly.

Bam! The sound had come from behind. Blade turned after hearing the sound and saw Gatlin. He hit Nazi across the back of the head, knocking Nazi out cold.

"Having problems with the neighbors, honey?" Gatlin asked Blade.

"I'm so glad to see you, baby," Blade replied, pulling out one of her larger knives and hitting Gage on the head with the handle, knocking her out as well.

She then got up and ran to Gatlin, giving him a glad-to-see-you, I've-missed-you hug and a kiss on the cheek. "It's so good to see you. I thought they . . ."

Gatlin interrupted her. "Save it for later, babe. I love you too. Now let's get these two out of here before someone else shows up. I believe I know where we can put them," he said.

Blade and Gatlin dragged the two back to room 1502— Gatlin and Blade's room. Gatlin tore the curtains down and tied the two losers up while Blade got the rest of her gear on.

"Stay right here," Gatlin told Blade. "I'll be right back. I've got to go get something. I'll leave the door open."

Moments later, Gatlin returned with Chris, "Hey, babe, I'm back. I have someone I want you to meet," he called.

"I'll be out in just a minute. We really have to come up with a plan because Gorman and Jackyl will be reaching the others anytime now. I know that there are three of them that are hurting pretty badly right now. But I also heard two other voices below me and seen Wrath. Oh yeah, and Grunge is here as well, and of course Gorman and Jackyl, plus these two. None of them are leaders, except for Nazi. He has to be answering to someone else, or he wouldn't have been on recon," said Blade.

A few moments later, Blade, her gear and suit on, returned from the bathroom to the main room where Gatlin and Chris were.

"Sweetheart, this is Chris, my new friend and, probably, besides us, the only person walking around here, maybe even alive," said Gatlin.

"Hello, Chris. It's nice to meet you," said Blade.

"Hello, ma'am. I don't mean any disrespect to anyone, but you are the most beautiful woman I've ever met. Pardon me, but you look extremely sexy and awesome in that suite. Are you guys, like superheroes or something?" asked Chris.

Blade smiled. "Well we just enforce the law and try and keep these most powerful mad men from actually taking over the world," she replied. "I don't consider myself a superhero, just an enforcer of the laws, with some special abilities and state-of-the-art weapons. Some of the others in the force, not naming their names, consider themselves superheroes—like the guy next to you.

"Oh and thank you for saying those nice things about me it makes a girl feel good when she has a swollen eye and a busted lip," Blade added.

"For what it's worth, I've worked here since before the hotel was even open," Chris said. "My uncle owns it. I helped him and my dad wire the entire hotel for telephone and cable TV, and we put in the alarm system and the security cameras. I know the ductwork, as well as a bunch of hidden access doors where there is wiring and things like that. If you think that that might help you, I would be glad to show you. You can get just about anywhere in the entire hotel in the ductworks and through some hidden halls and doors."

"Do you want to be a hero?" Gatlin asked Chris. "You can work with us. With who is running around in this hotel, I just don't like the idea of leaving you anywhere. Every one of them is a heartless, cold being. You stand a better chance of coming out of this alive. We can protect you, but you are going to have to do exactly what we tell you, when we tell you. You will, in return, help us navigate this huge building, until we at least come up with a better plan or get some help over here. What do you say, Chris?"

Chris accepted the challenge and offered his knowledge of the hotel in return for his safety. "Although if I had a weapon, I could be a better help to you guys," Chris added. "Plus it would make me feel like I was actually helping."

"Okay, little dude, here. This is the MFG-25 semiautomatic pistol—made especially for me. There is no other like it; nor is there another similar weapon as powerful. It has a twenty-five round clip. Here are ten more clips. Put them away and don't lose them. MFG doesn't stand for what you think it does. I saw you kinda laugh. It stands for, made for

Gatlin, and of course, twenty-five stands for the number of rounds the clip holds.

"First, you're going to have to change those clothes," he added before Chris could respond. "You stand out like a sore thumb. My God, they make you wear that? Damn, I can hear you when you are standing still. Jeez, man, why don't you just tie bells around yourself and carry floodlights with you. Damn, that is pitiful."

"Well, there's no way you can wear anything of Gatlin's, so you will have to wear something of mine. Here, wear this," Blade said, handing Chris a pair of black sweat pants and a black T-shirt. "No one should be able to see you that easily."

"Thank you, ma'am," Chris said.

"Oh yeah, Chris, here; put this vest on. I only wear it when I go out to the shooting range. It will hold your weapon and your clips, as well as anything else that we find along this journey," said Blade.

After Chris got changed and reappeared, he thanks Blade again for the clothes and Gatlin for saving his life. He then thanked them both for letting him join them in the fight of good versus evil. He finally thanked them for trusting him and for just being nice to him.

"Easy, Chris," said Gatlin. "What are you going to do—sing us a love song? Easy, man. Relax. You'll be fine. Now here's the plan. Chris, you will go with Blade, maneuvering her and yourself through the ductwork, as well as anywhere else you got that will let you guys travel undetected. I'm too big. There's no way I can fit in those vents. Blade will use communicators to talk to me and send me in the right direction according to what you two can see. I'll have to travel the halls. We are fully equipped with what we brought, so let's just pray that it's enough to get us through this mess. Y'all be safe, swift, and quiet, and most of all, be as lethal as possible. Just don't get yourselves killed. Good luck." Gatlin gave Blade a kiss on the cheek and then shook Chris's hand.

"Chris, one more thing; you do what I say, not what I do, and you will be fine and we will all be able to go home soon. I guarantee you. You take care, and let's go kick some ass," said Gatlin.

With that, Chris led Blade up to the roof, where they came to the air ducts. Chris went in, followed by Blade.

Meanwhile, Gatlin began to move down the stairway to the fourteenth floor, combing for Legion members. The sweep was on. The hunted had just become the hunters.

*   *   *

As Gatlin, Blade, and Chris began their mission, Gorman arrived downstairs carrying Jackyl in his arms.

Psycho asked, "What in the hell happened to him? Did he meet an unhappy guest or a disgruntled employee or what?" He giggled.

Gorman put Jackyl down and then, in a rage, picked Psycho up off the ground with one hand. Unable to speak, Gorman roared very violently and convincingly. Psycho understood that Gorman was extremely angry and concerned about his unconscious friend Jackyl.

Psycho got Gorman to let him back down. Then he began to examine Jackyl. Gorman stood right beside his fallen friend throughout the examination. Psycho finishes patching up Jackyl. "Now we just have to wait until he comes to so that we can find out exactly what in the hell happened upstairs," he said.

Gorman just couldn't get Psycho to understand.

Psycho tried to get in contact with Gage and Nazi; they were yet to report back to the lobby. Unable to get in contact with either of them, he called Ram and Mynx, who were just now leaving the fourteenth floor.

"Ram or Mynx, come in. Over."

"Ram, go ahead, Psycho."

"Yeah I want you to go check floors 5, 10, and 15 and find out what in the hell happened to Jackyl. Then find out what in hell Nazi and Gage are doing and tell them to report as soon as you find them," Psycho ordered.

"What's wrong with Jackyl?" asked Mynx.

"Well, Gorman carried him down here all beaten, battered, bloody and unconscious," said Psycho.

"Copy that. We will find out about it all and handle it," Ram replied.

"Yeah, well, copy this. Do not return to the lobby without answers," Psycho barked.

Neither Ram nor Mynx replied; they just got down to the business at hand.

*   *   *

Gatlin finished the sweep of the fourteenth floor; he saw no one around, good or bad. Gatlin checked in with Blade and Chris. "Fourteenth floor clear, moving down to the thirteenth."

"Copy that. We are over fourteen. We will be your eyes on the thirteenth in about four minutes. Gatlin, please wait on us. Do not be a hero this time," said Blade.

"Okay, I'll wait on the stairs between fourteen and thirteen for you two to catch up. Over," replied Gatlin.

As Gatlin was waiting, he heard someone coming up the stairs. Now not only was he unable to call Blade, he couldn't even wait on her and Chris to get to him like he'd promised. Gatlin hunkered down and listened. *Sounds like just one set of footsteps.*

In just moments, Ram entered the stairway, his weapon drawn. He walked by Gatlin, who was behind the stairway. Gatlin couldn't allow Ram to see him first. As Ram reached the thirteenth floor, WHACK! Gatlin hit Ram square across the back of the head. Ram, seemingly unfazed, turned around and faced Gatlin. *BAM*! Gatlin punched Ram in the nose. Ram's head snapped back and immediately returned, once again focused, unhurt by either of Gatlin's blows.

"Oh shit!" cried Gatlin. "You have got to be shitting me. What in the hell are you made of?"

Ram then punched Gatlin in the face. Gatlin fell back five or six feet into the wall behind him, cracking the wall. As Gatlin tried to get to his feet, *BAM*! Ram slammed his head and shoulder into Gatlin, like a linebacker tackling a running back in football.

Gatlin hit the floor extremely hard, Ram falling on top of him. When Ram picked himself up off of Gatlin, he noticed Mynx coming down the hallway very quickly, making her way toward the action.

When Mynx reached the two, she called Psycho and informed him that they had found the problem. "It's Gatlin, and right now, Ram is kicking the shit out of him. We are on the thirteenth floor. Still no sign of Nazi and Gage," reported Mynx.

Gorman, hearing this, got up from sitting next to Jackyl and stormed up the stairs toward the thirteenth floor to get some revenge of his own.

Ram wasn't giving Gatlin any room or any chance to use his mighty guns, which Legion members had feared for a long time. He picked up what seemed to him to be Gatlin's limp body and threw Gatlin into the soda machine, right next to where Mynx was standing and watching the royal ass whooping. Gatlin landed hard once again.

Mynx scraped Gatlin's back and side with her killer claws, digging them in just under his body armor and cutting him open like a stuck hog. Gatlin, now bleeding everywhere from the wounds inflicted by Ram and Mynx once again tried to get to his feet. The warrior, the will to survive, came out in him, as well as the will to kick these two's asses. Gatlin noticed his two opponents hugging one another.

"You're a sick bitch," he told Mynx. "Look at that ugly bastard. He hits like a pussy. That's probably why you like him; you're both pussies. I'm fixin' to kick his ass right in front of you, to show you that he really is just a mutant pussy with a hard-ass head." Gatlin jumped to his feet, glaring at Mynx and Ram.

As Ram reached for his gun, Gatlin unloaded his mighty 30mm cannons upon the now shocked Ram. Gatlin's rounds ripped into Ram's lower half, shredding his legs; blood, flesh, muscle, and fur flew all over the place, literally painting the walls and carpet with chunks of flesh and blood, giving them new color and texture.

Ram finally got off a shot. He hit Gatlin in the left arm. Not missing a beat or allowing a gunshot wound to the arm to slow him down, Gatlin focused on what he promised to do. He continued to walk toward the now gun-less Ram. This time, he didn't waste time and energy hitting Ram in the head. Instead, he hit him in the throat, chest, ribs, and kidneys. As Gatlin worked Ram over, blood from both of them flying everywhere, Mynx looked on in shock. Soon Ram was no longer moving or trying to protect himself.

Mynx swung at Gatlin with her claws. Gatlin reached up and grabbed Mynx's hand and, in the same motion, broke her arm like a toothpick. Mynx's bone ripped through her flesh, and now her blood too spilled onto the carpet. Mynx fell to the blood-soaked carpet, in obvious pain and screaming like a cat being swung by her tail. Unable to handle the screams of Mynx, Gatlin picked her up by her hair and punched her in the face. Her blood once again sprayed, this time painting the walls, as she fell, knocked out cold. Gatlin dropped her motionless body onto the floor.

*   *   *

Blade and Chris heard the gunfire and the screams.

"Get me there now," Blade said. "That was Gatlin's guns; he's in trouble."

Chris led Blade double time through the air ducts. "Tell Gatlin to get to the fourteenth floor snack area, back by the cigarette machine," he told her. "Tell him to get there now!"

Blade relayed the message to Gatlin. "Are you okay?" she added. "Are you hurt? Are you able to get to the snack area? Do you need me to help you?"

"No, no problem," Gatlin answered. "They didn't lay a hand on me. I'm fine. I'll see y'all at the snack area."

*   *   *

From downstairs, Legion also heard the awesome sound of Gatlin's cannons. Psycho ordered Mite, "Get up there and check it out. Then give me a status report as soon as you know something."

Up the stairs the little lady ran. Mite headed toward the sound.

Psycho called his people to find out what was going on.

Wrath answered. "Grunge is still with me on the eleventh floor," he reported. "The shots came from the thirteenth or fourteenth floor. I'm not real sure, but we will find out."

"Ram and Mynx were last known to be on the thirteenth floor. However, the two never called back to report the results of their encounter with Gatlin. Now they don't even respond to my calls. I will be up that way in fifteen minutes," said Psycho.

Gorman was now on the eleventh floor, and Mite was just leaving the ninth; they would converge on the spot where Ram and Mynx lay soon.

*   *   *

Gatlin made it to the fourteenth-floor snack area. Behind the cigarette machine, the ceiling opened up.

"Hurry, get up here," Chris called. "But don't get blood on the wall. That will give our position away real fast."

Gatlin climbed into the ductwork air vents, without getting blood on the wall. Although the air vent was very large, Gatlin barely fit.

"Oh my God," Blade gasped, seeing Gatlin. "You're bleeding everywhere. What in the hell—no who in the hell—did this to you?" She rubbed her fingers over his side, searching for the wounds. "Those scratches oh no, don't tell me; Mynx is here. Who else could cause these wounds? I know she's a quick, tough, and downright mean little bitch, but she didn't do all of this to you," Blade concluded.

"No, Ram did most of it," Gatlin told her. "Mynx just scratched the shit out of me. Ram is one tough bastard. I really didn't think I was going to be able to take him. If he hadn't thrown me, I probably would be static right about now. But he gave me new life with his throw. Then out of nowhere, that cat bitch scratched me. I thought about not ever seeing your pretty face again, and that's all it took. I blew Ram's knees to kingdom come. He will live, but I bet we don't have to worry about him for a long time. Ram is going to need at least two new knees. Hell, he might bleed to death.

"You see, Chris," he said, turning his head toward the bellhop, "the code states that we don't kill them. However, we can beat the shit out of them, and if they die of their wounds, well too damn bad for them. We can kill anything else that they use against us, other than regular Legion members, but that is a totally different story all together. They do come up with some shit at times." He sighed.

"We have to get some medical supplies for you, or you are going to get in real trouble with those wounds and gashes," said Blade.

"I can get some medical supplies downstairs, out of the security office," said Chris.

* * *

The Legion members who were on recon, arrived at the thirteenth floor.

Wrath called Psycho. "We found Ram and Mynx. They're here on thirteen," he reported. "It looks like they did find Gatlin, and he kicked the shit out of them both. They're both in very bad shape. But he has to be hurting also. There's just way too much blood here to be just Ram's and Mynx's."

* * *

Now above the Legion, in the air ducts above thirteen, Chris overheard the conversation between Psycho and Wrath. He overheard Psycho telling Wrath that he would be there in a few minutes, but first he was going to contact Malakai with a progress report.

It dawned on him that Blade and Gatlin may be able to use their uplink to call in some reinforcements. Chris turned around and headed back toward his new friends.

* * *

"We have the hotel, but Gatlin is in here somewhere causing a bit of a problem," Psycho told Malakai. "I have five members down or missing and may need reinforcements. But right now I'm sending Ratchet up to assist in the search and destroy mission."

Malakai didn't respond to Psycho's progress report or lack thereof.

* * *

Upstairs, Wrath was angry. "It's one damn guy!" he burst out, facing his fellow Legion members. "We can't find him or stop him when we do find him? Fuck me, man!"

*   *   *

Now back with Gatlin and Blade, Chris told them about the possibility of getting some help here using Legion's uplink down on the first floor.

"Gatlin, will you be all right by yourself?" Blade said. "I'm going with Chris. While Chris gets the supplies that we need to fix you up, I'll contact Tommy J so he can get us some help over here—if we can find the uplink and there aren't any Legion members around."

"I heard that Psycho guy tell the others that he would be up here in a few minutes," Chris told them. "So maybe the coast will be clear. I would bet that they are using the radio in the main office in the lobby. It has the best range and abilities to do something like that. It is located near the supplies in the security room. I can get the supplies, and Blade can call your people and we can watch each other's backs in the meantime."

"Sounds like a plan," said Gatlin.

"We can get down to the lobby in the air vents in about thirty minutes. But we can get there in about thirty seconds using the laundry chute. The only small problem is that, when we land, we will be a couple hundred feet from the front desk. But with all of them being up here looking for you, Gatlin, we should be able to get in and get out without being detected," Chris suggested.

"Hey, Chris, these guys play for keeps," Gatlin said. "They use real bullets. Some of them are scary; some are stinky; some are big, and some are small; and their women are all very beautiful but, in most cases, more lethal than the men or the mutants. So stick close to Blade. You two take care of each other. Be careful, be quick, and be back."

Blade and Chris took the laundry chute from the fourteenth floor. At the bottom, Chris landed on his foot very awkwardly. It hurt like hell, but they were now at ground zero and there was no turning back. He would just have to suck it up.

Blade had been on her own during missions, but never had she had a civilian with her who she had to keep an eye on while, at the same time, doing her job. *This could turn out to be harder than it has to be, and now he has a hurt foot*, Blade thought to herself.

As the two worked their way to the front desk and the security office, the lobby was empty. Things were going great.

* * *

Back on thirteen, Psycho had Grunge and Gorman carry Ram downstairs as he, himself, helped Mynx to her feet and down the stairs.

"We need to get Gage and Nazi. Where in the hell are they? I want every door kicked in and every room searched until they are both found," Psycho ordered the others. "Don't worry about locating Gatlin right now. We will do that when we have found all of our people—and have enough people to cover every floor at once. Now find Gage and Nazi!"

* * *

Chris pointed Blade in the direction of the radio and then headed toward the supplies. As Chris loaded the supplies into the vent, using a chair to reach it, he glanced over at Blade, who was now talking to Allied Force's base.

Chris noticed the closed dining room door and decided to peek inside. To his surprise, the room was full of guests.

"There are people in here," Chris told Blade. "I'm going to release them."

"Make it quick and quiet," said Blade.

Chris returned to the door of the dining room and opened it. "Listen up," he told the guests. "I'm here to get you people out of this situation, but all of you are going to have to be very quiet. If you're not really quiet, this will not work. The bad guys will most definitely return if they hear noise from down here. Once you reach the doors leading outside, do not hesitate. Just get the hell out of here ASAP. I know that not all of you have keys to your vehicles, but if everyone will help each other out, then everyone will survive. We will have everything inside taken care of real soon, and then you all can return and claim your belongings."

With that, Chris led the guests to the front doors, like a schoolteacher leading his young students to lunch. The guests were surprisingly quiet and quick.

Just as the last guest exited the lobby doors, Blade finished her conversation with Tommy J. She was surprised to see Chris relocking the front doors, like nothing had happened. Chris made sure that the lobby looked like it had when he and Blade had arrived. Blade watched, surprised that Chris hadn't left with the guests when he had a chance. Instead, Chris finished covering his tracks and then motioned for Blade to hurry. He would help her back up into the ventilation system once more.

BAM! Blade was struck over the head with a computer monitor, knocking her to the ground and really loosening up her brains. When Blade turned to see who had attacked her, *BAM*! This time she took a punch to the head. Blade was down and not moving anymore.

Jackyl had been lying down in the computer room. Neither Chris nor Blade had seen him. When he'd come to and looked up to see Blade, Jackyl had snuck up to her from behind. Blade had never known what hit her. So Jackyl had gotten his revenge on Blade.

Chris, seeing this, ran to help Blade. Jackyl blew fire at Chris, stopping Chris's pursuit. Chris pulled out the

MFG-25 and shot out both of Jackyl's knees with one very precise and very lucky shot. Jackyl fell to the floor right next to Blade. Chris being thrown to the floor of the lobby on his backside by the massive recoil of the mighty MFG-25 knew he couldn't hesitate; he figured that someone had to have heard the giant sound of the mighty pistol. He ran to Jackyl and hit him in the head with the pistol, not once but twice, making sure that Jackyl would not get back up for a while.

* * *

Chris was right, Psycho and the others did hear the shots. On the sixth floor, Gorman released Ram to Grunge. Knowing that Jackyl was downstairs, Gorman raced down the stairs.

* * *

Chris tried to revive Blade, but his attempts were unsuccessful. Realizing that he had to get Blade and himself out of harm's way, he picked up Blade's limp body and put her over his shoulder.

Chris knew that he would never be able to get Blade's body back up into the vents, so he darted toward the stairs. He hoped the little guy hadn't seen Blade and him getting out of the laundry chute or him putting the supplies up into the ventilation system. Picking a stairway, he kicked the chair from under the vent over into the corner and headed toward it. Seconds later, he was making his way up the stairs with Blade over his shoulder, trying to get some space and time between him and Legion so he and Blade could once again use the ventilation system.

Chris knew that he was way too outgunned to be walking the halls. As he reached the fourth floor, he figured he'd picked the correct stairway to come up. He made his way to the snack area. Blade was still out cold. Chris climbed up onto the cigarette machine and opened the ceiling to the ventilation system once more. He then returned to the floor to get Blade.

With every muscle and every bit of strength that he had, Chris was finally able to get Blade's limp body back into the ducts. As he was climbing up to get himself inside the vents, he heard a noise.

"Gatlin, damn, you scared me. She needs help," he added without pausing. "The supplies are still in the vent in the lobby. I'll go after them when I get back up in the vents so you can take care of Blade. I'm sorry I didn't take care of your girlfriend, but neither of us saw the little guy. She did make the call, and we did get the supplies, though. Oh yeah, we released the guests from the dining room." He looked down and swallowed hard. "If I hadn't been messing with the guests, Blade wouldn't have gotten attacked."

"It's okay," Gatlin assured him. "Blade has been a lot worse off than this. You have to keep in mind that these ladies aren't your girls next door; these gals kick ass, a lot of ass. Hell, you've seen Blade in action, so don't feel guilty."

Chris moved to climb back up into the vents with Gatlin and Blade. Just then, he heard movement, "Oh shit, Gatlin. I hear someone coming. I'm not going to make it in time. Close the vent. I'll lose them. Then I'll catch up with you later. Go get the supplies and fix the two of you up," Chris said.

"Damn it, boy," said Gatlin, as Chris dropped back to the floor in the snack area. "Get your ass . . ." Gatlin stopped short, as he heard the footsteps. He had only one choice—to close the vent and protect the unconscious Blade.

Chris turned from the snack area to the main hallway, acting like he was just a guest and didn't know anything about what was going on in the hotel.

There she was, a little woman, who drew back her wrist rocket full of darts.

"Hey, cutie," Chris drawled. "Whoa, what do you have there? Don't shoot me. I'm just getting something to munch on. But the machine took my money, so I'm headed back to my room to get more change. Do you want to come? What's going on? Where is everyone? Am I missing something or what?"

Chris didn't know who this pretty little oriental lady was, but her weapon told him she had to be one of the bad guys.

"How you get out dining room and up fourth floor of stairs?" asked Mite in her broken English.

*   *   *

Gatlin watched and listened from the vents. He knew that if he dropped down now, without Blade's help, he probably wouldn't be able to get back into the ventilation system. So he decided to wait it out and watch Chris closely. If anything went wrong, then he would help. As for now, he would just have to trust Chris.

*   *   *

"I wasn't ever in the dining room," Chris said, doing his best to look confused. "I've been on my balcony getting high. Then I fell asleep. Hey, cutie, you want to get high? We can go back to my room. I've got some real good smoke."

*   *   *

Wrath opened the door to room 1502. There he found Gage and Nazi tied up with the curtains from the room.

As Wrath untied his two battered allies, they told him that Gatlin and Blade and some little guy in sweats and a black T-shirt had tied them up.

*   *   *

Psycho received a call from Mite, "I find another guest," she informed him. "This one is roaming the halls on four. I bring him down now."

Before Psycho could respond to Mite, Wrath contacted Psycho. "I found Gage and Nazi. They were tied up in 1502," he reported. "They seem to be okay. They just both had the shit beaten out of them. They tell me that Gatlin and Blade are here and roaming the halls with a young man in black sweats and a black T-shirt. So instead of one person, we have three people to search and destroy."

*   *   *

Mite, overhearing the description of what obviously was the young man in front of her, drew her weapon on Chris. "Get on floor!" she ordered.

She contacted Psycho. "I have number three people. Man in black shirt in front of me now."

As Chris made as if he was working his way down to the carpet, he pulled his own weapon from the back of his vest. This time, Chris fired the MFG-25 on Mite. He hit Mite in the arm. After recovering from one hell of a kick from shooting the mighty weapon with just one hand, Chris aimed again, only to catch one of Mite's poisonous darts in the lower abdomen. Chris managed to get off another shot, as did Mite, at close range.

Chris's shot hit Mite directly in the wrist rocket, totally destroying it and blowing the top of her hand off. As Mite spun and fell, her second dart scored a hit, piercing Chris's shoulder near his chest.

Mite got to her feet in terrible pain. She stared at her hand; one of her wrist rockets had been completely destroyed—by a normal.

Gatlin dropped from the vents, and within a fraction of a second, he has the little lethal Asian in a sleeper hold. He put her out cold in seconds. Gatlin fixed the ceiling where he had come out and went back for Chris.

Chris just looked up at Gatlin all swimmy-headed. "Maaan, you're awesooooome duuude," he slurred.

"Can you run, Chris? 'Cause we really need to get the hell out of here now. We need to get up at least a couple more floors. Then I can put you back up into the vents. But you're gonna have to help me by runnin'. Can you run, Chris?" Gatlin asked.

"Noooo," answered Chris. "I can't even seeee." It was obvious that the powerful drug from Mite's darts was taking full effect on Chris.

Despite the shape Gatlin was in, he picked up Chris and laid him over his shoulder, scooped up the MFG-25 and tucked it into the front of his pants, and ran up the stairs.

Unbeknownst to Gatlin, Wrath and Ratchet were now on their way to the seventh floor. The question was who would get there first?

Gatlin reached the seventh floor and lowered the vent cover, all the while knowing that Legion had heard the powerful pistol fire off two rounds at Mite. Gatlin knew his enemies were coming; he just didn't know when they'd get there, who would be among them, or how many he would face. Gatlin pushed the now totally asleep Chris into the ventilation system and places the MFG-25 next to him and reclosed the vent cover.

Out of the corner of his eye, he saw, at the other end of the hallway, Wrath, accompanied by Ratchet.

They also saw Gatlin.

*   *   *

Psycho had ordered Gorman to help get Gage and Nazi, as well as Mite, back to the lobby. His pursuit of Gatlin would have to wait. Once again, he shared the task of carrying the wounded down to the lobby with Grunge.

*   *   *

Without hesitation, Gatlin fired on Wrath. Ratchet stood behind the cloaked enemy.

Wrath raised his hands, and, in response, pictures flew from the walls and doors flew from their hinges. Hovering in the air, these objects were the perfect shields for Wrath and Ratchet. Wood and glass flew through the hallway as Gatlin's assault shattered the pictures and splintered the doors, rendering his effort to get to his enemies vain. Unfortunately for Gatlin, not one round made it through to his enemies.

Gatlin stopped his assault. The remains of the pictures and doors fell harmlessly to the hallway floor, opening up the range of sight for Ratchet. As the debris hits the carpet below, Ratchet opened fire on Gatlin.

The shots ripped into him, blowing a chunk of flesh from Gatlin's left shoulder, just under his body armor, and another from his right leg. The rest of Ratchet's spent ammo ricocheted from Gatlin's armor. However, the assault took a toll on Gatlin's body armor as well.

Gatlin fell to the floor. Wrath held a hand up, stopping Ratchet's assault. He moved closer to Gatlin.

Gatlin's foes were now only fifty feet from him. He pulled himself to his feet and stumbled into room 712 for some cover. There were no more doors on any of the rooms, but he would use the walls for protection.

Just as Gatlin tucked himself into the room out of Ratchet's line of fire, the room suddenly began to shake. The furniture, under Wrath's power, began to fly around the room, at times coming very close to hitting Gatlin. As the furniture swirled around the room faster and faster, making greater arcs, it began to strike Gatlin.

At first, it wasn't too bad; the phone hit Gatlin in the head. Gatlin smashed it with his guns. Then the nightstand flew at him and struck him in the right shoulder, knocking Gatlin to the floor. Above him, the furniture circled through the air.

Wrath, who remained in the hallway positioned in front of room 701 at the opposite end of the hallway from Gatlin, increased his torment of Gatlin. The furniture began to fly faster and faster, spinning out of control and making it very hard for Gatlin to figure out which piece of furniture was going to attack next. Wrath motioned Ratchet to move down to the doorway of room 712 and end the torment for Gatlin with a round to the head or something.

Ratchet moved toward the room.

Gatlin was able to dodge the dresser, but not the air conditioner; it struck him in the midsection, slamming both it and Gatlin through the sheetrock and into the adjacent room, room 710. Shortly thereafter, the other dresser crashed into Gatlin's head and shoulder, cutting his forehead open.

Disoriented from the furniture attack, Gatlin nevertheless managed to shake the cobwebs from his head. "To HELL WITH THIS SHIT!" he roared as he opened his mighty cannons on the furniture.

Like the doors in the hallway, the furniture was soon being reduced to splinters, except for the large air conditioning unit. It seemed to wait or hover until Gatlin was still before it came at him.

Ratchet made it to the front of room 712. Gatlin saw the robotic foe in the doorway, posed to fire at Wrath's command. Pressed against the light switch next to the doorway that Ratchet had made his post, Gatlin saw the air-conditioning unit once again coming at him. He dove in front of Ratchet and, a split second later, dropped to the floor in the splits.

Catching Ratchet completely unaware, the air conditioner slammed into the robot with such force that it knocked him out of the doorway and into the wall behind him, cracking the wallboard halfway down the hallway.

"YEAH, BITCH, HAVE SOME FUCKIN' FURNITURE ON ME FOR A CHANGE!" Gatlin yelled.

Wrath stopped the air conditioning unit midair, and it crashed to the floor. Ratchet got back to his feet. He looked at Wrath and then down at the unit. Then with his laser, he blew the unit to pieces. Ratchet proceeds to cross the hallway back to room 712.

Gatlin was pretty banged up, and he was facing a very powerful enemy in Ratchet, with the help and wizardry and heartlessness of Wrath. Gatlin tried his best not to laugh at Ratchet, but the urge overtook him. As he laughed, he opened his cannons up on the awesome Ratchet from only about ten feet or so away. The shots blew the lethal lasers off the robot and struck the armor all over Ratchet's body, which prevented Ratchet from getting a good fix on his position.

Ratchet could not pinpoint his target if there was interference, such as hundreds of 30mm cannon rounds bouncing off of him. The onslaught drove Ratchet back out and into the hallway. Gatlin didn't let up, and the continuing assault forced the robot backward. Now Gatlin was blowing hoses off the giant machine. Ratchet began to smoke from a couple of different places. Gatlin didn't know what he had hit on the machine being. Nor did he care, He didn't let up.

Furious with the effort of Ratchet, Wrath began to move the robot with his wizardry. Gatlin saw that Ratchet was coming forward again. Just then, as always seemed to happen to Gatlin, his guns began cutting out, the indicator at orange and nearly plunging into the red. Red indicated complete shutdown, designed to prevent excessive heat from destroying the guns.

Seeing Ratchet approaching, Gatlin decided to turn to the wall that separated 710 and 712. With his guns, Gatlin widened the existing hole in the sheetrock and then burst through the wall to the other room. Inside room 710, he once again encountered flying furniture. "Oh bullshit!" he muttered to himself. "No fuckin' way! Are you kidding me?"

He jumped to his feet and, as he'd done a moment ago, opened his weapons up on the sheetrock. Then he was in 708. Now Ratchet was in 712. Gatlin fired a few more rounds into the robot that seemed to be struggling to get around.

Ratchet turned to Gatlin and opened his 45mm cannons. Gatlin dove to the floor, and the rounds blew holes in the wall of 706, as well as in some flying furniture in rooms 710 and 708. Apparently, Gatlin was going to face flying furniture in every room that he entered. And Ratchet wasn't letting up. With his assault, furniture was blown to pieces, as was the wall to 706.

Seeing an opportunity, Gatlin rose to one knee and fired off several covering rounds for himself. Then, using the holes Ratchet had created, he leaped through to 706.

Ratchet continued his relentless barrage of 45mm cannon rounds. The rounds flew through the rooms, burrowing their way as far as the outer bricks that covered the outside walls of the luxurious hotel. As Ratchet continued to pursue him, Gatlin used the holes made by Ratchet's powerful rounds, along with a few of his own rounds, to break through to the next room.

As in all of the other rooms, flying furniture swirled around 704. Ratchet, now in room 710, was about to burst through to 708.

Gatlin went to the open doorway of room 704. Wrath, still in the hallway, notices him and fired, tearing the doorjamb to shreds but somehow not hitting Gatlin at all.

"You dumb shit, you can move everything you want to but your own damn bullets," Gatlin taunted. "What an asshole. Face it, Wrath, you suck!"

As Ratchet moved from 708 to 706, Gatlin busted through the next wall, entering 702, the last room on the floor on this side of the hallway. Glancing toward the hallway, Gatlin saw Wrath just outside the door.

Wrath hurried out of the way, but it was too late. Guessing basically where Wrath was and his guns now indicating yellow, Gatlin opened up, ripping through the walls of the hotel. He fired shots up and down the wall that separated Wrath from his vision.

Gatlin's guns began to cut out again. As he pulled them down, Gatlin heard the thud of Wrath's body hitting the floor just outside room 702 in the middle of the hallway. With that, the furniture fell from where it was hovering, crashing to the floors of all the rooms. Gatlin heard someone coming up the stairs just outside room 702.

He hunkered down against the outside wall and watched Ratchet coming ever so close. The robot was now in room 706 and still firing his mighty 45mm cannons as he moved toward 704. He would soon be in the very room where Gatlin was sitting against the wall with, yet again, overheated guns.

His fuckin' guns don't heat up. That's bullshit, Gatlin thought to himself as he rested and waited. He was bleeding from the head wound and shoulder and leg wounds that he had accumulated in this battle. To go along with his already wounded body. Gatlin was a tired man.

*   *   *

In the vents above the fourth floor, Chris began to come to, and Blade was just finishing getting herself bandaged up and trying to rid her head of the pain and the cobwebs.

"Hey, good to have you back. How are you feeling?" said Blade, wrapping his ankle with an ACE bandage.

"Oh man, I don't know. We are really in trouble, aren't we? Where's Gatlin?" Chris asked.

"I hear him up a few floors; well, I don't hear him, but I can hear his guns. We are going to have to get our shit together and get back in the game," said Blade.

"Are you ready?" asked Chris.

"Yeah, are you sure that you are?" asked Blade.

"Yeah, I probably will be by the time we get to where Gatlin is," Chris answered.

*   *   *

As Ratchet could no longer see Gatlin, he stopped his assault.

Gatlin remained on his butt with his back against the outside wall of room 702. His wounded right leg lay flat and his left leg was bent at the knee. He was waiting to see which would happen first—Ratchet reaching him or his guns cooling so he could put up some kind of defense.

*   *   *

Back in the lobby, Psycho looked at his wounded group of villains. He shook his head as he surveyed the various wounds inflicted by Gatlin and Blade; even Chris had gotten into the action of putting the hurt on Legion.

Gorman and Grunge, the only two uninjured warriors that Psycho had left in this group, following Psycho's orders were steadily making their way toward Gatlin and/or Blade. The rest of the team was waiting for reinforcements to arrive and take out Blade and Gatlin, as well as their newfound friend, Chris.

Psycho knew that his team had failed him in the effort to this point and that he would have to answer to Malakai. He would get the blame or the glory, and right now, it looked like it would be the blame, unless his two giant warriors, Gorman and Grunge, were successful in stopping Gatlin, Blade, and Chris.

Psycho could no longer hear the awesome gun of his number one protector, Ratchet. He assumed that either Gatlin was down or Ratchet was down. But given the way things had been going on this operation, he felt that the gunfire upstairs had stopped because Ratchet was no longer able to fire his weapon and Gatlin had taken Ratchet out as well. Psycho would just have to wait to see how this operation unfolded from here on out.

Other than Ram and Ratchet, Psycho knew that Gorman and Grunge gave him the best chance to take Gatlin down. So Psycho simply awaited the outcome of the battle between Gatlin, Blade, and Chris versus Wrath, Ratchet, Gorman, and Grunge. On paper, there was no contest. His giants would crush the three much smaller and weaker members of Allied Force. In addition, Malakai was sending, Psycho hoped more members to finish the job, if Psycho and his team couldn't finish it themselves. Psycho could only hope the four remaining members of his team stopped Gatlin, Blade, and Chris before the backup arrived. Psycho knew that was his last chance to claim victory.

*   *   *

Ratchet was now in room 704, and he'd be in 702 soon. Gatlin looked at his guns. They were still too hot, indicating only a yellow light. Gatlin knew that he was going to need the green light, full power, to stop Ratchet.

Gatlin saw that Ratchet was beginning to cross through the enormous hole in the wall between rooms 704 and 702. With no defense and not enough time or ability to run with his wounded leg, Gatlin would do what he had to and hope that it worked.

Now in the same room with Gatlin, Ratchet scanned the room for his victim. As he honed in on the wall adjacent to the outside wall, he found Gatlin on the floor not moving and bleeding, his eyes closed. Ratchet bent down and picked up the apparently lifeless body of his foe. He made his way through the door-less entryway of room 702 and out into the hallway.

Gatlin could still hear the rumble of someone very large coming up the stairs toward them. He knew it wasn't anyone friendly, so he decided that he had to make a move before whomever it was arrived and he wouldn't stand a chance of escaping.

As Ratchet moved from the room toward the stairway, Gatlin quickly raised his guns and from point-blank range, opens all of his remaining mighty barrels of fury into the unsuspecting robotic giant.

Ratchet took round after round to his head and upper body. The sheer flurry of the rounds disabled his ability to hone in on his attacker. Nor was he even able to be aware that he was holding Gatlin as he took the royal ass whooping from his smaller foe.

Gatlin unloaded just about all the power that his guns had into Ratchet. Finally, the giant dropped Gatlin to the floor. Ratchet began to move around very awkwardly, not putting up any defense. Gatlin decided to fire upon him again. This time, the power of the assault forced Ratchet to fall down the stairway. Ratchet landed so awkwardly that he was no longer able to move, and he seemed to be leaking fluids from everywhere on his body.

Gatlin could now hear, as well as feel, the pounding of steps on the floor of the seventh-floor hallway. Gatlin did figure out that the footsteps that were marching up the stairs toward him were coming from the other end of the hallway. Gatlin braced himself against the outside wall of the hallway and waited to see who was coming for him.

He looked down at his guns. "Orange! Shit!" he said to himself. Gatlin did the only thing that he could. He waited for his cannons to cool down once again. Orange wasn't going to cut it with what was heading his way. Again, he would need the total power of the green light.

*   *   *

"Did you hear that, Chris? That's Gatlin's guns. He's in trouble. Get us there now!" ordered Blade.

"Hang in there, Blade. We are traveling as fast as we can in here. If you want, we can get out of these vents and try our luck in the hallways—if you think we stand a chance against the remaining Legion members" said Chris.

"No, we can't go down now. Gatlin told us to remain in the vents regardless of what we heard. He would get us out when the coast was clear enough to do so. Just get us there as fast as you can, so that we can at least see from up here what's going on. And if he needs our help, we will be there, because Gatlin will never ask for it—ever," said Blade.

"Okay. Just follow me. We'll get there in about . . . Hell I don't even know how far away Gatlin is right now. But we will get there as soon as possible. I promise," Chris told her.

"Chris, that doesn't help me much. Just lead the way please," replied Blade.

Chris didn't say anything. He just led the way in the direction from which they'd heard Gatlin's massive cannon moments ago. Following behind him, Blade was very concerned about what was going on with Gatlin.

*   *   *

Gatlin stood against the wall at the end of the seventh floor of this once luxurious hotel waiting to see what it was that was approaching him so rapidly from the other end of the long hallway. All he could think is, *whoever it is is huge and plenty pissed off, to say the least.*

Blood from a gash above Gatlin's left eye dripped into his vision, alerting him that he was cut. *Oh great, another scar*, he thought. He wiped his forehead. His hand was covered in blood. He looked down at his guns again. "Still too damn hot. Come on, man. Cool down, babies," he whispered. "I'm gonna need you both really soon. Don't do this shit to me—not now."

The footsteps got louder; whoever was coming was close now. Gatlin reached for his MFG-25. As he touched the empty holster, he remembered that his MFG-25 was in the hands of Chris, who was now in the ventilation system with Blade. He wasn't sure where they were. His headset must have gotten broken during the battle with Ratchet and Wrath. All that Gatlin was certain of was that he was standing out in the open with his primary weapons too hot to do much good—and apparently not getting any cooler—and his backup weapon nowhere in sight. Gatlin was beaten down but not yet beaten up. He knew that he was on his own, and something was going to show itself at the other end of the long hallway in just a few seconds, if not sooner. *It can't get much worse* Gatlin thought.

After several more very long seconds, the source of the violent ascent of the stairs appeared at the far end of the hallway.

Oh shit. Not Gorman. Damn, this just keeps getting better and better, Gatlin thought. *Son of a bitch, what's next? I'm facing a pissed-off giant gorilla man with my guns too damn hot to do me any good. I'm all beat to hell.* He knew that, as soon as Gorman spotted him, the battle would be on.

Just as Gatlin finished the thought, exactly that happened. It was inevitable—Gorman saw him. The gorilla man focused on Gatlin. Realizing who was at the other end of the 250-foot hallway, Gorman let out a bloodcurdling scream. He slammed his fists into his own chest and then into the walls on either side of the once beautiful hallway. Gorman had found what he had been looking for. Gatlin wasn't number one on his hit list, but Gorman knew that Gatlin was associated with the beautiful young lady who had inflicted so much pain upon his dearest friend, Jackyl. So Gatlin would just have to do.

"Oh shit, he saw me. Great, he wants to dance with me. I don't know that step, but it's a nice one, Gorman. Oh shit mania, there is no way I am getting out of this one," Gatlin muttered. "Come on, you big ass body of rage and muscle, let's see what you have in store for me. I guess the least I could do is stand up. Damn, this is gonna hurt—a lot!"

Gatlin knew that the only thing he could do was stand and fight. His injuries prevented him from running in order to buy himself and his guns some time. He would simply have to face the much larger and stronger opponent. Gatlin's leg wound was getting really bad. That went for all of his wounds. Gatlin was deteriorating much more rapidly than he would like.

Gorman, on the other hand, appeared to Gatlin to be in top shape with no wounds at all. It was just a matter of time before Gorman began his charge toward Gatlin and the fray between the two warriors would be under way.

*   *   *

"Oh Shit! That's Gorman. He doesn't scream and roar for no reason. He must see Gatlin or something is happening. Oh my God. Please, Chris, you have got to get me to Gatlin now!" said a very nervous Blade.

"We're above the fifth floor right now, Blade. We'll get to Gatlin in just a little bit. I'm guessing he's on either the seventh or eighth floor. Just stay with me and stay close. I promise that we will get to him" Chris assured her.

"I believe you, Chris. It's just, like I said earlier, Gatlin will never ask for help with anything—especially when it comes to fighting. He'll fight to the finish—I mean to the death—if someone isn't there to stop it or help him or his opponent. I can say that, in the past, it has been someone having to help his opponent. Oh, Chris, there are just too many of them this time, and Gatlin is hurt. I know that he's a lot worse than he would ever let either of us know—especially me. So I'm right here, right behind you, trying not to lose my mind while we work our way to him. It's nothing personal, Chris. It's just that he's the one—the only one for me. I want so badly to marry this guy. I have never felt this way about anyone in my entire life. So please don't take it personally," said Blade.

"Don't worry about me, Blade. I know that you're worried about Gatlin. You love him. I'm worried about him as well, and I only met him a few hours ago. He's really a special kind of person. I'm glad to hear that the two of you are so much in love with one another. You're a very lucky lady, and Gatlin is a very lucky man to have such a strong, caring, smart, beautiful lady like yourself to love him back in the same way that he loves you. You two will make a great married couple. I really mean that. If it hadn't been for both you and Gatlin, well then I would probably be a hostage or maybe even dead. What you two have done for the people in this hotel is truly remarkable," said Chris.

"Thank you, Chris. That really means a lot to me, and it would to Gatlin too, if he heard it. So when we meet back up with him, you'll have to repeat to him just what you told me. Besides, I can tell that he really likes you also, Chris. Gatlin doesn't make a friend in a matter of moments, the way that he did with you," Blade told Chris.

"Really, he seems so even-headed to me. But I appreciate that, Blade. That was a very nice thing for you to say. What do you say we go get to our friend Gatlin's position and help him end this nightmare?"

"I'm following you. Lead the way," Blade answered.

So Chris continued to lead Blade to Gatlin's position on the seventh floor. It was now just a question of who would reach Gatlin first—Chris and Blade or Gorman. Only time would tell.

*   *   *

Gorman slowly worked his way out into the middle of the hallway. He again let out a furious roar/scream. He began to walk—then trot. Then finally, Gorman broke into a run.

The walls shook. Debris from the pictures, doors, and furniture that had been destroyed during Gatlin's battle with Wrath and Ratchet bounced off the floor with every one of Gorman's heavy strides. The ten-foot-high ceilings made it easy for the seven foot four, 420-plus-pound Gorman to charge in a dead run toward the waiting Gatlin. The set of double doors that were located right at the halfway point of the hallway were only a bit higher than eight feet from the floor. Gatlin hoped that Gorman would knock himself out on the iron crossbeam. But, in keeping with how Gatlin's day had been going so far, Gorman cleared the crossbeam by a few inches. So Gatlin would have to do all of the knocking out of Gorman, if that was going to happen today, on his own.

Gatlin knew there was no reason to begin wishing for miracles. He just braced himself against the wall behind him, watching as Gorman, with every stride, got closer to a very close confrontation with him.

The enraged gorilla was now only ninety feet from impact. Gatlin's heart began to pump faster and faster with every one of Gorman's ever-approaching large strides toward him. Now only sixty feet from impact, Gatlin could hear Gorman snorting and see the beast slobbering.

"GREEN LIGHT! HELL YEAH!" Gatlin raised his mighty guns. Gorman was now within fifty feet of impact. Gatlin opened up on the giant.

Rounds sprayed the enraged beast. Blood, fur, and flesh flew from wounds to Gorman's abdomen, chest, arms, and legs. Gatlin even hit his face and head. Yet Gorman didn't break stride, as if he were oblivious to getting filled with hot lead from Gatlin's powerful guns.

"Son of a bitch!" Gatlin swore, not letting up for a split second. He continued to fill Gorman with 30mm cannon rounds of hot lead. Blood and tissue continue to fly throughout the hallway.

Fifteen feet until impact, ten—Gatlin still fired; Gorman still charged—six, five, four, three, two. Gorman lowered his massive head, covered in blood, in a tackling position.

Then suddenly, from Gatlin's right, something emerged. Before Gatlin could figure out what was going on, Grunge had thrown himself from the stairway in an effort to tackle Gatlin. Grunge made his move at the very moment that Gorman finally made impact. *Boom*! All three bodies collided. The 7 foot four inch muscular Gorman hit Gatlin from the front just as he was blindsided by the six foot nine, 335-pound, muscular and powerful Grunge—the two giants combining to deliver a sort of sandwich tackling technique and totally engulfing the six foot six, body armor-covered, ass-kicking Gatlin.

The three mighty warriors hit the wall Gatlin had been leaning against with such force that, on the outside of the seventh floor of Farrah's Hotel and casino, bricks actually broke away from the construction and fell to the sidewalk below. The wood and sheetrock were totally destroyed, as well as several wall studs on the inside of the luxury hotel.

* * *

The walls on other floors shake, as did the entire ventilation system.

"OH SHIT. WHAT IN THE HELL WAS THAT?" cried Chris.

"I don't know but you can bet that, more than likely, Gatlin is involved," answered Blade.

"Damn, it sounds like they knocked out the walls and maybe even the floors of the hotel," said Chris.

"Just get me there now, please," Blade replied. "We have to get there and see what the hell that was and whether Gatlin was, indeed, involved.

"Oh, God, please let him be all right," she added quietly. "I don't hear his guns anymore. Please be okay."

"We are now, best that I can tell, passing over the sixth floor, and there is no sign of anyone," Chris told her. "That means they must be on the seventh floor. That has to be where that giant earth-shaking noise came from."

* * *

Moments after the incredible impact, not one of the three blood-pumping freight trains was moving. Gatlin was laying a few feet from where he had been standing before the awesome collision. He wasn't moving, and his breaths were very shallow and inconsistent. Gatlin's body armor, mainly his chest and rib armor, was crushed in on his body. His right arm had snapped in two just above his gun and below his elbow. It was being held on only by the flesh and some tissue. Gatlin was now bleeding from his nose, ears, mouth, and some blood even trickled from his right eye.

Gorman's right shoulder was lying on Gatlin's right knee. Gorman was facedown, and blood pooled out from under his massive body. Gorman too was breathing very sporadically.

Grunge was in a sitting position, his back and his upper body resting against the very badly damaged wall. His left collar bone protruded through his shoulder flesh. His right ear was bleeding, along with his mouth and nose. His legs were slightly spread apart, and his right leg was turned very awkwardly. It was obviously broken in several places. Grunge's eyes are open, but he kept choking on the blood that continued to build up in his mouth. Gatlin's shoulders and head were resting on Grunge's inner thigh. It was one very large pile of badly wounded and broken warriors.

*   *   *

"We're here. We're at the seventh floor" Chris told Blade.

"Let's get down there and help Gatlin before he does something stupid," Blade replied.

"Okay, he should be just right up here. That's where we heard the big . . . Oh shit!" Chris seemed to have frozen.

"What? What is it? Is it Gatlin? Can you see him?" asked a very upset Blade.

"You don't need to see this. Let me go down and check things out first. Then you can come down," Chris told her.

"What? What in the hell are you talking about? I'm the hero remember. You just work here. Now get us down there, or I am going to bust through the ceiling tiles and get there myself," Blade cried, both indignant and worried.

Chris led the two of them down to the hallway of the seventh floor. Blade ran ahead of Chris before he could stop her. Seeing the pile of motionless bodies Blade ran to her boyfriend's side. Kneeling beside his head, she looked him over and then held his head in her hands. Blood continued to pour from his wounds as he lay in Blade's arms, totally unaware of anything and anyone around him.

"Gatlin, can you hear me? This is Blade. Talk to me. Do something to let me know that you aren't dead. Don't you die on me, you big hardheaded ass. Please, honey, say or do something. Tell me what I can do to fix you up." In her hysterical state of mind, Blade was oblivious to anything but the fact that her boyfriend wasn't responding. "Oh, Gatlin, damn it, do something. Don't you dare just lay there and do nothing. You better fight for your life. You better fight for us. I'm here now, baby. Come back to me. Please, Gatlin."

"Blade, someone is coming up the stairs. We have to get some cover somewhere," said Chris.

"I am not leaving him like this," Blade protested. "I'll stay with him and die with him if that's what it takes. But I'm not leaving him here like this."

"Well, okay, if you're not leaving, neither am I. I owe my life to the two of you, so let's guard him with our lives," Chris replied resolutely. "I'll take cover behind the big greenish dude." Chris drew Gatlin's MFG-25, which Gatlin had told him to use in emergencies, and hunkered behind Grunge and beside Gatlin and Blade. Blade placed Gatlin's head in her lap and sat behind his body, staring at the stairway, just beyond Gatlin's feet. Blade picked up Gatlin's arm and held it close to her.

As Blade and Chris awaited the arrival of whoever was coming up the stairs toward them, they were both in the wide open, but neither of them was going to leave the side of the fallen Gatlin.

The two wait several seconds before two Legion members appeared in their line of sight. Psycho—followed by Wrath, who had gotten himself back into the fray once again—reached the top of the stairway. Chris spotted him at the same time that Psycho spotted Blade. With his 9mm pistol, Psycho took aim on his lady target.

Chris fired the MFG-25, hitting Psycho in the shoulder, arm, and hand and grazing his neck. The recoil of the awesome weapon prevented Chris from scoring a kill shot, but it did knock Psycho back down the stairs.

"I'm out," Chris told Blade. "No more rounds in the gun, and I lost the clips that Gatlin gave me when he was carrying me up the stairs earlier, I guess Blade. We're in deep shit, girl. There's still one coming."

Just as Chris finished speaking, Wrath emerged from the top of the stairway, firing on Chris's position. He hit Grunge several times before finally hitting his target. Hit in the right arm, right leg, and left hand, Chris fell back behind Grunge's giant body and out of the line of fire from Wrath's 9mm automatic pistol.

Wrath stopped his attack on Chris when he noticed that Blade was sitting on her knees holding the fallen Gatlin's head on her lap without a weapon in her hand. The only thing that Blade had in her hand was her boyfriend's arm. Gatlin was in no shape to defend himself or protect his beautiful lady, Blade, from Wrath's attack. "So little princess," Wrath snarled, "I see that you have made a new friend, and just in time because your old friend Gatlin is leaving this world and he will be entering the world that I control." He raised his weapon, preparing to fire on Blade and the helpless Gatlin. "I will enjoy bringing the two of you back to this world as my slaves. Don't worry. It won't hurt a bit. I plan to put one in the middle of your forehead. You shouldn't feel a thing, my little beauty.

"When I execute someone, I like to do it right," he added. "So if you have any last words, please, the time is now to share them with whomever you think is listening. You are going to meet your maker. Then you will become mine—body and soul. Oh what a body it is."

"Oh please, Wrath, please allow me to say just one thing to my Gatlin before I go to the dooms of your world," said Blade.

"Yes, by all means, enlighten us with your last plea in your final hour," replied Wrath.

"All I have to say is something to Gatlin," said Blade. She rose up Gatlin's arm as if to kiss it good-bye.

When she'd gotten the arm just high enough she yelled, "PULL THE TRIGGER, BABY. PULL THE TRIGGER NOW!"

Gatlin did as his lady asked; he squeezed the gun trigger with every bit of strength he had left in his body. With the aid of his number one lady, who was aiming his weapon right at Wrath's head, Gatlin unleashed one more assault. The shots ripped into Wrath's upper body, as well as his already horrific face.

Whereas, before, Gatlin was unable to hold the mighty weapon up, much less aim it with any kind of accuracy, with Blade's help, the assault was enough. Wrath's faceless body fell back against the wall behind him and then slowly slid down the wall to the floor. Wrath's body came to a stop in a sitting position across from the three beaten and battered good guys.

"Oh, good job, baby. I knew you weren't done yet. I love you so much. Don't you go back out on me. You stay awake; we can get some help," said Blade to the barely conscience Gatlin.

Gatlin was only able to look up at Blade and give her a half smile.

"Baby, I'm not leaving you. I just have to check on Chris. He was hit several times by Wrath, if you didn't see it. Please stay awake for me. I'll be right back." Blade looked at the now awake but incoherent Gatlin.

"No, Blade, you stay with him," Chris called. "I'm hit in three or four places, but, hell, I'll survive. It just hurts like hell. I'm coming over to y'all." Chris began to crawl and pull himself over to his two newest friends.

Moments later, the three heroes are reunited once again in the hallway just above the stairway. The three of them just looked at one another and laughed and held each other.

Then from the stairway down which Psycho had fallen after Chris's assault, they heard something they didn't want to hear at this time. They'd had enough, but evidently Legion had not yet had enough fighting.

"They're all upstairs. Take them all hostage and let me finish them off," came Psycho's angry voice. "I'll kill the young nonmember one first. He's the asshole who got us all shot up like this, and he's out of ammo. I heard that beautiful sound of the empty chamber clicking after he filled me with that damn hot lead. Then I'll kill Blade because she's the one who started all of this shit in the first place. Then there's the famous Gatlin—the unkillable hero of the world. Well, he will die today by my hand only. I need this to get me out of the shit I'm in with Malakai," said Psycho.

Then appearing at the top of the stairs along with Psycho were Armageddon, Manaconda, Bulge, and Mammoth, as well as Witch, Torchess, and R.I.P. with her six demon troopers.

"Well, lookie here; we have the three menaces to my plan all in one tight little spot, and you all are either out of ammo or are in no shape to use the ammo that you do have. Isn't that right, Gatlin?" said Psycho.

"Go to hell, you piece of shit. You couldn't even defeat the two of us and a civilian with half of the entire Legion force. So kiss my fuckin' ass, you big pussy," Blade snarled.

"Well said, Miss Blade. I would love to kiss your perfect ass, but since I can't trust the three of you, I will just have to kiss it after you're dead; no offense. Pick her up, and get her away from Gatlin and the other one," ordered Psycho.

"Well hell, Blade and Gatlin, we gave them hell," said Chris. "I just want to say that I had a blast blowing the shit out of these losers. I wouldn't change one damn thing. I love you two. You are what goodness in the world is all about. Thanks for everything."

"Enough bleeding-heart shit. Separate them from one another, and do it now!" Psycho barked.

"Get your damn hands off of them, or we will open an entire barrel of whoop ass on you pieces of shit! I guaranty that none of you will like it one bit. So move the hell away from them before we unload on you and your team of low-life shitheads."

The command had come from Bolt-action, who was standing at the far end of the hallway, along with Recoil, Nuke, Amphibian, and Nitro. From behind Psycho and his Legion members emerged GrizzLee, Zeke, Torch, Crosshairs, and Shadow. Then the outside wall behind Gatlin, Blade, and Chris, along with Gorman and Grunge, was blown out. Standing there was Stealth in The Crow with her guns locked on Legion.

With Bolt-action's squad converging on them from one side and GrizzLee's group from the other, Legion was completely surrounded. Psycho and his team were forced to surrender.

"Okay, Psycho, this is how it's going to go down," Bolt-action said. "We're going to evacuate our team without incident. I would do the same if I were you because, right now, not one of you will survive a firefight with us. You know it, and I know it. I promise that we will shoot to kill, and not one of us will be hit. Do you follow me?"

Psycho did not respond verbally. He just motioned for his outnumbered and outgunned team to retreat back to the lobby. From there, they would collect the wounded and return to South America where they belonged—as well as where he would have to answer to Malakai.

Soon Legion had all its members loaded up and ready to make the long flight back to their base. The Allied Force team did the same.

Both Blade and Gatlin insisted that Chris went along with the team back to South Carolina.

The team began to work on the three heroes—Gatlin, Blade, and Chris. "Well, big guy," Bolt-action said, raising his brows at Gatlin, "it looks like I have saved your ass again. Now I believe that we're just about even in that category."

"Oh, hell, Bolt-action, you didn't have to come. We were just about to get on top of them and put them in their place," replied Gatlin, just before he went out from the morphine.

"Yeah, we hear ya. Whatever it takes for you to sleep at night," said Bolt-action, as The Crow and the crew take flight into the wide-open, early morning Arizona sky en route to South Carolina and Stealth slid in Fuel for their listening pleasure.

THE EXTRADITION

I T WAS early Wednesday morning when the report came to Tommy J's office. It read as follows:

*** GAGE HAS BEEN LOCATED IN OLD LA. *** END OF REPORT

Tommy J called Gatlin into his office to inform him that Gage had been located and that he wanted Gatlin to fly to Old LA to apprehend and escort her back to the base in South Carolina for holding until trial.

Blade overhearing the conversation, and furious with the idea stormed into Tommy J's office. "If Gatlin goes, I go," she demanded. (Now Gatlin's fiancée and knowing what Gatlin and Gage had shared in the past, Blade was allowing her jealousy to overtake her professionalism.)

Tommy J explained to Blade that Nitro would accompany Gatlin during this mission. He also reminded Blade of her own mission in Germany, with Crosshairs, Bolt-action, and Pistol Smoke, adding that it would be impossible for him to reassign everyone new missions because of her insecurities with Gatlin and Gage.

Blade stormed out of the office, using some choice words for both Gatlin and Tommy J. Gatlin asked, "T. J. is there anyone else who can accompany Nitro on this mission?"

Tommy J went down the list of missions and personnel. "The team member's personal specialties are the reason it's almost impossible to change the scheduling at this time. The people already have their orders and, at this very minute, are preparing themselves and their equipment, not to mention their states of mind. Hell, Gatlin, you know as well as I do how these minds work around here. They don't like change, just like you and me."

Silence hung in the air for a few moments as the two sat thinking.

"There's Nuke!" said Tommy J.

"Oh shit, come on, T. J. He's my kid brother. He's not ready to go out on his own. He's too green," Gatlin retorted.

"Damn, Gatlin, you can't keep the kid down. He's been doing a lot of good things around here. You taught him well; hell, everyone has taught him well. I recall before you went on your first mission, you was just as cocky, just as young minded and gung-ho as Nuke. I had to let you stretch your wings. Gatlin, it's no damn different. The boy is ready. Let him go. Let him make you proud. Let him make us all proud, if not for you, for him," Tommy J said.

Gatlin reluctantly decides to allow his kid brother to go on the mission. He realized that Nuke was probably ready and that Nitro was a proven hard-ass lady who would take good care of Nuke.

* * *

In the briefing room prior to take-off, Nuke and Nitro got their orders. Tommy J explained to the two, with Gatlin present, "The two of you will be taking the Phoenix, along with a Cougar."

The Phoenix was a four-man fighter jet that could travel at speeds up to 1,200 miles per hour. It was fully loaded with everything a small army would need during a battle. It was the little sister of The Crow. Cougars were fully armed assault vehicles with retractable guns in the front and rear. It was also the little sister of the Puma.

As the two boarded the Phoenix, Nitro turned to Gatlin. "I'll take care of him," she promised. "Don't worry. We'll be fine."

Nitro and Nuke departed from base in South Carolina heading to Old LA, California, and the rest of the team ensuring Gatlin all the while that everything was going to be all right.

*   *   *

Everything went well on the flight to Old LA. As Nitro and Nuke landed, they transferred from the Phoenix into the Cougar. The search for the very beautiful and dangerous Gage was on. Intelligence informed them of Gage's whereabouts; she was expected to visit an underground nightclub on the south side of town.

Nuke, who had not yet shut up since the trip began, continued to reassure Nitro that she wasn't alone. "I'm amped for this mission. I never thought I would see the day when I would be hunting for the person who, at one time, may have become my sister-in-law," he said.

After about three hours of surveillance, they finally hit pay dirt. Into the nightclub strutted Gage, looking gorgeous and apparently unarmed.

Nitro ordered Nuke, "Get the Cougar and pull it around to the front door. I'll have Gage out here in just a couple of minutes."

"Yeah right, you expect me to believe that you are going to bring Gage, one of the baddest babes on the planet out to the car, just like that? How the hell are you gonna do that?" asked Nuke.

"Watch and learn, F.N.G. Watch and learn," said Nitro.

After a few minutes, Nitro walked up to Gage, a syringe in hand. She put her arm around the Legion lady, at the same time sticking Gage in the hip and said, "Hey there, stranger; long time no see."

Gage reached for something in the back of her shorts, but Nitro grabbed her arm. "Not so fast. Have a seat. I have something to tell you and someone who wants to see you outside right now."

"Oh shit," said Gage as she began to get very drowsy.

As Nitro escorted Gage out to the parking lot, Gage asked, "Is it Gatlin out there waiting for me?"

"Yeah, princess, you bet it is," replied Nitro.

"Oh yeah!" yelled Nuke. "How did you . . ."

"Just shut up and help me get her in the car. This will only last about thirty minutes, and we are twenty—five minutes from the airstrip and the Phoenix. So let's move," interrupted Nitro.

The two got Gage into the Cougar and sped off into the darkness toward the airstrip. Upon arrival, they pulled the Cougar into the Phoenix and unloaded Gage, tying her to the cargo net in the back of the plane and removing the Desert Eagle that she had tucked into the back of her shorts.

"You keep an eye on her. I'm going to prep this bird for take-off and notify Tommy J. that we have our package and are returning to base," said Nitro.

They taxied to the grassy runway.

* * *

Gage began to wake up. As her head became clearer and clearer, she determined that she was on a plane heading God only knew where. After struggling to get free for a couple of seconds, she saw Nuke.

Before losing her cool, as she was known to do, she tried her seductive beauty on the young man. "Hey, Nuke, man, you look better than your big brother ever did. Where have you been keeping yourself, cutie?" she cooed, toying with Nuke.

As the Phoenix began lifting off, she convinced Nuke to come sit by her during the flight, because she was scared of flying. Nuke committed and sat by Gage. After sharing some small talk, about ten minutes into the flight, Nuke felt comfortable with Gage and with the situation.

BAM! Just like that, Gage had her legs around Nuke's neck and was squeezing him unconscious. After she felt he was good and asleep she used her long, beautiful, and powerful legs to pull Nuke's motionless body toward her. She leaned down and, with her mouth, removed Nuke's shoulder KABAR knife and began to rapidly cut through the cargo net.

Incredibly, after only three or four minutes, the net was cut and the ropes around her wrists were baby food. Gage was free.

She checked Nuke. He was still out but breathing. Remembering him when he was just a kid, she didn't have the heart to finish the job. Who would have thought, Gage actually had a heart.

Now her focus was on Nitro. But she didn't know how to fly a plane, so she had to come up with something besides taking Nitro out. She checked the cargo area for weaponry, grabbed a 9mm automatic rifle and her Desert Eagle off of Nuke, and headed to the cockpit to handle Nitro.

BAM! Gage kicked in the cockpit door and immediately fired several rounds at the radio. Not knowing anything about airplanes, she hit and destroyed the plane's control panel.

Nitro turned but was strapped into her seat. Gage struck her in the forehead with the butt of the machine gun and demanded that Nitro turn the plane around and head back to the airstrip.

"How in the hell do you expect me to do that, you stupid bitch?" Nitro screamed. "You destroyed the controls, you *dumb LA whore*!" She kicked the gun out of Gage's hands.

"Now we're going to crash, princess," she added, punching Gage in the jaw.

As Gage was falling, she pulled out her Desert Eagle. And as the plane began descending rapidly she shot (though not as accurately as the gun-wheeling arms specialists she was famous for being, due to the abrupt change in gravity) hitting Nitro in the leg at close range. Nitro fell back into the control panel in obvious pain.

Gage, in a panic said, "You two get buried in this plane, but I'm not."

She dashed to the back of the plane and put on a parachute. Then she opened the cargo door and tossed the rest of the parachutes, along with an inflatable raft, out, and then threw herself out behind it.

*   *   *

As the plane continued its descent to the earth below, Nitro got to her feet and yelled out to Nuke again and again; there was no answer.

She found him unconscious. In a split second (and relying on great training), she returned to the cockpit and retrieved the pilot and copilot's parachutes. Wounded and badly bleeding, she put one on herself and then returned to the cargo area and put the other parachute on Nuke. Nuke's size—he was a very good-sized boy and much bigger than she was—made doing so quite a struggle. Time was quickly running out. Nitro knows that she has to get Nuke and herself out of the plane within the next few seconds or there would be no chance for either of them to survive.

All Nitro could think about was her promise to Gatlin. *I'll take care of him . . . I'll take care of him.* She dragged Nuke's motionless body to the cargo bay door and pushed him out. Then she jumped right behind him. As they raced toward the earth, she dived toward Nuke. Reaching him, she pulled his rip cord, followed by her own.

Just moments later, the Phoenix smashed into the side of a mountain and evaporated.

Nitro turned her attention back to Nuke; he was going to hit very hard. (Nitro and Nuke were going to hit the ground, whereas Gage had landed in the water.)

After Nitro landed safely, she saw Nuke lying in a very awkward position about 200 yards from her. She ran to him screaming his name and saying a small prayer. Though she knew it couldn't be good, she hoped for the best.

As she reached his side, she heard Nuke choking. He was alive but all busted up inside, and he seemed to be bleeding internally.

*   *   *

Back in South Carolina, Stealth notified Tommy J and Gatlin, who was standing right beside his godfather, "The Phoenix went down. Moments ago, it just disappeared off radar. Without a distress call, something is badly wrong."

Furious, Gatlin told Stealth, "Get your ass in The Crow. We leave in five."

Tommy J, not rocking the boat, backed the decision of his number one man and the older brother of one of the fallen comrades.

In the hangar, Gatlin got his troops in order and had them board The Crow. Along with Gatlin, the rescue included Stealth, the best pilot in Allied Force; Xtract, a great mind and fine doctor; and Amphibian, the military's finest Navy SEAL who ever took the challenge and a fine field physician.

During the entire trip, Gatlin's comrades tried to calm their out-of-character leader; it did no good.

"There they are!" yelled Stealth.

"Put it down," ordered Gatlin.

"I'm trying."

"Damn it! Put it down now!" demanded Gatlin.

"Okay, okay, sir. I'm putting her down now." answered Stealth.

After the crew had landed safely, Gatlin rushed to his little brother's side. "Oh God, not Nuke!"

Turning his attention to Nitro, he grabbed her by the shirt and screamed, "You fucking bitch!" He dropped her back to the ground.

Turning, he ran back to The Crow, fired up one of the Pumas, and blew out of The Crow like a madman. He flew past his team with a very determined look on his face and fire in his eyes. They all knew that he had only one thing on his mind—and there was no stopping Gatlin once he was fully armed and focused on one thing—Gage.

*	*	*

"You know it's a setup," Xtract told the team. "She'll be waiting for him, to kill him. She always said that, if she couldn't have him, nobody else would either. And she's one who will keep her word."

As the team worked on their two comrades, they discovered that Nuke had multiple broken ribs, a concussion, a broken leg, a strained neck, a broken nose, a possible punctured lung, and several scrapes and bruises. But he would make a full recovery.

"Well, Nuke, I know that you probably can't hear me right now. But you're going to make it, buddy," said Xtract. "This is Xtract's special dose of morphine should make you feel nothing until we get back home. I say that you'll only miss approximately fourteen weeks of the grind. You're lucky, dude. Nitro saved your life, man. We love ya. Hang in there."

"Well, pretty lady, wipe those tears away," said Amphibian "We all know how Gatlin gets—especially when it comes to Nuke and/or Gage. Please, sweetheart, don't take it personally. You have a nice clean gunshot wound to that sexy leg of yours and a concussion and a few scrapes and bruises. Looks to me like you'll be out of action for at least seven weeks, girl. But what you done with that bird and our young friend over there, not to mention yourself, well hell, girl, you're my hero, for what it's worth." Amphibian hugged the shaken Nitro, and he and Stealth helped her to The Crow.

"We have to get this news to Gatlin before he does something to stupid," said Stealth.

After loading both Nitro and Nuke onto The Crow, the team attempted to contact Gatlin.

*   *   *

Gatlin heard the call from his team coming in, but he paid them no mind. He had revenge on his mind and revenge only.

It was now 3:30 a.m., and he was storming down the beach at speeds exceeding 100 miles per hour. (It was a good thing the beach was relatively empty, or who knows what could have happened).

After about an hour of searching the beach, Gatlin spotted the raft Gage had used to make her escape. He followed her footprints until they disappeared into the streets of downtown. He figured she had about a six and a half hour head start, depending on where she'd landed in the ocean and how fast she'd paddled the raft. Knowing Gage as well as he did, Gatlin knew that she could beat and had beaten many women and men who were bigger and stronger than her in several various competitions on the water.

Gatlin began his search at the nightclubs, trying to find out if anybody knew Gage or her whereabouts.

A big, burly guy accompanied by some of his friends approached Gatlin. "Heard you're looking for Gage?"

"Yeah," Gatlin relied. "Do you know where I can find her? It's really important that I speak to her."

"Look, you Commando wannabe, I ain't tellin' you shit—other than get the hell out of my club before my buddies and I kick your ass out."

"I'm sorry I bothered you, sir," Gatlin replied.

Gatlin turned as if to walk away. *BAM*! Gatlin punched the fellow square in the nose. He fell to the floor, totally knocked out, his face rapidly turning black and blue.

The other two grabbed Gatlin and one punched Gatlin in the face as hard as he could. Gatlin turned back to the man. "Somebody leave a door open?" he said. "I feel a draft!"

With all of his might, Gatlin forced his arms around to the front of the man who was trying to hold him with such force that it dislocated the man's shoulders. The man screamed in agony as he dropped to his knees in dire pain. Gatlin then grabbed the throat of the man who had punched him in the face, picking him up and dangling him some six to eight inches off the floor. "I'm going to ask you one more time," Gatlin said. "Where in the hell can I find this bitch?"

The man was in such distress and shock at the sheer madness and unbridled strength of this stranger, he only had one option—tell Gatlin everything that Gatlin wanted to know. "Okay man I'll tell you what you want to know and what I know about your lady friend. The lady is a mercenary or something. She stays in the underground world in the old subway tunnels. She is a badass—a real basket case. Nobody messes with her. She runs that underground world."

"Just point me in the right direction, you slug, and I'll handle the rest," said Gatlin.

The thug told Gatlin where he could find Gage and also warned him of the danger that he might encounter down in the underground world.

Gatlin thanked the man for the information. "I'll let you live," he told the shaking man. "But you need to get your buddies to a hospital and get their wounds tended to. Oh and by the way, when your broken-face friend comes around, tell him I'm not a Commando wannabe; Commando is a Gatlin wannabe."

Standing in a puddle of his own urine, the shaking man just looked at Gatlin and nodded his head.

*　　*　　*

While Gatlin worked his way down the destroyed subway, he removed his guns and body armor from his backpack and strapped them on. With his guns and armor, he was ready for anything.

After he'd been walking for several minutes, he heard an all-too-familiar voice. "Hey there, pretty boy. I knew that you would come looking for me. Oh by the way, how are our friends doing?" She let out a laugh. "Especially your cute ass little brother Nuke?"

"Show yourself, bitch. I'm not leaving this shithole of a place without you," said Gatlin.

"Ooh, sounds like a date," said Gage. "But you look tense from where I'm standing, baby."

"I'm not going anywhere. Show yourself so that we can get on with our lives," said Gatlin.

"Without you, baby, I can't get on with my life," replied Gage.

"Hang that shit up. I'm in love with Blade, and you and I are history. Now get over it," yelled Gatlin.

"Well, sweetheart, if that's the way you want it . . ." BOOM, BOOM, BOOM.

Gage was firing her hip rockets. A hip rocket was a projectile shot from a special gun that only a weapons' specialist like Gage could have come up with. It had power equivalent to a small grenade and pinpoint accuracy.

Gage's shots were strategically placed. The first hit just in front of Gatlin's feet and the second, just to the right of him. Unfortunately, the third struck Gatlin right in the middle of the chest armor, knocking him down and hurting him.

Gatlin rolled out of what he thought was harm's way. Gage began a barrage of heavy arms fire on him, hitting him in the leg and shoulder. Gatlin now in a lot of pain and disoriented, not knowing where the shots were coming from. He found a hole in the subway wall and dived into it. Bullets continued to fly all around him, but they were no longer hitting him.

"Is that all you got, Gage?" he yelled. "I'm not even scratched," yelled Gatlin.

"No, baby, I've got plenty more where that came from," answered Gage.

Gatlin kept Gage talking so that he could pinpoint her location. After she'd unknowingly given up her position, Gatlin rolled out; firing both cannons at the area he felt Gage was in. He heard her moan, but that didn't stop him from his mission. He continued his own barrage, sending 30mm cannon rounds into the location where Gage seemed to be, all the time yelling profanities at Gage. Gatlin was literally caving the walls down around the evil vixen—until she caved.

"STOP! STOP! DAMN IT! YOU WIN! I'm coming out. Don't shoot at me anymore with those damn guns of yours, please!" Gage pleaded as she worked her way down to where Gatlin was. "Okay, okay, you win," she said when she'd reached him. "I bet it really makes you feel like a big man when you can whip a woman's ass, huh, stud?"

Gatlin grabbed her by the arm, slung her to the ground, and pressed his boot to her throat, holding his guns just inches from her pretty nose. Gage could see the fury in his eyes. "You psycho bitch," he spat out, "prepare to meet your maker—which has to be Satan."

Fear was clear in Gage's eyes. She knew she was about to die, right here and right now. Nobody was around to hear her cries, and none of her comrades were there to help her. And this man who had once loved her was so pissed-off at her that he was planning to rip her apart with his fury.

Gatlin's radio crackled. "Gatlin . . . Gatlin . . . Come on, damn it. You know you can hear me. Nuke is going to be all right. Repeat, Nuke is okay. Come in," Tommy J pleaded with Gatlin.

Gatlin heard exactly what he wanted and needed to hear. He drew his mighty weapons back and helped Gage to her feet, instantly giving her an elbow to the face that knocked her out cold.

"Gatlin, go ahead, T. J.," he answered.

"Did you copy my last? Nuke is going to be fine. So is Nitro. Get Gage and get her back here to see your brother. He has been asking about you. That is an order," ordered Tommy J.

Knowing this new development, Gatlin removed his guns, placed them back into his backpack, lifted up the limp body of Gage, and tossed her over his shoulder like a sack of potatoes. Then he worked his way back to the Puma.

Now the only thing left to do was to transport Gage back to South Carolina in the Puma. The trip would take the remainder of the day and well into the next day. Gatlin realized he wasn't going to make the entire trip without sleep. Besides, he had some wounds to tend to before they got too far out of hand. So he stopped at a hotel in western Arkansas to rest and fix himself up.

He carried Gage, handcuffed, into the room and placed her on the bed and cuffed her to the bedpost. Then he worked on his wounds. While he was cleaning himself up, Gage came to. Gatlin walked out of the bathroom wearing just his pants, with bandages on his shoulder and thigh and his ribs wrapped tightly (several seemed to have been broken by the rocket shot fired by his new roommate).

With Gatlin, you could never tell if he was in pain or not. He was just that tough. He never complained about his own pain, just about the imperfections of his team, himself, and the never-ending problem with his guns overheating. He was a true man's man.

"Hello there," said Gage.

Gatlin gave her a look that said, 'Go to hell.'"

"Say, Mr. Body, I need to get cleaned up and get my wounds licked, if you know what I mean," said Gage.

Gage had continued to hound Gatlin about taking a shower and getting her wounds looked after when he decided to oblige her. He uncuffed her from the bed and escorted her to the bathroom, where he allowed her to get undressed, and the entire time reminding her to give him a reason to shoot her.

A few moments later, Gage informed Gatlin, "I'm now undressed. Would you like to see?"

Gatlin entered the bathroom. There stood the beautiful vixen, stark naked. Gatlin grabbed her arm and handcuffed it to his, and at the same time, he strapped one of his guns on the other arm and ordered Gage, "Get your ass in the shower and make it fast."

The entire time that Gage was in the shower, Gatlin had his gun on her through the shower curtain. After Gage finished her shower, she stepped out and asked, "Gatlin, are you going to dry my back off?"

"Not in this lifetime," Gatlin replied. He uncuffed himself from the beauty, telling her, "Leave the door open. You have five minutes to get dry and dressed."

As Gatlin turned to leave the bathroom, Gage using her towel, jumped on his back and tried to strangle him with her towel. Gatlin very calmly reached back, grabbed her by the hair, and pulled her over his shoulder. In the same motion, he punched her in the same spot, directly in the middle of the forehead, and once again, Gage was out.

After Gatlin patched up the wounds on Gage's body, he called into base to let them know that he had Gage and was in Arkansas and would be heading back to base. He would see them when he got there. He didn't mention that he had wounds, not to mention the severity of them. He could hardly get around with his ribs and shoulder in the shape they were.

After another day and a half of traveling,(a bit longer than Gatlin originally estimated) the two finally reached the base. As Gatlin pulled into the hangar, Tommy J, Xtract, Recoil, Stealth, and Amphibian were there to meet them. They unloaded Gage and escorted her to the holding cell, where she would remain until trial.

Xtract told Gatlin the news about Nuke and Nitro's progress and insisted, "Let me look at those wounds, Gatlin. They look pretty bad."

"Not before I see Nuke. They can wait," answered Gatlin.

"Sure," said Xtract. "I understand."

"Good to have you back boss." said Amphibian.

"Oh, man, it is so damn good to be out of that car and away from that crazy ass psycho bitch," Gatlin told him. "You have no idea, Amp."

"Hey, I'll holla at ya later, man," said Amphibian.

"Yeah, man. Later."

*   *   *

Gatlin went into Nuke's room. "Hey, little brother," he said, a tear rolling down his face, "how are you doing?"

Nuke turned to his big brother. "Man, Gatlin, I'm sorry. I thought I was ready, but I guess I learned that I'm not even fuckin' close. Sorry I let you down."

"Nuke, you done just fine," Gatlin told him. "Look what she did to Nitro; hell, what she did to the Phoenix—now we don't have one—not to mention what she did to me."

"She did that to you? *Damn*," said Nuke.

"Damn straight. Now you know why I dumped her crazy ass. She has a hell of a temper," says Gatlin.

"Speaking of tempers and Nitro, I think you owe her an apology. She did everything she could. Hell, she saved my life before she saved her own," Nuke told his brother.

"You get your rest now, little brother. I'll be back to check on you tomorrow night," said Gatlin as he gave Nuke a hug.

As Gatlin leaves Nuke's room he knew that he had to go do something he wasn't very good at—apologize.

"Knock, knock" Gatlin said as he entered Nitro's room. Nitro turned to him, "How are you feelin', girl?" asked Gatlin.

"Could be better, but I really can't complain, I'm surrounded by great people, people I love more than anything in the world," answered Nitro.

"Yeah, hey look, Nitro . . ."

"Gatlin you don't need to apologize. I understand your state of mind at the time. It goes with the job. I didn't take it personally," said Nitro.

"Well, will you at least let me thank you for looking after Nuke and doing what you told me that you would do and, most of all, for saving his life?" said Gatlin.

"Uh no I'd expect you to do the same for me and everyone else around here. Gatlin, you are our leader. You are made of everything that Allied Force stands for. Yeah, Tommy J is the founder and we all owe him a lot for what he has done for all of us, including you. But I'll tell you that every person and/or mutant who is a part of this elite group wishes they had half the leadership and guts that you display on a daily basis. Gatlin, you're the boss; we are supposed to get mad at you and even hate you at some point. But I guarantee we will always be beside you no matter what. Man you are *Billy badass times ten*. With all that said, I accept your apology." Nitro held her arms out.

Gatlin went to her, and they gave each other a long, firm hug. "I won't tell anyone that you're crying, Gatlin; just don't get any snot on me. I really couldn't handle that," said Nitro.

The two laughed.

GORMAN'S RAGE

DEEP IN the southeastern portion of South America just outside San Juan in a very dense jungle with an extraordinarily beautiful panoramic view of the Andes Mountains as a back drop, was a small but very functional jungle laboratory. It was ran and owned by the twisted mind of none other than Psycho.

"Okay, Gorman, we are just about ready for your injection," said Psycho.

"Do you really think that this injection will change Gorman back to his normal self?" asked Jackyl.

"I don't know how normal he once was. However, the injection will remove the gorilla DNA, which now occupies over 85 percent of his total being," Psycho explained.

Jackyl coached Gorman onto the table, in preparation for the experiment. Together, Psycho and Jackyl began to strap Gorman to the cold, bare surgical table. Jackyl continued to keep his close friend, Gorman, as calm as possible, while reassuring him that he would be more man than gorilla when this was over, because Psycho had said so.

Psycho began the injection.

"How long will it take before he begins to change?" asked Jackyl.

"Just a few minutes and we should see some results," Psycho told him.

*   *   *

Approximately fifteen minutes had past, when Gorman began to shake and convulse. Soon, he was out of control.

"What in the hell is going on, Psycho?" asked Jackyl.

"He is transforming into exactly what we want him to become," answered Psycho.

At that same moment, Gorman busted the supposedly unbreakable straps that had once bound him to the cold, uncomfortable table. Gorman then let out a very horrific roar of pain and anger—a sound that not even Jackyl (who had spent each and every day beside the beast and who knew his every move and sound)—had ever heard.

Jackyl looked at Psycho in awe. Psycho wore a crooked smile that made Jackyl very uneasy.

Jackyl then turned to Gorman; he wanted to try and settle the beast down. Gorman looked at Jackyl as if he had never seen Jackyl before. Then he tossed Jackyl to the side. Jackyl fell into a set of self-standing shelves, housing chemicals, bottles, and various books.

Gorman then turned and busted through the wall, heading wildly into the jungle—an out of control, terrifying beast clearing a path of destruction and roaring the entire way.

Jackyl knows that Gorman is heading for nothing but trouble. *Is there anyone or anything that can stop Gorman now?* He wondered.

*   *   *

After several hours of plowing through the jungle, destroying everything in his path Gorman arrived at a small village just north of Valparaiso. The small village consists of farmers and old world families that had lived there for generations. There was a small police force that consisted of ten to fifteen members, most of which were either guerilla soldiers or local young men.

As Gorman arrived at the outskirts of the small village, the villagers begin to scream, yell, point, and grab their frightened children. En masse, they ran toward the other end of the village at the sight of the awesome and very frightening part man, part gorilla. (On this day, there wasn't much man in Gorman's heart or mind.)

Gorman looked at the villagers in a very confused way. In a way, he could relate with the villagers, but he didn't know how.

The small police force was on the scene in just a few minutes, but not before Gorman had destroyed about half the village and inflicted bodily harm on some of the village men who were trying to protect their families from the raging beast. Some of the injuries were very serious; others had simply been tossed aside out of Gorman's way like rag dolls.

"Halt," one of the police officers ordered the out-of-control beast.

Gorman stopped his tantrum and bloodcurdling screams and roared. Gorman looked at the police force. The officers had their guns aimed at him from all angles. Gorman was surrounded. He continued to look around at the soldiers and their weapons. The small village didn't have much firepower; it had never really needed any.

Gorman was looking at some semiautomatic pistols, shotguns, and a handful of AK-47 automatic rifles. Gorman's mind began to wander again. Was he scared? Were these people friends? What had he done to get all of this attention?

Then as fast as the thoughts came to him, they disappeared. And like the beast that he was becoming, Gorman continued his reign of terror through the small, peaceful village.

"FIRE!" ordered the chief of police, Varza.

The soldiers fired on Gorman, hitting him just about everywhere imaginable—in the head, chest, back, stomach, arms, and legs. Gorman saw small pieces of himself fly from his body as round after round continuously made contact with his body from every angle. Gorman felt the sting of the small arms fire entering his body.

Gorman then rushed in his own defense toward the soldiers. Some soldiers retreated; others misjudged the speed and quickness of the massive beast and were tossed to the side as others were thrown through walls, doors, and windows. Some arms and legs were snapped like twigs in the process.

Chief Varza retreated to the small, three-cell police station and radioed the San Juan police force and army for assistance. All the while Chief Varza heard gunfire, screams, roars, and a few small explosions now and then. The longer that Varza talked on the radio, the fewer gunshots he heard. The roars became louder and closer to his end of the village.

*   *   *

Jackyl screeched his jeep to a halt just inside the village. He looked at the mayhem and destruction. Some small fires were burning; debris was everywhere; and injured villagers, as well as police and soldiers, lay everywhere, crying out for help, with broken bones and bleeding. Jackyl witnessed the out-of-control Gorman, as just then Gorman was finishing his reign of terror on the small village by attacking the outside of the police station/jailhouse. Gorman then simply walked back into the jungle at the opposite end from which he'd entered the village.

Jackyl asked a group of locals and soldiers, "Where in this village can I make a telephone call?"

A man rendering aid to one of the soldiers pointed to the police station at the end of the village. Jackyl took off in his jeep, driving to the police station. Upon Jackyl's arrival at the police station, Jackyl looked one more time at the destruction that Gorman has inflicted upon this peaceful village. Jackyl witnessed villagers returning from hiding. Men, women, and children begin to help one another with the wounded.

Jackyl entered the police station; there he found Chief Varza lying on his side with blood trickling from his scalp. "Hey, are you all right?" Jackyl asked the chief.

"Who in the hell are you?" asked Chief Varza, his very prominent South American accent.

"That's not really important at this time. Are you all right? Is there any way that I can contact the States from here?" asked Jackyl.

"I'm fine; just a bump on my head from the wooden shutters that flew through the window as that damn beast pounded my station. I was trying to contact San Juan for some help. The beast ripped the antenna from the wall outside, along with the wiring, slamming my radio against the wall with such force that I think it's now in pieces. I was unable to contact San Juan or Valparaiso, so we're on our own with that monster out there somewhere on the loose," said Chief Varza.

"I'm really sorry for what happened to your village and your people. But if there is a way that I can get in contact with the States, I can promise you and yours help," said Jackyl, concern for his dear friend, Gorman, forefront on his mind. "They will apprehend Gorman. He is not a raging beast. A very bad man has made him like this. If you help me contact some help, I will prove to you that Gorman is just a mellow being that is very misunderstood."

"Yes there's a phone at the medical center across the road there. But I intend to use it to get help here," said Varza.

"Sir, you know nothing about what you're dealing with. You can't stop him with your weapons and your army. I can, with the help from the States; I guarantee this. So please hold off on your army. Just help your people and let me handle Gorman. He will not return. He does not mean harm; he doesn't know what he's doing at this time. If he did, all of you would be dead. So, please, let me help you," Jackyl pleaded.

"Okay, we can try your way first, but if it doesn't work or it takes too long for your friends to get here, well then, I'm going to do it my way. We will level the jungle if we have to," said Varza as he pointed Jackyl in the direction of the only telephone in the village.

"Fair enough, thank you Mr. Varza," said Jackyl as he left the police station and went to the hospital across the street.

*   *   *

"Hello. Hello?" said Jackyl.

"Yeah, who is this?" said the voice on the other end of the call.

"Tommy J?"

"Uh no, this is Recoil. Who is this?" asked Recoil.

"Please, Recoil, I must speak to Tommy J immediately. This is Jackyl. Gorman has destroyed a village about forty miles into the jungle west of San Juan. The villagers are now threatening to kill him. Please let me speak with Tommy J," pleaded Jackyl.

"Damn, that sounds like a real pisser there, Jackyl. Hang on," said Recoil.

Moments later, Tommy J picked up the phone in his office. "Jackyl, what is it?"

"Oh, Tommy J, please, you must help me. It's Gorman he's out of control and is completely unresponsive to me. Psycho gave him an injection that he told Gorman and I would help Gorman become more human than gorilla. But all it did was make Gorman out of control.

"After the injection, Psycho had this look in his eyes as if he meant to do this to Gorman. Please help me, Tommy J. I know no one else to contact, and the authorities are going to hunt him down and destroy him." Jackyl was clearly very upset.

"All right, Jackyl, calm down. Where is Gorman now?" asked Tommy J.

"He's headed west toward the mountains heading from the village that he destroyed, where he hurt many villagers and soldiers. I don't believe that anyone was killed; thank God for that," said Jackyl.

"Okay, Jackyl, we are scrambling Stealth and The Crow. She'll remove some seats from The Crow so that GrizzLee and Zeke can ride with her and a Cougar to you. They will be departing in a couple of moments. Do we need to send aid as well?" asked Tommy J.

"Yes, I'm afraid so, Tommy J," Jackyl answered.

"All right, Jackyl, The Crow is in the sky. Expect them in about two hours or less. I am sending Xtract and the Raven with Nitro, Recoil, and Misti, along with food and aid. They'll arrive a couple hours later. Stay where you are so that Stealth can find your location, and they will start the recovery of Gorman from the village," Tommy J finished.

"Oh, thank you so much, Tommy J. Gorman means too much to me to let anything happen to him," said Jackyl.

"Yes, I know, Jackyl. The team will have weapons; that's why GrizzLee and Zeke are coming. Keep in mind that, if need be, we will use weapons to prevent bodily injury to ourselves or anyone else," Tommy J warned him.

"Yes, sir, I understand. Again, thank you, Tommy J," said Jackyl as the two hung up their telephones.

*   *   *

Jackyl, Varza, and the other villagers had been tending to the wounded for an hour and fifty minutes, when they heard the air blow the treetops, followed moments later by relative silence. Then The Crow appeared over the village, searching for a place to set down.

"Don't be alarmed," said Stealth over The Crow's PA system. "We're here to help. I am Stealth; this is The Crow. We will be landing and helping y'all. I have on board with me a couple of people who are going to help out as well. They are GrizzLee and Zeke. Please do not be alarmed; they will not harm you."

Jackyl motioned to Stealth, indicating where she could put The Crow down.

The Crow was the fastest and deadliest craft in the history of aviation. It was silent in its approach. It could hover, as well as land and take off, vertically. The Crow was the number one attack plane in Allied Force's arsenal. It was Stealth's invention; therefore, she was the pilot.

In a couple of seconds, The Crow was on the ground. The rear bay door opened, and out walked GrizzLee, followed by Zeke—making two more giants that this small village would see today. Some of the villagers screamed in horror as they witnessed the two powerful mutants.

Following GrizzLee and Zeke from the rear of The Crow was Stealth, driving the ground assault vehicle. The .50 caliber machine gun had been removed from the back of the vehicle so that the very large GrizzLee and Zeke were able to ride with Stealth. Neither GrizzLee nor Zeke could drive. This vehicle was made for speed, and it was known for its incredible all-terrain abilities. This assault vehicle was second only to the awesome firepower of the Puma. But in this case, the operation called for the smaller, quicker, and much better all-terrain vehicle; Xtract had recommended using the Cougar to get the job done.

Jackyl met the three members of Allied Force at the rear of The Crow. "Thank you for helping Gorman," said Jackyl.

"Yeah, hey no problem. Tell me, though, how could you allow Psycho to do this to your dear friend, Jackyl?" asked GrizzLee.

"Save it, little man, for someone who gives a shit about you and your kind. We are here for Gorman, a creation that has been nothing but manipulated by your leaders," Stealth said before Jackyl could reply. "You regulars are villains by choice. The mutants are forced into it by your sick-ass minded leaders. So get bent, tool, and get the hell out of my face."

GrizzLee just looked at Zeke and Jackyl as he and Zeke boarded the Cougar, with Stealth behind the wheel.

"Come in, Xtract," said Stealth from the radio in the Cougar.

"Xtract, go ahead, Stealth."

"Yeah, X, we're on the ground and will be moving out momentarily. I would like to give these people an ETA on the aid and food. Can you give me that, please?" asked Stealth.

"Yeah, Stealth, ETA about two hours forty-five minutes, roughly. Over," said Xtract.

"Copy that, Xtract. Be careful. We'll see you a little later. We are moving out. Over and out," Stealth replied.

Stealth relayed the message to the people of the village. Then she returned to the Cougar and began following the obvious path that Gorman had made through the jungle.

*   *   *

After several minutes, Jackyl decides to follow the Cougar from a distance. He intended to ensure that the Allied Force extraction team did not hurt Gorman or use weapons on him.

*   *   *

Stealth, with GrizzLee and Zeke, traveled the rough path that Gorman had made through this beautiful landscape for over two and a half hours.

*   *   *

Meanwhile, back at the village, Xtract, with the Raven and his team, arrived. The Raven, being much larger wasn't as fast as, nor could it maneuver like, The Crow. It did have the ability to land and lift off vertically. The Raven was Allied Force's assault transport craft. It could carry the entire team, as well as enough ammunition and supplies to outfit everyone and all the vehicles needed to transport the entire team on the ground during any operation.

After the Raven made a successful landing, the rear bay door opened, and Recoil and Nitro exited the craft, driving Pumas. Recoil had Misti with him, as well as food and supplies, first aid, and plenty of fresh water. Recoil drove over to the makeshift hospital that the locals had set up just outside, as well as inside, what appeared to be the schoolhouse for the children.

Nitro awaited Xtract at the rear of the Raven as Xtract finished shutting everything down. Now Xtract was in the Puma with Nitro. They drove to the schoolhouse to lend their expertise to the situation. Xtract and Nitro were both extremely well-schooled in the medical field, as well as being field surgeons. Recoil and Misti were very good in the field as assistants to Xtract and Nitro.

Nitro just looked at the mayhem that surrounded them, while Xtract contacted Stealth and informed her that they were on the ground and were rendering aid to the wounded. "Man, I can't believe that Gorman would or even could do this to any humans, not to mention villagers. Hell, he's from the jungle. Something is very bad wrong here. Gorman doesn't do this shit. This is bad, very bad, for not only Gorman but also Lee, Zeke, and Stealth. I hope they can handle him," said Nitro.

"You and me both. I'm not sure that T. J. was completely informed as to the destruction and devastation that Gorman imposed on this village and its people. The scary thing is that he did all of this with his bare hands with automatic weapons firing at him from all angles and, from the looks of the blood and fur, hitting him a lot," said Recoil.

"Well, Stealth knows that we're here if they need us. And as much as I don't want to, we may have to use lethal force and take Gorman out for good," replied Nitro.

"Yeah I know," said Recoil.

"Let's get these people stable enough to transport them to the real hospital in San Juan so they can get back on their feet," said Xtract. He turned to the man who was clearly the chief of police. "We need some of your people to help us, chief. They can begin handing out food and water, getting bandages, and helping those with injuries that aren't so serious to the hospital. We'd really appreciate it."

"Yes, sir, we'll help," Varza assured him. "My name is Chief Varza."

"Okay, Varza, I'm Xtract. This is Misti, Nitro, and over there is Recoil. We are here to help. Nice to meet you," said Xtract.

Varza began to give orders to his remaining force, as well as to some of the villagers, to help get the wounded food and water and get them transported to the hospital. Varza also ensured the villagers that "these people" were here to help.

The locals began to help and trust Allied Force. They all worked together, and shortly they really had something going between the two entirely different worlds. One thing that these two very different worlds had in common was that, when help was needed, help was there.

"Hey, this is really working well," said Recoil as he wiped his sweat from his brow.

"Yeah, the entire world should see what we are witnessing. They could damn sure learn from this," said Misti.

*   *   *

Stealth, GrizzLee, and Zeke, with Jackyl close behind, tracked Gorman well into the night. The trio came to a dried-up river.

"Awe shit, we can't go through that," said Stealth. "It's way too soft. We'll sink to the damn axles in a couple seconds. Then we'll be just shit out of luck, not to mention in the middle of the jungle without transportation.

"We can't go around 'cause there isn't any way of knowing how long that that will take, not to mention the fact that we've gotten this far because we've been following Gorman's trail. The jungle is just too dense to even try going around," she concluded.

"Well, then we go on foot from here," replied GrizzLee.

"Yeah it's the only way. But I think that you should sleep first Lee," said Stealth.

GrizzLee was 60 percent grizzly bear and 40 percent man. GrizzLee still had to hibernate, but because he also had human DNA, he didn't have to hibernate all winter like regular bears. He did, however, still have to sleep every day for at least six to eight hours (preferably eight plus hours) to regenerate his strength.

"What time do you have, Stealth?" asked GrizzLee.

"It's almost 1:30 a.m. Get some sleep. I'm sure that Gorman will have to rest as well, so we shouldn't lose too much ground. I'm going to get some sleep myself. We can get Zeke to take watch for the night," Stealth suggested.

"Sounds good enough to me," said GrizzLee as he motions for Zeke to guard the Cougar and them as they slept.

Zeke moved over toward the path that Gorman had made through the jungle and stood between the path and the Cougar.

Zeke was a medieval being. No one at Allied Force, including Tommy J could explain his existence. The only thing that Tommy J and Xtract could come up with was that Zeke was from anywhere from the sixteenth century to the early eighteenth century, according to his dress, his helmet, and his two large weapons of choice. His first weapon was the bardiche, a Russian poleax used during that time period. His second weapon of choice was a poleax with a hammer head, a weapon used by the Swiss back in the sixteenth century.

Zeke made an excellent lookout or guard because, for unknown reasons, Zeke did not sleep—ever. This could be one reason that he was so very close to GrizzLee, a sort of protector of GrizzLee while GrizzLee slept. Zeke did not speak, even though GrizzLee, as well as the other members of Allied Force, had tried to teach him to speak. Zeke only made rough noises and occasional grunts when things were heavy or he got hurt.

GrizzLee and Allied Force had learned in the past that Zeke would never quit fighting until either himself or his foe was dead. Zeke possessed the remarkable ability to heal himself; he could regenerate himself somehow. Zeke was truly a mystery. However, Allied Force wouldn't change a thing about him. He was very loyal to his teammates, especially to GrizzLee. Zeke would die to keep any of his fellow members alive; he was that kind of being. Although a bit frightening to the rest of the world because of his size, he was almost infantile in his knowledge of everyday life in this era. But when it came to battle, Zeke was one of the best to have on your side.

*   *   *

At 6:00 a.m., Zeke saw Gorman returning along the trail he and his companions had been following. Gorman was still enraged; he continued to roar and scream bloodcurdling screams of anger and agony. Gorman's screams awakened both Stealth and GrizzLee from their sleep.

Zeke walked toward Gorman to start the inescapable battle that was about to begin.

"Oh my God, that is Gorman?" said Stealth.

"He is very strong," said GrizzLee. "I'm not so strong right now." He sat up in the back of the Cougar and watched Gorman, who was now about fifty meters down the path.

Zeke looked at GrizzLee and then at Stealth and then back at Gorman. Seeming to understand, Zeke resumed his walk toward the enraged Gorman.

"I'll keep an eye on him for you, Lee," said Stealth. "You need to get more sleep."

Stealth knew she couldn't help Zeke with Gorman. Gorman would kill her in a matter of moments in the rage he was currently in if she didn't use her weapons on him. So all she could do was watch this one.

*   *   *

Gorman's screams also awakened Jackyl, who had pulled off the path about twenty-five meters behind the Cougar and tucked himself out of sight of Stealth, GrizzLee, and Zeke.

Jackyl watched as Zeke walked straight toward Gorman; he is now within fifteen meters of Gorman. Gorman had yet to notice Zeke coming toward him. He was looking around as if lost physically as well as mentally. Gorman seems totally oblivious to Zeke's presence, not to mention Stealth and GrizzLee and even the Cougar.

A few moments later, Gorman seemed to have heard, or maybe smelled, the presence of someone or something. The man/gorilla looked around for a couple of seconds before focusing in on Zeke walking toward him, now only ten meters away. Gorman raised upright and began to roar even more loudly than he had been. He threw his arms into the air in a threatening way.

Gorman barks at Zeke a few times in a gorilla manner and then charged Zeke. Zeke drew back his mighty bardiche. As the two got within a couple of meters of each other,

Zeke swung the giant Bardiche, slashing Gorman across the shoulder and chest. Gorman screams out in agony, so loudly the entire jungle awakened, as did GrizzLee, after only about five hours and forty-five minutes of sleep.

GrizzLee wasn't at full strength, but it would just have to do if Zeke couldn't take down Gorman alone. GrizzLee sat up once again in the back of the Cougar, and he and Stealth watched the fray between Zeke and Gorman.

Unbeknownst to them, Jackyl was also watching the battle of the two giants.

Zeke turned and, once again, swung his bardiche, once again striking Gorman, this time in the back, causing another large, deep gash in Gorman's flesh.

This time, Gorman turned and hit Zeke in the chest with a mighty right-hand blow; as he did so, he fell back and into the undergrowth of the jungle. Zeke was knocked back ten feet, causing him to drop his bardiche.

"Damn, I have never seen anyone or anything knock Zeke backwards, not to mention that far back," said Stealth, with a very concerned look on her face.

GrizzLee said nothing. He just continued to look on.

Zeke was now looking straight into Gorman's eyes. Gorman was, in turn, returning Zeke's gaze. Zeke pulled his poleax with a hammerhead from the back of his sheath and tossed it to the ground, away from the battle. This one was going to be hand to hand.

"Oh no, Zeke, not this time. Don't go one-on-one with Gorman today, sweetheart," said Stealth.

"He will fight fair. He knows no other way. Nor does he know that Gorman is juiced today," said GrizzLee.

Gorman began to get back to his feet just as Zeke charged him again. This time, Zeke lowered his shoulder and drove it into Gorman's midsection. The two of them fall back to the jungle floor. Gorman then grabbed Zeke, who stood six foot six inches tall and weighed a little better than 350 pounds, and threw the medieval being. Zeke landed nearly eight feet away on the jungle floor. Gorman reached over to a broken tree, about three feet in diameter and approximately seven feet long, and pulled it from the ground by its roots. As Zeke was getting up, Gorman swung the tree like a baseball bat, striking Zeke in the chest and crushing Zeke's armor chest plate.

Gorman swung the tree at Zeke again, this time hitting Zeke in the front of his full face armor and severely damaging Zeke's face mask. Zeke was bleeding badly from under his helmet and mask.

Gorman went to Zeke and, once more, picked Zeke up and threw him into the trees and undergrowth. Zeke, very slowly and extremely unstable, tried to get to his feet.

Gorman had nothing on his mind right now but Zeke's death. He picked Zeke up, this time holding the shaken man above his head. Zeke was, at this time, in very bad shape and barely able to fight back.

Bam! Gorman was kicked in the back with such force that he dropped Zeke to the ground and hit the ground himself, fast and hard. Gorman tried to get to his feet, but he was kicked once again, this time in the backside. Gorman fell back to his face. GrizzLee then grabbed Gorman by the hair on the back of his head and begins to pound his fist into Gorman's skull.

After several blows to the head and face, Gorman in his fury, rolled over onto his back. In doing so, he lost a very large handful of fur from his scalp. Gorman took another blow square to the nose.

The next punch GrizzLee threw missed its aim. Gorman caught his hand. He outmuscled GrizzLee and tossed the bear-man over to the side. Then somehow, after a beating like that, Gorman jumped back up to his feet.

Gorman again picked up the tree that he'd used to hit Zeke and awaited GrizzLee's effort to get back to his feet. As GrizzLee was rising up, Gorman swung the tree downward as if it were an axe and he was chopping wood, right into GrizzLee's back. As Gorman prepared to bring the tree up for another swing, GrizzLee turned as only he could. GrizzLee was a mixed martial arts specialist who also happened to stand seven foot three inches tall and weigh 345 pounds.)

As Gorman tried to keep up with the GrizzLee's unmatched movements, GrizzLee used a spinning heel kick to splinter the tree that Gorman had been swinging. Gorman looked at the tree in awe. Immediately, GrizzLee delivered a front flying knee to his opponent's chin, knocking the beast off his feet again.

As GrizzLee approached Gorman, he noticed Jackyl out of the corner of his eye. Evidently, Jackyl had made his way down to the battle of these three Titans without anyone noticing. While GrizzLee was looking at Jackyl, Gorman got back to his feet. He ran and tackled GrizzLee to the ground. Gorman once again saw a large tree stump beside them. He grabbed it and lifted it over his head, ready to slam it down onto GrizzLee.

TOOF, TOOF, TOOF. Three darts flew through the air and landed in Gorman's neck. Still standing over GrizzLee, who had hit his head when Gorman tackled him and was bleeding from a large gash above his right eye, Gorman paused. GrizzLee rolled over onto his back and, with his hands over his head, he thrust his feet up and into Gorman's chin, knocking Gorman back and causing him to drop the stump just inches from GrizzLee's head.

"Step back," yelled Jackyl. "I can stop him now. These are elephant tranquilizer darts. In a few seconds, he'll be out like a baby. Just don't hurt him anymore, please."

After a few seconds, Gorman did begin to settle down. Eventually, he fell over and was out of it. Jackyl rushed to Gorman's side and began to inspect his friend's wounds. Jackyl then told GrizzLee, "Your friend over there doesn't look too good. Maybe we should get them out of this jungle and back to the village for some medical treatment."

"Yeah," said GrizzLee.

"By the way," Jackyl added, "come to think of it, you don't look so good yourself."

As GrizzLee, Jackyl, and Stealth began getting Gorman prepared for the long, rough trip back, Zeke got back to his feet. He walked over to GrizzLee and Stealth and just stood by them, his weapons back in place. It was obvious to both GrizzLee and Stealth that Zeke's legs weren't as sturdy as they normally were, and he wasn't breathing too well. Blood still trickled from under his helmet. GrizzLee knew that his buddy was in very bad shape.

But in the past, Zeke had been able to heal himself. Like a lot of mutants, he had the capability of regenerating his health. GrizzLee was hoping that Zeke could again do that for himself. Zeke wasn't just like all other mutants. The minds of Allied Force barely understood him. But one thing was sure; as always, Zeke could be hanging on to his last breath, and he would put his pain on hold when he was needed and guard his teammates. And now he stood by Stealth and GrizzLee, looking over them as they strapped Gorman's limp body to the back of the Cougar.

After the team had Gorman stowed away, Jackyl asked, "Can I ride with Gorman back to the village?"

"I guess so," GrizzLee replied. "I may need you to help me with this giant in case something goes wrong.

"Oh yeah," he added, giving Jackyl a puzzled look, "why didn't you shoot Zeke and me with those tranquilizers? You could have made Psycho very proud, bringing back such a catch."

"Because I knew you weren't out to kill Gorman. You were out to get him back and out of harm's way. There was no telling what would have come and hunted him down if . . . oh I don't even want to think about that. And you have helped me, so in return, I helped you. We aren't all bad all the time.

"Gorman is childlike and innocent. He's helpless to their experiments and injection without me, just like I am helpless without him to the meanness of Legion and torment of others in and outside Legion. Psycho takes advantage of the mutants. I will never let him get his hands on Gorman ever again." Jackyl's eyes narrowed. "He lied to us. For that, he will pay."

The Cougar was now turned around and heading back to the village. "Well yeah you're right," said Stealth. "Psycho will pay for what he has done to Gorman and for causing havoc in the jungle community, especially to Chief Varza and his village. But Gorman isn't going to be able to assist you in anything for some time. I know as well as you do, that you can't take on Psycho by yourself. So this time it's on us, Allied Force."

"No problem," Jackyl replied. "When we get back, I will personally show you guys where Psycho's lab is in the jungle. Then you all can do what it is that you all do best. Just let me have Gorman."

"Gorman isn't at fault here. He's a victim, and we will handle that accordingly," said GrizzLee. "So don't worry about Gorman and yourself; you just concentrate on getting your big friend here better.

"Then you both should consider coming over to the good side. T. J. does good things for mutants," he added.

For several miles, nothing else was said. But there was now a mutual respect present between the two very different sides. For Jackyl, it was the wisdom of the mutant, GrizzLee that was responsible for this newfound respect. As for GrizzLee, it was the comradeship between Gorman and Jackyl and Jackyl's determination to help his friend find a cure.

*   *   *

"Come in, Xtract, over," said Stealth.
"Xtract, go ahead, Stealth," said Xtract.

"Yeah, we are returning to the village. We're heavy one very large, but calm and sleeping package, as well as his sidekick," Stealth reported Stealth.

"Copy that. It's good to hear your voice. We were getting a little bit worried about y'all. How is everyone? We have all the wounded transported to the hospital in San Juan. The rest have been fed, and we are looking pretty good right now. Everyone is helping everyone else, feelin' real proud to be a part of this," said Xtract.

"Damn, Xtract, you sure are long-winded this morning," Stealth replied. "Anyway, ETA fifteen minutes. It was a successful hunt. Lee has some wounds. Zeke has some pretty bad ones, but you know, apart from blood, Zeke doesn't even look bad. Well you know Zeke; he probably doesn't even know that he's hurt. And if he does know, he doesn't care. Honestly, X, I'm a bit worried about Zeke. His breathing doesn't sound good at all, and believe it or not, he looks tired to me also."

"Hey, Stealth, I don't mean to freak you out, but get Zeke here as quickly as possible," said Xtract. "You said that he looks tired. Do everything and anything that you can to keep him alert."

"Copy that, X. We are haulin' ass as it is. Over and out," said Stealth.

* * *

Back in the village about twenty minutes later, Misti heard the Cougar approaching through the jungle.

"Here they come," said Misti.

As the Cougar pulled into the village, the team noticed something very strange. Zeke was riding on the front hood of the Cougar.

"What the hell?" said Nitro.

"What is Zeke doing on the hood?" Recoil asked GrizzLee.

"Well, Xtract said to keep him alert. So I told Zeke to get on the hood and watch out for any more danger. I thought the fresh jungle air would do him some good and keep him alert, at least until we got back here. Besides, Zeke thinks he's doing something good," GrizzLee explained.

The group unloaded their cargo. They placed Gorman in the concrete cell at the police station. This time, they tied him down, using anchor chains made of titanium that they retrieved from the cargo hold of The Crow. All the while, Allied Force tried to convince Chief Varza that Gorman would not get loose again.

"What do we do with this one?" asked Xtract, pointing to Jackyl.

"Nothing," answered GrizzLee. "He poses no threat. He helped in the apprehension of Gorman. He has information about the whereabouts of Psycho and his laboratory. In return, we will fix Gorman up for him, and the two will be released," answered GrizzLee.

"OH BULLSHIT! Lee, let me wax both these bastards right here, right now and get it over with," said Recoil. "I didn't come down here just to watch you catch and release. This ain't no fuckin' fishin' show."

"Relax, Recoil, you will get your shot tomorrow to blow stuff up and, as you put it, kick some ass," GrizzLee said. "But for now, you are going to have to just hold tight and sleep on it. That will give us a chance to get rested and heal our wounded. Your action is tomorrow. I'll let you know then. As for now, let's just help these people and ourselves to get better and stronger."

*   *   *

As the dawn of a new day appeared, Gorman began to wake up. Sitting just outside his cell was Jackyl.

A few huts down from Gorman, GrizzLee was preparing for the day. After getting up and around, GrizzLee went to check on Zeke.

"Good morning, Lee," said Xtract.

"Is it a good morning?" asked GrizzLee.

"Well our medieval friend made it through the night," Xtract replied. "He let me change his dressings every time. But he's still always on guard. You're going to have to work on that. You know, get him into the present era. I really think that that would be beneficial for him."

"Well, Xtract, I believe in the old saying, 'If it isn't broke, don't fix it.' Besides, he knows no different and I like him that way. He's extremely loyal, and you know as well as I do that that's a good thing," GrizzLee said.

"Well anyway, this big ole guy is going to make it. I don't know how, but he is," said Xtract.

"Well as much as I would like to stay and chat, I have orders to give," GrizzLee said.

"Oh by the way," Xtract said before GrizzLee could leave. "Nitro and Recoil have been working on Gorman. They both assured me that we would be able to get him back to his old self by the end of the day."

GrizzLee just looked at Xtract without replying and then turned and walked out the door.

Xtract, with a grin on his face, watched GrizzLee and Zeke leave. Xtract and all of Allied Force knew that GrizzLee and Gorman were as close to hated rivals as you could possibly get. And Xtract knew that it had to be killing GrizzLee to have to follow orders and let Gorman go after hunting him down and what he'd done to his friend, Zeke, and tried to do to himself.

From the main street of the village, GrizzLee called out to Stealth, Jackyl, and Recoil, so that they can go over their next operation—the search and destruction of Psycho's jungle laboratory. As GrizzLee went over the plan of attack, there are obvious mixed emotions among the group, primarily in relation to having to travel with the enemy, Jackyl.

The team all knew the code: "We are to follow orders, whether we agree or disagree." It went with the job.

*   *   *

The Crow was lifting off; the plan was set. GrizzLee watched as the awesome jet disappeared into the jungle sky. GrizzLee then turned his attention to the cleanup at hand. He dived right in, right alongside his teammates, volunteers, and the villagers.

Soon Varza and what was left of his force, which consisted of a few wounded, diehard soldiers, were also helping out. Chief Varza had lost about 85 percent of his force, as the majority of his officers were now in the hospital recovering from wounds sustained during the raid of Gorman, who was being housed just up the street from their location.

The men, women, children, and the remaining members of Allied Force worked side by side to rebuild the village and mourn their losses. From all directions of the jungle, people of all tribes, cultures, races, and ages came to the aid of the fallen village.

"Wow, I thought only good news traveled fast," said Chief Varza.

"It does, my brother," said GrizzLee, "but bad news travels even faster."

"AMEN!" said Nitro.

"Oh, my gosh," added Misti, "look at all of them. We are truly blessed here. Your people will not mourn long, Chief Varza. This village will be back and standing stronger than ever before in no time."

*   *   *

On The Crow, Jackyl directed Stealth to Psycho's laboratory. As Stealth climbed to 12,000 feet, she saw the laboratory and flew on by. Then she silently lowered the craft for deployment.

Stealth stayed with The Crow while Recoil took Jackyl with him on this unusual search and destroy operation, so that Jackyl could point out the best way to enter the small complex without detection.

The two arrived at a safe distance from the complex. Recoil ordered Jackyl, "Stay put until I return."

Recoil worked his way up to the laboratory; he spotted his target.

Recoil kicked the door down and rushed Psycho. Within seconds, Recoil had Psycho's ass kicked, gagged, and tied up. He wanted so badly to take this low-life scum out, but followed his orders. Recoil made Psycho watch as he destroyed all of Psycho's work, his formulas, and everything else that was in the laboratory.

Psycho, known for wetting on himself, didn't disappoint. He moaned and groaned as he watched all of his crooked work go up in flames.

Recoil, grabbed Psycho and dragged him by his lab coat to a safe distance. Then he returned to the laboratory and placed C-4 explosives throughout the complex, enough to bring down a small town. After the C-4 had been placed, Recoil returned to Psycho and, at gunpoint, made Psycho press the button to set off the C-4 charges himself.

With many quick but large explosions, the laboratory was completely destroyed. What was once a laboratory was now just a very large crater in the jungle floor.

*   *   *

Stealth saw the smoke and felt the vibrations of the blast. She knew that was her cue to evacuate Recoil, Psycho, and Jackyl.

On the flight back to the village, Recoil worked out on Psycho a little bit. As The Crow arrived back at the village, Psycho looked at his captors. "You idiots," he snarled, blood coming from his mouth and nose, "what are you going to do to me? I know Tommy J will not allow you to kill me. All that you can do is maybe lock me up. I will eventually get out, and you can bet that I will never forget this day for as long as I live."

The team said nothing. Stealth just calmly landed The Crow in the middle of the street.

By now, Gorman was up and around and, fortunately for the world, he was back to his old self once again. Jackyl joined Xtract in escorting Gorman out to the streets. As was expected, the villagers begin to scream in fear at the sight of Gorman.

Xtract offered up an explanation. "It wasn't Gorman who caused this tragedy in your peaceful village, but that man." He pointed to Psycho.

With his hands tied behind his back, Psycho was a sitting duck.

GrizzLee instructed Jackyl, "Get Gorman and head back to get your jeep. And get yourselves out of this part of the country, maybe this part of the world."

As the two disappeared into the jungle, GrizzLee turned to his team. "Okay, load 'em up and let's go home."

The teams boarded The Crow and the Raven.

"What do you want me to do with this madman?" asked Chief Varza.

"Ask your people. I'm sure they can come up with something. But here's a hint, don't kill him or allow him to die. We wish you well, my friend. We are sorry for your losses, but you can and will rebuild. You know who to call if you need us. Good luck, friend," said GrizzLee.

As The Crow lifted off, shortly followed by the Raven, the team could hear Psycho pleading for the team to take him with them. Moments later, the team noticed that the villagers were all crowding around Psycho. Shortly thereafter, they saw a large cloud of dust rise into the air. Then all they could hear was Psycho screaming.

"I feel sorry for that man down there," said GrizzLee.

"What the hell? You must be losing your edge, Lee," Recoil exclaimed. "I hope that they kick the living shit out of him."

"No, I didn't mean Psycho. I feel sorry for Chief Varza. He's gonna have to break them up every day so that they don't kill him," explained GrizzLee as Stealth slid in some 3 Doors Down for the team's listening pleasure during the flight home.

TIME TRAVELERS

I<small>N</small> S<small>OUTH</small> America, on November 20 at 10:00 a.m. Malakai was holding a meeting with his top advisors, as well as some of their next in charge in the Legion meeting room. He addressed the group. "As you know," he told them, "the reason for this meeting is to discuss the termination of Allied Force. We must crush them. They are interfering in Legion's ability to take over the world. Therefore, I am here to discuss any ideas—new weapons, equipment, and the like—that could aid us in once and for all successfully terminating Tommy J and Allied Force."

For awhile Malakai continued the meeting of new ideas.

Out of nowhere, Nazi spoke up. "B<small>ULLSHIT PLAN</small>!" he yelled. "It's bullshit. I'm so damn tired of hearing these lame ass ideas about how to rid the world of Allied Force and Tommy J. I know, hell everybody knows, that you and Tommy J are old college buddies or whatever. And I know that you want him alive, to get from his mind all his ideas, formulas, and knowledge. Well, we are tired of going into battle against Allied Force with our hands tied behind our backs, so to speak. I say to hell with Tommy J and Allied Force. I've got a plan that will indeed rid the world of Allied Force and Tommy J at the same time, giving us control of the entire world, along with the many space programs that you want to get your hands on. With a little help from

Psycho, I can give us the world and beyond by Christmas," he concluded.

"Okay smartass," Malakai snapped. "First, what business I have with Tommy J is none of yours. Second, if you ever interrupt a meeting of mine by screaming out and talking to me or anyone else on the panel who doesn't report directly to you like that, I assure you, you will not like the repercussions at all. Third, enlighten me, as well as the rest of the panel, with this great idea, including what you have planned for Psycho. You know that you can't just pick my people out and give them orders without discussing your idea with me first. That's how it works. I'm first in charge. You are second in charge. That's how it is. If you don't like it tough shit. Deal with it or hit the damn road."

Nazi told Malakai and the panel his idea. It involved a lot of firepower, equipment, supplies, personnel, and even a warper for time travel. "With me leading the campaign rather than the people who did it the first time, we could change history," Nazi promised. "I, along with several of your people, could travel back in time, to August 29, 1939, over seventy years ago. Travel back to World War II. This time, we wouldn't fail." Nazi took a drink of water. "I was there before, as was Bulge. With what we know, along with the personnel and weapons and equipment that we now have, we could change the way the world is now.

"Instead of this shitty democracy, we could have Communism, or what I refer to as Nazism. When we get back to 1939, we could win the war before the damn Americans are even in-country, thus saving the Japanese and all the other powers that were stirred into the mix a lot of hassle. I know the mistakes that my mother country, Germany, made along with the Axis. Once we accomplish this very dangerous, large, and extremely controversial mission, upon returning to the present day and time, the world will be mine . . . ours.

"I could be president, and you, Malakai, could be ruler of all worlds. Since you are so in love with your mother country, the United States, Malakai, you could live anywhere in the States that you wish to, without having to worry about Allied Force. The only thing that you will have to worry about is what you are going to do with all of your new real estate."

Malakai again reminded Nazi of who made the decisions, who was number one, and who number two was. "I will not tolerate back talk from you, Nazi, or anyone else for that matter, in that way again. However, I like the idea. It's not bad, not bad at all.

"Psycho, make a list of materials that you'll need to construct this warper or time traveling machine. You have until Thanksgiving Day to make this happen, which will be appropriate as I'll give thanks for my new world.

"Nazi, you and I have a meeting to finish, along with some very big plans to make in limited time. As for the rest of you, you will hear from me when Nazi decides who he'll need on this mission in order for it to be a successful one. This meeting is over. Dismissed," Malakai ordered.

"Oh, Malakai, a time machine isn't all that complex of an instrument," said Psycho once the others had left. "In fact, it's quite simple. I believe that I could have it ready by the deadline. I'll get help from my very much improved helper, Ratchet. He will make a superb lab tech assistant, with the state-of-the-art chip in his mainframe, along with our computer system and some pushing of the proper buttons and keystrokes. Hell, we will be in 1939 in time for Thanksgiving if you wish."

"Yeah okay, whatever. Just get it done. Then get Ratchet, as well as any other new toys that you might want to try out, geared up, primed, or whatever it is that you need to do and be prepared for World War II relived," Malakai ordered.

"One other thing, guys," Psycho said. "How big do you want the machine to be? The size will not slow down or speed up the construction of the machine. I can use a closet to send people one at a time or an entire room so that we can all go at once. Better yet, why don't we use the airplane hangar? That way, we can all go, along with our equipment, supplies, and even transportation, at one time. What do you think?"

"Sounds great," said Malakai. "Get on it."

* * *

It was Thanksgiving Day. The entire Allied Force team was present at headquarters, Tommy J's house in South Carolina. They all give thanks to the good Lord for what they had, what they now lived for, and their abilities and leadership. At the conclusion of their prayers, each and every one of the members thanked the Lord for each other and for Tommy J. All of Allied Force's team members, as they did twice a year, for Thanksgiving and Christmas, enjoyed each other's company.

For some members of the team, these were the only times they all could see each other. They never had the same assignments. Some of the team reminisced about old times and battles. Most just rested and relaxed. It was a very special day, considering the jobs that they all possessed.

Most importantly, primarily for the animal mutants, at these gatherings, Tommy J updated everyone on the progress of his research into each of their unique cases, returning them back to 100 percent human if possible.

Unfortunately, today's news wasn't what they had hoped and prayed for over the past year. But all of them knew that, if anyone could find a cure, it would be Tommy J. One day, Tommy J would find cures for all of them. They all understood and thanked their leader for his constant, as well as grueling, efforts to cure each and every one of them.

Tommy J was just that dedicated to his people. The entire team knew that, if they could only somehow dispose of Legion, they would free up about 80 percent of Tommy J's time. And they all understood their individual roles as an Allied Force member.

*　　*　　*

Back in South America, it was now 3:30 p.m. The warper was complete. Psycho had tested it. He had been to 1939 Germany and returned to the present date and time.

"The landing area is in a large pasture some thirty miles from the Poland border," Psycho told Malakai and Nazi. "That's where you wanted it, Nazi, so you can finish the war before it even gets started. That's the way we should do it—short and sweet, so we can eliminate the possibility of all the different countries getting involved. Then we'll get back here to the present to reap the rewards. There's only one thing I have left to do."

"Yeah, what's that?" asked Malakai.

"I will have to surgically implant a chip into each of us who will be going. It's a simple procedure, as well as quite painless. The chips will be injected into everyone's neck, using this injection gun. In Ratchet's case, I just have to reprogram his existing chip. The chip will ensure that each of us will not be affected by what happens in the present time. Regardless of what happens—or whoever gets killed, including soldiers, civilians, and even animals—the events and deaths will not affect any of our people's existence, once we return to the present time."

Malakai and Nazi both raised an eyebrow.

"Chances are that someone or something that survived the first World War II won't survive the second World War II," Psycho explained. "Therefore, there's a chance that some of our Allied Force friends will be terminated. And while I said that whatever happens during our return to German history won't affect *our* present there is a caveat. Once we've returned, we will have approximately thirty minutes to reset the time to the exact time that we left, in order for our new events to overturn the actual events of the first World War II in the way that we intend them to. Does that make sense?" Psycho continued.

"Just get me back here safely, and I'll do the rest," he concluded when he realized that Malakai and Nazi weren't quite with him.

*   *   *

As the members that would be going back in time gathered for their implants, Psycho reminded Nazi of the chips' importance. "Think about it, Nazi, only those with chips implanted can go. That way, we don't end up ending one of our own lives while we are taking over the world. So do the math. Make sure that you have enough firepower, and let's fly.

"Oh by the way," he added, his pride clear "I have already installed one chip. I finished the newest member of Legion. He is going to be Ratchet's partner. He's awesome. He stands eight foot eight. He is four and a half feet wide across the shoulders and three and a half feet in girth in the upper body from chest plate to spine. He is 80 percent machine and 20 percent man. So he can think for himself, make his own decisions, and work with Ratchet. His head, which is the majority of the 20 percent man, is protected by the same steel that his chest is constructed of. It's housed in a solid steel helmet that covers both back and sides. His face is protected by the same steel, only in a cage with a mesh covering."

Psycho's excitement was palpable as he continued to list the merits of his newest creation. "He can take orders as a soldier, and he can give orders as a platoon leader. He knows no fear, although he does understand circumstances.

"Each shoulder is a three-part mechanism. The outer third is responsible for the total movements of the arms and shoulders, much like the rotator cup of a human. The middle third allows for the full rotation and movement of the 60mm cannons that are mounted on each shoulder; the ammunition is housed in his back hull, which holds thousands and thousands of automatic loading rounds. Then finally, the baddest of the bad, the inner third, is the tank turret. It has full 360-degree turning capabilities. His upper body houses up to sixty rounds for the mighty turret and the retractable barrel, allowing him to shoot at various distances and taking up limited space for maneuverability with no hesitation. The turret is housed in his back, which opens up allowing the turret to rise very quickly up and over his head. Like the shoulder cannons, the turret is controlled, aimed, and fired by his control panel, which is housed inside the armored hands of the machine and fired by human hands, the other part of the 20 percent human.

"He isn't quite as fast as Ratchet; still, he can move about 20 miles per hour. I have a chance to try out my new toys, per Malakai, so here he is.

"I haven't had a chance to name him yet. Since we are going back to World War II and you are leading the campaign as well as being a German, I was thinking a temporary name would be Panzer. What do you think?"

"I like it. I like him a lot. Thank you so much, Psycho." Nazi looked over the iron giant and newest member of Legion. "The name is perfect," he added. "Thanks again."

Psycho nodded his acknowledgment of the praise and then moved on. "How many chips are you going to need? It takes about twenty-two seconds to duplicate one. At this time, I've made two thousand chips. You have six Hell Knights, four Rams, twelve Demon Troopers, and better than 1,500 Zombie Commandoes. That should be enough. I'll save the rest for another trip if ever needed. They will be in my database."

"I have exactly 1,536 soldiers under my command on this operation," Nazi told him. "They consist of six Hell Knights, three Rams, and twelve Demon Troopers. Then there are the seventeen Legion members. That makes for 1,574 troops in all. That will be enough chips; very good. Oh and thanks again for Panzer."

"He's mine," Psycho said under his breath, suddenly angry at the realization that Nazi thought Panzer was his. *Oh well, I'll let him break him in*, he told himself. Then when they returned, he'd simply reprogram Panzer. He would change his new creation's name to something not so Nazi-ish. Then he'd have both the new machine and Ratchet to protect him. He loved his intelligence.

*   *   *

Legion's equipment was loaded. The chips were implanted. Everyone was in the hangar. It was 6:40 p.m.

"We will see you in about a month our time and about two days your time," Psycho told Malakai. "By the way, we will be completely cut off from any communications with you—to or from," he added. "If anything goes wrong, I have left everything that you need to know and use in the database and in the lab safe." He paused for a moment but thought of nothing else he needed to convey to his leader. "Well that's about it. Wish us well."

Moments later, just like that Legion was in Germany, 1939.

The seventeen Legion members on this very twisted and demented mission were Nazi, Ram, Bulge, Psycho, Witch, Mite, Jackyl, Gorman, Gage, Staft, R. I. P., Maiden, Mammoth, Mynx, Plague, Torchess (the identical but evil sister of Allied Force's Torch) and, last but not least, Grunge.

At 6:45 p.m. in South Carolina, Xtract went back inside for some more ice tea. He overheard Tommy J's alarm going off at the computer tracking and scanning base. Curious, he went to the control room. Seventeen Legion members' dot indicators and names flashed on the screen.

Xtract rushed back out to poolside, where everyone had gathered for an evening swim. "I hate to break up a great party," Xtract told Tommy J, "but I think you need to see what's up with your computer."

Tommy J rushed into the control room. "What the hell?" he exclaimed upon looking at the screen. "Get Stealth and Gatlin in here now! Malakai is up to something very strange."

Stealth and Gatlin, as well as some other members arrived in the control room. "Stealth, get on the terminal. See if we can figure out what is going on," Tommy J ordered. "It's strange that all of these names are coming up terminated. Malakai's name hasn't come up yet. Stealth, get The Crow fired up and prepare for take-off. Xtract, do the same with the Raven. Something very big is going down, or something very bad is happening. Gatlin, get dressed, geared, and loaded. You're all going south, to South America."

"C'mon, T. J., they're getting terminated. Ain't that a good thing? Someone else is taking over the bad side. Right?" Nuke suggested.

"No, Nuke it is not good," Tommy J replied. "Stop dripping water all over the floor. Go get dried off and changed."

"How many members do you want to deploy?" asked Gatlin.

"Well the screen is currently showing well over four hundred terminated and still counting. That includes Nazi's Zombie Commando troops. Let's see, together the Raven and The Crow can transfer twenty members and their gear, with Pumas, equipment, ammo, and rations. Shit, fill 'em up," Tommy J concluded.

"You heard the man," Gatlin told the others. "Let's get our shit together. Damn this was a good party."

The twenty members that Tommy J was forced to send on this mission of mercy were Gatlin, GrizzLee, Nuke, Pistol Smoke, Amphibian, Zeke, Crosshairs, Stealth, Blade, Optic Blast, Nitro, Shadow, Mack T, Jon Henri, Drazil, Xtract, Recoil, Torch, Fusion, and Bolt-action.

*   *   *

It is now 9:30 p.m. as the team departed. Legion terminations continued to come up on the screen.

"Now better than 1,100 members and soldiers, still no Malakai," Tommy J reported.

*   *   *

By 10:00 p.m., the team was over Georgia and, at 11:00 p.m., Tommy J radioed in another progress report. "The total is now 1,485, still no Malakai."

"We are an hour and a half from destination. Everything going well," Stealth replied. "Raven is on my wing. Xtract is giving me the thumbs-up. Team is ready although very uneasy about what is going on or what to expect at destination. Over," said Stealth.

"Sending the Raven ahead to monitor complex at four-mile altitude, above and beyond Legion's radar," Stealth continued. "Closing in on one mile; switching to T-sight." Thermal imaging allowed them to see into the base. After a short pause, Stealth continued the report. "Showing four persons—one at sublevel and two outside complex probably guards, can't make out who they are at this time. The final person is on level three; appears to be lying down in bed; must be Malakai. At least someone is getting some rest tonight.

"Doesn't appear that there is any structural damage, complex is totally intact. No sign of disturbance that any of us can see at this time. You can probably tell us who the people are by looking at who isn't on that list in front of you. Over."

"Total missing is at 1,574," replied Tommy J. "No Malakai. Do whatever is necessary to get to him undetected. Be swift and sharp; it may be a trap. Find out what is going on, then report to me immediately. If you do not know who these people are, take prisoners. The names that I have compiled as candidates for the person's on property are Armageddon and Wrath, along with Manaconda and, of course, Malakai. Don't be surprised if the two guards are Armageddon and Manaconda. The person at sublevel is more than likely Wrath doing what it is that he does. The person lying in the third-floor bed is more than likely Malakai. I'm not a betting man, but if I were, that is what I'd bet on. Handle them and report."

* * *

"Come in, X."

"Xtract, go ahead, Stealth."

"Yeah, we are going to need a disturbance to get these guys out in the open and get some movement so we can see just exactly who in the hell we're dealing with. Do you think that you could do that for us?" said Stealth.

"Yeah," Xtract replied. "Roger that, Stealth. We are presently four miles east of target and approximately three miles up. Let us know. We are standing by."

"Okay, SOT bad asses, load shock rounds and prepare for deployment, on Stealth's mark," ordered Gatlin, gearing up the special operations team.

"Xtract, deploying team at this time. Give us that disturbance in one," replied Stealth. "Don't worry about hitting anything. Malakai owns all of this property— something like ten thousand acres or some shit like that. Over."

"You got it, Stealth," replied Xtract. "Starting the clock now."

The seven-member team landed in total darkness behind the hangar. Complete silence filled the property. The members quickly took up their positions. Five, four, three, two, one . . .

Xtract fired two missiles from the Raven into the mountainous terrain below. *Boom! Boom!*

The complex immediately came alive. Air raid warnings sounded off all around the complex. Just like the Allied Force team had planned, the two guards emerged from around the house. The guard at the west entryway was the giant Armageddon; the other guard, who emerged from the back of the mansion, was none other than Manaconda.

With guns full of shock rounds (nonlethal stunning ammunition), the team opened fire on the confused guards. Gatlin, Nuke, Amphibian, and Crosshairs all peppered Armageddon. He returned fire, spraying the property with live, high-powered rounds from his cannons and hitting only timber. Soon, the barrage of stun rounds began to take their toll on the enormous Armageddon.

From the shadows, Nuke and Amphibian emerged and shot the high-voltage, nonlethal stun netting over the giant mutant man being. Gatlin and Crosshairs continued to fire round after round at the mountain of a man. Finally, Armageddon was down. Shortly thereafter, he was apprehended, and his weapons were removed.

In the backyard much of the same was taking place, as the rest of the SOT team—Pistol Smoke, Bolt-action, and Optic Blast—took care of Manaconda, in much the same way as the first squad had taken down Armageddon.

From the opposite side of the house, Wrath emerged, apparently trying a sneak attack on the team. As he worked his way around the enormous mansion for his surprise attack, he was suddenly caught in the sunlight brightness of The Crow's floodlights.

"I've got lock on you Wrath," Stealth said into the PA system. "Stop and surrender your weapons, or I will end you right here, right now. This is Stealth in The Crow, fully armed and capable of dropping you and everything around you in a matter of seconds. Face it; you're a deer in my headlights.

"Tell me, Wrath how do you like being on the other side of demands?" Stealth continued, seeing that Wrath had not yet dropped his weapon. "Remember Blade, Chris, and Gatlin back at the hotel in Arizona? Well, look, once again, you get to meet The Crow—the world's most silent killer. She's the world's fastest, deadliest, and—did I mention?—quietest attack jet. I designed her myself. She makes the other so-called silent planes sound like freight trains. Anyway, I'm so glad that you got to meet her up close and personal."

Just as Stealth finished, the team moves in from all sides. Seeing that he was surrounded and obviously alone and outgunned, Wrath reluctantly dropped his weapons and surrendered. Nuke fired several shots, hitting Wrath all over his upper body and head with stun rounds.

"HOLD YOUR FIRE!" ordered Gatlin. "DAMN, BOY!"

"I hate that bastard," said Nuke. "I couldn't help myself."

The team left the three stunned Legion members, who would be out of it for several hours and headed inside the mansion for some answers.

"Turn on the lights, Malakai," Gatlin bellowed, "or we will light this place up our own way! I have Stealth just outside, about a half mile up. Xtract is only a mile away in the Raven. They have the capability and authorization to turn this beautiful home into a junkyard in seconds. This is Gatlin, with six members. We are very pissed off, I'm going to count to three and the lights better be on and your sorry ass down here. One, two . . ."

The lights came on.

"Now get your ass down here," Gatlin yelled. "And don't try anything stupid. I'm very irritable at this time. I don't want to be here. You have broken up a great party and forced me and my team to work on our day off. Now move your ass!"

Malakai was downstairs momentarily. When he reached the bottom of the stairs, Malakai was immediately grabbed at each arm from behind by Amphibian and Nuke. Crosshairs walked up to Malakai and held her guns some three or four inches from his head. Bolt-action, Pistol smoke, and Optic Blast all aim their weapons at Malakai. He had so many red lights on his face and head he looked like a Christmas tree.

Gatlin got in Malakai's face. He shoved his gun barrels up under the Legion head's chin. "Believe it or not," he began, "this is a peace mission from T. J. Consider yourself the luckiest bastard alive. Now I'm gonna ask you just one time, what in the hell is going on and what happened to your people? Where are they? Don't dick with me. I will pull this trigger, and they won't even be able to tell what you used to be. So spill it or I am going to spill you."

Malakai knew that there was no way out of this mess and that, unlike Nuke; Gatlin knew that Malakai had had Nazi kill his parents. Malakai also knew that Gatlin would pull the trigger and blow him to pieces. So Malakai reluctantly told Gatlin and his team everything that they wanted to know, even about the warper, the chips, and how to use them both.

"You sick son of a bitch!" cried Amphibian. "You can't change the past. The soldiers that fought and died in that war are heroes, and whether you believe it or not, they made this world one hell of a better place than it would have been if they had not done what they did."

"Bolt-action, you and Amp go check out the hangar," Gatlin ordered. Then he turned to his radio. "Stealth, Xtract, come in."

"Stealth; go ahead."

"This is Xtract; go ahead, big guy. It's getting really boring up here."

"Go ahead and bring 'em in," ordered Gatlin. "I guess we're gonna do some time traveling."

"Roger that," replied Stealth.

"No shit, that doesn't sound good," came Xtract's reply. "Copy that."

Amphibian's voice came over the radio. "Gatlin, everything checks out. It's all here just as he said," he reported. "He's done it. I don't believe it but he has. I've seen it all. Bring him down here and give me three minutes with the sick piece of shit. Just let me kick the shit out of him for messing with history, our lives, and God only knows what else."

"I appreciate that, Amp, but there is really no time for that right now. B. A., you get in contact with T. J. and let him know what's going on here as well as where we are going. I'll figure something out to take care of this mess. We have to get injected for this one," said Gatlin.

* * *

In disbelief, Tommy J wished his team well.

Bolt-action injected himself and then began injecting the rest of the team. Meanwhile, Gatlin, still standing in front of Malakai, began removing his guns. As the team heard Gatlin's guns hit the floor, they all know that it was too late.

"I've got one more thing to do before I go," Gatlin told Malakai.

BAM! Gatlin punched Malakai in the nose.

As Malakai fell back, Gatlin went after him. From his back, Malakai leaped to his feet in one motion and dropkicked Gatlin in the face. Then he jumped on Gatlin's face and began whaling away on Gatlin.

"Oh shit, it's on, baby!" yelled Nuke.

Gatlin was taking punches in the face left and right. "You are a boy in a fight with a man," Malakai told him.

With that, Gatlin slung Malakai off of him.

The entire team watched the fight between the two leaders—a battle playing out between good and evil once again. The team also knew there was no stopping Gatlin.

"He has to do this," said GrizzLee to the others. "You would do the same thing, given the chance."

Gatlin got to his feet. Blood trickled from Malakai's nose. Gatlin had blood in his mouth and in his nose, and blood gushed down his face from a huge gash under his left eye. His face was covered in blood.

Malakai again kicked at Gatlin's head. This time, Gatlin grabbed Malakai's leg in midair with his left arm and, in the same motion, with his right arm—and all his power and anger—punched the inside of Malakai's knee, snapping Malakai's leg nearly in two. Gatlin dropped the leg and, with a roundhouse right, punched Malakai in the left side of the head, knocking Malakai to the floor. The Legion boss was in agony, having suffered a very serious fracture to his leg and to his jaw as well. As soon as Malakai hit the floor, Gatlin was on one knee beside Malakai, rapidly punching his opponent in the face. Blood flew in all directions, hitting the wall, the floor, and Gatlin's body armor and even his face.

GrizzLee grabbed Gatlin off of Malakai and held him up about three inches off the floor. "Man, boss," he said, "Malakai has had enough. We have to get going. Finish this later when we aren't so pressed for time."

"Okay okay," Gatlin agreed. "I'm cool, really. Lee, I'm cool."

GrizzLee released Gatlin. Gatlin charged Malakai again, just as Malakai was trying to get back to his feet. Gatlin kicked Malakai in the face, ending the fight for Malakai, but not for Gatlin. Before Zeke or Nuke or even GrizzLee could get to Gatlin and wrestle him to the ground, Gatlin had already kicked Malakai in the ribs and stomach three of four more times.

Malakai wasn't moving; he was just breathing and bleeding.

"THAT'S A BOY KICKING A MAN'S ASS—FULLY!" Gatlin roared at Malakai's motionless body.

"Damn, boy, chill out!" Nuke said.

"I hate that bastard. I couldn't help myself," replied Gatlin as he smiled and winked at Nuke.

The team was now ready for the warper and to travel back in time—to 1939 Germany. The team, was about six hours behind Nazi and Legion, said their prayer.

Then just like Legion hours earlier, Allied Force was suddenly in 1939. As the team landed, Amphibian and Recoil, with help from Zeke and Drazil, disabled the C-30 that belonged to Legion. The team then begins to unload the Pumas.

The Puma was an armored assault vehicle that could carry up to six allied force members. It had, mounted on each of the four fenders, the two in the front as well as the two in the rear, 30mm cannons that could be fired from the cab, either by the passenger or the driver. Centered in the back of the Puma was a retractable Howitzer/80mm cannon. From the operator's seat, someone could operate the awesome duel weapon from a vantage point above the cab and over the glass. It also houses an extremely powerful laser in both the front and rear chassis. These could also be fired from the cab by either the driver or the passenger. This machine was the most elite ground assault vehicle on the planet and in the history of humankind.

"Listen up, people," said Gatlin, the overall leader of Allied Force field teams, "this is how we are going to split things up. In P-1 will be Bolt-action and Nitro, P-2 is Amphibian and Torch. Optic Blast and Mack T, you're in P-3. P-4, Nuke and Fusion; P-5, GrizzLee and Zeke; P-6, myself and Blade; P-7, Stealth and Jon Henri; P-8, Pistol Smoke and Shadow; P-9, Xtract and Crosshairs; and in P-10, it will be Recoil and Drazil.

"I know that this is the first time we've all had a chance to work together in the same theatre. So I split us up into two battalions. Each battalion will have five Pumas and ten members. The first battalion will be lead by Bolt-action, and the second battalion by myself. It may take a little while to get use to each team. Let's work together and find Nazi and his team. Keep in mind that we are way outnumbered; so be smart.

"In this campaign, we will be shooting to kill and destroy. Take no prisoners and leave no wounded. We can kill them all out of this world, so forget the code.

"Do not fire on any troops from other countries, unless they fire on you first or you feel threatened and there is no other option but force.

"Some of us may fall. We must get our people back to the real world when we are done here. Leave your locators on. If your Puma becomes disabled, destroy it. We will send someone to get you. Remember who we are and what we stand for. Do not get caught up in the war. We are here on one primary objective; that is to stop the aggression of Legion. If we stay within ourselves, as well as our plans of attack, we will come out victorious. Any questions?"

"Yeah man, I got one," said Nuke. "You don't even look like you've been in a fight with Malakai. Does your face hurt?"

"No, I feel great," replied Gatlin. "I don't even feel like I've been in a fight."

"Yeah well, whether you feel it now or not, sweetheart, you are going to definitely feel it when we get back to the present day and time," said Blade. "I guarantee you that, baby."

"Yeah, thanks for reminding me, doll face," replied Gatlin sarcastically.

Gatlin faced the group. "Okay, people, let's synchronize our watches. Keep in contact. Bolt-action will follow Nazi's trail along with 1st Battalion. Then I will take 2nd Battalion, and we will flank 1st Battalion a hundred meters to the east. It's officially August 29, 12:00 a.m. Remember, they have about a six hour lead on us, so Bolt-action, lead the way; let's move 'em out. We have a lot of ground to cover. Let's do this right."

The team loaded the ten Pumas in theatre. Bolt-action and Nitro picked up Nazi's trail easily. Apparently because he didn't expect Allied Force to be in-country, Nazi had failed to cover his tracks, so to speak.

As the team moved, up ahead in the distance, they saw a bright orange sky, evidence of war.

"I wonder if that's our boy," said Optic Blast.

Soon, the team reached a very small village that looked like it may have been a German command post or something because of the flags, some still partially hanging, others laying all over the ground scorched. The building nearest them was more or less a pile of rubble. The tracks that the team was following led right to the village. Apparently, Nazi was responsible for this.

Bolt-action stopped the convoy. GrizzLee got out seeing if he could figure out how Nazi was traveling, how many vehicles he had, and how many soldiers were on foot.

Boom!

GrizzLee was shot in the shoulder.

"Sniper, Sniper! In the building at the end of the road!" yelled Nitro.

Nitro raised the 30mm cannon on the front of P-1 and fired into the building. After the blasts had literally ripped the building's walls down, the sniper fell to the ground.

"Damn, Lee, are you all right?" asked Nuke.

"Yeah, I'm okay. It doesn't hurt much," answered GrizzLee.

P-1, P-2, and P-3 moved toward the building and the outskirts of town up ahead. P-4, Nuke and Fusion, stayed back with P-5, GrizzLee and Zeke. As Fusion patched GrizzLee's shoulder up, Nuke and Zeke went on foot to check and clear out the rest of the six-building village.

"Hey, Zeke, you think that Nitro got the sniper or that he just shit himself when she opened up on his ass with those 30s and had a heart attack?" asked Nuke. "That stupid son of a bitch didn't know what the hell he got himself into. He ain't ever seen any firepower like that shit before. You don't talk much. I'm gonna have to take you out on the town when we get back and loosen you up—maybe hook you up with a couple of ladies.?"

Zeke just stopped walking and looked at Nuke and then started walking again.

*   *   *

Through the woods on the east side of 1st Battalion was 2nd Battalion. They had come to a large lake and, unable to cross, were forced to reroute. They crossed the road, about a mile south of the village that 1st Battalion was now in. Now 2nd Battalion was on 1st Battalion's west flank, approximately a mile behind them.

Gatlin and 2nd Battalion see the town up ahead about two miles or so. They heard weapon fire.

"That sure as hell sounds like Legion's weapons," said Blade. "I hope Legion is still all together, or this could be a longer mission than we expected." She pointed out that, if they were to encounter only a portion of Legion's in-country team, that portion would inform the others of Allied Force's presence. "And that could become a long game of cat and mouse," she concluded.

*   *   *

As 2nd Battalion continued to push forward, moving across the countryside toward the town, 1st Battalion was pressing forward, following the road. About a mile prior to reaching the next town, 1st Battalion could actually feel the earth shaking as heavy artillery pounded the town ahead. They could also smell the gunpowder.

Bolt-action got on the radio. "P-1 to P-6. Come in, Gatlin."
"Go ahead," answered Gatlin.

"Yeah, Gatlin, I've got good news, bad news, and even worse news. Good news is we encountered a sniper in a small village a few clicks back. It was, unfortunately a German soldier, not Legion. The bad news is, he hit Lee in the shoulder before Nitro could spot him and take him out. Lee says that he is all right. Fusion stayed back to patch him up, while Nuke and Zeke finished sweeping and clearing the village; they are going to catch up directly. The worse news is, we are following these tracks, and at my location, there is a fork in the road. As luck would have it, the tracks turn off to the east, northeast toward the Poland border. According to the imprints in the dirt road, it appears that a lot of Legion went this way. Do you want us to come into town and give y'all a hand, or do you want us to continue to follow these tracks toward Poland?" Bolt-action asked.

"Ain't that just some shit," said Gatlin. "You go ahead and follow those tracks. We're going to head into this town and see what's left to do. Good luck. Let me know what you find. Over."

"Roger that, Gatlin. Be careful. We will see you soon. 1st Battalion movin' out," replied Bolt-action.

*   *   *

As second battalion entered the town, gunfire flew from seemingly every direction. It was now 1:45 a.m. on August 29, 1939. The team split into two squads; P-6, P-8, and P-10 went straight into town, while P-7 and P-9 flanked both the east and the west sides of the main road.

The team immediately begins to encounter very heavy resistance; 2nd Battalion was now in a firefight with infantry, armor, and snipers. For the moment, the team was immobilized. The battalion faced three tanks, two MG42s, and dozens of German infantry.

As P-7 and P-9 waited on the wings of the town, P-6, 8, and 10 began to defend themselves, having no choice, in their own fashion, as ordered by Gatlin.

"All personnel get on foot," Gatlin ordered. "There is an abundance of ZC foot soldiers."

"Shadow," he added, "you man the howitzer on P-8 and keep the big boys off of us while we clean out the damn ZC."

The Zombie Commandoes were Nazi's own personal soldiers that Wrath had brought back from the dead for him to command. And soon, Gatlin's battalion was confronting a whole hoard of them.

*   *   *

Blade was getting a lot of action. She returned fire with her G-11 automatic assault rifle. She was taking out the oncoming ZC, when she found herself pinned down by German soldiers in front of her, while approximately twenty-five ZC were closing in on her from behind. "Shit, we are here to help you, you stupid asses," Blade said to herself, wishing the German soldiers would understand. "Kill the ugly bastards."

Blade had no place to go. The ZCs were now within thirty feet of her location. She was unable to return fire. She called for some support from her headset, all the while not knowing if anyone could even hear her with all the explosions and nonstop gunfire surrounding her and her team. Blade waited in hope a few more seconds. There was no response.

Boom! Boom!

The ZC began falling, as well as flying through the air, some on fire and some in parts. It was Stealth, dropping the ZC with the 30mm cannons from the front of P-7, as well as with its laser.

Jon Henri, with his massive 60mm cannon, picked off a few more for good measure before he took two rounds to the leg.

Jon Henri dived behind the large pile of rubble and debris that Blade was behind. He made sure Blade was all right, and then he stood up and returned fire.

Stealth continued to fire on the ZC and the German troops. Behind her Puma, a German Tiger tank began to turn its turret toward her. Caught up in the firefight in front of her, she didn't see it.

Boom! Boom! Boom!

The tank was toast. Shadow had blown the top of the tank almost completely off with her precision shooting with the howitzer.

Jon Henri grabbed Blade and literally carried her under his massive arm to the safety of the P-7.

Stealth, who was operating P-7, greeted Blade. "Hey, girl, how are you? Why don't you grab the controls of the 30s while I get us the hell out of here."

"Jon is hit," replied Blade.

"How bad?" asked Stealth.

"I'm all right, ma'am. Let's just get out of here and finish clearing the town," said Jon Henri, who was bleeding all over the back of P-7.

*   *   *

"It's Plague," Xtract screamed, "with some two hundred and fifty ZC!

"There he goes," he told Crosshairs. "He's got his big-ass 80cal with him and about fifteen snipers. Looks like everyone on his little sniper team is carrying a 30mil. We have to get him out of there before he gets a chance to hunker down. He'll be able to tear a whole lot of us up from that vantage point."

The remaining two hundred or so ZC remained just outside the large building that now housed the first known Legion member, Plague. The ZC set up bunkers just outside the front of the old hotel, as well as on both the east and west sides of the hotel. They even had a good-size bunker located on the first floor in the lobby. Once their bunkers were up, they all begin to fire on Allied Force.

"Go with P-9," Crosshairs told Xtract. "Set between those two buildings. Fire ZC on out of building—use cannons. I'll work get shot on Plague other ZC inside building."

Deciphering Crosshair's broken speech as best he could, Xtract followed her lead. He set up and began to fire on the hotel. "Damn these guys can shoot," he muttered to himself.

Crosshairs worked her way around and got a good line on the hotel. She set up behind some bales of hay in a field on the west side of the hotel. As she did best, she immediately began scanning the structure for Plague. She saw no sign of Plague right away. However, she did spot two ZC setting up a bunker with a 30mm cannon on the third floor.

Crosshairs fired on them with her 20mm cannon. One of the rounds blew the chest completely out of one the ZC. The only way to kill a ZC was to hit it in the chest or the head or to blow it to pieces; otherwise, they wouldn't die . . . again.

Looking over at his dead partner, the other ZC reached for the 30mm, Crosshairs fired another 20mm round. This shell blew the second ZC's head to pieces. Thinking nothing of it, Crosshairs returned to scanning the hotel for Plague, picking off ZC and their 30mm bunkers on almost every floor of what appeared to be an eight-story hotel. Before long, eight ZC were dead inside the building; eight rounds had been fired. Crosshairs was named for her unmatched accuracy.

Xtract's firefight with the ZC outside the hotel had been successful up to this point; he had dropped a dozen of the undead soldiers. Then he began to take fire from his right flank.

As he turned, he saw approximately forty German soldiers afoot being escorted by a half-track and a Panzer tank. They were within sixty meters of him.

Boom! Boom! The tank fired on P-9, hitting it and blowing the vehicle up. As the soldiers rushed the burning Puma, the tank turned its assault onto the ZC bunkers in front of the hotel.

The ZC returned fire on the half-track, and the soldiers fired back at the ZC from behind the half-track. Pistol Smoke opened up on them both, dropping seven in a matter of seconds, including two from the back of the half-track, with his H&K MP5.

Pistol Smoke was then forced to take cover, as twenty or more German soldiers began to fire on him. He returned fire, dropping two more.

The tank continued to blow ZC to pieces every which way.

In P-7, Blade told Stealth, "I can waste that tank from here. Should I take the shot or let them kill more ZC and take the chance of the tank turning its assault onto some of our own?"

"Blow it up," Stealth answered resolutely. "We can't take that chance. I don't know where Xtract and Crosshairs are. P-9 is blown to shit down there between those two buildings."

Boom! Boom! Boom! Down went the mighty Panzer tank.

Then, from out of nowhere, another half-track fired on P-7, hitting Blade in the shoulder with its 20mm cannon. Blade fell back into the back of P-7, and Stealth punched the accelerator. The P-7 jumped from the half-track's line of fire. Unfortunately, it jumped onto the street where the other half-track was located.

The second half-track began to fire on P-7. Stealth fired back with the laser, blowing the half-track and approximately fifteen soldiers to pieces.

This helped out Pistol Smoke. He fired on the remaining four soldiers, hitting and killing one of them and leaving three who were now only about ten feet from him. Pistol Smoke was now pinned down.

In the couple of seconds it took for them to reach him, the three remaining soldiers were dead. Gatlin had finished them off.

The half-track that shot Blade found its way to the street. Jon Henri tried to get on P-7's howitzer, while Stealth tried to get the P-7 turned around in the congested street.

Boom! Boom! Boom! The half-track threat was over.

Shadow had scored another hit. She offers Gatlin and Pistol Smoke a ride, and the two gladly accepted. Now the three were in P-8.

* * *

Crosshairs, who had continued to pick off ZC in search of Plague, now found herself in trouble. The remaining ZC outside the hotel had found her location. They all opened fire on her at once, ripping her hay bale bunker to shreds.

Xtract, who had taken some damage from the explosion of P-9, was trying to get to her. He crawled his way into two German soldiers. The soldiers stared at Xtract, who didn't have a gun. Both men took aim.

Slash. Out of the shadows, Drazil had appeared and, with his large, razor-sharp, retractable claws, had sliced one of the soldier's throats. Blood shot all over Xtract. Then with the other hand, Drazil stabbed the second soldier through the nose and into the brain, killing him as well.

Drazil then helped Xtract get back to his feet, gave him his M5, and said, "Stay here."

Drazil pulled out his Beretta 9mm pistol and made his way toward Crosshairs.

Recoil arrives at Xtract's side to help him.

Crosshairs continued to concentrate on locating Plague, even while ZC forces continued their assault on her crumbling bunker. Suddenly, she noticed that the ZCs were too close. She fired laser bursts, tearing up the field and catching it on fire. While she was doing this, the last ZC from a 30mm bunker fired on her, ripping into her midsection and ribs and dropping her.

Drazil, who was coming from her right, began picking off as many oncoming ZCs as he could. He dropped seven before they hit him in the leg, side, and tail.

Xtract covered Recoil as he went to get Drazil out of the line of fire. He dropped ZCs as they come into the open field. Recoil reached Drazil and dragged him back to Xtract, behind a small, burned-out building.

* * *

Shadow and P-8, with Gatlin and Pistol Smoke now aboard, begin firing on the hotel. P-7, carrying Stealth, Jon Henri, and Blade followed. Together, the two Pumas rolled side by side up the middle of the street toward the hotel blowing the ZC to God only knows.

* * *

Crosshairs was still down, but at this point, no one was shooting at her.

* * *

Boom! *Boom*! From the hotel, relentless .80 caliber cannon fire rained down on the two approaching Pumas, blowing the laser off of P-7, as well as a 30mm cannon off the front of P-8.

The two Pumas returned fire, not knowing exactly where the assault was coming from.

"Nobody on the howitzers or 80mms," Gatlin ordered. "Stay inside until we can locate the shooter."

*   *   *

Crosshairs found her number one target—Plague. She switches to sidewinder missiles, locked onto Plague's helmet, and fired.

By the time Plague noticed the laser guide on him, he turned to his left to catch the lethal six-inch projectile in the eye.

Boom! Plague's head exploded. His lifeless body fell to the street below.

At the same time, Crosshairs fell back onto her back.

*   *   *

The two Pumas in the middle of the street unloaded on the hotel. As they reached the front doors, Pistol Smoke, Gatlin, and Stealth rushed the building on a search and destroy.

On the second floor, Pistol Smoke found a ZC who had been hit several times but was still alive. Pistol Smoke finishes him off with one round to the face.

*   *   *

Daylight began to top the tree line and then gradually and gracefully shone on the bombarded remnants of the East German town where Gatlin and his team found themselves. What had taken place here over the past several hours began to horrifically come to light. The team could see all the mayhem that they had been forced to take part in. The stench of gunpowder, fuel, and war lingered heavily in the morning air.

The team finished the sweep of the devastation. They make sure that all of the ZCs were accounted for, as well as killed properly.

As the "All clear!" sounded, Stealth, Jon Henri, and Pistol Smoke went back to the other side of town to retrieve P-6 and P-10.

Xtract was still a little dazed and bad of hearing from the tank blast that had destroyed his Puma, P-9. Nevertheless, he began working on the team. Gatlin sat with Blade as Xtract bandaged her up. Blade would now be one armed for a little while, as Xtract placed her injured arm into am immobilizer. Blade was in pain, but she still had her right arm, and she would make it.

Recoil told Gatlin, "I need some help getting Crosshairs in. She's in pretty bad shape."

Recoil and Gatlin went to find and bring back Crosshairs.

Stealth, Jon Henri, and Pistol Smoke returned with P-6 and P-10.

Drazil had a hole in his side just above his waist, three holes in his right leg, and a hole in his tail. He probably wouldn't be able to walk very well for the remainder of this operation. He would have stay on P-10's guns.

Jon Henri's leg wounds looked bad, but he assured the team that he was fine.

"Hell, he's a big ole boy," said Pistol Smoke. "He probably won't even walk with a limp."

Gatlin and Recoil returned with Crosshairs. She appeared to be in pretty bad shape. Stealth begins to work on her immediately, and Xtract assisted.

The rest of the team did inventory and destroyed anything they couldn't take with them.

Gatlin got in contact with Bolt-action. "Well, we have five wounded, P-9 is destroyed, P-7 lost its front mount laser, and P-8 lost the front 30 on the driver side," he reported. After filling Bolt-action in on Crosshair's condition, he reported the tallies for the other side. "Best estimate,

279 ZC dead and one Legion member, Plague, dead. We encountered heavy resistance and extreme firefights with both Legion and the German Army. We took out five tanks, three Tigers, and two Panzers, along with four half-tracks, six bunkers, and seven MG42's. All in a day's work. How did y'all do?"

"We traveled throughout the night, up until about forty-five minutes ago. We're getting some pecks now," Bolt-action reported, referring to food. "Nazi must be moving fast and dropping troops off at strategic locations. We haven't seen any signs, other than these tracks, and they haven't split. GrizzLee tells me that, as we go, the convoy we're following continues to get lighter.

"It's pretty slow going, though. We had to shut down twice to allow German troops to pass through without giving away our position. I guess we've traveled about 140 miles or so, in just under six hours. Yeah, I guess that would be about right. It's just about 8:00 a.m."

"We're going to push north," Gatlin replied. "Shadow just informed me that there are another set of tracks heading north. She knows that they have to be Legion's because that style of tire tread wasn't even around in 1939. So I guess we'll see y'all soon. Be careful. If you need us, just whistle. We all wish you well. But I have to tell you, I would love to get The Crow with Stealth and Crosshairs up. We may still have to eventually send Stealth after The Crow before this thing is over. Right now, we just can't take the chance of getting her shot down. Getting back to South Carolina in the Raven with all of our equipment would be extremely difficult. But you know, desperate times call for desperate measures. So let us know what's up. Contact me tomorrow, unless you need to before. Over and out."

*   *   *

Stealth gave the status report on Crosshairs. "She's going to make it. She just lost the ability to cool her guns and use her laser bursts on her laser. But she is as tough as they come. She is our superior cyborg killing machine.

"To keep Crosshairs as operational as possible, she should ride with me and Jon Henri in P-7," she informed Gatlin. "Xtract can ride in P-10 with Drazil and Recoil. That way, Recoil can man the howitzer while Drazil is on the 30s, and Xtract can do the driving.

"And Xtract would like to keep an eye on Drazil," she added. "With Drazil being the type of mutant that he is, his wounds look really bad—well, at least to the human eye."

"No problem," Gatlin replied. "Y'all do what you think is best for everyone, and let's move north."

And so, at 8:30 a.m., 2nd Battalion, now some 350 miles from The Crow and Raven, began its push north.

*   *   *

Approximately 270 miles due east, 1st Battalion, finished their pecks and then continued moving east.

Awhile later, 1st Battalion pulled over for another rest and to change GrizzLee's dressings. Amphibian and Torch went to the tip of what turned out to be a cliff. They looked two hundred feet down to the valley floor.

"Man, isn't that a beautiful view," said Torch. "You can almost see everything from this point."

Amphibian, using binoculars, noticed large troop activity. "It's Legion, in the valley below," he exclaimed. "It appears to me that they are preparing to move out. PAY DIRT! It looks like better than five hundred ZC troops, Ram and his three brothers, Maiden, Mammoth, and Grunge are all down there." He paused for a moment, taking the numbers in. "Well I guess those'll be the odds. What a matchup—Allied Force, 10; Legion estimated 507. That seems fair."

"Look over there," said Torch. "It's their pathway down the mountainside. Nothing shows on the locators. SHIT! The locators don't work in 1939. That sucks. We'd better get back to camp before Legion tries to move on us again. Let's move."

Upon returning to camp, Amphibian told Bolt-action and the rest of the team what he and Torch had discovered. "Seventy meters up, that trail drops off into a valley—a valley full of Legion," he announced. "It appears that Ram is heading up a regiment. I guesstimated five hundred ZC and counted seven Legion members. I say that we hit them now, if we're going to. Hell, we chased the fuckers this far. Now that we caught them, let's do it."

"How do you want to handle this Bolt-action?" asked Optic Blast.

Bolt-action thought for a moment. Then he faced his team. "Okay, we are way out numbered but not out-manned. They have seven members; we have ten members," he told the group. "The ZCs are just targets. They don't really count. They're like the body of the snake. We take out the seven Legion members—the head of the snake—and the body is harmless.

"So here's the plan. We have the advantage of being at an elevated position. Done properly, they're fish in a barrel. We set the Pumas up all across the top of the ridge about ten meters back from the edge and just out of sight of Legion, until ordered up. We'll space them thirty meters apart, so if they're seen, one good rocket or missile doesn't take out more than one at a time.

"Manning the guns will be as follows—and don't forget to hit the PTO, so you can drive the Puma from the howitzer chair—P-1, Nitro in the chair; P-2, Torch; P-3 is Mack T; P-4, Fusion; P-5 will be Zeke. Make sure that headsets are on.

"The rest of us are going down the mountain path, to get up close and personal. Pumas' primary targets will be ZC. Clear them out first. Then, if you have a shot on a Legion member, take it. After you've thinned the ZC out, concentrate on their vehicles and their artillery.

"Lee, you okay? Can you move enough? We really need you on that mountainside and valley floor," he concluded.

"I'm fine. Don't worry about me," replied GrizzLee. "Just finish the plan and let's get home."

Having instructed the shooters, Bolt-action turned to the rest of the team. "We'll have assigned targets for the squad on the valley floor," he told them. "Amphibian, you'll take out both Brown and Red Ram. Optic Blast, take out Maiden. Nuke, you've got Black Ram and Grunge. Optic Blast will assist if you need her to. Lee, I'm giving you Mammoth. And I'll take Blue Ram and Ram himself."

Seeing that everyone understood his or her assignment, Bolt-action addressed his battalion. "Gear up, ammo down; leave everything behind except for weapons and ammo. Nitro, you'll move the Pumas up on my command. At that command, I want an endless barrage of howitzer, 80mm, laser, and 30mm blasts into that valley floor. Do not stop until I give the order or you run out of targets. Give us twenty minutes to work our way down, and then be on standby. It's now 3:30 p.m.; everyone knows their objectives.

"Let's get down there before they try and move out on us again," he ordered.

"HELL YEAH!" said Amphibian. "You heard 'im. Let's move. This is what we get paid for, baby."

Bolt-action, Nuke, Optic Blast, Amphibian, and GrizzLee worked their way down the mountain trail. As the team reached the valley floor, just seventy-five meters in front of them, they saw better than five hundred Legion troops.

"Its 3:47," Bolt-action told his team in the valley. "We need to get some cover and find our targets. The Pumas will be moving up in about three minutes."

The team spread out in every direction, in search of cover and their targets.

Bolt-action looked at the equipment—seven obviously confiscated half-tracks, along with nine jeeps each housing .50 caliber machine guns. He also saw bazookas, RPGs, four portable howitzers, and five pull-behind 80mm cannons.

Looking around he saw believe it or not, Blue Ram. Bolt-action had an open shot, so he took aim with his .80 caliber rifle. He fires one shot, hitting his unsuspecting target right between the eyes.

The Pumas had now moved up into position, and as Bolt-action took the shot, he ordered Nitro, "Open them up fully."

When Bolt-action's .80 caliber round struck Blue Ram between the eyes, blowing the hideous beast's gray matter into the air, Blue Ram's lifeless body fell harmlessly to the valley floor.

"It's on," Amphibian said to himself, as ZCs scrambled for weapons and shelter and searched frantically to determine where the assault was coming from.

Some three hundred ZCs, on Ram's order charged the mountain side.

P-1, P-2, P-3, P-4, and P-5, on cue, unleashed an awesome barrage of firepower—a display of that this era had never seen before and would never see again—into the valley floor. The initial onslaught blew crater-sized holes in the valley floor, destroying two half-tracks. ZCs began falling everywhere, cluttering up the valley below. But they continued their desperate charge toward the mountainside. Some of them stopped and began to man the 80mm cannons and the howitzers and even half-tracks.

* * *

Mammoth grabbed an 80mm cannon and took cover behind one of the disabled half-tracks. He raised his massive and mighty weapon up toward the top of the mountain, honing in on one of the Pumas parked along the ridge.

*   *   *

In P-4, Fusion continued to fire into the valley, totally oblivious to the fact that Mammoth was about to unload on her vehicle and her position.

*   *   *

Mammoth fired relentlessly, ripping the winch, laser, and both 30mm cannons from the front of the assault vehicle. His rounds climbed and ripped their way across the front hood off the Puma.

*   *   *

Suddenly, P-4 was taking heavy fire. Before Fusion had time to react, the rounds reached her. She was hit in the arms and chest, and then two rounds found their way to her face, blowing the back of her head out. Fusion fell back and off of the P-4.

*   *   *

Seeing that he'd successfully hit his target, Mammoth turned his assault onto the Puma next to the one he'd just destroyed.

*   *   *

GrizzLee couldn't locate his targets; ZCs were all over him. He raised his 60mm cannon and began to mow ZC down, all across the nearby valley in front and around him.

He was rewarded by a second wave of ZC, approximately fifty of them, heading for his location. With nowhere to go, he began to toss grenades as well as fire his awesome weapon. GrizzLee continues to kick some major ass, not realizing that he had been hit nine times.

But before long, he began to feel the effects of the punishment that his body has taken over the past few minutes; he first felt light-headed. The ZC continued to move in toward him. GrizzLee fired back a few more times, hitting only earth before he fell, first to his knees and then all the way to the ground.

About sixty meters from GrizzLee, Nuke saw a group of ZCs within twenty feet of GrizzLee, who was lying down on the other side of a huge boulder. Nuke turned his assault onto the remaining forty-five plus ZC rushing GrizzLee's location. With a combination of RPG rounds and his M4/M203 over and under automatic rifle with grenade launcher, Nuke soon blew the oncoming ZC to pieces. For the time being, GrizzLee was out of harm's way.

Nuke then got some attention from Black Ram, who, using an M60, forced Nuke to jump behind a large, fallen tree. Black Ram was tearing and blowing the bark, along with limbs, off the tree that Nuke was using for shelter. Black Ram was literally chopping into Nuke's shelter with M60 gunfire.

Nuke made a decision to rise up and fire his modified handheld RPG, even though he didn't know exactly where Black Ram was. Nuke raised his body and fires. Just as he pulled the trigger, he saw Black Ram out of the corner of his eye. Nuke's RPG round hit and destroyed a transport truck, killing two more ZC, and Nuke took a few rounds from Black Ram's M60 to his shoulder and arm. He fell back behind the fallen tree.

Black Ram charges toward the tree, unloading on it and through it as he ran. From his left side, Optic Blast cut Black Ram in half with her headband laser. Black Ram's upper body continues to shoot for a couple more seconds before it fell over.

Optic Blast got to Nuke, and the two now found themselves pinned behind the enormous fallen tree.

*   *   *

Mammoth fired again. This time, he knocked the right cannon off his target.

*   *   *

With the right cannon blown off his Puma, Mack T lowered the mighty barrel of P-3's howitzer and fired on Mammoth, blowing the half-track that Mammoth was using as shelter into the air. The vehicle immediately exploded. After it touched back down to the beautiful valley floor, Mammoth came running out from behind the blazing vehicle, still firing his 80mm canon.

*   *   *

From his position on the valley floor, Bolt-action saw an explosion. Suddenly Mammoth, engulfed in flames, emerged from behind the half-track that had blown up, firing his weapon.

Bolt-action took aim again and fired his brutal .80 caliber rifle, blowing the top of Mammoth's head into the air. The huge mutant's body fell harmlessly to the burning ground around it.

*   *   *

Amphibian found Brown Ram about fifteen meters from him. He turned his M5 assault weapon on the big, horned mutant.

BAM! Amphibian was tackled from his blind side by Red Ram.

Brown Ram turned on Amphibian and raised his guns, both M41A/M203, one in each hand.

Then *Boom*! Brown Ram was blown to a mist. From above the valley floor, Zeke had nailed him directly in the chest with a howitzer round.

Red Ram grabbed Amphibian and began to strangle the much smaller Amphibian, with just one hand. Amphibian shoved his compact M5 assault rifle into the ribs of the huge monsterlike mutant and fires away, blowing Red Ram's guts and insides out through the many, many holes in his back. Red Ram's nerves forced him to pull the trigger of his M60E, and one of the rounds grazed Amphibian on the side of the neck.

*   *   *

Nitro and Torch continued to blow away ZC from atop the mountain. Mack T and Zeke began destroying equipment and vehicles in search of any more targets.

*   *   *

Bolt-action, moved into Legion's makeshift camp and began to destroy vehicles and equipment with grenades. Amphibian joined Bolt-action in what Amphibian referred to as "the fun."

Optic Blast spotted Maiden, along with a couple dozen ZCs. She fired on Maiden, and Maiden fell and rolled under a jeep. Her ZCs protected her, firing on Optic Blast and Nuke. Optic Blast caught a round directly in the headband, knocking her unconscious.

Maiden climbed to the .50 caliber machine gun in the back of the jeep, and a ZC jumped into the driver's seat. The two headed for Nuke and Optic Blast's location.

Bolt-action fired on Maiden, hitting her in the leg several times and completely shredding her upper thigh. Maiden turned her gun onto Bolt-action and unleashed on him, hitting him all over the front of his body and dropping him in his tracks.

* * *

Out of the corner of his eye, Amphibian, who had been using grenades to blow up Legion's equipment, saw his battalion leader go down. Suddenly, Grunge had grabbed him from behind. Grunge squeezed so hard that Amphibian dropped the grenade in his hand. In terrible pain, Amphibian was about to black out.

With his last strength, Amphibian stuck his 9mm behind his head and to the side of his neck and fired into Grunge's throat. Grunge dropped Amphibian and immediately grabbed his throat, black blood spraying from his wounds.

Amphibian reached down and grabbed the grenade he'd dropped. He pulled the pin, shoved it into Grunge's ribs, and took cover. Grunge was holding his throat and stumbling around.

BOOM! The grenade went off, blowing Grunge to pieces.

Amphibian took cover in one of the transport trucks. Amphibian called Nitro. "Get down here with everything you've got. I think I might be the only one still standing, and there are still about fifty ZC, Ram, and a very pissed-off, wounded Maiden."

* * *

Nitro, Torch, Mack T, and Zeke headed toward the valley floor that they had been bombarding for almost an hour and a half.

Zeke stopped at P-4 and picked up the dead body of Fusion. He gently placed her in P-4's cab, looking at his fallen comrade for a few seconds before continuing on down with the rest of the Pumas.

The foursome continued to take ZC fire all the way down the mountainside trail.

"The hell with this shit," said Torch. She stopped her Puma and climbed into the howitzer chair. Switches the mighty weapons from howitzer to the much faster-shooting weapon, the 80mm cannon, she returned fire on the ZC.

*   *   *

Maiden emerged from the smoke firing the .50 caliber machine gun at the approaching convoy of Pumas. As her driver headed toward the Allied Force assault vehicles— right past the transport that Amphibian was in—Maiden focused her fire on Torch, the stationary target at the time.

From behind Maiden, Amphibian fired two 9mm rounds into the back of her head. Maiden's attack came to an abrupt halt as her body fell forward. She still clutched the .50 caliber, firing thoughtlessly as she fell. The stray rounds caught her driver in the back of his head, exploding his skull across the inside windshield of the jeep, just moments before the jeep went out of control, flipping end over end before exploding into a giant fireball.

*   *   *

The truck that Amphibian was in the back, of pulled away. He heard Ram; the driver radio Nazi to inform Nazi that Allied Force was now in-country. Ram gave Nazi a full report, telling him which Allied Force members were present, who had been wounded or killed, and where Nazi could find Allied Force.

Amphibian listened as Nazi asked Ram what he has left. Ram replied, "Fourteen ZC, myself, three jeeps, two 80mms, one howitzer, and this truck carrying grenades and missiles."

"Meet me at the rendezvous point in four hours," Nazi told Ram. "We'll rebuild your army and revenge your losses against Allied Force."

Amphibian turned his headset off and decided to ride it out. One jeep was in front and two were behind the truck he was in. He couldn't bail out; it was only 5:45 p.m. and not dark enough to provide him cover. Amphibian was an intelligence specialist and an SOT member; he would play spy for a while. This battle was over.

* * *

As the convoy reached the valley, the team saw what they had taken part in. The battlefield was littered with body parts of both ZC and Legion members. Everywhere they looked, vehicle debris was strewn across the expansive valley floor. Small fires burned everywhere, and every so often small explosions erupted.

The convoy stopped near the center of the battle-stricken valley that, just a few short hours ago, had been a beautiful and colorful natural landscape. In Bolt-Action's absence, Nitro took over command of 1st Battalion. "Search and rescue!" she ordered. "Let's find our people and get them some help."

The team spread out across the valley on the hunt for their wounded. Allied Force's Number one nurse, Nitro stayed back and returned to the top to retrieve Fusion's body. Before she'd gone far, Torch found Bolt-action. "Here's Bolt-action," she called. "He's out but alive."

Given Bolt-action's proximity, Nitro ordered Torch to leave him and locate the others.

Mack T found Nuke and Optic Blast. Nuke, who was bleeding from what appeared to be every place on his body, was trying to revive Optic Blast. Mack T loaded both warriors onto the Puma and returned them to what had become camp for the night.

Nuke told the others where to find GrizzLee. "He's in the worst shape of us all," he said.

Torch went back to Bolt-action, and Mack T had headed toward GrizzLee, when he noticed Zeke carrying GrizzLee toward camp. GrizzLee's giant body lay lifeless in Zeke's massive arms.

*   *   *

Still assuming command in Bolt-action's incapacitation, Nitro after returning to the valley floor with Fusion's body gathered the team. "Okay, listen up. Here's where we stand. We searched the entire valley, and there's no sign of Amphibian. It's close to 7:30 p.m. and too dark to continue the search tonight. We have to stay the night any way; we have wounded who need attention and can't travel right now. And we're all in desperate need of rest."

She paused, softening her voice softly before continuing. "Some of you may already know that we lost one of our own today. Fusion was killed in action, fighting for freedom, against the aggression of Legion, and to preserve the history and future of humankind the way that we know it—in a damn war that has already been fought and the outcome decided," she added. "We all know that she will be missed. Let's take a moment for prayer."

After the group had shared a mournful silence, Nitro finished her address. "Lee is in critical condition. I'm not sure that he'll make it through the night. Optic Blast will be okay. She was knocked out and has a concussion. She also lost the ability to use her laser from her headband. Same with Bolt-action, outside some broken ribs, he will be fine. He also lost his ability to use his body armor." Bolt-action had a type of unexplained body armor in his skin that could reflect most small arms fire. "Nuke was shot up all to hell, but he assures me that he will make it back to the squad very soon, so I have to take his word for it.

"We will stay here tonight," Nitro concluded. "Come sunup, we will continue the search for Amphibian. In the meantime, we will listen for him and try to get in contact with both him and 2nd Battalion. I'm extremely proud of all of us. We kicked ass, a lot of ass, but we also paid one hell of a price. Let's do inventory."

The battered team completed its inventory; 1st Battalion remained unable to get in contact with either Amphibian or 2nd Battalion. The deep, black sky of Germany fell heavy on the team. In every direction they looked, the group could see the dreaded orange sky that depicted the war raging on throughout the night.

At 9:45 p.m., Zeke mounted up on the P-5 howitzer chair to stand guard over the exhausted and wounded team—only after he had spent the last forty-five minutes by his best friend's side, waiting for GrizzLee to wake up.

After Bolt-action and Nitro had completed the very emotional duty of bagging Fusion's body, the two went over the events of the day, discussing both the team's status and the plan of attack for the following day. They were still unable to make contact with either Amphibian or Gatlin and 2nd Battalion.

"What do you think happened to Amp?" asked Nitro.

"I don't know, but I don't think that we have to worry about Amp too much," Bolt-action replied. "He obviously isn't here, and Ram, I'm almost positive, wouldn't take prisoners. Amp is probably trying to infiltrate Legion as we speak. I've got the utmost confidence in him, as I do in all of our people. I expect to hear from him, if not tonight than in the morning sometime.

"If you'll check on the wounded, I'll go check with Zeke. Then I'll meet you back here to wrap things up."

"Sure thing," Nitro agreed. "You know, we are really going to miss Fusion until this thing is over," she added, tears filling her eyes.

"Yeah, I know, but let's keep our heads and get back home so that her death isn't for nothing," said Bolt-action. "That's what she would have wanted."

Before Nitro entered the makeshift sick bay—the back of a transport that had been abandoned by Ram and his team—she stopped and looked around at the group of people who she loved so much. She saw Bolt-action walking over to Zeke on P-5, Torch sleeping in the cab of P-2, and Mack T kicked back on P-3's howitzer chair. She guessed that Optic Blast was sleeping in the cab of P-3.

Nitro turned and entered sick bay. Nuke, who was hooked to an IV drip that was administering some fluids, vitamins, and a slow morphine drip, woke up.

Nitro looked at GrizzLee. To her, he looked like a giant teddy bear. Hoses from his nose delivered oxygen, and his chest dressings needed to be changed again. She and Bolt-action both thought that GrizzLee had a punctured lung. A six-inch chunk of flesh, fur, and muscle were missing from his shoulder, and both his legs were bandaged up. He was supporting two bullet wounds, approximately three inches apart, in his upper thigh. He was very lucky that the chest wound wasn't any higher and closer to his heart. His left wrist and hand both had bullet wounds; his wrist was shattered, and the bullet was still lodged in the bone. The wound to his hand had been made by a different caliber weapon than the other wounds on his body; it had been made by a 30mm fired at relatively close range. The round had entered that palm and exited through the back of the hand, destroying it; his ring finger and pinkie finger were just barely hanging on by flesh.

Nitro and Bolt-action had put GrizzLee back together the best that they could with what they had to work with and in the conditions that they are under. GrizzLee was so bandaged up that he looked like a mummy. Seeing GrizzLee, such a sweet and gentle being all the time, filled Nitro with sadness, adding to her sorrow over the death of

Fusion. The team needed the two fallen warriors for not only their unique abilities but because the two offered a wide variety of language skills. Besides English, Fusion had spoken Russian, German, French, and Spanish. GrizzLee could speak Chinese, Japanese, Vietnamese, French, and Spanish. He could even communicate with Zeke, who didn't speak in any language.

Nitro began to change GrizzLee's bandages.

"Hey, girl, how are ya holdin' up?" asked Nuke.

"I'm dealing with it. How about you? How are you feeling?" she asked.

"Oh, I'll be ready to go by morning. Hell, I'm ready now, but after today and what we lost, I'd better do what you and Bolt-action told me to. So I'm lying here being fed—what you say that I need. By the way, every so often, Lee will moan and then call out in sort of a growl, but he doesn't move. Is he gonna make it?"

"That's the morphine; it's probably giving him nightmares. He had quite a bit of trauma. But to answer your question, I really don't know if he's going to make it or not," Nitro said gently. "We've done all that we can for him; the rest is up to him and the good Lord. I pray he doesn't take this gentle giant of a warrior. He has already taken one of us. The good Lord knows what we are trying to do here. We need this big one here." Having finished changing GrizzLee's dressings, Nitro broke down in tears.

Nuke reached out to her and gave her a hug.

"I'm not sure about this mission anymore," she confided. "I mean I felt really confident at first. But this, this is a whole lot more than I ever imagined. You realize that we only have ourselves. Every country involved in this war will take us as the enemy. So we'll face them, along with having to battle Legion and that sick-minded fucker, Nazi; excuse my language. I have to admit, I'm a little scared. I really don't know what is coming up for us, Nuke. Damn, I wish this hadn't happened."

"It's okay Nitro," Nuke said, his tone comforting. "Hell, I'm scared too. I know if everyone was honest, we'd find out that they're all scared as well—well except for Zeke, but that's an entirely different story all together. You and Bolt-action have done all that you can for us, and believe me, we all appreciate it. You have to know that there wasn't anything that anyone could have done for Fusion. She died protecting us, the way she wanted to die, the way that she had to die. I feel better already. Bolt-action and Optic Blast are out there right now, ready for whatever lies ahead. Amphibian is fine—I'm sure of that—wherever he is. I've been on the S.O.T. with him for going on six years. He always disappears. That's why we always call him the invisible man."

Nuke met Nitro's gaze. "Don't worry," he told her. "We're heroes. And you're one also. I won't let you out of my sight, starting tomorrow, I promise. Hell, you know that I haven't taken my eyes off of you since the first time that I saw you. Do you really think that I am gonna start now?" Nuke kissed her on the forehead and squeezed her a little tighter before releasing her.

"Thanks, Nuke. I guess I really just needed to talk. I'm going to make you keep your word about watching over me," she added. "I feel a little flakey. I've got to get back to Bolt-action and then try and get some sleep."

Nuke opened his blanket. "You can sleep right here," he said with a grin.

Nitro just smiles and slapped Nuke on the arm, "Yeah right, in your dreams," she said.

"I know; every night you're in my dreams," replied Nuke.

"Get some sleep, Romeo. Oh, and by the way, if Lee wakes up, talk to him a little bit but don't mention Fusion. They were very close friends. Good night," said Nitro.

"Okay," Nuke agreed. "Good night."

* * *

When Nitro met back up with Bolt-action, she asked about Zeke.

"Oh well, you know Zeke. He seems to understand about Lee, but you can't ever really tell because he never changes his facial expressions. But we don't have to worry about anything. Zeke is always focused. He never once took his eyes off that road the entire time that I was talkin' to him. Lee sure does mean a lot to him.

"Speaking of Lee, how is he doing, as well as the rest of the team?" "The rest of the team is sleeping with weapons at arms' reach," she reported. "Nuke tells me that he will definitely be ready by tomorrow. He told me that three times. Lee is still not showing any movement and doesn't respond to my voice at all. He doesn't seem to be getting any better, but he doesn't seem to be getting any worse either. Let's see, it's 11:40 p.m. Lee has been in sick bay for four hours. We really need to see something out of him by morning. Nuke did say that Lee cried out, though. He wasn't very loud, but Nuke did hear him nevertheless. So that tells me that either Lee feels pain or he is having bad dreams. Either way, this is a little encouraging, compared to what kind of shape that he was in when Zeke carried him up to me."

"Why don't you get some sleep? We can go over this stuff in the morning. I really don't think that Legion is going to try anything tonight. Personally, I don't think that we will see them again, until we go after them. And that's exactly what I intend to do. I'm gonna hit the sack myself," Bolt-action told her. "I'm gonna try Gatlin one more time first" he added.

"If it's okay with you, I was going to sleep in P-1 and park it behind sick bay, with the windows down" said Nitro.

"No problem; good idea," Bolt-action agreed. "I'm gonna man the turret on P-4, beings that there are no guns left on the vehicle besides the turret, Howitzer and 80mm. It is all shot to hell and smokes like a chimney but she still runs and we need transportation and firepower so hopefully she will last a bit longer for us. That way, we'll have someone on all Puma's, just in case. Oh and hey, Nitro, I was really impressed today at your leadership on the ridge, and especially after you got down here. You've done a great job. Keep it up."

"Thank you, sir. You need to get some sleep yourself. Good night, sir," replied Nitro.

"Good night," said Bolt-action.

*   *   *

Bolt-action finally got in contact with Gatlin and 2nd Battalion. Bolt-action updated Gatlin on their battle with Legion. He reported their losses, the injured, and the victory, as well as the numbers of Legion and ZC dead. Then he broke the news about the loss of Fusion.

"I hate to hear that about Fusion," Gatlin said. "Damn it. I'm sure my team will feel the same way. I'll tell them in the morning. How is Lee taking it? Or does he even know about it?"

"No, Lee is still out of it from his injuries and the heavy meds that Nitro has him on. We'll figure out a way to tell him in the morning," said Bolt-action.

"Well that is some real bad news," said Gatlin. "We'll pray for Fusion and the wounded. We haven't had any action or luck catching up to Legion. We are currently on a SSE heading. Every place we come to has been abandoned and destroyed. We've been one step behind Legion but unable to intercept them. It's frustrating, but the lack of action has been real beneficial for our wounded, giving them some time to get back to their normal selves. But you know as well as I do that they're ready to go no matter what kind of shape they're in.

"We've come to a three-way intersection of rock roads, right near the border between Germany and Poland. The rocks are making it impossible to track Legion as well as we could back on the dirt roads. So I'm getting three recon teams together and sending them down each road about twenty miles; then they will report. The recon teams will be heading out at 6:00 a.m. I'll get in contact with you for a status report at around noon tomorrow. If you don't hear from me, well than you'll know that we're getting it on with some Legion, somewhere.

"Hey, bud, again, I, as well as my team, feel the pain of your loss of Fusion. But just remind the team that we will get her back when we end this thing, the sooner the better. Take it easy and get some sleep," said Gatlin.

"Yeah okay, you do the same," said Bolt-action. "Over and out."

*   *   *

As the sun rose over the beautiful countryside, during this ugly time in history, all seemed peaceful for the first couple of days for 2nd Battalion. It was very quiet you can say that serenity is amongst the team.

Gatlin gathered his battalion and told them, "I'm very tired of this place and time, as I am sure that all of you are. We have way too many wounded, and 1st Battalion is in even worse shape than we are. We lost Fusion yesterday during a conflict with Legion, apparently led by Ram. First Battalion took most of them out, but at the cost of one of our own. Lee is in real bad shape. Optic Blast and Nuke are wounded, but they tell me that they will be good to go by this morning. Amphibian is MIA.

"With that being said, let's all take a minute before we head out this morning and remember Fusion and pray for Lee, as well as Nuke and Optic Blast. Stay within yourselves. Remember, we are playing for keeps this time, as is Legion; you can bet on that. So be safe, be smart, and be back.

"I'm splittin' us up into three recon teams." He explained his plans, saying that once each team had completed its objective, everyone would meet back in their current spot for the next plan of attack. "So listen up, here are the recon teams. In P-7 will be Stealth, Jon Henri, and Crosshairs. You three will recon east and report, no more than twenty miles. P-10 will be Xtract, Drazil, and Recoil. Your squad will be heading down the south-southwest road. The third squad is P-6 and P-8; P-6 will be myself and Blade, and Pistol Smoke and Shadow will take P-8. We will recon to the south-southeast.

"I know that we are running a little low on fuel, and we really didn't bring any, as I was sure that we could find some in this country somewhere. But I am sure that we have enough for these recons and that we'll make it back to The Crow and the Raven. I will make sure of that.

"Okay, with that, let's all give our Fusion a moment of silence."

The team paused to reflect on the fallen Fusion.

"Let's move 'em out!" ordered Gatlin.

As the three recon teams took off in their designated directions, all were in pretty high spirits considering what they had done, lost, and seen, not to mention that they were everyone else's enemy in this war, and they were the "good guys."

*   *   *

After traveling about twelve miles, P-10 reported from the SSW. "Yeah, Gatlin, we are about twelve miles down and we have already located none other than Nazi, Bulge, Staft, and some giant tank-looking dude, along with six Hell Knights and approximately two hundred ZC. They've got some very heavy confiscated artillery," reported Recoil.

"Monitor the situation and report any changes immediately," Gatlin ordered.

*   *   *

At 7:10 a.m., P-7 radioed with a report. "Sixteen miles out, I spy Psycho, Gage, Torchess, Ratchet, a dozen Demon Troopers, and about fifty ZC, as well as heavy artillery" said Stealth.

Gatlin gives P-7 the same orders as he had P-10.

*   *   *

At 7:25 a.m., approximately nineteen miles out, P-6 and P-8 came upon a discovery of their own. Ram, Mite, Jackyl, Gorman, and an estimated three hundred ZCs had set up a base and were in possession of a heap of heavy artillery confiscated from the German Army.

"All units and squads back to base camp," Gatlin ordered. "Repeat, all units return to base camp ASAP.

Gatlin contacted Bolt-action. "Hey, man, according to my calculations, our recon teams have located the remaining Legion members and their equipment. Each recon team has reported back, and it appears that Legion is setting up what looks like camps in three different locations. Seems to all of us that they are waiting for something or someone; it doesn't appear that any of them are planning to move out any time soon."

Gatlin gave Bolt-action the coordinates to 2nd Battalion's base camp, "I think it's time to join forces and become stronger. We're gonna need all the help that we have at our disposal," said Gatlin.

*   *   *

After taking a closer look at the coordinates that Gatlin had given him, Bolt-action realized that Gatlin and 2nd Battalion had been on a SSE course. Gatlin had just made a big circle and was heading straight for 1st battalion's current position." On paper, Bolt-action figured the two battalions were only about forty-five or fifty miles from each other. He decided that he'd lead 1st Battalion on an alternate route to avoid any further conflict with Legion before meeting up with the others.

"Gatlin, this is Bolt-action; we will be taking an alternate route to your position. We will be there in about two or two and a half hours."

"Copy that. Be careful. If need be, give us a call," Gatlin replied.

* * *

Back at 2nd Battalion's base camp, Gatlin made a very tough decision.

"Get prepared," Gatlin ordered Stealth. "We're gonna strip P-7 down to nothing but Puma and guns, for more speed. You should be able to get up to 90 miles per hour or better. The catch is that you will be traveling alone, back to get The Crow."

"I have no problem with that," Stealth assured him. "I have been missing my baby anyway. I should be able to get there in about three hours or so, without any trouble or involvement. Ten minutes to load P-7 and prep her, then about thirty minutes fly time. So in about three and a half hours, we will have The Crow with us."

Ten minutes later, the P-7 was stripped; it was now 8:30 a.m. "I'll see ya about 1:00 p.m.," Stealth said as she pulled away in P-7, excited for the race ahead of her. "Don't start without me."

As he watched Stealth and P-7 disappear over the hillside at a very high rate of speed, Gatlin gathered the rest of his team. "Okay, 1st Battalion should be here between 9:30 and 10:30, barring any accidents or problems."

The team was psyched, but an uneasy feeling also hung in the air around the camp. The team knew that, in the past, if they were losing or in trouble, they always had the luxury of reinforcements. Plus, up until this point, they were never fighting to prevent the change of world history as we know it. They know that if they failed, the world they would have to return to would be a terrible place—one likely led by Malakai and Legion. The team knew that, if Malakai did control the world, the world would die of hatred. They had never had to fight for so long, with so many members in so many directions, facing so much firepower, and remaining, by a long shot, the underdog.

The team stayed busy, preparing and refueling the vehicles and loading and cleaning all weapons. The team went over which targets to hit first, second, and third and what to do if they were in the heat of battle with one group of Legion and another group of Legion joined.

"What we must accomplish seems very impossible right now, and maybe it is," Gatlin told his team, "for now we are definitely outgunned and outnumbered. But remember, ZCs probably can't pose much of a threat by themselves. However, as long as they are being led by Legion, they can shoot and fire any and all weapons in Legion's arsenal with great accuracy." Not wanting to hold back any punches, Gatlin told the team the score. "We will be facing a Legion force an estimated eight hundred strong; that is close to ninety times our own force."

The team didn't like the odds. But being who they are and given what they represented and what they were fighting for, the Allied Force warriors were willing to give it everything they had. Maybe that would prove to be enough to overcome the tremendous odds. Only time would tell.

*   *   *

"It's 9:50 a.m. I hope 1st Battalion makes it here soon. And I wonder how Stealth is doing," said Recoil.

"Stealth to Gatlin; come in, Gatlin."

"Ask and you shall receive," said Gatlin as he picked up the radio. "Yeah Stealth, go ahead; this is Gatlin. Read you loud and clear. Over."

"Copy that. I am showing 9:52 a.m. We didn't sync watches prior in the rush. According to my odometer, I have traveled 110 miles, no problems. This little jewel can really lay it down when she needs to. I officially take back everything that I ever said about her and all of her sisters in the past. I'm going to have to join the SOT so I can have one or these babies all the time. I've gotten up to 120 miles per hour. I just about lost it a couple times. I figure that, on average, I'm traveling about 80 miles per hour. I just about lost it once when the road curved without notice. I hit some small trees and a road side sign. If she got damaged, it hasn't affected her performance at all. The second time, I almost hit some cows.

"Gatlin, I need to sign off and concentrate on the road. Traveling at 115 miles per hour; odometer reads 118 miles per hour. Estimated 182 miles remaining. It's beginning to rain and may snow by the looks of these clouds. Should reach The Crow if all goes well in approximately two hours. I will contact you if there are any changes. Over and out," reported Stealth.

"Come in, Gatlin."

"Go ahead, Bolt-action."

"We are traveling along down this road, haven't seen any signs of Legion or soldiers of any kind. I figured that we would be at your location by now, but still looking . . . Got a visual on you now. Over and out."

As 1st Battalion pulled into base camp, it was 10:15 a.m. The two teams reunited. It had only been a few days, but it was a few days that not one member would ever forget. The two teams embraced and then got down to the business at hand.

Gatlin, with his second in command, Pistol Smoke, and 1st Battalion's leader, Bolt-action, along with his newly second in charge, Nitro, gathered at the back of P-6, the makeshift war room. There they went over the plan of attack.

Recoil rushed in. "Hey, guys, you have to see this," he burst out. "I know why Nazi has his troops on all three roads and waiting. I'm looking at this map that I got out of one of the German half-tracks back in town, right, for an alternative route. And there it was. These three roads are referred to as, ironically, "The Crow's Foot," because, if you look at them on the map, they resemble a crow's foot. Anyway these three roads all lead into this larger road or highway that connects Germany to Poland. In the first World War II, that road or highway was used by the German Army. Now hear me out. This road was used by the largest regiment or whatever they called themselves back then. Anyway, on September 1, 1939, Germany used this road to conquer Poland—hence, the start of World War II, well, after the false radio crap or whatever. I'm talking like thousands of troops and hundreds of tanks, jeeps, and half-tracks came through here, on these very roads. Nazi would know this, as would Bulge, from being here when it actually happened, the first time.

"I'm willing to bet everything that Nazi is going to let those troops get on the road and then he is going to hit them with everything that he has. Those soldiers have never faced the state-of-the art weaponry that Legion possesses. The soldiers will be slaughtered; they don't stand a chance. Nazi is going to stop them and then fight the war his way. Why else would he have all of his equipment and men at three very close locations to each other? It makes sense, doesn't it?"

"I'll be damned," breathed Bolt-action, taking in the gravity of what Recoil had just revealed. "Good work, Recoil. Do you happen to know exactly what date in history this big push of the Germans passed through this area?"

"No, sir, I just remember the basics, maybe from a documentary or something. But by the looks of it, we have some time. The Legion forces are probably forty miles from the main road," Recoil explained. "I think if it was going to happen real soon, they would be closer to the road. It's going to take a couple of days to get all that equipment and that many troops in position for an attack of that size, right? And it looks to me that they are pretty settled in right now. I'd say that they will be mobilizing by tomorrow afternoon at the latest. It will be August 31st, and World War II started for Poland on September 1, 1939."

Recoil paused, looking around at the team's leaders. "We can do this right," he said, "without rushing into it. Well, with that being said, I'll leave the rest up to you military minds."

"Recoil, you and Optic Blast go out on a search and rescue for Amp. He is probably ready to come home now," said Bolt-action.

*   *   *

At 10:45 a.m., Recoil and Optic Blast loaded into P-3 and went in search of Amphibian. Nineteen miles later, Recoil and Optic Blast were looking at one of Legion's camps. The P-3 was parked off the road in some trees approximately a quarter mile back. They each scanned the camp area for the whereabouts of Amphibian with binoculars equipped with range finders. They were looking for a holding pen or cell that Legion may be holding Amphibian in.

All they saw were Legion members clowning around and cleaning weapons and equipment that they had obviously taken from the German Army.

"The big idiot is alive," Recoil suddenly said, pointing. "There he is; he's still in camp. Hell, they don't even know he's there. He's either very lucky or very good. Look. Do you see 'im over by the tent next to the row of trucks?"

"Yeah, I see the moron," said Optic Blast. "What in the hell is he doing? Oh my gosh, he is stealing their canteens. Wait, he is pouring the water out and filling them with sand. Are you seeing this? He's down there playing around. He's going to get caught. Those Hell Knights will pick up his scent, and then he'll be toast. Get a hold of him and tell him to get over here," ordered Optic Blast. "Playtime is over. It's time to get back to work."

"I love that guy," Recoil said, chuckling. "He's ruthless. You have to admit, he's good, even fun to watch. Hell, he's our best infiltrator that we have by far. As for those Hell Knights, they can't smell him. Amp doesn't give off anything that they can pick up on. Amp gives off no body smells what so ever. Damn he's a maniac.

"Come in, Amp. This is Recoil. If you can hear me, I can see you. Optic Blast is with me, we are at your six. Find us and get over here before they see you and us. We have to get back to camp."

"Copy that Recoil. I'm heading yawl's way," whispered Amphibian. "I have to make a couple of stops on the way."

As Amphibian worked his way very methodically to safety, he stopped at several trucks and half-tracks.

"What in the hell is he doing now?" asked Optic Blast.

"Oh shit, he's placing C-4 charges on their equipment. He is as cool as the other side of the pillow. We're lucky to have him on our team," said Recoil.

Optic Blast shook her head. "You guys are never going to grow up. You all are always acting like little boys with your games, antics, and all your practical jokes. I just don't understand how you all think, the whole bunch of you guys."

After about twenty minutes, Amphibian finally reached Recoil and Optic Blast. "Hey what brings you two down to this neck of the woods?" he asked.

"We are here to retrieve you," said Optic Blast. "We're going to hit them soon. Gatlin, Bolt-action, Pistol Smoke, and Nitro are all working on a plan as we speak. We need to get back to camp. Are you okay?"

"Oh yeah, I'm fine. I had a good time playing with those tools back there," said Amphibian as he winked at Optic Blast and pounded fists with Recoil.

The three reached the P-3 and began their fifteen-minute drive back to base camp.

"So we're gonna hit 'em," Amphibian said enthusiastically. "When? Hell, I'm ready now. I set some charges on I believe about a dozen of their vehicles. I can detonate anytime I want to. Hell I poured out most of their food, and I put sand in their canteens; I even took a leak in a few of them. I let air out of the tires of the pull-behind howitzers and 80mm cannon trailers, and I unhooked a lot of their trailers. I knew that y'all would be coming for me directly. I just figured I'd stay busy in the meantime."

"Well I don't think that you know we lost Fusion," said Optic Blast. "Lee is in real bad shape. Gatlin and Bolt-action are working on a plan of attack right now. Stealth took P-7 and went back to get The Crow. Gatlin has something very big planned."

Amphibian turned serious. "They killed Fusion? Oh fuck that. It is on now. Those assholes have just signed their death warrants, motherfuckers. It is so fuckin' on now. Get us back to camp. We have a revenge factor that comes into play now, something that we have never had in the past. Oh those bastards. Forgive my language, Optic Blast. Does Lee know about Fusion?"

"No; well at least he didn't when we left. He was still in pretty bad shape. I believe that Gatlin was going to tell him when he thought it was a good time. So right now we are two people short, as if the odds weren't already so far in Legion's favor. I hope that Gatlin and Bolt-action come up with one hell of a plan," said Recoil as he sat back in the passenger's seat.

Not another word was spoken for the duration of the short trip back to base camp.

*   *   *

"Come in, Gatlin."

"Hey, go ahead, Stealth."

"I'm at The Crow, loading P-7 on board, and shutting bay doors. Man, I have to tell you, that that porthole, warper, or whatever it's called looks extremely inviting right now. I'll prep The Crow and see y'all in about thirty minutes," said Stealth.

"Roger that, Stealth. Be careful, and we'll see you then. I promise that we won't start without you. Over and out," said Gatlin.

The rest of the team all let out a collective sigh of relief—relief that Stealth had made it to The Crow safely and relief that The Crow was going to be in on the fight.

"Yeah, it's time to kick some ass again," said Amphibian. "They are gonna pay for what they did to Fusion and Lee."

Gatlin knew it was time to fill his team in on the plan. "Gather around, people!" he called, radioing Stealth so she could be in on the meeting. "Here's the game. One team, Legion has better than eight hundred men with heavy artillery. The other team, us, has eighteen members, nine vehicles, The Crow, one hell of a plan, and more importantly, attitude. I like our chances."

The entire team agrees. Everyone was in very high spirits and ready to get it on, regardless of the odds. Gatlin was the best motivator in the business. He would definitely have to live up to that title in true form on this day.

Gatlin would talk to his entire team one more time before Allied Force embarked on the task at hand.

"It's 12:45 p.m. Are you with us, Stealth?"

"Yeah, I can hear every word that you're saying," she replied. "I'm one minute from putting her down. Go ahead."

"Like always, we are the underdogs, and this is no exception," Gatlin continued. "But like I said, we are always the underdog. We have always, since the beginning some eighteen years ago, been smaller in numbers compared to Legion.

"I'm gonna give y'all the prewar statistics. This is not going to be a battle. Believe me, it is going to be war, we will not take the Legion camps on one by one. I, as well as all of you, want to get out of 1939 and the sooner the better, so why not just one ass-kickin' war? No stopping; just keep fighting until the end. That's why I'm giving you these stats. When this thing is over and we stand victorious, then and there, we can compare apples to oranges—their power versus our power. On paper, it looks like we already lost, so let's prove the paper wrong once again. Did you hear everything, Stealth?"

"Yes, sir, I heard every word," answered Stealth walking toward the team.

"Well, we are glad to see that you made it back," Gatlin said. "Good work on getting The Crow. As I was sayin', we may be the underdogs, but we are eighteen of the baddest bad-asses ever assembled together at one time."

The entire team exploded in a cheer of agreement.

"Uh, I believe that you mean nineteen of the baddest bad-asses ever. Don't you?"

"You're up," said Nitro, turning to GrizzLee as he joined the group.

"How ya feelin', mummy man?" asked Nuke.

"I'm light-headed, in a bit of pain, tired, hungry, and ready to—what y'all say—kick some ass. Just put me on a gun somewhere and give me my guns, and I'll be fine. Nobody say a word, 'cause it will not work; I'm going with or without you. I've got a debt to collect, for my dear friend and yours, Fusion. So give me some food and my guns," GrizzLee concluded.

"You heard the man; give him his guns and feed this man," said Gatlin.

"You got it, big guy. Hell yeah, you got it, Lee," said Bolt-action.

"Okay, now here's what we're up against," Gatlin said. "People, this is a true army, led by a man who knows war and how to lead troops in a war. We're up against roughly eight hundred soldiers, according to our intelligence from Amphibian."

"Excuse me, Gatlin, but isn't that an oxymoron? Intelligence and Amphibian?" said Torch, laughing.

"Oh yeah, good one, girl," said Blade, giving Torch a very unorthodox fist punch.

"Yeah, very funny, ladies. I'll have you know that I risked my life for that Intel," said Amphibian.

"Oh please, Amp. Recoil and I both watched you through binoculars play around at Legion's camp for several minutes. No telling what the hell you were doing before we got there," Optic Blast retorted.

"Okay, enough, people. We had our laughs. Amp, you will not answer that. Can I be in charge again?" said Gatlin. "As I was saying, the Intel is fantastic, and frankly, neither I nor any of y'all should give a shit how he got it as long as he got it. We all know that Amp does things his own way, so we will leave it at that.

"We also need to thank Recoil for his knowledge of the area and World War II history. Without him, we wouldn't even have a plan to use the Intel that Amp gathered. So thanks for that, Recoil.

"Now, if I may continue—if that's not too much to ask—I myself would really like to get this thing going and get it decided, and get the hell out of here. Okay, according to Amp's numbers, Legion has six hundred and seventy grenades; seven hundred and eighty missiles and/or rockets; sixteen tanks, Tigers, Panzers, and Panthers; forty half-tracks; thirty six 80mms; fifty-six 30mms; fifty-nine bazookas; sixteen RPGs; forty-four jeeps, now with .50 cals mounted; eleven portable 20mms; twenty-two portable howitzers; seventeen transport trucks; and most of all, a leader who has no heart for lives, enemy or innocent."

The team was in awe over the power display that Legion possessed. They all knew that it would be directed at them within the hour. Gatlin, trying not to allow reality to hit his team so hard, added quickly, "Sounds like Nazi has a bunch of firepower lying around that he won't get a chance to use. Keeping him from using most of it's gonna be a piece of cake, good cake, really good cake, the kind Mom use to make.

"Listen up, people, it's almost time to get geared up mentally and physically. We will win this thing. It isn't a question of how; it's a simple question of when. Stealth, we are counting on you and your skills with The Crow to get this game kicked off; get the odds as even as you can, as fast as you can and get The Crow back on the ground. There are just too many enemies around here to have her up for a very long period of time. You hit your targets and you hit them good and hard. Return and hit them again, a second time. You are to only fly two sorties per and report.

"As for the rest of us, we have nine vehicles and three target areas; that's three vehicles per target area. We've numbered the three targets. Nazi's camp is target number one, or T-1; Psycho's camp will be T-2; and Ram's camp is, of course, T-3. Stealth will hit these targets in this order— T-1, T-3, and then T-2. Because of distance, that will be more efficient for our ground troops.

"Here is how we're gonna work it by squads, each squad having three Puma's. Squad number, S-1, will attack T-1, S-2 will attack T-2, and S-3 will take on T-3. Pretty simple; I hope I didn't lose anyone on that tough numerical stuff. The squad members are as follows: S-1 will be P-1 with Bolt-action and Nitro, P-4 with Nuke and Recoil, keep an eye on P-4 Recoil and Nuke she is pretty banged up, and P-7 with

Jon Henri and Crosshairs; S-2 is P-2 with Amp and Torch, P-6 with Blade and myself, and P-8 with Pistol Smoke and Shadow; and in S-3 will be P-3 with Optic Blast and Mack T, P-5 with GrizzLee and Zeke, and P-10 with Xtract and Drazil. T, you will have to drive P-5 out to the sight for Lee and Zeke, but Lee can maneuver it around once he's there."

"No problem," said Mack T. "I'll get them there and put them in a good spot."

"On this one, it's the final hit it and get it," Gatlin told the team. "So we're taking everything with us. There is no more. So hit what you're aiming at and stay focused. It will seem overwhelming at first and maybe throughout and, hell, it may even seem impossible. But remember home as we know it and love it. Stay within yourselves. We are all heroes. You don't have to prove it. No one will be impressed. Just stay focused and do the best that you can to keep their guns off Stealth. She's gonna be the key that opens the door to the ass kickin'; we just have to turn the knob and enter the fray. Okay, let's pray."

After a moment, the group was ready.

"Okay, squad leaders, let's move 'em out," said Gatlin. "Good luck. We are going on Stealth's mark. We do not attack target until Stealth attacks target. Headsets on. LET'S RIDE!"

*   *   *

S-1 took position; the howitzers in all three Pumas were up and ready to fire. In P-1 was Nitro with Bolt-action on the 80mm cannon; Recoil drove P-4 with Nuke on the portable howitzer, and in P-7, Jon Henri was in the chair and Crosshairs was armed with sidewinder missiles and three boxes setting next to her.

Bolt-action gave the team one more boost. "Let's kick their asses," he said with a roar. "Shoot until you run out of targets. Let's use up all of this stuff; no reason to take it back with us. Good luck. I love all of you."

Moments later *Varoom, Varoom*—thirteen, fourteen, fifteen, sixteen times. The battle was on.

*　　*　　*

Stealth fired sixteen rockets or missiles on her first sortie into each of Legion's three camps.

Moments later, her second and final sortie went as planned. She fired fourteen more of the same on strategic targets, with pinpoint accuracy.

Stealth and The Crows attack had reduced Nazi's arsenal from sixteen tanks to only three, ten half-tracks to four, nineteen jeeps to twelve, seven howitzers to five, six transport truck to just three, two hundred ZC to sixty ZC, six Hell Knights down to just two. Unfortunately Nazi, Staft, and Panzer were still present. Bulge died in his tank.

*　　*　　*

Approximately seventy-five meters apart from each other, the three Pumas hunkered in the north east portion of the dense tree line that surrounded three sides of the Legion encampment. Either a portable howitzer or a portable 80mm cannon sat between each Puma. Following Stealth's second and final sortie, the S-1 team unleashed their fury into and onto Legion, just as fast as their guns would reload.

Bolt-action, Nitro, Nuke, and Jon Henri were all stationary. Crosshairs grabbed an extra box of her specially designed sidewinder missiles—twenty-four per box—put them on her back, and moved through the woods in search of the three Legion members at T-1, Nazi, Staft, and the tank-looking guy known as, Panzer.

Bolt-action was dropping ZC everywhere with his .80 caliber. Nitro was concentrating on the heavy artillery.

She destroyed two jeeps with .50 caliber machine guns mounted in them and a half-track before they zeroed in on her location. A tank and two half-tracks turned their attacks toward her location, blowing the woods to splinters around her. Nitro took out one more half-track. Then the Puma was peppered with both .50 caliber and 80mm rounds.

Nitro could no longer stay in the chair of the P-1, so she slid down the side of the Puma and grabbed a borrowed RPG. Strapping it to her back, she grabbed ten grenades, a 60mm as well as a 30mm, and took shelter from the P-1 about thirty meters away, in a hole from a large, uprooted tree that had recently fallen.

Just as she got set up with her 60mm in place and began manning the RPG, the P-1 was destroyed by tank fire. Nitro rose up when she heard the explosion and saw a tank and Demon Troopers heading toward her Puma. She took aim with the RPG and fired an antitank missile, hitting the tank in the front. The tank stopped. She heard screaming coming from the tank as she fired again, this time hitting and destroying a jeep.

The Demon Troopers and the other half-track begin firing on her with 20mm cannons and tossing grenades in her direction. Nitro dropped back inside the giant hole in the earth just as four, five, six grenades exploded all around her. Once again Nitro rose up, this time dropping the RPG and manning the 60mm machine gun. She began ripping into and shredding Demon Troopers, soon taking down six, seven, and then eight.

Then the half-track fired on her; two jeeps were very close and closing; from roughly eighty feet away, they opened up on her position with their .50 caliber machine guns. Nitro was pinned down, in a bad way.

She grabbed six grenades and the RPG. Seeing that her 60mm cannon had been blown to pieces, she grabbed her 30mm cannon and retreated deeper into the woods, heading toward the densest part so the half-track and jeeps would no longer be able to give chase, all the while firing her 30mm cannon back at the three or four Demon Troopers still on her tail. The half-track and the two jeeps continued to fire on her from afar. She was hit from behind in the left forearm. The impact from the shell twisted her body and caused her to fall to the ground.

Nitro turned and fired her 30mm at the three Demon troopers that she saw taking cover. From the ground, she tossed two grenades, blowing one of the Demon Troopers up and keeping the other two pinned down. Nitro then fires the RPG at the stationary half-track that had, evidently, lost sight of her. She put two RPG rounds into the vehicle, totally destroying it. Once again, the jeeps fired back at her, and once again, she was pinned down.

Nitro rolled over to some large rocks and trees for cover and sat, waiting for the other two Demon Troopers to show themselves. The jeeps continue their assault, hitting only rocks and trees. The Demon Troopers moved in. Nitro picked them both off with her 30mm cannon. With two shots remaining in the RPG and three grenades, she decided to toss one of her grenades toward the closest jeep. After it exploded, she fired the RPG, destroying the jeep. Nitro began to receive even heavier fire from the last jeep. She was pinned, and the firing didn't stop.

Nitro made a decision. She threw her last two grenades, and as she was throwing her last one, she fired her 30mm. A slug slammed into her left shoulder, and she fell back in pain. She heard her final grenade go off. She tries to fire the RPG's last round, but the pain in her shoulder didn't allow her to raise the heavy weapon. So she grabbed her 30mm and began firing. Peering from her hiding spot, she saw that the grenade had actually blown the jeep up. Nitro just sat back against a tree for a minute and relaxed.

*   *   *

Bolt-action on the 80mm was killing everything in sight. He had taken out fourteen ZC, two jeeps, and a transport truck. He was running low on ammunition, so he threw grenades, blowing up two howitzers.

Bolt-action was tossing grenades, when he was ripped nearly in two by Staft in a half-track. She had taken out 1st Battalion's leader.

Three ZC came for Bolt-action's weapons. As they rolled him over from his stomach, Bolt-action pulled the pins on two grenades, and *Boom*! He and three ZC were dead.

* * *

Nuke continued to blast artillery with the howitzer. He had blown to pieces two transport trucks when he saw Staft in her half-track with a tank and two jeeps trailing her. He tries to turn his portable howitzer around to flank Staft and take her out.

Staft tore into Nuke with 20mm from the half-track. Nuke fell to the ground. The jeeps continued to fire on him, and he was hit two more times. Nuke lay motionless, the jeeps still firing. On his way to death, as the small convoy passes him, Nuke rose up to his knees and tossed a grenade, stopping Staft's half-track. Nuke then fired his 30mm cannon into her, tearing her to shreds.

In doing so, Nuke took several more .50 caliber rounds from one of the jeeps, three or four to the head. Nuke's fight has ended but so had Staft's.

* * *

Recoil, seeing the convoy that had just killed his partner, turned his chair in P-4. Yelling profanities, he began bombarding the convoy. He took out one jeep and then a second jeep.

The tank turned and fired on the P-4. A mighty and powerful shell fell just short of hitting the Puma, but it's collision with the earth was enough to knock Recoil from atop his seat. Dirt and debris filled the air as Recoil struggled to regain control and get refocused. The tank continued heading for him.

They must think I'm dead, Recoil realized. They were still coming, but they were no longer shooting at him. Recoil thought to take aim on the oncoming tank when he notices that he was full of shrapnel and his left arm, from the shoulder down, had been completely blown off his body.

Just then, he began to receive small arms fire from his right flank, hitting both him and the P-4. Instead of returning with small arms fire, Recoil took what they were giving him—a chance to climb back up and into P-4's howitzer chair. In doing so, Recoil was hit a half a dozen more times all over his body.

Finally reaching the chair, Recoil launched a desperate assault on the tank and the troops, though he was becoming weaker and weaker. The pain and blood loss were causing him all sorts of problems. Recoil fired relentlessly at the tank, blowing ZCs, as well as the earth around them, to pieces. Then he finally manages to hit the tank three, then four times, stopping its assault and ending its threat for good.

The ZC ground troops continued to fire on him, and Recoil was hit several more times. He was full of lead. The only thing keeping him fighting was his heart. Recoil turned the chair, all the time taking hits.

Just as he got turned, he saw a Hell Knight that, evidently, had already seen him. As Recoil completed his turn, the Hell Knight's lava projectile struck Recoil directly in the face, knocking half of Recoil's head off. Recoil died, still sitting in the P-4 howitzer chair, his one arm still grasping the gun. Recoil had taken over twenty rounds.

*   *   *

From the howitzer chair, Jon Henri was firing away. He blew the last half-track up, and in it, a Hell Knight.

Jon Henri took a round to the right leg. He turned and saw four ZC on foot. He fired back, blowing all four ZC completely apart. Jon Henri then turned his attention on a howitzer that was apparently firing on Crosshairs. With just one precision shot, he ends the howitzer threat to Crosshairs. Jon Henri then spotted the "tank man," Panzer. Jon Henri fired on the mighty Panzer, hitting him in the chest and blowing part of Panzer's iron helmet off. The giant tank like man fell back onto the floor of the battlefield. From behind the fallen Panzer, another Hell Knight emerged, firing two razor projectiles at Jon Henri, both of which hit Jon Henri on either sides of his chest. Knocked backward, he fell from the P-7's chair all the way to the ground below.

From the ground, Jon Henri saw Nazi's tank roll into the battle, running over a disabled jeep and several dead ZCs. Jon Henri grabbed his 60mm and began to fire on the Hell Knight that stuck two razor projectiles in either side of Jon Henri's chest just moments earlier as the Hell Knight walked across the battlefield. A few rounds hit the Hell Knight, and he falls and then got back to his feet, as did Panzer. Nazi fired a couple of tank rounds at P-7, just to destroy it. Two ZC emerged from behind Panzer, along with a jeep. Jon Henri fired his 60mm, taking out the two ZCs with no problem. The jeep fired on Jon Henri's position. He couldn't move. He was pinned down for the time being.

Jon Henri dropped to his knees, pain throbbing from his wounded leg, and began to crawl through the underbrush and fallen trees.

BOOM! The tree that Jon Henri had just been behind, exploded from a tank blast by Nazi. After being rained on by tree debris, Jon Henri turned and fired, taking out the oncoming jeep. Panzer spotted and then fired on Jon Henri's position, hitting the ground and trees all around him. Jon Henri was forced to get back to his feet and take off running in retreat, the best that he could with the hole in his leg. Panzer's rounds and missiles followed him, tearing the woods to shreds in front, behind, and all around Jon Henri.

Nazi fired a tank round right in front of Jon Henri, knocking him off his feet and causing him to fall and roll into a shallow creek. Jon Henri gathered himself and climbed back up the creek bank, just in time to see Nazi's tank explode, along with the last howitzer; the jeeps, one with a mounted .50 caliber cannon; and several more ZCs. He also witnessed several blasts ricochet off Panzer's body armor. Crosshairs had fired the shots that had caused the explosions; the ricochets were from the 30mm of Nitro, who was coming from the other side of the camp.

As Panzer turned on Nitro, Crosshairs fired a sidewinder missile and scores a hit on Panzer's turret, just as it was rising to fire. The missile blew the turret half off. Again, Panzer hit the ground. The last Hell Knight began to fire on Nitro. Jon Henri gets out of the creek and headed toward the clearing. Two ZC opened fire on him, hitting him in the right shoulder and hand and causing him to drop his 60mm. The ZCs were dropped immediately to their deaths by Nitro and her 30mm cannon.

The Hell Knight fired razor projectiles at Nitro. One hit her just above the hip, causing her to also drop her weapon. She hit the ground very hard in agonizing pain.

In just moments, Crosshairs had blown the Hell Knight to pieces. Jon Henri took care of the last couple of ZCs, just as Crosshairs fired another missile. This one flew just two or three inches in front of Jon Henri's face.

Boom! The missile slammed into the giant robot, hitting him right in the midsection. Panzer was down once again. This time, he was on his back.

Jon Henri looked at Panzer, back at Crosshairs and then again at Panzer. He just smiled and shook his head. Then he pointed at Crosshairs. She had pulled off another unbelievably incredible shot. Her guns spun and reloaded themselves. Crosshairs worked her way to Jon Henri.

Nitro got back to her feet. "Is that all of them?" she yelled. "Yes, ma'am. That's all of them," answered Jon Henri.

Nitro worked her way up and onto the hood of the jeep that no longer had a .50 caliber machine gun on it. She just sat and waited as Jon Henri and Crosshairs walked across the battlefield to her. As Jon Henri and Crosshairs walked by the downed Panzer, Jon Henri stopped and looks down at the fallen giant. He pulled two grenades out, focused on the hole in Panzer's face mask—a result of the earlier howitzer blast—and looked at Crosshairs. He pulled the pins from both grenades and then stuffed the two live fragment grenades into the hole in Panzer's mask. He and Crosshairs walked away.

Boom!

"See if you can get up now," said Jon Henri.

The two reached Nitro.

"Are we all that's left?" asked Crosshairs.

"Yeah, I'm afraid so," replied Nitro softly. "Let's get Bolt-action, Nuke, and Recoil loaded up, Jon. Crosshairs, you destroy all of our immobile Pumas and equipment."

"Yeah, okay, sure thing," said Jon Henri, sighing as he and Nitro moved solemnly toward the sad task of bagging and loading their own dead comrades.

Crosshairs used C-4 to destroy the remnants of the Pumas and equipment that didn't belong in this century. When she had destroyed everything that they couldn't take back with them, she helped Jon Henri and Nitro as best she could to gather gear, ammunition, and weapons and do inventory.

With the smell of smoke and burning diesel fuel still heavy in the air, Nitro went over the inventory with her two remaining comrades. "I have a list of what we have here, from what is left. We still have P-4—in descent shape somehow, although she is still smokin'. We have a portable howitzer hooked to it, fourteen grenades, three bazookas, two 60mms, one portable 80mm, one RPG, and thirteen rockets. We also have that jeep that the .50 cal got blown off of. It'll still run, so we can use it. We'll pull the 80mm with it.

"Jon being that I only have one arm that is functioning at 100 percent, I'll have to drive P-4 and switch the transmission from standard to automatic. Crosshairs will ride with me. We will put the rest of our team in the back of P-4. You can drive the jeep and pull the 80 can't you?"

"Yes, ma'am, I can do that," said Jon Henri.

"Okay, let's get them loaded and get this thing turned around," said Nitro. "You can follow us back to base camp so we can drop everything off for now. After we get some medical attention ourselves, we can get back into this thing before it's over. Let's go."

Jon Henri and Crosshairs just nodded their heads and began loading their fallen comrades into the back of P-4. They loaded all of the gear, weapons, ammunition, and the 80mm cannon onto the jeep.

*   *   *

At T-2, second squad watched Stealth finish her second sortie. The team—Amphibian and Torch in P-2, Gatlin and Blade in P-6, and Pistol Smoke and Shadow in P-8—found themselves still facing Witch, Gage, Torchess, Ratchet, two Demon Troopers, 120 ZCs, twelve half tracks, five jeeps, three howitzers, and two transport trucks.

Gatlin had set his squad up in a staggered formation. From left to right, Amphibian was on the front line fifty meters to his right and thirty meters back. Torch was on the P-2 howitzer. Fifty meters from Torch was Gatlin with his mighty cannons. Fifty meters down and thirty meters back was Blade on the P-6 howitzer. Fifty meters down and thirty meters back was Pistol Smoke with an 80mm, and fifty meters down and thirty meters back of him was Shadow on P-8's howitzer.

"RAIN DOWN ON THEM!" roared Gatlin.

The howitzers opened an unforgettable barrage of fire on their enemy. Gatlin, with his 30mm arm cannons, and Pistol Smoke and the 80mm cannon sprayed their fury onto the now very active battlefield. Amphibian, with his M60 and plenty of ammunition, an RPG on his back, dozens of grenades strapped to him, and his detonator did what he does best. He took off into the fray.

*   *   *

With narrowed eyes, Witch took in the onslaught befalling the Legion base camp under her command. She ordered eight half-tracks, each manned by four ZCs, along with three jeeps, each with .50 caliber machine guns and carrying three ZCs, to charge the howitzers. "Locate targets and do not stop firing until I give the order or I will destroy you myself," she screamed. "MOVE!"

She turned to a group of thirty ZC troops. "Enter the trees behind the camp," she commanded. "Split into two patrols, scramble, and go on search and destroy."

*   *   *

Torch's howitzer rounds were scoring hits on their targets. She had confirmed kills on the other four half-tracks, one jeep, and eighteen ZCs.

*   *   *

Now in Legion's camp, Amphibian tossed grenades and fired his M60. He had already scored kills on one howitzer as well as two armored transports, with three ZCs manning the guns, and eleven ZC foot soldiers when he took a round in the ribs on his right side from a Demon Trooper.

Amphibian returned fire with his M60, ripping the Demon Trooper to shreds as he continued to maneuver through Legion's camp.

* * *

On P-6's howitzer, Blade fired at the oncoming Torchess in her half-track. Three other half-tracks, along with eleven ZC ground troops, followed her. The menacing attack force headed straight for Blade and the P-6.

Blade managed to destroy the first two half-tracks, as well as all eleven of the ZC foot soldiers, just before one of Torchess's shells finally found its mark. It hit directly in the side of P-6, rupturing the fuel tanks and causing the Puma to explode. Blade flew from her seat, slamming into the tree that stood close to twenty feet behind the now flaming machine. Blade lay splayed on the ground. She was full of shrapnel and just about every bone in her body was broken.

Witnessing his girl blown into the air, Gatlin—in a very "un-Gatlin" like moment, lost his cool in battle. He left his post and ran through the woods, firing his powerful guns. One jeep exploded. Another lost its gunner and then the driver. The four remaining ZC foot soldiers took cover and returned fire on Gatlin.

* * *

"I need three more half-tracks up and on the point, after Gatlin in the tree line, NOW!" ordered Torchess.

Torchess, with her trio of half-tracks, fire into the woods at Gatlin, tearing and shredding the woods as trees burst into pieces all around him.

* * *

Gatlin heard Blade calling out to him. "I can't help you, Gatlin. I don't have a weapon." She coughed up blood as she spoke.

"Oh, Gatlin . . . you . . . Please, you've got to help." she pleaded. "It hurts so badly; it hurts all over, baby." She coughed again, choking on her own blood. This time her blood was very dark, almost brown.

"I'm gonna help ya, babe. But, Blade, you're gonna have to be quiet," he told her. "They're only a couple hundred feet away. They're gonna hear ya. Be still. I'm gonna get you out of here; I promise. Just hold on. I have to clean up some trash first, babe."

Gatlin slowly looked around the tree that he was behind. He sees two half-tracks that were no longer in the clearing. Moving through the woods now, the two vehicles knocked down smaller trees as they worked their way toward him and Blade. The other two half-tracks, one with Torchess on board, were traveling on the outskirts of the woods in the open area of the battlefield. The four ZC foot soldiers were easing their way toward Gatlin's position.

Gatlin was armed with his mighty 30mm arm cannons that everyone wanted to get a hold of, his MFG-25, and four grenades. Gatlin looked over at Blade again; he was still thirty feet or so away from her. Blade was trying her best to suck up the unbearable pain and be quiet for both of them; she was slowly and very painfully dying. Gatlin figured that it was time. He waited for just another moment until the two half-tracks that were in the open area got a little closer. He didn't believe they knew exactly where he was.

When he felt that the half-tracks were close enough, he tossed two grenades. The first grenade landed right in the back of the half-track, killing both of the ZC and totally destroying the cannon. The second grenade landed and went off just in front of the second half-track. As it turned toward him, Gatlin saw that it was Torchess' half-track.

Blade was now located between him and the half-track of Torchess. Gatlin opened up with his 30mm cannons on the oncoming half-track. Rounds found their targets, in both the heads and faces of the driver and the navigator. Torchess' half-track stopped twenty feet from Blade and fifty feet from Gatlin, with trees blocking Torchess' line of fire.

Gatlin turned his attention on the other two half-tracks in the woods. They were now within eighty feet of Gatlin, too far for an accurate grenade throw, and he was down to just two grenades. So he concentrated on the four ZCs afoot in the woods behind him, all the while keeping one eye on Torchess as best he could. Out of the corner of his eye, he saw that Torchess had now pulled her dead driver out of the half-track's cab and was driving it herself. He hoped that the other two half-tracks would get into the open and close enough before he was surrounded. These thoughts raced through Gatlin's head. He found himself facing what appeared to be overwhelming odds.

Gatlin sees two ZC without them seeing him. He opened up on them with his 30mm cannons, ripping both of them into several pieces and spreading them throughout the woods. The two half-tracks in the woods begin to fire on Gatlin's location. They were now only approximately sixty feet away, and Torchess was closing in, only about forty feet away. Gatlin knew she would continue to maneuver until she got a clear shot on him.

From behind a very large tree, Gatlin fired with his left arm cannon at the two half-tracks in the woods, and with his right hand, he tossed a grenade. The grenade hit the hood of the half-track and bounced straight up and forward toward the bed of the vehicle. It exploded in midair, blowing the gunner's head off. The gunner's headless body continued to fire the 20mm cannon from the back of the half-track as the body fell, shooting and killing the other gunner in the other half-track and thus momentarily ending the threat of the two half-tracks inside the woods.

Gatlin took in the events in the woods in front of him in shock. Suddenly, he felt the slam of small arms fire across his body armor. "Damn it," he swore when a couple of the rounds actually found flesh, burrowing into his left bicep under his armor. He looked down at his arm and then out where he believed the shot had come from.

He saw the two remaining ZC foot soldiers working their way toward him. Glancing toward Torchess, Gatlin saw that she was not yet a huge threat, and the other two half-tracks with the remaining two ZCs were currently incapacitated. So Gatlin walked toward the oncoming foot soldiers with his guns blazing. The two ZCs, with their backs to the wall, tried their best to hold Gatlin off with their AK-47s, but their attempt at defense didn't work. Gatlin did more damage to these two than he had to the others because these two had inflicted pain on him. He unloaded on the two until he'd reached them, firing for about thirty-five feet, and when he finally finished, you couldn't tell where one ZC ended and the other began; it was such a mess.

Gatlin turned his attention back to the two half-tracks in the woods, now mobile again. They stopped, and the driver of one climbed out and climbed into the back of the other, manning the 20mm cannon mounted there. Gatlin threw his fourth and last grenade; it exploded under the half-track, disabling the vehicle. The gunner continued to fire the weapon but without an open shot, and now his half-track had been immobilized by the grenade.

The two ZCs apparently realized the inadequacy of this situation and decided to get back into the other half-track, which would both drive and shoot. Gatlin just watched as the two scrambled. *This is like a silent picture show from the 1920s*, he thought.

A few seconds after the ZCs made their move toward the second half-track Gatlin found his perfect opportunity.

He fired on the driver, blowing his chest out from behind, just as the ZC was reaching for the door handle. Moments later, he fired on the wannabe gunner, just as he touched the 20mm cannon in the back of the half-track. The ZC's head was cut in two, from his forehead to his neck.

Tree bark and debris flew around Gatlin. Torchess was now back on her 20mm cannon in the back of her half-track. She scored major hits on Gatlin, ripping into his armor and again into his left arm and down and into his mighty left arm cannon, destroying his left mounted weapon. Gatlin fell back in pain.

Blade broke her silence. "Are you all right, Gatlin?" she cried.

Hearing Blade's voice, Torchess found her lying against a destroyed tree. Torchess just looked at the helpless Blade and turned her weapon on the injured warrior. She filled Blade with dozens of hot lead rounds from less than twenty feet away. With the awesome firepower of the half-track's 20mm mounted cannon, she ended Blade's battle, as well as her suffering.

"You BITCH!" Gatlin roared. He charged and fired on Torchess, hitting her across the chest and stomach. Gatlin reached Torchess' half-track to find her crawling in the back of it toward the rear, in an attempt to get out. Gatlin picked her up by her hair and slung her back into the back of the cab. She hit the seat and fell back to the floor of the bed. As Gatlin walked up to her, Torchess pleaded for her life. With his arm-mounted weapon, Gatlin punched Torchess in the mouth, knocking out most of her teeth. Torchess just looked up at Gatlin, barely clinging to life.

"Sorry I had to knock out all your teeth, BITCH! But I had to make sure that this fit." Gatlin ripped a grenade from her vest and shoved it into her toothless mouth. He pulled the pin and jumped off the side of the half-track.

Boom! Torchess was sprayed all over the half-track.

*   *   *

Pistol Smoke continued his battle, firing the 80mm and defeating both the first and second wave of Witch's attack. He now faced the third round. Eight ZC foot soldiers and two half-tracks, one driven by none other than Witch herself, came at him.

Pistol Smoke took some small arms fire from the ZC foot soldiers. He returned fire with his M60E, taking out three of the eight ZCs. Then emerging from behind him, the two half-tracks fired on him, Pistol Smoke returned fire on them both, hitting and killing the gunner of the first half-track, just before Witch in the second half-track fired and destroys Pistol Smoke's bunker, along with his 80mm cannon.

Pistol Smoke, now on the run, grabbed his 9mms, shouldered his M60E and an RPG, and carried his 30mm in hand. He backtracked into the woods where Gatlin had destroyed the two half-tracks earlier. Pistol Smoke took cover behind them, both to gather himself and to get his bearings.

From his position he watched the first half-track on his trail stop and pick up a ZC foot soldier to replace the gunner. Pistol Smoke, with only the two spent half-tracks for cover, threw four grenades, causing only minor damage to the first half-track but killing one more ZC foot soldier.

The second half-track fired on his position. Pistol smoke heard what was left of the glass on the two half-tracks he was using as cover shatter. Then the tires popped as the high-powered rounds found their mark. He lays his M60E down and swung the RPG around to fire. With no clear shot, he was forced to shoulder the RPG again. Once again, he began tossing grenades.

The grenades fall short, causing no damage. He tried the RPG again. This time he took on small arms fire. Once again, Pistol smoke had to sling the RPG back up to his shoulder. Now, he armed his 30mm cannon. He took one

ZC out right before the other dropped him with multiple leg shots. Pistol Smoke could feel the deep burn of the hot lead in his bloodstream. He was now in a lot of pain and bleeding badly. He tosses three more grenades.

The grenades slowed the attack but did not stop it. Witch and the two ZC pressed forward. With his M60E now in hand, Pistol Smoke fires on the half-track's front grill, climbing his rounds up the hood to the windshield. Ultimately, they reach their target, Witch. The firing from Witch's half-track stopped, and Pistol Smoke continued to keep Witch pinned down in the rear of her half-track as he works his way over toward her.

Within fifteen feet now, Pistol Smoke was relentlessly firing his weapon as he walked. He paused just long enough to toss a grenade into the back of Witch's half-track.

Witch leaped from the rear of the vehicle, her M41A/M203 firing wide open as she fled from the half-track. Pistol Smoke stopped his march and took cover behind a fallen tree and some debris. He slung his M60E around to his back and began pulling pins and tossing grenades—his last four. The flying ammo herded Witch back toward her vehicle. Out of grenades and with just a couple rockets left, Pistol Smoke quickly surveyed the scene. *Now is as good as time as any to use this piece of shit*, he thought.

He took aim on the spent half-track. He had seen that Witch had taking cover behind a burned-out jeep parked very close. He fired on the unmanned half-track, hitting it directly in the fuel tank and destroying it. The vehicle flew straight up in the air ten to twelve feet.

Pistol Smoke's next target was no mystery. The only mystery was why Witch wasn't putting up any type of resistance at all. It was unlike her or any Legion member not fight to the death. *I'm not here to solve mysteries*, thought Pistol Smoke. *I'm here to kick Legion's asses at all costs*. Witch happened to be Legion. "So suck on this, bitch," he said out loud as he fired his second and final RPG round into the two burning jeeps, blowing them into many large pieces.

Witch proved his guess that she was still behind the two jeeps right. She emerged from the flames and smoke covered in diesel fuel, shrapnel, and blood. She was limping very badly, missing her right arm from just above the elbow, and appeared to be disoriented. Pistol Smoke passed by her and unloaded on her with his 30mm, just about blowing her spine through her chest. Witch was no more.

*   *   *

The battle raged on. Shadow was perched in P-8's howitzer chair and operating the vehicle from there. As she maneuvered through the battlefield, two ZCs crossed her path. They fired on her but missed. As Shadow returned fire with her M5 machine guns, a third ZC emerged from behind a pile of fallen trees and hit Shadow in the right hand, ripping her wrist and hand nearly off of her arm.

In terrible pain, she fired on the ZC with her left hand, tearing up the debris but not killing the ZC. She was then hit again, this time in the right knee. She spotted the ZC this time and blew his head completely off his body.

In very bad condition, Shadow turned the Puma around and began her search for the two remaining ZCs. She heard shooting coming from her right flank and looked over to witness the two ZCs struggling to their feet, only to be gunned down shortly.

"Hey, cutie, miss me?" called a familiar booming voice. "Don't shoot. It's me, Amp!"

Shadow grinned. "Are you okay? I . . ."

BOOM, BOOM, BOOM!

Right in front of Shadow's eyes, Amphibian was torn into three pieces. He fell to the ground. Shadow was motionless for a few seconds.

As she regained her composure, she saw Ratchet coming through the woods firing his laser, the very laser that had just killed her friend and teammate right in front of her eyes.

Shadow turned the howitzer toward Ratchet to open up on him. Then BOOM, BOOM. She was being fired upon from behind. Glancing over her shoulder, she saw Gage.

This time Shadow was hit in the back and the same knee that was already wounded. Her knee was no longer functional. She struggled to get back up to fight on and defend herself, just in time to see Gage's jeep blow up and flip end over end.

Seeing Shadow in trouble, Gatlin fired his mighty cannon, the only one he has left to fight with.

Ratchet turned his assault on Gatlin. Six and then seven times, Ratchet hit Gatlin in the body armor, knocking Gatlin back and to the ground. All the while, Ratchet was taking 30mm fire from Gatlin all across the upper body. Gatlin's assault on Ratchet slowly forced Ratchet backward. Shadow opened up on Ratchet with the howitzer in tandem. She hit the towering robot one, two, three, four times. The first rounds struck Ratchet in the midsection, the second in the leg; the third round misses him, but the fourth round nailed Ratchet in the head, knocking him to the floor of the battlefield.

Torch, now on foot, emerged from the trees to check on Gatlin.

"I'm okay," he told her. "Go check on Shadow."

Torch took off toward P-8. From under the rolled jeep, Gage peppered Torch on the dead run with her 20mm pistols. Rounds penetrated Torch's chest and head, killing her before she could reach Shadow.

Gatlin and Ratchet both got back to their feet at the same time. Shadow maneuvered for a clear shot on Gage. She would just have to push through the terrible pain and leave the Puma. Dragging one leg behind her, she worked her way through the debris-riddled battlefield.

Seconds after Shadow left the P-8, *BOOM*! Ratchet blew the Puma fifteen feet into the air. It landed back on earth, sending shrapnel into the air. Some landed on Shadow's back, knocking her to the ground. The hot metal burned her flesh and tissue, and she lay on the ground in terrible pain and unable to remove the scorching hot metal from her body. Shadow was in very bad shape.

Ratchet saw Shadow's struggle. He moves in for the kill. Gatlin once again fired on the machinelike image of himself, ripping Ratchet up.

Ignoring Gatlin's assault, Ratchet continued to move toward Shadow, intent on finishing her off. But Gatlin continued to slow Ratchet's advance with his powerful weapon and accuracy.

Gage turned on Gatlin and began firing on her former boyfriend. Gatlin moved to take cover.

BOOM!

A round ripped through the back of Gage's head, blowing her very beautiful face apart. Pistol Smoke reloaded his RPG with a rocket from a dead ZC. He took aim again, this time firing on Ratchet. The rocket found its mark, hitting and putting a huge dent in the head of Ratchet and ending Ratchet's threat with one desperate but fantastic shot.

As Ratchet fell his guns blazed wide open, and one rogue 45mm round found its way to Pistol Smoke's abdomen. Pistol Smoke doubled over in pain, holding his stomach. Blood poured from his wound, and he fell to one knee and then to the ground.

"Is that all of them?" asked Gatlin.

"No. There are a couple of jeeps with 50s on them, close to thirty ZC, two more howitzers manned by ZCs, and a damn Demon Trooper to the west of us," replied Shadow.

"Okay, cool. You and Smoke stay here and stay low. Take care of one another, I'm gonna end this thing right now. How about that RPG?" said Gatlin.

"Sorry, man. It's empty," Pistol smoke gasped.

"Oh well, I guess I'll just have to do it my own way. Stay down and quiet. I'll be back for y'all," said Gatlin. "Wish me luck and stay alive until I get back. I need you guys."

Gatlin heard the powerful howitzer firing off in the distance. He stopped and listened for a few seconds and then worked his way toward the thunderous sound of the mighty weapon. A couple of minutes later, Gatlin found the howitzer bunker. As he was moving in for an open shot, he saw a jeep pull up. What was it doing?

"They must be lost without their leaders," he muttered to himself.

Gatlin decided to get started. He fired on the gunner in the jeep, blowing his head completely off his body. The driver reached for his sidearm, and at the same time, the howitzer began to turn in Gatlin's direction. Gatlin fired a second time. He killed the driver of the jeep as cleanly as he'd taken the gunner. Without missing a beat, Gatlin fired on the howitzer gunner, nearly cutting him in two—but not before Gatlin took two rounds, one to the shoulder and the second to the chest under his armor.

Gatlin falls down to one knee, *Shit! I'm hit again. Where in the hell did that come from?* he asked himself.

Gatlin worked his way back to Shadow and Pistol smoke. Shadow was lying on her stomach with her shirt off as Pistol Smoke removed the shrapnel from her back and sides.

"You were right," said Gatlin. "Close to thirty ZC are spread throughout the woods, along with a jeep with a fully functional .50 cal. And I know of at least two more half-tracks that are still going."

He reached for his headset to call Stealth. He soon realizes that his headset is wasted. As Gatlin was known to do, he removed the headset, crushed it in his hand, and tossed it into a creek. "Piece of shit," he growled. "Son of a bitch, I hate when things don't work. Does yours work, Shadow?"

Shadow gave Gatlin her headset. "Damn its 6:45 p.m." he swore. "It's gonna be getting dark soon. Stealth, come in; come in, Stealth. Copy, respond!"

* * *

Stealth couldn't quite make out all that Gatlin was saying, but she did make out, "No Crow . . . Dead and wounded throughout the area."

Stealth tried to respond, but in return, she got nothing but static.

She grabbed her weapons. With no other choice, she ran on foot in the direction of the T-2 battlefield.

* * *

Nitro, Crosshairs, and Jon Henri, heading back to base camp, had heard the broken conversation and figured Stealth would be moving toward T-2 on foot.

Nitro, on her headset, told Stealth, "Hold on, girl. We'll be there in approximately three minutes. We'll drop off our dead, and you can ride back with us. Hell, we'll all go."

* * *

Just inside base camp, Stealth eagerly awaited her ride into the battle.

* * *

"Give me a hand with Shadow, if you can," Gatlin directed Pistol Smoke. "We need to get her behind P-8. Then you stay with her and I'll work my way back to P-2 and try and draw their fire.

"Not to worry; I will be back. You know that," he added before Pistol Smoke could protest.

Gatlin attempted to leave his two injured teammates in their new positions—Shadow behind the P-8 and Pistol Smoke just thirty or so feet from her, but he was immediately taking fire from the woods surrounding the large battlefield. He dropped back down a few feet from Pistol Smoke. The three Allied Force members were way outnumbered now. Suddenly, directly in front of Gatlin, a jeep, followed by a half-track, stopped. They had clearly also located the three's position. Gatlin, Pistol Smoke, and Shadow found themselves out of everything except their primary weapons.

"OH SHIT!" yelled Gatlin. "RETURN FIRE ON 'EM NOW!"

Shadow sat with her very badly injured back against P-8, shooting her 20mm automatic pistols at the ZCs in the woods. Pistol Smoke, with his powerful M60E, and Gatlin, with his one good 30mm cannon and his MFG-25 on his hip, concentrated on the jeep and the half-track that were in front of them firing armor-piercing rounds. Meanwhile, the rest of the ZCs, along with the other half-track, cut across the battlefield. There were about twenty ZCs on foot.

Gatlin told Shadow and Pistol Smoke the obvious bad news. "Well, hell, it looks like we're gonna fight 'em all right here. Right now!"

Shadow took out four ZCs before she took a single round directly between the eyes.

Pistol Smoke began mowing the woods with his M60E; hitting and killing two more ZCs. Gatlin destroyed the oncoming jeep. Its explosion took out three more ZCs.

Then the squad begins to encounter howitzer rounds; the howitzer was zeroing in on their position.

Pistol Smoke killed two more ZC foot soldiers running around in the woods and working their way to the battlefield. Gatlin took another hit, this time in the lower back, again just under his body armor. Pistol Smoke, without missing a beat, turned on the shooter and ended his threat with a round to the ear.

But the woods were just too congested and the ZCs just too spread out their endless assault like a bad rash. Finally, the onslaught took Pistol Smoke down. He'd taken on several rounds, and the barrage was too much for his vital organs. He died on his way over to cover Shadow. He fell approximately twenty-five feet shy of P-8 and Shadow's position, not knowing that Shadow was already dead.

The ZC's endless attack scored more hits on Gatlin, to his leg and to his side. Gatlin turned and was able to cut one of the charging ZC in two. He was in the middle of the battlefield with no cover and clinging to life. He rolled over to his stomach and began to pick off the charging ZC—one, two, three, four . . . seven, eight . . . ten. Meanwhile, the half-track sprayed the exposed Gatlin with fire, throwing earth and debris into the air and onto Gatlin.

Suddenly, the half-track exploded, followed shortly by the second half-track. Crosshairs and Stealth, with the unmatched accuracy of Crosshairs's sidewinder missiles stopped the armored charge toward Gatlin. Stealth took out the other seven ZC foot soldiers, just as the howitzer finally zeroed in on Gatlin's position, totally destroying his position, as well as him.

Stealth turned her Puma toward the howitzer, while Crosshairs finished checking on Gatlin, Pistol Smoke, and Shadow.

Stealth located the howitzer bunker. Using an M203 grenade launcher, she destroyed the bunker and everyone around it. The fighting had stopped. She then went in search of Torch, Amphibian, and Blade.

After an hour of searching, Stealth had Gatlin, Amphibian, Pistol Smoke, and Shadow loaded on the Puma. Crosshairs had found Torch and Blade. Stealth drove across the bloody battlefield to meet up with Crosshairs. As Stealth stood next to her closest friend, Crosshairs, looking down on her six dead teammates and remembering the fallen one's back at camp with the wounded Nitro and Jon Henri, the truth dawned on her. "You know, Crosshairs, this is really war. I mean we are in a war—a battle for life and death. The four of us are going to have to do exactly what Gatlin said before all this started, leave everything out on the battlefield. Because he was right, without a doubt, this is definitely war."

Crosshairs nodded. Her weapons automatically locked and loaded. The battle-scarred women hugged each other tightly. With Crosshairs riding shotgun, Stealth turned the P-2 around and headed back to base camp. They had to leave the other Puma behind because Crosshairs couldn't drive or operate any machines.

Stealth would have to drop off their dead once again. And she'd need to pick up Nitro and Jon Henri so they could return and Jon Henri could drive the other Puma.

*   *   *

Third squad's battle raged. The group was facing Ram, Mite, Jackyl and Gorman, along with 217 ZCs, eight half-tracks, six howitzers, and four transports. Led by Optic Blast, third squad included Mack T, Zeke, Xtract, an injured Drazil, and a very badly wounded GrizzLee. GrizzLee is on P-5 howitzer because of his immobility. Zeke roamed the battlefield carrying his 80mm cannon. Drazil, because of his wounds, remained on P-10, about thirty meters down from GrizzLee. Xtract was the gunner for the portable 80mm cannon approximately forty-five meters from Drazil's position. While Optic Blast drove the P-3 over the battlefield, she manned the 30mms from inside, and Mack T, from the chair had both the howitzer and the 80mm cannon at his disposal.

Driving with one hand and firing with the other, Optic Blast dropped one ZC after the other, while Mack T destroyed equipment with the awesome howitzer. Mack T took some small arms fire and was hit in the arm and in the leg. But he continued his relentless assault. The tandem's tally stood at twenty-seven ZC foot soldiers dead and two howitzers, one jeep, and two half-tracks totally destroyed.

*   *   *

On a .50 caliber machine gun mounted in the back of a jeep, Mite fired on GrizzLee. The P-5 was being peppered with .50 caliber rounds.

Seeing his friend's situation, Zeke turned his attention on Mite. With the unmatched power of his 80mm cannon, he ripped into eight ZC accompanying the lady Legion warrior and destroyed Mite's jeep. Mite flew from the vehicle and plowed face-first into the ground.

GrizzLee gave Zeke the thumbs-up. Just as Zeke turned, he was hit across the chest and shoulder by Jackyl in a half-track escorted by eighteen ZC and Jackyl's sidekick, Gorman, carrying a 60mm cannon. Zeke was down, and GrizzLee was extremely pissed-off. He fired back at Jackyl's half-track, killing four ZC. Gorman fired back at GrizzLee. The shots ripped into GrizzLee's already wounded leg, shredding it even more than it already was, as well as scoring three gut shots.

P-3 emerged from the dust and gun smoke cloud. With her 30mm cannons, Optic Blast literally tore the legs out from under Gorman. Mack T switched from howitzer to 80mm cannon and fired into the cab of Jackyl's half-track, killing his driver and another eight ZC foot soldiers.

"Hold on while I take these other three ZC's out!" Optic Blast called to Mack T. She slammed into reverse, ramming the Puma into Gorman, who was on the ground.

Seeing this, Jackyl unleashed on her. His rounds found their mark, hitting her in the forearm and shoulder. Mack T turned, switching from the 80mm back to the howitzer and took aim on Jackyl. But before Mack T could fire, he was nearly torn in half by Ram's 60mm cannon.

With Gorman now in front of the Puma and not moving much, Optic Blast took the liberty of finishing the giant gorilla man off with the 30mm cannons mounted from both of the Puma's front fenders. The gruesome attack tore off half the beast's face.

Just as soon as she is done with Gorman, Optic Blast saw Jackyl's half-track heading directly for her. Then it exploded, throwing what remained of Jackyl all over P-3's hood and windshield.

"You okay?" GrizzLee asked. "Anything else I can do for you?"

Optic Blast, not knowing the severity of GrizzLee's wounds, answered, "I would have you clean the front of my ride off, but I am a little busy right now. Just keep up your timely shooting, big guy. I owe you one now, sweetheart."

Optic Blast contacted Mack T in the chair above her.

"I think I'm pretty bad," said Mack T.

Optic Blast stopped the P-3 and got out to see about Mack T.

"Why don't you come inside and ride for a bit," Optic Blast suggested. "You can fire the 30s for me. What do you s—?"

Boom!

Mack T's head, hit by Ram's 60mm cannons, flew off. Optic Blast was covered with blood and gray matter as Mack T's headless and lifeless body fell to the floor of the Puma.

"Oh my god!" Optic Blast screamed. "Shit, I shouldn't have stopped; I know better than that. Shit, baby," she said, holding back tears, "I am so sorry. Son of a bitch; I got you killed."

In the heat of the battle, her shock and sorrow turned to rage. *Motherfucker, Ram. You will fuckin' die for this one; I swear to you. You bastard*! she said to herself as she spun out and got back into the battle as best she could.

*   *   *

Drazil and Xtract had bombarded the battlefield with unbelievable precision and accuracy—killing an estimated thirty-five ZCs and destroying their armored transports, two jeeps, three howitzers, and two half-tracks—when, from behind them, the very badly wounded Mite, with half her face still on the battlefield, shot them both in the back with her crossbow armed with poisonous arrows. In just moments, both heroes were drugged out.

Mite, small in stature, but very large in hatred for Allied Force, slowly worked her four foot eight body up to the drugged Allied Force members and, with her Desert Eagle, took them both out of the battle, execution style, a single round to the back of the head.

*   *   *

As Zeke stumbled around, he took two rounds, one to the leg and the second to the chest, knocking him down. Optic Blast stopped the Puma in front of him. Zeke climbed into the howitzer chair, and the two took off in search of Ram.

During their search, they took out three more half-tracks, along with sixteen more ZC foot soldiers. Then Optic Blast, who kept firing the 30mm cannons from the cab, realized that neither the howitzer nor the 80mm cannon had fired for some time. She knew what had happened, but the area was just too hot to stop right now. She had this terrible feeling of being all alone in this mess.

Before long, P-3 started to run badly, and smoke rose from under the hood and trailed behind the assault vehicle. The Puma had sustained multiple bullet rounds and much abuse over the past couple of days. Optic Blast turned P-3 around and retreated, moving toward P-10.

In a half-track, Ram was gaining on her. And so were the last dozen ZC on foot. Legion's last howitzer fired on the Puma. Each round got closer and closer. Stealth, Nitro, Jon Henri, and Crosshairs were still twenty minutes away. This was now a race against time.

Optic Blast reached P-10. With Ram approximately sixty meters behind her and gaining. Ram fired relentlessly, as did the ZC foot soldiers and the mighty howitzer. Optic Blast doesn't have time to get set up and man P-10's howitzer chair, so she simply climbed into the cab and pulled away—just as the howitzer finally struck its deadly blow, destroying P-3, as well as Mack T and Zeke's bodies.

Optic Blast retreated moving back toward the camp. As she passed P-5, she spotted a humped over GrizzLee in the chair. Was he dead? She couldn't look long; Ram was now only thirty meters back, and the howitzer, with its deadly rounds, was still on her tail as well.

Optic Blast heard a crash. She looked in the rearview mirror just in time to see Ram's half-track flip over end on end. With his .44 automatic pistol, GrizzLee had shot and killed Ram's half-track driver. GrizzLee then turned the howitzer chair in the direction of Legion's mighty gun, but again he was sprayed with small arms fire from the ZC foot soldiers.

Optic Blast whipped the Puma around and began dropping ZC—four and then five were down.

GrizzLee, with better than twenty-five wounds and all he had left, fired his last four howitzer rounds from P-5. The first two rounds got very close but the last two rounds were right on the money, hitting and destroying Legion's mighty howitzer, as GrizzLee fell over for the last time.

Optic Blast remained in P-10's cab. As the ZC foot soldiers showed themselves, she made them pay one at a time, until the last three had been cut down by P-10's 30mm cannons and her own precision shooting.

She took a deep breath and waited for Ram to show himself from the half-track wreckage.

Optic Blast's radio crackled to life.

"Hey, girl," came Nitro's voice, "Stealth, Jon Henri, Crosshairs, and I are en route; ETA seven minutes—plenty of backup. How's it going? Don't hear any shooting. Is it over? Have we won? Over."

"Copy ya, Nitro. I believe that it's down to just Ram and me. The howitzer stopped firing for some reason. Maybe Lee took it out? I'm just waiting for Ram to show himself. Then I'm going to kill him slowly," said a very emotional Optic Blast as she scanned the body—and vehicle-littered, smoke-covered battlefield. "The rest of my squad didn't make it."

"We can see the smoke and even smell the gun powder," Nitro replied. "We are four minutes out. KEEP RAM AT BAY! Over and out."

As Ram showed himself, Optic blast ordered him, "Drop your weapons. It's over. You lost again."

Ram tossed his 60mm cannon to the side and put his hands on his head, apparently surrendering. This wasn't part of Legion's creed. Strapped to his back and out of Optic Blast's sight was Ram's 20mm pistol. Ram was thirty feet from Optic Blast.

"Get down on the ground on your face," she ordered. "Allied Force is leaving 1939. The reason that I am not killing you is because you will have to go around to each battlefield and retrieve your dead, if you plan on returning to the present day along with us. You know as well as I do that Malakai will kill you if you return without your people."

Hearing footsteps to her right, Optic Blast turned. There stood Mite, shooting at her. The shot hit her in the shoulder. Optic Blast returned fire, both shots hitting Mite in the head and dropping her dead.

Ram rips the 20mm pistol from his back and fired into P-10's cab and right through Optic Blast's eye. The entire third squad was now dead.

Ram walked over to the P-10 to claim his prize, the Puma, and return it to Malakai.

Stealth pulls up, sliding sideways with her pulse pistols out the window and firing. She blew Ram's hand completely off his arm, with the pistol still in it.

"Don't kill him, Stealth!" Nitro ordered.

Jon Henri and Crosshairs jumped out of the Puma. Crosshairs kicked Ram in the face, and Jon Henri straddled Ram's back and grabs his massive horns. Crosshairs once again kicked Ram in the face. With her broken language, she blamed Ram for all of Allied Force's deaths.

Stealth grabbed Crosshairs and pulled her friend back away from Ram.

"You lose," Nitro told Ram. "Legion loses. When will y'all realize that evil will never defeat Allied Force?"

"You stupid bitch," Ram spat back. "I enjoyed watching all of your people die. If I had it to do all over again, knowing that it would end this same way, me having to pick up all my dead by myself, I wouldn't change one damn thing, you fuckin' idiots." He spat blood to the side and laughed at Nitro.

"Kill him," ordered Nitro. "Let Malakai figure out what to do with them."

With that, Jon Henri twisted Ram's horns and snapping his neck.

Crosshairs did her duty by destroying any and everything that Allied Force couldn't take back, while Jon Henri, Nitro, and Stealth gather up third squad and got them all loaded.

"Jon, you drive P-5. Stealth, you take Crosshairs in P-10, and I'll drive P-2 back to The Crow," Nitro said solemnly.

Four of the twenty members who'd come to 1939 traveled back to The Crow, in three out of the ten Pumas they'd brought. Their only thought now was getting back to the present day and time. They hoped that Psycho's machine worked so that they could get their members back safe and sound and, more importantly, alive.

*   *   *

Allied Force, those alive, those dead, and those in pieces in body bags, all returned to the present day and time. They did exactly as Malakai had instructed before their departure just a few day's prior. Stealth and Nitro set the time and day and pushed the proper buttons on the warper. Then the four living members removed the body bags that held their team members who had fallen in a battle that had taken place decades earlier. Still struggling to wrap their brains around all they had seen, done, and experienced, the team worked in silence to unzip each bag.

Just like Malakai had said, within a few short minutes, the fallen members began to come around, one after the other. Finally, the entire team was back and reunited in the present day and time. All twenty members were accounted for and in good health, just as they had been when they'd left this very spot just a few hours but many memories, earlier.

The team heard the distinct sounds of hammers being pulled back on guns. They turned to see Manaconda and Armageddon aiming down on them.

"I wouldn't worry too much about us, if I was you," said Nitro. "I would be figuring out a way to get the rest of my team—*my dead team*—back from Poland and Germany, 1939. You have twelve hours from right now to do so. When the twelve hours expire, whether you and your people are back or not, we will destroy this time machine. This warper or whatever the fuck you and Psycho call it will be *toast*, and so will you if you ain't back. So my advice to you two dipshits is to lower your weapons before we all draw down on you and finish Legion, right here and right now.

"My team has had a very long couple of days, and we are a little moody and damned tired of Legion and y'all pointing fuckin' weapons in our faces. So take my advice. Lower your weapons and go fetch your team before the time expires.

"I will blow this thing in twelve hours," she said again, making sure they understood the deadline. "I DON'T GIVE ONE GOOD SHIT ABOUT THE CODE AT THIS POINT! I'll come up with some sort of story to tell T. J. The clock is ticking, dickheads."

Armageddon and Manaconda exchanged a brief glance before following Nitro's advice. The decision was confirmed by Malakai as he came down to the hangar to see what was happening, staying at a distance on his crutches.

As Manaconda and Armageddon stepped into the warper, headed for 1939, Malakai ordered, "Find Nazi or Psycho and bring them back first. They can show you where the rest of the team is located."

And thus, Legion's search and rescue—a race against time—began.

As Allied Force headed out of the hangar, Stealth turned to face the injured Legion head. "One of these times, Malakai, we're going to rain down on you, and not a soul—or in your case, a soulless person—on the planet will be able to help you. We will help your mutants and bring them to our side, and as for the rest of your people, well; they can all burn with you. I've seen just about every one of my team members die, and I will never see that again," she yelled. "Gatlin isn't the only one you have to watch out for now. Now you have a very pissed-off woman watching every move that you make. So walk softly, you asshole!"

Allied Force boarded the Raven and The Crow for their flight back to South Carolina. Everyone was back to normal and looking fine, except for Gatlin. The evidence from his fight with Malakai began to reappear on his face. The rest of the team was soon trash-talking Gatlin, teasing him about his swollen face.

Stealth got in contact with Tommy J. "We have the entire team loaded on both birds and are en route to home base. Legion has once again been defeated, but it took everything that we had to do so. We lost seven Pumas, but neither the Raven nor The Crow were hurt. Nitro has C-4 charges set for all the documentation, blueprints, and the warper to blow in just under twelve hours. Malakai is aware of the time frame, so he will just have to get his people the hell out of the hangar. Nitro told me that when she blows, she's gonna blow big."

"Copy that. I'm just glad to hear your voice, Stealth, and very happy that everyone made it back," replied Tommy J. "Great job, everyone. Please relay my message to the team for me. Over and out."

"Yes, sir, I will. Over and out."

She turned to the others with a grin and nodded toward Nitro. "I do have to say one thing, Nitro. You all missed it, except for Crosshairs, Jon, and me. Y'all should have seen Nitro steering the Raven into the warper; that was priceless. But she got it in there and that's all that matters, right girl."

"Hey I never said that I was a pilot," Nitro said. "That's Xtract's bird, not mine. I just drove it, sorta like a car. But I finally got it in there. I guess it must've been pretty funny to watch, though. I was getting really pissed-off at it and myself. I just knew that we were going to fall under attack right there at the warper because I couldn't get the damn Raven into the stupid machine."

"But you got us all here," said Amphibian, "and now we're all back to our old selves and going home. It just seems weird that we did all of that and it's now only a couple hours later than it was a few days ago. That's a trip." He sat back, ready to enjoy the flight back home.

Silence filled the craft for a moment before the radio crackled to life. "Stealth to Xtract; come in."

"Xtract; go ahead, Stealth."

"I know that we aren't supposed to do this, but on this one, I say we leave the PAs open so we can all talk to one another if we want to on the way home. What do you say?"

"Sounds good to me," Xtract agreed. "Everyone seems to still be coming to grips with the whole thing anyway."

Copy that," said Stealth, and she pressed play on the CD player. This time, the entire team sat back and listened to Led Zeppelin on the flight home.

WRATH'S LAIR

A T HOME base in South Carolina, Tommy J opened an e-mail from an old friend in China. It read:

Old friend, we are in need of your help in a desperate way. Villagers, hunters, and wildlife are being threatened. One man hospitalized, four others still missing, presumed dead. Search called off two days ago, after six-day search unable to find lost. Man in hospital in stable condition, shock, was not part of missing party but local hunter. He tells of giant stone men, which he called mountain men and strange noises from high in the mountains. Please help. Sorry I don't have more information for you.

The e-mail concluded with detailed directions to the area where the man in the hospital had made the last sighting.

"Gatlin, report to control room immediately," ordered Tommy J over the mansion's intercom.

*   *   *

What now? Gatlin wondered as he got up from reading his superhero comic book.

When he entered the control room, he found Tommy J and Nitro huddled around the computer.

He walked in one door just as Stealth walked in the other door.

"What's goin' on?" Gatlin asked Tommy J.

Tommy J held a finger up in the air, motioning for Gatlin to hold on for a second. Then he gave Nitro coordinates so that she could come up with a flight plan, as well as an attack strategy.

"Gatlin, you come with me. Stealth, you get with Nitro and come up with something that we can use, pronto," said Tommy J as he walked into his office with Gatlin following close behind.

"Close the door, Gatlin. Listen up, I just heard from an old friend in southwest China, via e-mail. After reading the e-mail, I felt it very important I call him on this one. Well, here read it." Tommy J handed Gatlin a printout of the message from China.

"Wait a minute, T. J. You want to send us here? To freakin' China?" asked Gatlin.

"No, Gatlin," said Tommy J, "I don't want to; I have to on this one."

"Why?" Gatlin asked. "Why do you have to? Don't they have authorities over there that can handle this sort of thing?"

"Well yeah, they do; they have a lot of authorities over there for this sort of thing, when it doesn't involve a Legion member. But this one does. That's why we are going to handle it for them," Tommy J replied.

"What do you mean a Legion member?" Gatlin wanted to know. "Who is it? And how does that friend of yours know that it's a Legion member?"

"It is, indeed, a Legion member," Tommy J assured him. "It's Wrath. Wrath has evidently been hiding out in that region off and on since the conflict back some time ago when you and Blade were on vacation at Farrahs in Arizona. And my old friend knows that it's a Legion member because he knows all about Legion, as well as all about us. My dear old friend is the father of one of our own. He's Lee's father. He keeps in touch with me as I do with him on the progress of Lee's case. He also checks on his son, but he doesn't want Lee to know about it, so this information does not leave this room, understood?"

"Yes, sir, I understand," Gatlin replied. "I had no idea that Lee's father even existed. Do you keep in contact with any other team member's parents or family members?"

"Yeah, I talk to a few every so often, but that has nothing to do with this operation. So assemble your team. It will take a six-man team to accomplish this one we think, according to Nitro's figures. Stealth will fly you in and return in three days to fly you out. Unfortunately, there is no place to land The Crow. The terrain is very rough in that region, so it will be a hover drop. We can only get you in as close as a hundred to a hundred and twenty miles, depending on weather— snow, ice, winds, you know, the usual stuff that falls over there around the Himalayan Mountains," said Tommy J.

"You want to send us where?" asked Gatlin.

"I told you, southwest China," Tommy J replied. "My friend is in Saga, China. The problem is in the Himalaya's, well a mountain in the Himalayas called Dhaulagiri. It's actually located in Nepal, on the border of China and Nepal to be exact. You are to leave in two hours. You can brief your team or I will; it's up to you. So get to roundin' 'em, up and prepare for another round with Wrath."

"T. J., you know that this is some shit. But being's we don't have a choice in the matter, we will be ready in time for departure," said Gatlin as he walked out of Tommy J's office and past Nitro and Stealth.

"I am so sorry," Nitro mouthed as Gatlin walked past her.

Gatlin just shrugged his shoulders and walked out of the control room and down the hall to his first team member his little brother, Nuke, to deliver the good news.

As Nitro worked on the supplies, gathering gear, ammunition, and vehicles, and ensured they had sufficient fuel to complete this operation, Gatlin arrived at Nuke's door. Gatlin banged on the door, but there was no answer. He kicked the door open. Inside, he found Nuke playing a video game, without much success, and using some choice words for what Nuke called the "damn cheating game."

"Get up!" Gatlin yelled.

When Nuke didn't respond, Gatlin realized that Nuke didn't even know he was in his room. His little brother had headphones on, likely jamming to Pearl Jam. Gatlin called out to Nuke again, this time slapping Nuke on the back of the head. "Come on. Get up and turn that off. We have to meet with T. J. about going to China. Don't you ever check your inbox or messages?

"Don't you ever clean your room? he added, looking around. "You're a slob."

"Yeah I clean my room," Nuke retorted, as the two headed down the hall to Pistol Smoke's room. "I clean it all the time. Hell, it's clean right now. I can find any and everything that I want. I like it just the way it is."

Pistol Smoke was no happier about the new assignment than Gatlin had been. "What in the hell is this?" he demanded as soon as Nuke and Gatlin entered his room. "I'm not a cold weather guy. What is this all about, Gatlin? I just got this damn message, and I am hoping that it's a very bad joke. Because I don't do cold weather, snow and shit like that. Nepal, c'mon man, that's like where they make fuckin' snow and freezin' ass temperatures, man. Fuck this, man. I am sick, dude. I can't go."

"Oh bullshit, you ain't sick," Gatlin replied. "Man up and get your shit screwed on tight. Borrow some pantyhose from Fusion or one of the other ladies so you can stay warm and meet us in the briefing room. You have ninety minutes."

"Oh, Gatlin, man, this is dog shit. I'm a sunburn, sand kinda guy. I like short pants and sunglasses, not fuckin' parkas," Pistol Smoke shot back.

"Well, if you want to, you can were short pants and sunglasses. I don't give a shit what you wear; just be in the briefing room in ninety. Have you seen or heard from Bolt-action, X, or Lee this morning?"

"I talked to Bolt-action earlier. He was going out to the gun range. Xtract is, I believe, in the lab with Recoil. And I haven't seen Lee; don't have a clue where he's at," Pistol Smoke replied.

When the three found Bolt-action at the firing range, Pistol Smoke handed Bolt-action the message informing them of the details of their next operation.

"What? Is this true," said Bolt-action, his excitement clear. "I've always wanted to return to the Far East—ever since my unit left, back when I was still in the corps."

"What? You want to go to the damn mountains?" asked Nuke. "That place is like Tibet—you know, Tibet, one of the coldest places on the planet. That Tibet."

"Yeah I'm aware of the area that we're going to. But according to this," said Bolt-action, pointing to the message, "the area that we will be in is south of Tibet, closer to Nepal, if not in Nepal. Y'all will love it; you wait. It's beautiful over there."

The four-man team returned to the mansion and headed down to the lab to find Xtract and look for GrizzLee in the process. When they reached the lab, they found Xtract with Recoil. The two had been sitting around talking about the same thing that the four of them had been talking about all morning.

Then Stealth's voice came over the intercom. "The Crow is ready. All vehicles are loaded and ready for departure. Lee is with me. We have everything that you boys are going to need on your winter wonderland getaway. I'm so glad that all I am doing is flying you boys in and flying you back out. Have fun. See y'all in the briefing room." She let out a giggle before the PA system clicked off, and the entire complex could hear her.

In the briefing room, the team waited for Tommy J to arrive. It was 7:45 a.m. eastern time. Stealth was in the back of the briefing room, making fun of the team. She found it highly amusing that the six men had to leave the near-perfect weather of South Carolina and travel across the Atlantic to the vast and brisk cold region of the Himalayas.

"Okay, men and women listen up," said Tommy J as he strode into the room. "Y'all know, as does the entire complex, that you are about to embark upon an operation—one I'm sure y'all will be able to overcome—that may seem to involve incredible odds and obstacles given the region of the world you'll be traveling to. I wouldn't be sending you if I didn't think that you could do it and if it wasn't extremely important to not only us, but to people of the area. I have the utmost confidence in each of your abilities as individuals and as a team.

"Stealth, as you all know will fly your team into the area. As was stated in the report, this will be a hover drop. You all will drop with the Pumas. We are sending three Pumas with you. A very reliable source tells me that there should be a very good-size opening in the Dhaulagiri Mountains, possibly a cave, where you will likely find Wrath.

"About the giant mountain men," he added, raising his eyebrows, "I don't know if the fellow actually saw one or was just suffering from dementia. The man wasn't part of the four-man hunting party that evidently disappeared in the same area where he claims to have seen the giant mountain men.

"Also, something that wasn't on y'alls report but that I obtained via telephone conversation—the same man reported hearing very loud and strange noises coming from the possible cave area, prior to seeing the so-called mountain men and before the hunting team went missing.

"The hunting team has now been missing for eight days and the authorities are presuming that they are dead but are not yet releasing that information. So the investigation continues, just not the search. The man in the hospital is an older man who has hunted, trapped, and lived in that area for many, many years. The locals all believe that he indeed saw something. They just don't know what. That, people, is where we come in."

"What are we supposed to do if we see this mountain man, or men?" Bolt-action wanted to know. "Take them out, I hope."

"I don't know about the mountain men. My concern is the cave that supposedly exists, which nobody recalls ever being there before. Nor does any archaeology literature confirm its existence. But to answer your question, Bolt-action, about the mountain men, if they seem hostile, yes, take them out."

Bolt-action looked around, and the entire team grinned back at him.

"But if the cave does indeed exist," Tommy J continued, "your job is to find out if it's Wrath's. You are to apprehend him, and destroy anything that's threatening that area, and return stateside. Here if he doesn't agree to our help, we will inject him so that he is mellowed out for several months—without Malakai knowing."

"That's it?" asked Nuke. "Just go over there, check out a cave, and bring Wrath back, if he's there?"

"You heard the man. Let's get it together," said Gatlin. "Let's pray and take to the skies."

After the team prayer, Gatlin moved his team to a private location so that they could all gather their own private thoughts about the upcoming operation.

The team and all they needed were aboard The Crow. The time was 8:45 a.m. eastern time as The Crow and the team lifted off—in flight and headed for the Himalayas.

After six and a half hours, Stealth with her copilot, as always, Crosshairs, talked to the team via The Crow's PA system. "Well, guys, we're about an hour from the drop zone, according to Crosshairs. Sorry I can't get y'all in closer to the area of the sightings, but with those awesome crosswinds, it's just too risky, even for The Crow. We could lose her and our lives as well.

"I'm sorry for laughing about your operation," she added. "Just a bit of humor, I'm sure that y'all will be fine. You have Lee; he knows this part of the world. Just stay warm."

"No offense taken," Xtract assured her. "It's kind of an unusual operation. We get to go to China and, you get to go to Egypt at the end of the month. Yeah, that seems fair."

"Ok team, listen up," said Gatlin. "Get your gear on. We are about forty minutes from drop zone. Let's get our heads together and make this op short and smooth."

For the next thirty minutes, the team didn't say another word. They each did what they needed to do to be prepared, both physically and mentally, for the operation.

"Six minutes till drop zone," said Stealth over the intercom.

"All right, let's get the Pumas ready for their drop," ordered Gatlin. "P-1 will be myself and Nuke; P-2 is Pistol Smoke and Xtract; P-3, Bolt-action and Lee. Xtract!"

"Opening bay doors," answered Xtract.

"Operate them out, Xtract," Gatlin ordered.

With the remote for the winch and release, Xtract pushed the button that started the Pumas in motion. The remote winched one vehicle at a time to the bay doors, where the vehicle was released from the winch, much like a paratrooper exiting the craft. Each Puma was released and their auto-chutes opened immediately after they were clear of The Crow.

"There goes the last one, Gatlin," said Xtract.

"Okay, fellas, let's do this," said Bolt-action. With high fives, fist punches, elbow slams, and pats on the back, everyone was fired up for the drop.

"Okay, let's move in three, two, one," said Bolt-action.

"Good luck, guys," called Stealth.

"Yeah, you two be careful going back," called Gatlin, and he leaped from the rear of The Crow, the last of the team to exit.

Shortly, the bay doors closed and The Crow was out of sight and gone.

On the snow-covered ground, Gatlin gathered the team together. Having removed the parachutes from the Pumas and rolled their own chutes up, they put all the parachutes in the Pumas' cargo areas. "All right, let's do a map check," he said, pulling out the map Tommy J had created using the information he'd received. "Lee, do you know the area we're currently in?"

"No sir." GrizzLee shook his head. "I'm afraid I don't."

"According to this map, we need to head north-northeast for what looks like a little more than a hundred miles before we reach the base of this mountain we're supposed to be investigatin'. From there, we are to follow a mountain trail to the cave. It's now 3:50 p.m. Let's get movin'. It gets dark over here pretty early, doesn't it, Lee?"

"Yes, sir," replied GrizzLee. "It gets dark around 6:00 or 6:30 p.m. That's when the yetis come out."

"Well, then, let's get moving," said Bolt-action.

"Hey, whoa!" Pistol Smoke broke in. "Wait a minute, man. Did you say yeti? Nobody said anything about yetis to me."

No one replied, as the three-vehicle convoy was already moving out toward its destination by the end of Pistol Smoke's protest.

*   *   *

The team had been traveling for nearly an hour and a half at 40 miles per hour, when the large mountain that was their destination came into view in the distance.

"Hey, Gatlin, let's open these babies up and see what they can do in the snow," suggested Nuke. "It's getting really boring putting around so damn slowly. We ain't seen nothing but a few snow hills and wolves. What do you say we get to where we're gonna camp for the night. I'm getting too damn cold driving around aimlessly, doing nothing."

"Listen up," Gatlin said over the radio. "Last one to the mountain takes first watch."

"Whoa!" yelled Xtract, as he downshifted and then took off beside P-1.

Nuke slammed the pedal to the floor, and the race was on. The team reached speeds of up to 90 miles per hour as they raced throwing snow fishtails into the air twenty to thirty feet high.

P-1 reached the base of the mountain first, followed by P-3 just as P-2 finished a very close third and won first watch for the evening.

*   *   *

At 7:00 p.m., darkness began to fill the valley as the sun lowered behind the mountains.

"Back in formation single file as we go up this trail," Gatlin ordered. "Stay sharp; keep your eyes open. Be careful. Let's reach our destination without incident."

"There won't be any incidents as long as those damn yetis stay away," said Pistol Smoke.

The team laughed at Pistol Smoke's fear of the never-before-seen creatures. GrizzLee just smiled at him.

The team had traveled more than an hour along a trail that snaked its way up the side of the mountain when they reached an enormous opening in the trail. It was enormous. About two miles long and about a mile wide, the clearing was very flat with mountains surrounding the valley floor. It is a very beautiful place.

"Well I guess we'll make camp here," said Gatlin. "It's nice and flat, and even though it's lighter up here now, it will be dark very shortly. We'll keep close tonight. Let's use the trail as our back door. We'll park P-1 at the northeast,

P-2 at the northwest, and put P-3 over at the southwest. This should give us a pretty stout and secure perimeter."

* * *

All the vehicles were in place, and camp was set up. The team had just finished eating and going over the plan for tomorrow. As P-2 had first watch, Xtract climbed into P-2's howitzer seat and switched the PTO (Pull to operate) so that he could fire the howitzer and/or 80mm cannon, as well as all four 30mm cannons mounted on all four fenders of the Puma. In P-1's howitzer chair, Pistol Smoke did the same.

Gatlin, Bolt-action, and GrizzLee looked over the map, trying to pinpoint possible locations of the cave they'd set out to find, while Nuke put away the dinner supplies, repacked the gear, and ensured that all weapons would be ready to go when the team was.

At 8:45 p.m., Gatlin stored the map away. "Let's get some shut-eye," he said. "At midnight, we'll change watch. Bolt-action and you, Lee, will relieve Pistol Smoke and Xtract. At 4:00 a.m., Nuke and I will relieve you two. Let's get some sleep."

The team agreed, and leaving the lights on, they turned in for the night.

* * *

It was 11:45 p.m. when Pistol Smoke heard what started out as a faint noise he couldn't quite identify. He shook his head and listened closer, certain he hadn't imagined the sound. After a moment, he recognized the sound of small pebbles, loosened from above and rolling down the side of the mountain. It wasn't long before both the sound and the size of the rocks hitting the valley floor increased.

"Hey, buddy, do hear that?" he called to Xtract.

"Hear what?" his friend replied.

"Man, I hear rocks and shit fallin' down the side of the mountain. Do you hear anything over there?"

"No, dude, I don't hear a thing. It's probably a mountain goat or some kind of cat. Why are you gettin' scared of the dark on me now?" said Xtract.

"Look, man, it's almost time to change guard," Pistol Smoke said, not quite hiding the nervousness in his voice. "Oh, man, you don't think that it's those yetis do you?"

"No, man," Xtract began. "It's just . . . OH SHIT! I hear it now, and I see the rocks." After a moment's pause, Xtract continued, nervousness now creeping into his voice. "Hell, the rocks are getting bigger and they're falling more and more frequently. I'm gonna stand watch. Get the others, just in case. I'll cover ya."

As Pistol Smoke made his way to the tent where the rest of the team was sleeping, ever larger rocks bounced ever more rapidly down the mountain wall. *What in the hell is that?* Xtract asked himself.

Huge figures began to take form, way up in the dark sky above the camp. The falling rocks turned from rocks into boulders.

Pistol Smoke saw the large figures as well; they seemed to be appearing everywhere now. "Gatlin, get up. All of you get the hell up; something is going on. Get out here now!" he yelled.

By now, some of the large figures were on the ground.

BOOM, BOOM! Xtract opened up the howitzer. He fired round after round into the large stone figures. As he hit one, it exploded and sent rocks of all sizes flying through the night air.

Bigger and bigger boulders continued to crash to the ground. Some hit P-3, totally destroying the vehicle. The assault vehicle and its vital weaponry and transportation capability now lay under a large pile of rocks and boulders.

"Fuck me, man," said Xtract. "These fuckers are everywhere. They're coming from up there somewhere. They're like stone giants or some shit made out of the sides of the mountain. What in the hell is that all about?"

The rest of the team was now outside in total disbelief of what they were seeing. This was definitely something that none of them had ever encountered before. Gatlin observed for a couple of seconds and then shouted out his order. "Fire! Fire! Blow them sons of bitches out of the sky. Don't let them touch ground!"

Nuke opened up on the stone giants with his 203, bazooka/tank killer. Gatlin followed suit with his awesome 30mm cannons.

When GrizzLee reached P-2, he ordered Xtract to get inside. "I'm taking the chair. You work 'em with the 30s and the laser from in there."

Bolt-action made his way to P-1, climbed up into the chair, and opened up on the multiple targets before him. Pistol Smoke joined him, climbing into P-1's cab and manning the 30mm cannons and the laser.

Gatlin and Nuke remained on foot, attacking what seemed to be an endless supply of these figures of stone that continued to appear, as well as land. From the ground, the brothers continued to blow the giants to pieces. From their respective chairs, Bolt-action and GrizzLee attacked the oncoming giants with the full force of their howitzers. And Pistol smoke and Xtract blasted away at the stone figures, rendering their attackers to piles of dust, with the front—and rear-mounted 30mm cannons as well as the Pumas' lasers.

The stone giants continued to touch down to the valley floor. There were simply too many of them for the team to be able to keep them from landing. The giants far outnumbered the six-man team; as fast as the team took one of the figures out, several more seemed to replace it.

Gatlin's guns begin to overheat and cut out. GrizzLee found himself suddenly surrounded by the giants. He continued to blow them away with the powerful gun, as well as taking a few of them out with some old-fashioned hand-to-hand.

At closer look, the team realized that the giants were swinging very large medieval weapons—swords, battle-axes, large wooden hammers, chains with spiked balls on the ends, and some nasty-looking knives. The giants now cluttered the valley floor; they were everywhere.

GrizzLee was struck from behind with a large sword that slashed open his back. As GrizzLee turned to fire some more, he was struck again, this time with a large hammer that knocked him off the chair and down to the valley floor. The giant who had knocked him down raised its hammer for another strike.

Boom! Nuke blew the giant to pieces.

As GrizzLee struggled to his feet, a second sword-swinging giant, who was about to slash GrizzLee from behind, got the same from Xtract. Xtract's awesome gun reduced the stone giant to a large pile of rubble, and the rocks rained onto GrizzLee, who was attempting to pull himself back into the howitzer chair.

With Bolt-action's help, Pistol Smoke was still able to stay on top of his attackers. Gatlin, still having problems with his guns overheating, was beginning to get overrun by the giants. Bolt-action turned his attack onto the stone giants surrounding Gatlin, blowing them away as Gatlin maneuvered around the valley. Nuke strapped his bazooka to his back and pulled out his 20mm automatic pistols and joined Bolt-action on his endeavor.

GrizzLee continued his struggle; this time, his struggle was getting back into the P-2 chair. Xtract was trying to keep the stone men off of GrizzLee. But, the giants would soon overtake P-2. GrizzLee was in trouble. Xtract got out of the Puma and began to take the figures out on foot with his M249, ripping the giants to pieces.

Seeing the giants beginning to take his fellow warriors over, Gatlin ran toward them, just as his guns cooled down. With guns blazing, Gatlin's attack was extremely effective, and stones flew in every direction.

As the rest of the team continued its assault, the tide began to turn in Allied Force's favor for the first time. The giants seemed to be retreating, going back to where they'd come from. They disappeared as fast as they had appeared. The last remaining giant took a final swing at GrizzLee—missing him but knocking the 30mm cannon from P-2's left front fender—before floating back toward wherever it had come from.

In a dead run, Gatlin reached P-2 and flung himself onto the massive back of the giant, trying to hold it down and keep it from escaping. But the giant continued to gain altitude. Realizing he couldn't prevent the giant's retreat, Gatlin, at point-blank range, fired with his mighty gun into the back of the fleeing giant's head as he held on with the other.

Gatlin soon found himself about fifteen feet in the black sky above camp, with rocks and debris flying everywhere. *This was a real good idea, dumbass, he told himself. You aren't gonna come out of this one a true winner.*

Shit; here goes nothin'. "Okay, bitch, it's just you and me now," he yelled.

"JUMP!" Nuke called to his brother. "You're getting too high."

Gatlin continued to fire hundreds of rounds into the back of the head and neck of the ever-retreating giant. At approximately twenty-five feet above the ground, the giant finally exploded, throwing stones of all sizes everywhere and Gatlin to the very hard valley floor.

The explosion destroyed the right side of Gatlin's body armor and damaged his right gun. Other than some nasty bruises and a sore back, Gatlin was all right—as was the rest of the team.

GrizzLee had a nasty gash across his back, and a very badly bruised chest, but like always, he insisted that he was fine.

All the stone giants had returned to the mountaintop or wherever they had come from. The team was in disbelief at what they had just encountered. P-3 was totally destroyed, buried under tons of boulders.

Xtract bandaged GrizzLee up, while Pistol Smoke and Nuke salvaged all that they could from P-3's wreckage.

"What in the hell were those things?" asked Bolt-action. "And damn, where did they come from?"

"Well I believe we just met the 'mountain men,'" said Gatlin. "That freaky shit just about guarantees that Wrath is here our next stop is the cave."

"Oh yeah the cave," said Nuke as he and Pistol Smoke returned to the others.

A little battered from the incredible battle, the team decided to stay awake for the remaining four and a half hours until dawn—at which time they would roll up camp and move farther up the mountain in search of Wrath's cave.

*   *   *

As the dawn of another day began to reach over the mountaintops, rays of morning sunlight shone down onto the valley floor and the camp. The team finished their pecks, rolled up camp, and made ready to continue their journey up the mountainside.

"Okay, everyone, listen up," said Gatlin. "Since we lost P-3, we will have to ride three to a Puma. I know that it's not gonna be that comfortable, but oh well. Xtract, you will ride in P-2 with Bolt-action and Lee. Pistol Smoke you will ride in P-1 with Nuke and me. Let's move 'em out."

*   *   *

The team had traveled a couple hours up the rocky, narrow path that the mountain offered them when Xtract stopped. "Check it out," he said, pointing to a partially hidden opening in the mountain wall. "Do you think this is the mystery cave we're supposed to investigate?"

"I believe that we are here men," said Gatlin. "Unsaddle and let's take a look inside."

"Man, I don't know about this, Gatlin," said Nuke. "It looks a little creepy in there—even for me."

"Hey look, guys, tighten up." Gatlin looked around at his crew, holding each of the men's gazes for a moment. "We are on this bitter cold-ass mountaintop to do a job, a job that we are being paid very well to complete, so we will complete this operation. Put your personal fears behind you. We are stuck with two options; one, we go in and finish what we came here to do or, two, we stay out here again in the freezing air and take our chances with the evil Stonehenge dudes from hell. I don't know about all of you, but I'm going in, with or without you. So what's it gonna be?"

The team gave Gatlin a collective answer. "Go in."

"Let's finish this thing and then let's get the hell out of this place," Pistol smoke added.

Gatlin led the team into the cave, using the spotlights from P-1. Nuke drove, and Pistol Smoke manned the howitzer. P-2 followed, Xtract driving, GrizzLee using the spotlights, and Bolt-action in the howitzer chair.

"Look on the walls," said Xtract. "There are torches. What do you think, Gatlin, light them?"

"Yeah, I guess we could," Gatlin agreed. "It'll help us see this dark, cold-ass, stinky place. Light 'em up."

Nuke and Pistol Smoke lit the torches on the cave walls.

"Hey boss if there are torches, there has to be someone occupying this cave," GrizzLee pointed out. "Maybe they're expecting company."

"Don't tell me that the yetis know how to use fire," said Nuke.

"This *was* definitely a yeti cave," said GrizzLee. "They were here at one time, but they've been either forced away or killed out."

"Oh great, now we could possibly fight Bigfoot. That's just wonderful," snapped Pistol Smoke.

"No, you're not listening," said GrizzLee, gesturing to the torches. "This isn't the yetis. They're not here. They once called this cave home but no longer."

"This cave has an eerie, dark, and unspiritual presence," he added.

"Stop talking about yetis and all the dark and unspiritual presence stuff; it's giving me the willies," said Nuke.

* * *

After the team had made its way approximately a mile deep into the cave, having lit all the torches along the cave walls and now reaching a place where there were no more torches to light, Gatlin stopped to gather everyone's thoughts. "We've traveled this deep and haven't found shit but a bunch of torches and no sign of life or Wrath," he said. He told Bolt-action, who was second in charge in the field in Allied Force's chain of command, to come to the hood of P-1, while the rest of team held their positions. "Xtract, why don't you change Lee's dressing," he added. "Nuke, equip all weapons with lights. Pistol Smoke, keep an eye on the rear from the back of P-2 and make sure nothing tries to come from behind us.

Midway between carrying out Gatlin's instructions Bolt-action stopped short, and so did everyone else. "Do y'all hear that?" he said.

"Yeah, but what in the hell was it?" Gatlin responded. "It sounded like a cat getting swung around by its tail."

The sound came again.

"Did everyone hear that?" Nuke asked rhetorically. "It sounds like it's getting closer and closer."

The sound grew louder and more frequent, and whatever was making it did, indeed, seem to be getting closer to the team.

"Arm up and take positions," ordered Gatlin. "Do not fire until I give the order."

More and more frequent, louder and louder, whatever this thing was it was definitely getting closer to them. Each of the team members took a defensive position, prepared for what would, it seemed to be another battle.

"It sounds like its right on top of us, but I can't see anything," said Nuke.

"Hold fire until we can see what the hell it is," ordered Gatlin. "Shit, it's right here with us. Stay sharp. On my mark."

VARROOM, VARROOM, VARROOM.

Small balls of fire began exploding all around the team. Whatever it was, was indeed above them.

"What in the hell is it? Gatlin, talk to me," said Xtract.

VARROOM, VARROOM.

Again fireballs flew through the inky black darkness of the cave. This time, a couple of the fireballs struck P-2, catching the vehicle on fire.

"Pistol Smoke, put out the fire I still can't see a damn thing. Hold fire," ordered Gatlin.

"There it is; it's some kind of bird!" yelled Bolt-action.

"Okay, the next time the thing comes around, open fire on its ass if you have a visual. Remember, short, controlled bursts," said Gatlin.

BOOM, BOOM.

GrizzLee opened fire on the bird or whatever it was. "It's too fast for the howitzer; switching to 80mil," he said.

VARROOM, VARROOM, VARROOM.

The flying creature fired again and again at P-2. This time, as Pistol Smoke was putting out the fire, one of the flaming balls hit him. "Oh shit. I'm hit!" he screamed. "I'm on fuckin' fire. Help!"

Nuke ran to help Pistol Smoke extinguish the fire, but not before the flames had burned Pistol Smoke's lower body, scorching his legs, feet, and midsection on the left side, thankfully, not too badly. Pistol Smoke was now out of the fight and in terrible pain, though. Nuke pulled Pistol Smoke out of harm's way, the best that he could tell.

"FIND THE FUCKIN' THING AND KILL IT," Gatlin boomed. "We have got to get this motherfucker down before it picks us apart. Fire everything that we've got!"

And they did just that—GrizzLee on the awesome 80mm cannon, Gatlin and his 30mm arm cannons, Xtract with his M249 automatic rifle, and Bolt-action using the 30mm cannons from the cab of P-1. Nuke kept Pistol Smoke covered keeping his friend, as best he could, from taking any more damage. Hot lead flew throughout the cave. The team could see the bird now, thanks to the fire that was coming from the barrels of their weapons, now so constant it lit up the entire cave.

They hit the bird again and again. Finally, it was down and out.

"What is that thing?" asked Bolt-action. "What kind of ugly-ass bird is that?"

"I'm not sure," said Gatlin. "You have any idea Lee?"

"Yeah it looks like a phoenix, but it also resembles a young dragon with its scale-covered body," GrizzLee said thoughtfully. "The phoenix is covered in feathers. However, both shoot fire and neither are harmed by it. It could be, but I'm not sure, a mutation of the two. I just don't know, boss." He shook his head, not at all sure what to make of the creature lying before him.

"Hey, can I get a little help over here with Pistol Smoke?" Nuke cut in. "He's in some serious pain, man. He's like burnt from the waist down, I think."

"Bolt-action, give Nuke a hand getting Smoke over here. X, set something up; we have wounded," ordered Gatlin.

"You got it, Gatlin." Bolt-action hurried toward his injured friend. "Damn, Smoke, I didn't even realize you were hit. Shit, man, don't worry; X will get you goin' again."

Gatlin walked away from the rest of the team, heading some sixty feet deeper into the cave. He stopped and looked down the pitch-black path with his night vision, part of the standard gear for all Allied Force members. Along with the night vision goggles, the team's head gear was equipped with radios and, sometimes, cameras, if the ops called for them. A team member could activate each of these devices by simply touching the one he or she wanted to use at that time.

The rest of team followed their orders. While Xtract worked on Pistol Smoke, Nuke held Smoke's hand and talked to him. Bolt-action was looking at GrizzLee's wounds also.

GrizzLee nodded for Bolt-action to look up and behind him, and Bolt-action followed his gaze. "Don't tell me that he's coming up with some sort of plan?" he said. "I can't wait to hear this one."

"That's probably only half of it, Bolt-action," said Nuke. "The real reason he's way over there is the fact that he has not one but two members of his squad injured on this one, and we just got started. You should know that better than any of us, Bolt-action. That sort of shit bothers the hell out of Gatlin."

"Yeah, man, you're right. I just wasn't thinking," Bolt-action replied. "Hell, besides, I didn't mean anything by it. Y'all know as well I do that I and everyone of you would go to battle in hell with that man."

"Amen," said GrizzLee, as Gatlin walked back toward the team.

"We don't have many options," said Nuke. "We can stay here, where it's a lot warmer but infested with dragon birds or some shit. Or we can turn around and go back outside and take our chances with those freakin' stone giants again."

Gatlin returned to the team. "How's Smoke?" he asked.

"Well, he's burned, fortunately not real bad," Xtract reported. "Some places are more severe than others. I have him on a morphine drip right now, and he's resting. The rest is up to him and God."

"Good. Keep an eye on him for me. How are you doin', Lee?" asked Gatlin.

"I'll be fine," GrizzLee replied. "What's on your mind, sir?"

"I want all of y'all to remain right here," Gatlin replied. "We'll call this base camp for the time being. I'm gonna walk down this way a bit to see how far these Pumas can travel. By the way, how bad is P-2?"

"It's fine. A little darker in color thanks to the fire-throwing chicken from hell over there, but the best that I can tell, she's sound as she was when she came into this place," answered Nuke.

"Uh, sir, no disrespect, but do you think that you going off by yourself is such a good idea? I could go with you and watch your back," suggested GrizzLee.

"No, Lee, I need you to stay here on the guns, just in case some of those dragon things decide to come back. Xtract will have to stay here and tend to the wounded. Bolt-action will stay and take over command while I'm gone. Nuke, you will help Xtract with whatever he needs. I'll be fine, and I won't be gone long. So hold the fort until I get back.

"Make sure that y'all stay close to camp. Get some rest and take advantage of this downtime and get something in your stomachs. I've got a feeling that this op is gonna be a long one, with much excitement," Gatlin added.

"Hey, Gatlin, make sure that your tracking device is activated just in case," said Bolt-action.

"Yeah, you got that buddy. Take care of the team and the wounded. I will return." With that, Gatlin turned and walked away from the team, disappearing into the dark cave and the unknown on a one-man recon mission.

"Hey, bro, take your MFG-25 with you since your gun is kinda messed up on the right side. Just in case," said Nuke as he caught up with Gatlin and handed him his very powerful semiautomatic pistol.

"Thanks. I'll bring you back a souvenir, if you're lucky," said Gatlin.

Nuke watched as, once again, his brother disappeared into the darkness.

* * *

Before he realized it, Gatlin had walked a lot farther than he'd planned to. He'd found more torches and had been lighting them along the way.

About another mile deeper, Gatlin reached what appeared to be a fork in the path. It was the only fork that he'd come across the entire walk. Gatlin decided to take the path to the left, as it seemed to be the main pathway. Another two hundred yards down the path he came to what seemed to be a dead end. Out of habit, he lit the torches that were on either side of the dead-end path.

He paused for a moment before something occurred to him. *What are torches doing at a dead end?* he wondered.

When nothing happened Gatlin turned around to return to the main path. Suddenly, the ground began to shake under his feet. He heard the ground shaking both in front of him and behind him. At the same time, he heard something in the distance. Moments later, to his amazement, he watched in total disbelief as forms took shape in the distance. He took a closer look; the forms were, indeed, exactly what he thought he'd seen. Skeletons armed with crossbows and assorted medieval weaponry, which somewhat resembled the weapons that the stone giants had used, were making their way toward him.

With no place to go and no place to take cover, Gatlin found himself surrounded. So Gatlin did what he does best;

he readied himself for battle, taking aim with his 30mm cannons. With the odds the way they were, a part of him hoped that he wouldn't have to use force. But the other part of him, the ass-kicking warrior, prepared for the worst.

Gatlin wasn't sure how many of these skeletal troops there are. They continue to rise from the ground. He knows his weapon is far superior, but again how many are there? Gatlin plays it cool, he just looks around, now there is approximately fourty that he can see, and more were still rising from the floor of the cave. They were approaching him more aggressively now, getting close and closer. In moments, there had to be more than seventy-five or eighty above ground, and they looked like they meant business.

The odds weren't getting any better, so Gatlin did what he was known for; he opened fire on them. As Gatlin slung lead, he saw that his weapons were reducing the bone army to nothing more than clouds of dust. "Oh this is fuckin' great," he yelled. "C'mon, assholes; bring it on, you dumb shits!" He laughed out loud and continued to blow the skeletons to dust. He was having a great time.

Then he noticed that there were a bit more of the bone warriors than he'd thought. The army had grown to what appeared to be upwards of 120 strong, and more skeletons were still emerging from the ground.

He suddenly found himself cut off from the rest of his team. He discovered moments later that his radio didn't seem to work in this cave. He was now in a battle with what appeared to be an endless supply of soldiers. The skeletons began closing in; they were much closer than Gatlin liked.

Then an arrow pierced Gatlin's left shoulder. Another sunk into his right side just under the body armor. Gatlin picked up the pace of his assault. Soon, Gatlin had demolished over 130 soldiers with no relief in sight. The skeletons continued to come and to fire at him. Most of the arrows bounced off his armor, but every so often, they found their target and Gatlin took another hit. One arrow found his left forearm just behind his arm cannon. Another hit his left ankle.

Gatlin continued his assault, but his guns were beginning to overheat and misfire. The "body" count was well over two hundred, and the skeletal soldiers were still coming. Gatlin's guns fired slower and slower, allowing the skeletons to get even closer. He pulled out his MFG-25 and began to pop their brittle melons once again. He was taking the soldiers out with every shot, but the powerful pistol just wasn't fast enough to keep up with the ever-growing army of skeletons. The pistol just didn't compare to the firing speed of his cannons.

Gatlin checked his cannons. "Shit," he said under his breath. "Still too hot."

His guns were just not cooling fast enough. He inserted another twenty-five-round clip into his pistol and continued to drop skeletons with every shot. Than he was hit again; again an arrow found its way into his right side just below his body armor, where the explosion with the stone giant had damaged it.

The army was now on all sides of him and closing in on him quickly. It appeared that fresh bone soldiers had stopped coming out of the ground, but the army was now only fifteen feet away. His cannons were still too hot. He was forced to pop in his last clip. Once again, he began to fire the powerful pistol for all it was worth, using choice words for his attackers as he took them out. He fired six, five, four, three, two, one; *click, click, click*. He was out of MFG-25 rounds.

The army was now within kicking distance, so that was exactly what Gatlin did. He had been in heavy hand-to-hand combat, taking out a dozen or so of the medieval soldiers when he was slashed across the back, cutting his shoulder wide open.

Out of the corner of his eye, he saw a green light flash. His guns were cooled. Gatlin raised his cannons and unloaded on the army of skeletons, blowing bones and dust all over the place, including all over himself, until he'd dusted the last one. The battle was over, but this warrior had taken a lot of punishment.

*   *   *

Back at base camp, Nuke couldn't help but stare into the darkness his brother had disappeared into. "Gatlin's been gone a long time," he told Bolt-action. "Way too long. Something isn't right. I'm going after him."

"No wait," said Bolt-action. "We'll all go."

"Well I hate to rain on your parade there, Bolt-action, but there is no way that we can move Pistol Smoke right now with the condition he's in," said Xtract.

"Noooo, maaan, youuu guuuys can move me. I'm fine and ready for any—" said Pistol Smoke before the morphine took him back out.

Bolt-action shook his head. "Shit," he finally said. "Okay, Nuke, you go. But you better be careful. I'll stay with Xtract, since he has to stay with Smoke and Lee. Follow Gatlin's tracker. Don't be a hero. And stick to the path," Bolt-action ordered.

After Nuke gathered what he thought he might need for this search and rescue, he was off down the dark and ever-deepening path, in search of his brother. Nuke knew that Gatlin wouldn't leave his team for this long without some kind of contact with them unless something had gone wrong. Nuke has never once had to go in search of Gatlin. He was, needless to say, very nervous.

Nuke checked the locators. According to them, he was right on target and closing in on Gatlin's location. A mile or so further down the path, Nuke knew that, by this time, he should have had a visual on Gatlin. Nuke just continued his quest, moving deeper down the musky path, unable to shake the feeling that something had happened to Gatlin.

Nuke walked another quarter mile down the path. He now had no sign of his brother on the locator, much less the naked eye. The tension in his body grew stronger and stronger as he imagined what might have happened to Gatlin. Nuke tried his headset radio. No good. "The radios don't freakin' work in this damn cave," Nuke said to himself.

Nuke found himself cut off from base camp and Gatlin. He was now on his own.

*   *   *

Back at base camp, Xtract was getting worried. "Bolt-action," he said, "they've been gone a long time. Nuke has been gone for almost two hours, and Gatlin's been out for close to four hours. I say we go after them. It's obvious that the locators and headsets aren't working in here. I guess it's the cave walls. They could be in trouble."

"I don't know," said Xtract.

"I just think that someone needs to go," Bolt-action insisted. "I'll go and you can . . ."

"Oh my god, Gatlin! Gatlin over here!" Xtract's cry interrupted him. "Damn let's give him a hand," said Xtract.

GrizzLee leaped from the chair of P-1 and runs to help Gatlin get back to camp. Gatlin was using one of the skeleton's swords from the battle as a makeshift cane and bleeding badly from the wounds inflicted during his battle. Gatlin stood at the beginning of the path, about to collapse from his wounds and exhaustion. He fell to one knee, just as Bolt-action and Xtract reached him.

Xtract surveyed the team leader. Gatlin's right shoulder looked very serious. His left shoulder was bleeding as well, but it seemed to be just a flesh wound; there was a lot of tissue, but it didn't seem to be as bad as some of his other wounds. Gatlin's left forearm was badly wounded.

A hole had been torn open, exposing muscle. His left foot and ankle were wounded, but not that badly, at least not that bad for a man with the heart, strength, and stamina of Gatlin.

GrizzLee, despite his own wounds, made his way through Bolt-action and Xtract. GrizzLee looked into Gatlin's eyes and said, "Hey boss, good to see ya. We were getting a little worried about you. Here let me help you up and get you back to camp, so these guys can get you all fixed back up and we can get on with this operation." GrizzLee tried to hide the concern he had for his leader, but everyone could hear it in his voice. Still, he wanted to keep Gatlin from realizing just how worried he and the rest of the team were. GrizzLee was giving Gatlin the same pep talk that Gatlin gave the team when they were in bad shape and wounded.

The entire team knew that Gatlin was in serious condition right now, but they wouldn't let him know that they were concerned. Gatlin realized that he was in pretty bad shape. But he would never let anyone know that he knows. That was just the way that he led his team—by example.

GrizzLee and Bolt-action get Gatlin back to camp. Xtract carried his weapons, body armor, and the medieval sword/souvenir that he was using as a cane.

"How do you feel?" Xtract asked. "What happened? What did you . . . GATLIN, STAY WITH US. *Gatlin*!"

Gatlin had passed out from exhaustion and loss of blood.

"We'll give him a little morphine so that he can rest; that'll give me a chance to sew him up and get him put back together," said Xtract.

"I wouldn't do that," cautioned Pistol Smoke, who was lying next to Gatlin in pain. "You know how he is. He will be plenty pissed if he finds out you gave him morphine during an operation."

"Well then, why don't you just tell me how in the hell I'm suppose to fix him up? Are you volunteering to hold him down while I patch him up?" asked Xtract.

"Uh no, I'm not getting in on this one," said Pistol Smoke. "But he's gonna be pissed when he wakes up feeling all drugged up. Plus, if Nuke doesn't get back before he wakes up, you know that there will be hell to pay."

"What? Wait, what? Where is Nuke?" demanded Gatlin.

"Well, buddy, Nuke went out looking for you. He left over two hours ago, and he's not back yet," explained Xtract. "We tried to get in contact with both him and you, but neither of you could or would respond. I'm guessing that the two of you never crossed paths. Nuke must have gone another way."

"There is no other path. There's only one way to go—no intersections or turns, except for the one I took, and it was a fuckin' dead end.

"You mean to tell me that y'all just let him go off alone. Damn you, Bolt-action. I left you in charge because I figured that you could handle the simple task of stayin' at fuckin' camp with everybody here with you. You let me down big-time. I'll never leave you in charge again, you can damn sure count on that shit," said a very angry Gatlin.

"Hey, big guy, you can't blame me for your little brother's actions. Nuke made the decision to go, regardless of what I or anyone else said. He listens to you and T.J., and that is it my friend. He is as damn hardheaded as you are. So you jump my ass for that? Hell, you trained him. He is you all over again, only younger and cockier. And forgive me, but a hell of a lot dumber. So back the hell off," retorted Bolt-action.

"I have to go after him," said Gatlin.

"Oh no, you're not leaving, not in the shape that you're in," said Xtract. "So settle down. Nuke will be back. Let me get you fixed up. You are no good to him or anyone else in this shape."

"If you think you can stop me, if you're man enough, have at it," growled Gatlin. "Otherwise, get the hell out of my face." Gatlin pushed himself to a sitting position.

"Help, Lee, help me put him down!" yelled Xtract.

GrizzLee grabbed Gatlin from the back while Xtract tried to inject Gatlin with morphine.

"Don't even try that shit with me, X. Let me go, Lee, or I will kick everyone's ass here," said Gatlin.

GrizzLee didn't let go of Gatlin, and Xtract struggled to inject the morphine, content with getting the needle anywhere into Gatlin at this point. As the two struggled, Bolt-action walked over to Gatlin and punched him directly in the nose, laying Gatlin out enough for Xtract to give him the shot.

"Oh, man, dude, I feel sorry for you when he wakes up. He is so gonna kick your ass for that," said Pistol Smoke.

"Yeah, maybe so, but he is our leader. And he can't make proper decisions in that state of mind. I'm in charge now. X, put big mouth over there"—Bolt-action nodded to Pistol Smoke—"out for awhile. I need to think."

The two wounded men slept soundly while Xtract worked on getting Gatlin put back together.

*　*　*

Three hours had passed since Gatlin had returned to base camp. There was still no sign of Nuke.

"Okay, let's get back to work and come up with a plan," said Bolt-action. "Gatlin will be waking up soon, and we all know that he is going to immediately want to go looking for Nuke at any price. So before we have to go through all of that again, we need to get organized. Xtract, you keep an eye on those two. Lee and I are going to do inventory. How do you feel, Lee?"

"I'm much better," said GrizzLee.

"All right, we'll do weapons check first. You take P-2 and I'll take P-1," Bolt-action ordered. "Just lay them all out so that we can get an accurate count. I'm not sure what all we got off P-3 that was salvageable."

"You got it, bud," said GrizzLee.

GrizzLee reported that, on P-2 were sixty fragment grenades, four M203 grenade launchers with twenty-five shells each, two M60Es with roughly seventy thousand rounds, four M249s with eight thousand-round drums, forty-five howitzer shells, two hundred thousand rounds for the mounted 80mm cannon, plenty of first aid, and food and water."

"On P-1, we have fifty fragment grenades, three 80mm cannons with eighty thousand rounds per, seventeen C-4 explosive packs with detonators, close to three hundred howitzer shells, four hundred thousand rounds for the mounted 80mm cannon, as well as plenty of food and water, supplies, and first aid. Fuel right now looks pretty good. We seem to still have a pretty powerful arsenal, so we should be fine for a while," said Bolt-action.

"Sounds good," GrizzLee agreed.

"All right, listen up. We are going to pack it up and get our wounded on their feet and roll. We're going after Nuke. Let's move," ordered Bolt-action.

*   *   *

In thirty minutes, the team had the Pumas loaded and ready for the search and rescue of Nuke.

"Okay, let's get this show on the road," said Bolt-action. "We have to make a move on this operation toward getting the hell out of here and getting our butts back home. As everyone knows by now, neither the locators nor the headsets work in this cave. And if everyone would look down at your watches, well, for some weird reason they don't seem to work in here either. Best estimation, we have a day and a half at best to find Nuke, finish this thing, and get back to the LZ for extraction." It was strange how far away the loading zone where The Crow would be waiting seemed just now.

"We'll catch that flight with Stealth back to our side of the world, and we'll complete this operation. More importantly right now, we will find Nuke," Bolt-action concluded.

"Oh, man, what in the hell happened to me?" asked a very groggy Gatlin. "I feel like I've been run over by a convoy of trucks."

"Hey, boss, good to see you up and around again," said GrizzLee. "You had us all a little scared there for a little while. Are you feeling all right?"

"Honestly, Lee, I feel like shit. Let's get this show on the road. Bolt-action, you're in charge for the time being. We have to find Nuke," said Gatlin.

"Well, thank you, Gatlin. Listen up. This is how we are going to have to travel because of our wounded. Smoke will ride in the cab of P-2, and I will drive, taking point. X will drive P-1; Gatlin will man the 30s. Lee will be in the chair. This time, Lee, 80mm first. If you think that you need to switch to howitzer, I will leave that up to you. Remember, we are in a cave. I don't know if the howitzer will pack too powerful of a punch for the walls or not. They may begin to crumble. I've never fought in a cave before. But before we pullout, Gatlin, you are going to have to tell us what you encountered down there. We have to know," said Bolt-action.

"Well if you must know, boss, at first the ground began to shake," Gatlin began. "Then from under the cave floor, through the dirt, an army of medieval skeletons emerged. Hundreds of them surrounded me in a matter of a few minutes. They would appear just as fast as I could kill them. They weren't hard to kill. In fact, it started out kinda fun. It was the seemingly endless number of them that posed the problem. I don't know where they come from or why they are here, but my guess is that they are guarding something or someone. We have broken through their first three lines of defense, whoever it is. First the stone giants, then the fire bird deal, and now the skeleton army. There is really no tellin' what in the hell we'll face next.

"I just about guarantee that we are not at all wanted here," Gatlin added. "So, Bolt-action stay sharp at point. I will tell y'all when we are getting close to where my battlefield was. Hell, you ought to be able to tell; the ground'll be littered with bones and bone fragments and weapons."

Gatlin climbed into P-1's passenger seat. The team is ready for whatever lay ahead. Although they were shorthanded, the team feared nothing, outside the mysterious disappearance of Nuke.

"Let's move out," ordered Bolt-action, as the two Pumas embarked on a mission of the unknown once again.

* * *

Bolt-action drew in his breath as the team arrived at the scene of Gatlin's battle. "Damn, Gatlin, you really had one hell of a conflict here. Now I know what you're talking about."

He also realized that Gatlin had been right; they hadn't encountered a single fork or turn in the path other than the one they were on now, which, indeed, led to a dead end.

"Did you ever go any farther to the right?" asked Bolt-action.

"No," Gatlin told him. "I took this left and found this dead end, and that's when the skeletons showed up and changed my entire thought process. After the ordeal, I didn't get a chance to go that way."

"Well maybe Nuke went to the right while you were in the battle with the skeletons. What do you think?" suggested Pistol Smoke, who was now awake again.

"No I don't think so," Gatlin objected. "He would have heard the gunfire, and he would have come and helped me dust the skeletons."

"Yeah, Nuke would have been the first one there at your side," agreed Xtract.

"All right," said Bolt-action, "we've seen enough. Let's move on and find Nuke. We are burning daylight."

"Daylight? Did you say daylight, Bolt-action? We haven't seen daylight in forever," protested Pistol Smoke. "How in the hell can we be burning it when it isn't even here?"

"Smoke, do us all a favor and shut the hell up before I do it for you," said Bolt-action.

"You got it," Pistol smoke said. "You just said daylight, burning daylight. I don't know what that means. What does that mean?"

"It's an old saying," said Xtract. "It means we're wasting time. Now shut up and sit there. You are such a lightweight when it comes to drugs, Smoke."

The team resumed the search for Nuke, this time heading along the path that led to the right.

*   *   *

Several hours had passed, and the team hadn't found so much as a clue as to Nuke's whereabouts. They remained unable to get in contact with him via headset. It was becoming obvious that they weren't going to find a spot anywhere in this cave where their communications would work.

"It's like he vanished," said Xtract. "He's somewhere in this cave. We just have to find him."

"I'm guessing we have twenty-six hours and some change to get Nuke, get Wrath, and get to evac," said GrizzLee.

According to the odometer, the team was now better than thirteen miles deep inside the cave. Still, they'd found no turns and no sign of Nuke. At this point, the cave seemed to go on forever. And the team had no idea what to expect around every new curve. The tension was growing, almost to the point of stress, but the team drove on. They had never failed an operation in all of Allied Force's eighteen-year existence, and they didn't plan to start now.

As the team reached the fifteen mile mark, according to the odometers in the Pumas—something that was actually working in the cave—the ground began to shake.

"Hold up, Bolt-action," said Gatlin. "The ground is shaking a little bit."

The team stopped.

"Do you feel that?" he asked. "That is exactly what I felt before the skeletons attacked."

"Okay, fellas, take positions. We are about to get it on again, it seems," ordered Bolt-action.

The team all took their positions. Bolt-action took the front flanks on foot, carrying his handheld MK2 aircraft mini-gun. The gun weighed 231 pounds, which meant only a few could handle it in action with their hands. It fired 550 rounds per second. It wasn't the fastest-shooting gun Bolt-action had in his personal arsenal, but it was one of his favorites.

Pistol Smoke, from the cab of P-2, would man the 30mm cannons and laser and take the front. GrizzLee would remain in the chair of P-1 and use the 80mm cannon, while Xtract and Gatlin covered the rear flanks, both with their usual—Xtract and his M249 Squad Automatic Weapon (SAW) and Gatlin with his 30mm arm-mounted cannons.

"Lock and load, fellas," ordered Bolt-action.

The team was now ready for anything that the cave had to offer. The ground continued to shake, more frequently now. The shaking seemed to be getting closer to the team.

"Stay frosty, people," said Bolt-action.

The floor of the cave began to open all around the team.

"On my mark!" ordered Bolt-action.

From under the ground emerged giant, two-headed serpents.

"FIRE, FIRE, FIRE, EVERYTHING WE HAVE!" ordered Bolt-action.

The team opened up on the serpents, ripping and blowing the giant snakes to pieces. Like the skeletons had, more and more of the snakes emerged as fast as the team killed them. For every snake the team killed, two or three took its place.

"They're all around us!" yelled GrizzLee as he blew snake skin and guts all over the cave walls.

The team continued their awesome barrage of firepower against the ancient serpents. The snakes began to spit what appeared to be some kind of acidic mucus at the team.

Gatlin noticed that the spit instantly burned holes in the cave floor on contact. "Oh shit, they're spitting acid shit at us!" he yelled. "Keep them at bay! Don't let them get any closer! Stay away from their spit!"

At this point, the team had destroyed fourteen serpents, and the ground continued to shake and rumble and eventually open. Now not only serpents were rising from the depths of the cave, but the medieval, weapon-wielding skeletons were back and rising once again. The team was now surrounded by nine more snakes and better than two hundred skeleton soldiers.

"Oh great," said Pistol Smoke. "Well the odds are the same as they always are—Allied Force not too many guys; assholes, a lot."

GrizzLee was literally blowing the skeleton soldiers to pieces. Gatlin and Bolt-action were concentrating on the giant serpents. Xtract and Pistol Smoke were killing whichever of their enemies crossed their paths, as the two of them now covered both the left and right flanks.

After almost forty-five minutes of battle, none of the Allied Force team had been wounded yet. At best estimate, four snakes and still well over one hundred skeleton soldiers remained.

"Hey, it looks like they've stopped coming out of the damn ground," said Gatlin.

Moments later, Xtract was hit in the leg by an arrow. As he turned to the shooter one of the serpents spat on him, hitting him in the left hand. The giant snake was charging his position. "Oh shit!" yelled Xtract. "This damn acid spit burns. Get this son of a bitch off of me!"

The serpent closed in. When the giant serpent was only thirty feet away from Xtract, Xtract heard Gatlin's voice. "GET DOWN!" Gatlin screamed.

Just as Xtract dropped to the floor of the cave, he heard the awesome 30mm cannon rounds fly very closely over his head, on their way to ripping the oncoming serpent to shreds.

As the blood mist from the snake cleared, Xtract and Gatlin could see more skeleton soldiers. Xtract unleashed his pain and frustrations on them, and Gatlin followed his lead. In seconds, the twelve or fourteen soldiers were dusted.

The team continued their bombardment of their enemies. The ancient serpents had now all been removed from the equation. The team concentrated on the couple dozen remaining skeleton soldiers. After about a minute and a half, the outgunned skeleton soldiers' threat was over as well.

"That's all of them," said Bolt-action. "Is everyone all right?"

"I'm hit, and I also got spit on by one of those damn snakes," replied Xtract.

"How bad are you? Can you handle it?" asked Bolt-action as he made his way back to the Pumas.

"Yeah, I need to stitch my leg and get something on my hand and wrap it up, but I'll make it. Is everyone else okay?" asked Xtract.

"Yeah I'm okay," shot Pistol Smoke. "I just have a very large amount of pain right now. Other than that I am doing pretty good and thank you for asking."

"Oh, man, shut him up," said Gatlin. "I believe we are all fine. We just can't see anything with all this damn dust in the air."

"Hey, guys, can I have your attention for a couple of seconds now please," said Bolt-action, "Since we can't go anywhere yet because we can't see anything through this thick bone dust."

The team all looked in Bolt-action's direction. "I know that this operation has started out like shit. And we are missing a very important member of our team, somewhere in this cave, and we will find him. But I just want to say that we have defeated another one of Wrath's threats. That gives us four. Each and every one of you guys was flawless in the execution of that battle. With the exception of the injuries to Xtract, which are very minor compared to the overwhelming odds that we faced, I say that we kicked some major ass just now. Thanks for being on my team. I'm proud of being a member of this team. So thanks again.

When the others nodded their agreement, Bolt-action continued. "Let's get patched up and get back on the road to finding Nuke. Finding him is our first priority, Wrath is secondary right now, and since I am in charge, that's how we're going to look at it. I will take the ass chewing from T. J. But Nuke's disappearance has changed this game for all of us. Again thanks. You all kicked ass."

"Hey, no problem, bud; we're all in this thing together," said GrizzLee.

The rest of the team agreed with GrizzLee. They all spread out around the Pumas and prepared to move out.

"Hold up. Everyone, hold up. Stop a minute. It's my turn to say something—especially to Bolt-action," said Gatlin. "It's gotta be tough being second in charge when the first in charge is a perfectionist, like myself. But I meant what I said earlier, Bolt-action, you are in charge of this operation until I feel that I can perform to my best abilities, and right now, I'm not there. You're a damn good leader. You got this battle going in the right direction right off the bat. Yeah we kicked ass, but we followed your orders. That victory was your first of many to come, my friend. I will go to battle with you any time and any place."

The team let out a collective cheer of approval.

"Was that an apology or something?" asked Pistol smoke.

"That was about as close as an apology that you will ever hear Gatlin say," replied Xtract. "I'm not sure that he knows that word or its meaning. But I guess you could ask Blade when we get back stateside if she has ever heard him say that he was sorry."

*   *   *

After traveling about another hour, the team was now twenty-two miles into the cave. They had still come across no forks, no turns, no intersections, and not a sign of Nuke. It appeared to the team that there was only one way in and one way out of this cave.

"HOLD UP! HOLD UP! Xtract," yelled GrizzLee from atop the chair of P-2.

Xtract stopped P-2. Bolt-action, seeing P-2 stop, stopped too. GrizzLee climbed down from the chair and to the cave floor. He began to examine the ground along the pathway.

"What are you looking at, Lee?" asked Gatlin.

"Sir, you might want to come see this," GrizzLee replied. "It looks like we are not the only beings in this cave. There are footprints. They're going down the same direction that we're traveling. I'm not sure when or where they began. I just noticed them. The tracks are going both down and up the path here, see."

"Man, what kind of tracks are they, Lee?" asked Gatlin.

Now the rest of the team was—except Pistol Smoke, who was still in P-2—was looking at the footprints as well.

"Sir, those would be, if I am not mistaken footprints of a group of yeti—possibly a family," answered GrizzLee.

"Oh, man, are they dangerous to humans?" asked Pistol Smoke. "Or are they shy like everybody is always saying on TV?"

"We don't need this—not now, not here," said Bolt-action.

"To answer your question Smoke, I am not really sure if they're dangerous," said GrizzLee. "I remember hearing my grandfather talk of the yetis when I was a boy. He never said that they were dangerous or aggressive toward humans. But with what we have found and seen in this cave to this point, I couldn't honestly answer that question. They are animals, and if they are being driven out of their homes or, worst yet, threatened by whoever is responsible for this madness in this cave, I would be willing to bet they might be scared or even mad. In most cases with animals, when that happens, they will become territorial and aggressive. So, yes, they very well could be very dangerous at this point."

"That's just great!" replied Pistol Smoke. "As if giant rock men; flyin', flame-throwing devil birds; medieval skeleton soldiers, and giant, acid-spitting snakes weren't enough, now we have to worry about Bigfoot and an entire colony of Bigfoots, or Bigfeet, whatever you would call them that may or may not be dangerous to humans. That is just fantastic. I'm going to personally kick the shit out of Wrath myself."

"Yetis or no yetis, we have to get moving, find Nuke, and finish this thing. I would say that we have about twenty-three hours at best until evac," said Bolt-action.

As the team moved out once again, GrizzLee asked Xtract, "What if Wrath has the yetis working for him somehow? They are extremely powerful creatures?"

"Man, I don't know, but I wouldn't put it past that sick, twisted bastard," replied Xtract. "I'm concerned about our team. We have some pretty serious wounds that really need to be taken care of in a hospital—any place but a cave. I can keep everyone going to this point, but I'm not sure about infections and things like that. Another concern is fuel. We have burned a lot of fuel on this one. We need to make sure that we have enough to get back to the LZ for pickup."

The path began to widen a bit as the team traveled deeper downward into the cave.

"Is it just me or is the path getting wider as we go?" said Xtract.

"It appears so," replied Gatlin.

The cave was becoming more and more of a mystery to the team. They had traveled deep into its bowels and there were still no signs or traces of Nuke. An uneasy feeling settled on the team. They all did what they always did—continued their own private prayers to God, praying they would find Nuke and that he would be fine and that all of them could return home alive.

*   *   *

"Hold up," ordered Bolt-action.

The team had come to the first fork in the path.

"What do you want to do, bud?" asked GrizzLee.

"Well, big 'en, I think it is time for a quick meeting of the minds. Gather up and let's get some kind of plan for this next move," Bolt-action ordered.

The team gathered for a tailgate meeting to decide what the next move was going to be.

"What do you think, Bolt-action?" asked Gatlin.

"Well, man, it's like this. We just haven't had a whole lot of success running recon teams during this operation. Our options are either send out a three-man recon team and have the other two hang back, or we just pick a direction and all of us go in that same direction. But if we choose the latter, we don't know how far the path goes or if we're heading in the right direction to find Nuke, Wrath, or get out of here. We are starting to run a little low on fuel, not to mention very short on time. So I'm going to leave this one up to you, Gatlin, and always I will trust your decision. I'm sure that I speak for everyone here when I say that. So this one is up to you, sir," said Bolt-action.

"Is that right?" asked Gatlin, looking around at the team. "Everyone, do you want me to make the call? Or does anyone else have any input on what we are faced with?"

"Boss, we all believe in you, even if you are wounded and a little out of it due to the drugs," GrizzLee assured him. "We trust you; whatever you decide, that's what we'll do. I'm with you all the way, always. I'm sure everyone else feels the same way."

Collectively and wholeheartedly, the team agreed.

"All right, then we go left. Bolt-action, lead the way," ordered Gatlin.

The team took the path to the left and continued to head deeper down into the cave.

The team rolled deeper into the darkness, lit only by flickering torchlight. After awhile, GrizzLee, atop the chair of P-2, had Xtract stop the Puma again. "Hold up. Do you hear that?" he said. "That's moving water. We're coming up on a body of water down toward the end of this path. I can smell it."

The rest of the team agreed that they could neither hear nor smell water. All they could smell was the musky cave.

"Y'all are just going to have to trust me on this one. I hear and smell water up ahead," said GrizzLee. "I'm sure of it."

"Well, you're the one with the animal instincts," said Xtract. "We believe you. Let's get moving."

"Yeah, let's get a move on and find out exactly what Lee is hearing and smelling," agreed Gatlin. "Let's go."

About a half mile deeper into the cave, the team reached a huge opening in the cave. Sure enough, approximately fifty yards down below them, they found a very large body of water being fed by an enormous waterfall, apparently from an unknown mountain river.

"GrizzLee was right on the money," said Bolt-action. He paused, taking in the scene. "Okay, so what is this all about?" He didn't have to point out that the huge pool of water being fed by a giant beautiful waterfall looked like a painting. "What does this mean?" he wondered.

"Well, I guess that's why we're here," he continued, thinking out loud, "to . . . *Oh my God*. Look over there, they're yetis. My God, they do exist. What are they doing?"

After a moment, he answered his own question. "They're dragging the pool for . . . *gold*," he gasped. "There's gold in the pool, and the yetis are working as slaves for Wrath. There is no other explanation."

"Wrath has found gold in the Himalayan Mountains. Who would have thunk?" commented Xtract. "How in the hell did Wrath know to look in Asia for gold in this particular cave?"

"Okay so he found gold. Who gives a shit how? I say we go down there and set the yetis free," suggested Bolt-action. "Hell, I can't see anything that is keeping them from leaving."

"Yeah, Lee, you could probably communicate with them," said Pistol Smoke. "You look more like them than anything that I have ever seen before. No offense, Lee."

"There's your answer," said Xtract, pointing to the left of the yetis. "Demon Troopers at 10 o'clock roughly a dozen and a half of them. They're all packin' small arms. Let's take the bastards out."

"Yeah, but you're looking at about twenty-five yetis. What if the yetis are on their side? Then we are way outnumbered," said Bolt-action.

"I'm not killing any yetis. No way. No matter what happens," GrizzLee said firmly.

"I don't know. What do you think, Lee? Will the yetis take a side in a battle if we attack those assholes down there?" asked Gatlin.

"I'm not sure. But from what I've seen, I'd conclude that Wrath has come into their territory and enslaved them. I think it's worth a shot. I say we take out the Demon Troopers and hope for the best," GrizzLee replied.

"Yeah that sounds good. Gatlin, you're back in charge of this op. Tell us where you want us and what you want us to do," said Bolt-action.

"Yeah, okay, listen up. Bolt-action, you take Smoke with you. Find a good spot and begin pickin' them off with your sniper rifles. The rest of us will join in and finish them off. Let's move," ordered Gatlin.

Bolt-action and Pistol Smoke were in position.

"On my mark," said Bolt-action. He had a Demon Trooper in his crosshairs. "Mark!" he said, as he squeezed the trigger. Pistol Smoke did the same. *Boom, Boom,* two shots and two headless Demon Troopers.

At the sound of the shots, the yetis all scrambled for cover. The Demon Troopers did the same.

"It's on!" yelled Gatlin as he and GrizzLee, along with Xtract, joined in on the slaughter of the Demon Troopers.

Bolt-action and Pistol Smoke continued to pick off Demon Troopers with eerie precision. In just minutes, it was over as fast as it had started. The air was full of the fresh stench of gunpowder.

"Good job," said Gatlin.

The team maneuvered its way down to the water's edge. While the team checked the dead bodies of the Demon Troopers, the yetis began to emerge from behind the team. The team simply looked at the very large, clearly strong, hairy beings. The yetis simply looked back. The two sides stared at each other for several minutes, not knowing exactly what the other group was thinking or whether they were friend or foe.

GrizzLee heard a voice. He followed it to a Demon Trooper that was not yet dead but very badly wounded. "What are you saying?" GrizzLee demanded as he picked the Demon Trooper's head up off the ground. "Say it again."

"The Digger is coming," the Demon Trooper gasped. "The Digger will kill you. He will kill you all," the trooper promised with his dying breath.

"What was he saying?" asked Bolt-action.

GrizzLee told the others what the Demon Trooper had said about The Digger. "Whatever that means?"

Waves and bubbles suddenly formed within the cave pool. The yetis all begin to retreat, soon disappearing from sight once again. The team gathered around the vehicles.

"What's going on now?" asked Xtract.

"I'm not sure, but arm up and take cover," Gatlin ordered his team. "Lee, get on the chair. X, take P-2's. The rest of y'all be prepared for whatever the hell is about to come out of that water."

"What in the hell is that?" asked Bolt-action.

As the team focused on the pool it became clearer and clearer to everyone that whatever the Demon Trooper had warned was coming would be here soon. The waves, now heavier and more violent, began to crash against the shore of the beautiful cave lake.

"Be ready," ordered Gatlin. "On my mark."

"What in the hell is that damn thing?" asked Pistol Smoke.

A head broke the surface. Within seconds, "The Digger" had emerged. Standing four stories tall, the creature towered over the team. Its hairless body and outer skin, tough and thick like that of an alligator, was covered with fishy scales. The apparently amphibious creature had extremely large, slightly webbed hands. At the tips of its giant fingers were unbelievably sharp and long claws, seemingly used for digging. The creature's face was like no other. Although it did have two eyes, two ears, a nose, and a mouth, the face was slightly deformed. The creature's eyes were yellow, and it blinked side to side, rather than up and down, much like lizards. Its mouth was very large, much larger than its other facial features, with gigantic teeth, some that were very sharp, some that looked to have been broken off, and others that were just jagged. The Digger's shoulders seemed as broad as mountainsides, its arms as wide, as large, and as strong as the great redwoods. The abs of the mighty creature reminded the team of the rolling hills of South Carolina. The last thing that astonished and amazed the team from what they could see at this time was the beast's thighs; they resembled two vertical zeppelins.

Whatever, this creature—this digger, this giant monster from the depths of the cave lake—none of the team had ever seen such a dominant-looking force. Never, in all of their battles, against all of the many foes they had faced, had they come up against something that compared to what the team saw standing in front of them now. This creature was an extraordinary being.

The team tried not to appear intimidated by their very impressive opponent. The harder they tried, the harder it became to not just stare in awe of this mighty digger.

Suddenly The Digger, for no clear reason, let out a bloodcurdling roar that literally caused rocks to fall from the walls of the cave and splash into the lake below.

"Everyone, move back, slowly," said Gatlin. "Do not make any sudden movements. Maybe his vision is poor. Stay sharp and close to your weapons. Do not let him know that we are not here as friends. Obviously, we are gonna have to take this thing out before we can move on. I'm just not real sure exactly how in the hell we are supposed to do that right now. Honestly, I wasn't expecting something like this. Wrath is pulling out all the stops on this one. That's for damn sure."

Just as Gatlin finished his instructions, The Digger let out another terrifying roar. This time, the creature began to move a little closer inland toward the team. Rocks again fell from the cave walls and ceiling, splashing into the lake below.

The team moved slowly to what appeared, at first, to be a safe distance from The Digger. GrizzLee remained atop P-1, and Xtract remained atop P-2. The rest of the team roamed on foot, looking for cover and an open shot on the giant.

The Digger, obviously able to see pretty well, watched the team. It was clearly surveying each member and totally aware of what was going on. It seemed to be sizing up the team, watching the men get into position for a possible attack. The Digger's head and eyes moved with speed and focus, and the team saw intelligence and no signs of confusion behind those eyes. Intelligence was something the team had never had to face in one of Wrath's creations.

The Digger continued to move toward the ever-shortening shoreline.

"Okay, guys," said Gatlin, "if he continues to move toward the shore, we're gonna have to take him down. The next step he takes toward either of us, open up with everything. And don't stop until he does. Remember, short, controlled bursts. We don't know how stable these walls are here. So be sharp. Stay frosty.

"Lee you and X take out those unbelievable legs, with nonstop 80mm fire. The rest of us will, hell, I guess hit him everywhere else and see what that does. ON MY MARK!" ordered Gatlin.

The awesome creature took another step, the step that started another battle for the team.

"MARK! FIRE, FIRE!" ordered Gatlin.

The team opened fire on The Digger. GrizzLee and Xtract began pounding hundreds of 80mm cannon rounds into The Digger's massive legs. Bolt-action and Pistol Smoke, from their sniper positions, began their assault on the impressive beast's head and neck area. Gatlin took his fury out on the digger's upper body, ripping large chunks of the monster from its chest and stomach.

The Digger roared and screamed in pain and confusion as the team continued its bombardment of awesome firepower into the creature. The Digger raised his mighty arms up and slammed them down into the water, pounding the shoreline with tidal wave-sized blasts of water. Blood and flesh continued to litter the water beneath the mighty beast, as the attack from the team was relentless.

Still, The Digger continued to move toward the shore. Bolt-action scored an eye shot with his awesome .80 caliber sniper rifle, which sat atop a 203 grenade launcher. The Digger once again screamed in agony, grabbing its left eye and swinging its head around toward the direction of the shot. Using all the strength in its massive and powerful right arm, the mighty Digger slammed its giant fist into the cave wall, hitting just below the spot from which Bolt-action had fired the shot. That really got things going. The cave walls began to crumble under Bolt-action's feet. Bolt-action struggled to regain his footing.

Unable to match the eye shot of Bolt-action because the beast had its back to him Pistol Smoke took a shot and hit The Digger in the left ear. All the while, GrizzLee and Xtract continued to try and cut the legs out from under the enormous creature with the awesome power of the Pumas' 80mm cannons. The pair of cannons was blowing huge holes in The Digger's legs.

Using his 30mm arm cannons, Gatlin was littering the lake below the creature with blood and flesh. All the while, he searched for the open throat shot that he hoped would drop this creation of Wrath's.

The Digger grabbed at its ear but only for a moment. The beast had only one thing on its mind, and that was Bolt-action. Bolt-action, at this point, was unable to put up any kind of fight due to his desperate struggle to regain his footing. He searched desperately for some solid ground to keep himself from falling to the floor of the cave below, or worse, into the cave lake that was now polluted with The Digger's blood, flesh, and bone.

Seeing that Bolt-action was losing his fight to regain his footing as the walls and floors around him crumbled, the team unloaded on The Digger in a desperate attempt to get the creature's attention off of Bolt-action. But there was nothing they could do for Bolt-action. Bolt-action fell to the base of the cave, not only destroying his number one weapon, but shattering his lower left leg. Now most of the bone was outside the skin.

Bolt-action lays right where he landed, in pain and unable to move as swiftly as he needed to. Seeing Bolt-action's struggle to find shelter, The Digger moved in for the kill.

GrizzLee switched from 80mm cannon to howitzer and began to blow even larger holes into the mighty legs of the aggressive giant. He had to draw the creature's attention off of Bolt-action and onto himself. The strategy worked. The Digger, now in even more pain became even more aggressive than before turned to GrizzLee. GrizzLee never let up.

The giant amphibious beast was now noticeably beginning to lose much of its mobility. Seeing that the howitzer rounds weren't causing much damage to the cave walls or ceiling and were causing major damage to The Digger, Xtract switched over to howitzer and joined GrizzLee in the new assault strategy.

Bombarded with the very heavy lead of the howitzer shells, The Digger began to slow considerably. Still, it seemed determined to reach land.

GrizzLee and Xtract continued their massive assault on the creature's legs; larger and larger chunks of the beast littered the waters beneath the enormous body. Some of the chunks of flesh and bone were even beginning to land on the shore. As the rest of the team continued the assault,

Gatlin waited for that throat shot. But the opportunity simply didn't present itself. So he continued to blow tissue and flesh from the ever-slowing beast as it tried to reach the shoreline.

Pistol Smoke continued to score hits to The Digger's head. He too was looking for the deadly shot that would end this battle and allow the team to go to Bolt-action's aid. Pistol Smoke's shots found the ear and the back of the beast's neck.

Once again, in great pain, the creature slammed its mighty fist into the ever shallower water of the cave lake. More rocks and boulders tumbled from the walls, some actually striking the hidden yetis.

The Digger was almost to the shore. Gatlin's 30mm assault finally began to tear into the beast's right shoulder, which soon resembled ground beef. There wasn't much left of The Digger's shoulders.

Gatlin's guns began to overheat and cut out just as he found an opportunity to hit a target that had been very hard to hit—the beast's throat. He wasn't even sure that a throat shot would stop this beast, but he damn sure wanted to try.

None of the team had ever seen such a creature take so much punishment and still be on the attack. With Gatlin's guns overheating and cutting out and Bolt-action lying unarmed and in bad shape and getting worse with every passing moment, The Digger reached the shoreline. After reaching the shoreline, The Digger just laid his upper body on the shore as if he was resting.

"HOLD YOUR FIRE! HOLD YOUR FIRE!" ordered Gatlin.

The team stopped firing. The creature lay on the bank, doing nothing but breathing and bleeding.

"I'm gonna go check on Bolt-action," said Gatlin. "If this thing moves or tries to get back up, end it." He made his way over to his fallen friend.

As Gatlin reached Bolt-action, he saw that his second in command's gun had been ruined and his leg was in bad shape. It looked to Gatlin like Bolt-action's leg was broken in several places. "I need to get you over to X, so he can take a look at that leg and get you fixed up," said Gatlin. "Hold on, man; I'm gonna carry you out of here. It's probably gonna hurt like hell, so hang on to me. I won't drop you, buddy."

As Gatlin worked his way back over to Xtract, Bolt-action over his shoulder and Bolt-action's destroyed weapon in one hand, the yetis began to emerge from their hiding places. There were twenty-five yetis in all, and three of them had been injured by falling boulders.

"Look, Lee," said Xtract, nodding toward the emerging yetis. "What do we do? Shit."

"Nothing," responded GrizzLee. "Don't do anything. Just go meet up with Gatlin and Bolt-action. I'll handle the yetis."

Gatlin laid his injured partner down on the shoreline, and Xtract knelt at the wounded warrior's side. "It's pretty clear that you have more than one broken bone there, dude," he said gently. "I'm going to have to put you in an immobilizer after I reset them the best that I can. I'll ask you before I do anything. Do you want morphine to ease the pain or do you want to ride it out?"

"What do you think?" said Bolt-action.

"So many badasses. Look, if you start to hurt and the pain is becoming intolerable, just let me know. I can give you a shot that doesn't have a lot of meds in it. You'll still be able to function and you won't feel so drugged up," said Xtract.

"I appreciate that, man, I really do," said Bolt-action. "Just reset the bones, so I can get back in action before something else happens. I don't want to be so vulnerable. You know what I mean, man."

"Gotcha," said Xtract. And he got to work resetting the bones in Bolt-action's leg.

Gatlin returned to the shoreline and stood next to GrizzLee. Together, they inspected the enormous body of the fallen Digger. "What are we supposed to do with this gigantic body of rage and destruction?" asked GrizzLee.

"I'm not sure about that one, Lee," replied Gatlin. "But what do you think we should do about the yetis?"

GrizzLee took a deep breath and met his leader's gaze. "Well, I think we just fix up the wounded yetis, if they allow us too. Then we let them go on with their lives. They pose us no threat, and I'm sure they're not hostile. If they were, they would have done something by now. I say we let them go and wish them well."

Just as GrizzLee stopped talking, one of the yetis walked up to GrizzLee and dropped something at GrizzLee's feet. "Hey look, Gatlin, its Nuke's headset," GrizzLee said.

"Where did you get this thing?" Gatlin demanded.

GrizzLee looked at Gatlin kinda funny.

"What am I sayin'? Son of a bitch, they can't understand a damn word I'm sayin'. Shit," said a very frustrated Gatlin as he looked at his brother's headset.

"I'll try and get something out of them, Gatlin. Just take it easy," said GrizzLee gently. "We'll see what we can do. Don't go ballistic on them or me. Please."

"Yeah, man. I'm sorry. I just need to find him, you know," replied Gatlin.

"We will find Nuke," said GrizzLee.

Gatlin just turned and walked away from both GrizzLee and the yeti. He had to wipe his face, so the team couldn't see the wetness under his eyes.

The team knew what their leader was doing, as well as how he was feeling. The entire team felt the same way. They needed to shed a tear for Nuke, and they all had or would on their own time and in their own place, each trying to keep one another from witnessing his toughness melt, his softer side revealed. Everyone knew the fact that Nuke was

Gatlin's little brother added another layer to their already, many layers of fears.

Xtract finished with Bolt-action, and the two found seats on the back of the Puma.

"What's going on, Lee?" asked Xtract.

"Not much, man. One of the yetis just brought Nuke's headset to me and Gatlin. Gatlin has it right now," answered GrizzLee.

"Hell yeah," said Xtract. "Do we know where Nuke is at or what?"

"Man, you're as bad as Gatlin. The yetis can't speak, and if they did, do you really think that we could understand? If they spoke at all, I would think they would speak Chinese, given where they live. And since none of us speak or understand Chinese, it really doesn't matter if they speak anyway, right," said GrizzLee.

"You're right man. Hell, Lee, I just wasn't thinking. What are we going to do? Do you have any ideas on how we can communicate with them?"

"I guess I could try and communicate with them by using sign language and some objects and movements," suggested GrizzLee. "But that's really all that I know to do. I just think that Gatlin is going to blow a gasket if we don't find Nuke soon, especially now that we have his headset."

"Lee, just do what you can, man. Gatlin will understand. Go on. Give it a try. Hell, it's better than anything the rest of us could or have come up with," Xtract told him. "I'll go and talk to Gatlin while you do your thing with the yetis."

"Yeah, thanks, man. Thanks a lot, Xtract," said GrizzLee.

"Lee, if you are successful, try and tell them that we will give their injured medical treatment, if they will let me," said Xtract as he turned and walks over to where Gatlin was standing alone, looking out over the clear blue-green waters of the cave lake.

"Hey check it out, Bolt-action. Lee is trying to talk to the yeti dudes," said Pistol Smoke.

"Right on, Lee," said Bolt-action.

"Hey, guys, you might want to get over here as fast as you can," GrizzLee called after a moment. "I believe that we have broken the communication barrier with our new friends here."

Gatlin ran over to GrizzLee, followed by Xtract. "What's up Lee? What have you found out so far?" asked a very excited Gatlin.

"Well, Xtract is going to administer medical attention to their injured. I believe that I got that across to them," GrizzLee said. "I believe that we understand each other enough that we have communicated that. I also think that they either know where Nuke is or where he was. I'm not sure, but I'm hoping that when we're finished helping their injured and they realize that they can truly trust us and that we're not here to harm them but to help them, they will either tell us where he is or maybe even take us to him.

"But, Gatlin, you have to understand I'm not sure about anything concerning Nuke. So let's try and not get too fired up about it. Pistol Smoke get the Puma over here so that Xtract can give our new friends some medical attention. Gatlin just bear with me on the rest. I will keep trying to get through to them on what we really need in terms of Nuke."

"I hear ya, Lee," Gatlin agreed. "I know you're doin' the best that you can for Nuke, me, and us. I'm sorry if I sound like I'm not grateful. I am extremely grateful for what you are doin'. I'm sure that no one else has ever communicated with a yeti. So just overlook any bad things that I might say or do. It's just me trying to cope with the situation. It's nothing against you or anyone else on the team, or the yetis, for that matter."

"No problem, boss. I know what you are like; you are very passionate about family and your team. I said it before, and I'll say it again. We are going to find Nuke, I guarantee you that" GrizzLee assured him.

Xtract began to work on the injured yetis shortly after Pistol Smokes arrived with the Puma. Pistol smoke helped out a little, but he couldn't get over the shock that yeti existed and that he was standing within an arm's reach of a family or community of them. "This is wild," he said. "I never in my life would have ever believed anyone could prove without a doubt that yetis exist, much less that I would be a part of the discovery. This is great. I think that I'm not as freaked out about them as I was earlier." Looking back at the Puma, he saw that Bolt-action was sleeping in the back.

*　　*　　*

Thirty minutes later, Xtract finished putting a breakaway splint on a small yeti's leg. Xtract's work was now done. The yetis' injured had all been cared for.

GrizzLee continued to communicate with the larger yeti who seemed to be the leader of the group.

When The Digger raised its head up, the team armed themselves once again. The Digger just looked at them and slowly slid its gigantic body back into the depths of the cave lake without incident.

Xtract helped the small yeti back over to the four other yetis that were standing in front of what appeared to be an opening in the side of the cave wall. The larger yeti stopped and looked back at GrizzLee. He looked back at the four yetis and the hole in the side of the cave and then once again turned to GrizzLee.

"Hey, Lee, the big one is trying to tell you something," said Xtract. "I think he wants you to follow him and his friends over there."

GrizzLee walked toward the yetis. The yetis all turned and begin to walk into what appeared to be another smaller cave. GrizzLee followed as the rest of the team looked on. All were still in a bit of shock that these mythical creatures not only existed but were communicating with one of their own. The yetis and GrizzLee disappeared into the smaller cave.

"If I hadn't seen it for myself, I would never believe this," said Xtract.

"Yeah no shit, X. You and me both," said Gatlin as he and Xtract walked over and joined Pistol Smoke and Bolt-action at the Puma.

For about fifteen minutes, Gatlin, Xtract, Pistol Smoke, and Bolt-action discussed their wounds, the most recent battle, and the yetis. From the smaller cave, the yeti group and GrizzLee reappeared.

"Gatlin," said GrizzLee as Gatlin got up from the tailgate of the Puma.

"What's up, Lee?" asked Gatlin.

"He's in there. Nuke is in there," GrizzLee said, holding up a hand before Gatlin could react. "He's all right. He's in some kind of holding cell. He didn't see me, but I saw him. We have to get in there and get him out before the Demon Troopers return."

"Oh, hell yeah guys thank God for that one fellas. Outstanding work; really, Lee, you are an amazing asset to this team." Gatlin took a deep breath before giving his orders. "Pistol Smoke, you stay here with Bolt-action. Xtract, you come with Lee and me. We're goin' after Nuke and getting that fucker Wrath so we can get home."

Moments later, the three-man team, gear and weapons ready, returned to the smaller cave. This time, the yetis remained outside. The trio reached the entrance to the holding cell area. It was covered with iron bars and the stone walls of the cave.

"Get on it, X," ordered Gatlin.

Xtract pulled from his belt a small cutting torch no bigger than a hot glue gun and began to cut through the iron bars. In just minutes, the two-inch iron bars were cut. There was now a hole in the bars big enough for himself and Gatlin to fit through. The entire set of bars weren't large enough for GrizzLee to fit through, so GrizzLee stayed back at the entrance to the holding cell area.

Xtract and Gatlin dropped into the holding cell. "Damn, this place is huge," said Gatlin.

"No shit," replied Xtract.

"Stay low and sharp," Gatlin ordered. "We have to find Nuke and get the hell out of here. I don't *even* like this place."

Two minutes passed. "Gatlin, check it out. There's Nuke. How in the hell are we supposed to get in there?" He paused and lowered his voice. "Oh shit, look, Demon Troopers. Four, five, six, shit six of them," he counted, "and they're armed with automatic weapons."

"I'll show you. Follow my lead," Gatlin mouthed back.

Gatlin grabbed the first Demon Trooper to pass their path. With one fluid motion, he snapped the trooper's neck like a twig. Gatlin then dragged the demon's lifeless body out of sight. He looked up at Xtract and grinned. "That's how we're gonna do it. No shooting. There's no tellin' exactly how many of these assholes there are down here. It's only you and me, and they have Nuke. We are on total stealth."

A couple of seconds later, three more Demon Troopers were coming down the hallway. They had Nuke with them. One walked in front of the group, followed by two on either side of Nuke holding each of his arms. Nuke was gagged, and his arms were tied behind his back. His feet were bound as well.

As the group approached, Xtract grabbed the leader and, just as Gatlin had done with the other trooper, snapped his neck in a single motion. At the very same time, Gatlin popped up behind the other two, grabbed their heads, and smashed their heads together. They also fell lifeless to the hallway floor.

Gatlin picked Nuke up from the floor and untied his brother's feet, though he didn't untie Nuke's hands or remove his gag. Meanwhile, Xtract finished the other two Demon Troopers off, snapping their necks as well.

The rescue was a success. The three returned to the hole in the cage's wall where GrizzLee was waiting. Gatlin and Xtract helped Nuke up to the hole, and GrizzLee pulled Nuke through. Xtract and Gatlin followed, GrizzLee helping both of them through.

GrizzLee successfully led the team back out to the shoreline. The six-man team was reunited once again, and for the first time in a long time, they were at full strength, not counting their various wounds. The team was now set to finish this operation and return home.

Back at the shoreline next to P-1, Gatlin finally removed the gag and untied Nuke's hands.

"Man, where in the hell have you dudes been?" asked Nuke. "I was going after Gatlin. Then I was struck on the back of the head by what I found out to be, after I came to, a damn shit-eatin' Demon Trooper. There has to be better than thirty of them shitheads down there. They took my weapons, I guess, 'cause I woke up in an underground freakin' prison with nothing but what you see—the clothes on my back. Man, it is so damn good to see y'all. I knew that y'all would come eventually, although, I have to say, it took you a hell of a lot longer than I thought it would. But what the hell; we're all here now."

Xtract began checking Nuke out and gave him something to eat. "Dude, you have no idea what the hell we've gone through to find your little ass. Remind me to tell you all about it when we are back home and I am kickin' your dumb young ass," said Bolt-action as he rubbed his hands through Nuke's hair, messing it up even more than it already was.

Just then, the larger yeti began to pull on GrizzLee's arm. GrizzLee looked at the yeti and then followed him back into the cave from which they'd just returned with Nuke.

"Where's Lee going?" asked Nuke. "Oh yeah, I was going to tell y'all that you don't need to be afraid of the yetis. They're actually pretty cool for something that doesn't talk or understand a damn word you say to them. I know they saved my life on a couple of occasions during my stay down there."

Nuke paused, he bit his lip. "Man, we have to help the others who are still down there. There has to be at least twenty-five of them still down there," he said.

"What all did you see?" Gatlin wanted to know. "Who is responsible for this? Is it Wrath by himself or does he have someone else besides the Demon Troopers helping him out?"

"No, the best that I could tell, it's just Wrath and the shit eaters," Nuke replied. "But, man, I think that they might kill the other yetis that are still down there. Wrath has enslaved them, and they are digging and working themselves to death digging all kinds of tunnels. There are all kinds of hidden pathways and tunnels all through this cave. They can travel all over without ever even being seen or using the main pathway that we were following. There's really no telling where in the hell they're all at—the yetis as well as the Demon fuckers."

"What do you want to do, Gatlin?" asked Bolt-action.

"Well, I guess . . ." Gatlin scratched his chin. "I'll be damned," he said when he saw GrizzLee and the yeti returning with Nuke's weapons and gear.

"Well here you go, little man," said GrizzLee turning the gear over to Nuke. "They had it put away and guarded by those troopers. I guess he must have gone down to where we got you. In about three minutes, he returned carrying all of your gear. I assume that the troopers that you guys took out were the same ones guarding your gear."

"Man, if I hadn't seen it for myself, nobody could have convinced me of what I just witnessed," said Xtract. "Hell,

Lee, you have friends in high places. I think they even understand you."

"Well, Xtract, from what I've seen the yetis seem to trust us all. It's not only me who has friends here. I'm thinking that we all have a lot more new friends," GrizzLee replied.

Gatlin was ready to get moving. He walked over to P-1, where Nuke was getting himself reacquainted with his gear. "Nuke," he asked, "do you know if those underground tunnels that you were in lead to Wrath? Or do we take the main path that we've been following ever since we got into this stinky, musky-ass place?" he asked.

"I don't know about Wrath, but I do know that a few miles down those tunnels, they do eventually come out to a pretty good-sized path, almost as big as a road. It could very well be the main path that we have been traveling, but I can't say for sure," answered Nuke.

"Can you get us there?" asked Gatlin.

"Oh yeah, no problem, but we have to free the yetis that are still down there," Nuke insisted. "I know that when the others find those dead Demon Troopers and realize that I'm gone, they'll be all kinds of pissed-off. They might kill 'em."

Gatlin just nodded and walked back to the others. "What's up, boss?" asked GrizzLee. "What's on your mind? You got a plan or something? I'm not going to be able to fit through that hole we cut in those bars. I know that the Pumas aren't going that way. Plus, we can't carry Bolt-action down through there."

"Yeah I know, Lee. This is what we're gonna do," Gatlin replied. "Nuke knows the tunnels well enough to lead a team through there and find out exactly what is goin' on. We will free the remaining yetis, and more importantly, we can take out the rest of the Demon Troopers. Nuke said there's about twenty-five or thirty of the yetis still down there. Nuke will show Smoke and me the way through the bowels of this cave, using the tunnels. Hopefully, the tunnels will eventually come out and join back up with the main pathway. That's where the three of us will meet back up with you three. Shit." He paused. "The only problem we have with that is that X is the only one who can drive, and we have two Pumas."

"Do you think that you can drive P-2, Lee?" asked Nuke.

"No, hell no," replied Bolt-action. "Lee can't drive a grocery cart. No offense, Lee. X can drive P-1, and I'll drive P-2. Lee can ride with me or X in the gunner's chair."

"No offense taken," said GrizzLee.

"Well that sounds all good and shit, but, Bolt-action, you seem to be forgetting that you have only one leg that's worth a shit," said Gatlin. "You'll have to switch to automatic transmission."

"Hell, man, it's the only way," replied Bolt-action. "I'll just have to stop and switch it back to standard so I can pull the PTO to fire the 30s and laser from inside. I can handle that.

"Y'all are not even going to leave me out of this one," he added. "So, Gatlin, make the call so that we can get on with the damn thing."

"Bolt-action, I've never questioned your toughness, so if you say that you can drive her, hell you got my vote," said Gatlin. "That's the plan. Let's get this show on the road."

"I can do it," Bolt-action assured him.

"All right, let's get goin' and get those yetis returned to their family, so that we can get on with what we came here to do—take Wrath and his army down," said Gatlin.

"You heard the man. Now let's move," said Nuke.

"Oh hell, Nuke, shut your young, dumb ass up. Nobody is listening to you," said Bolt-action.

"I know," Nuke said. "I just always wanted to do that, and the timing was right then."

"Oh my God, let's go," said Gatlin.

With that, the team motioned to the yetis that they were leaving and tried to show them their gratitude. Then the two three-man recon squads headed out on their individual missions. Nuke led the first squad back down into the tunnels, followed by Gatlin, with Pistol Smoke covering the rear, still limping very badly from his burns.

The second squad—led by Xtract in P-1, with Bolt-action driving P-2, despite his condition, and GrizzLee in the gunner's chair—waved good-bye, for what it was worth, to the yeti group and began working its way back to the main path. They hoped this path would lead them to meet up with first squad in about an hour or two. The team's spirits were high, but an uneasy feeling rested in the hearts of all the team members.

*   *   *

First squad was now right where Gatlin had snapped the first Demon Trooper's neck.

"We need to go right here, then left, followed by two rights, and then another left," said Nuke. "Then I'll have to get my bearings. But that will get us going and, I'm sure, some action."

"Okay, great. Nuke you stay behind me until I tell you different. You got that," ordered Gatlin.

"Yeah I got it, bro," replied Nuke.

Shortly after Nuke fell back and just as Gatlin had expected, six Demon Troopers appeared at the first intersection. Apparently, the troopers were just killing time.

"Okay, this is how I do it, but I better never catch either of you doing it this way," said Gatlin.

Gatlin fell in the middle of the tunnel hallway, landing flat on his face. Nuke and Pistol Smoke hung back in the shadows, out of sight. When the Demon Troopers saw Gatlin lying in the middle of the hallway floor, they left the intersection and came to find out what was going on. The six Demon Troopers reached Gatlin, and four of them got down on one knee. As the other two troopers stood guard, the four on the ground turned Gatlin's lifeless body over onto his back. Gatlin's eyes were open, but he wasn't moving. He just stared straight ahead blankly.

The Troopers tried to get Gatlin to his feet, but it seemed that his legs weren't working. The Demon Troopers decided that two of them were strong enough to carry Gatlin to a cell. One held his feet, and the other held Gatlin under the arms. The Demon Troopers were really paying close attention to the motionless Gatlin. After a few short yards of traveling with their newest inmate, the two Demon Troopers in front went ahead of the others, apparently to open up a cell to house Gatlin.

Seeing his opportunity, Gatlin reached up with his powerful arms and grabbed the neck of the trooper who was holding his upper body. In one motion, he snapped another Demon Trooper's neck. In the next split second, Gatlin used his mighty legs and the shock of the second Demon Trooper to his advantage. He wrapped both legs around the Demon Trooper's neck, pulling him to the floor of the cave. With his awesome guns, Gatlin fires two shots. Each round found their marks in the middle of the foreheads of the two Demon Troopers following, ending each of their days right then and there.

The two Demon Troopers who had moved ahead of the others turned at the sound of Gatlin's guns, and they got holes installed in the middle of each of their foreheads as well. Then with one good, quick twist of Gatlin's mighty legs, the sixth Demon Trooper lay dead. In a matter of forty-five seconds, the hallway was clear.

Pistol Smoke and Nuke reappeared from the darkness.

"Well that's six down and a couple dozen left," said Nuke. "We better get movin'. The others are bound to have heard the shots from that badass gun, which they all know the sound of far too well, Gatlin. Let's go this way."

*   *   *

Second squad was now back on course, traveling along the main pathway of the cave.

"Did you hear that?" said Xtract. "That was Gatlin. They must have met someone or something down there."

"Poor bastards," said Bolt-action. "Those troopers don't stand a snowball's chance in hell against Gatlin's firepower, not to mention that Nuke and Pistol Smoke are with him."

*   *   *

"Good job, dude," said Pistol Smoke. "What's next?"

"Well the best that I can remember is that there are some cells that some of the yetis were in just past this next intersection," said Nuke.

"Just show me the way. This time it's my turn," replied Pistol smoke as he attached suppressers on all four of his pistols. Two Desert Eagles were strapped to his thighs, and two 20mm semiautomatic retractable pistols were attached to each of his forearms, another invention of Stealth's.

The three reached the intersection. "You go to the right. I'm going left to free the dozen or so yetis down there," said Nuke. The main block of guards or whatever you call it is just down your way about thirty meters or so. There are usually about fifteen or more troopers in there at one time, so you should get your chance to show your stuff, Smoke."

Nuke headed off by himself to free the imprisoned yetis, disappearing into the darkness. Pistol Smoke took the tunnel to the right. Gatlin followed about twelve feet behind Pistol Smoke.

Nuke was right. Several Demon Troopers—eighteen to be exact—congregated in the blockhouse.

Pistol Smoke stopped, and Gatlin caught up with him. "Do you think you can take 'em?" asked Gatlin.

"I do believe that I can, big 'en. You cover my back," Pistol Smoke replied with a grin. "I love this shit, don't you, Gatlin?" He patted Gatlin on the shoulder and moved toward the doorway.

Pistol Smoke first took out the two Demon Troopers who were standing at the front door. Two shots, two dead Demon Troopers. The rest of the Demon Troopers took defensive positions. It was too late. Pistol Smoke rolled on the ground in front of the doorway by the fallen Demon Troopers, with guns blazing wide open. Six more shots produced six more dead Demon Troopers.

Without knowing what hit them, the remaining ten troopers returned fire toward the doorway, just as Pistol Smoke finished his roll to the other side of the doorway and stood up. He holstered his Desert Eagles and activated his 20mm retractable pistols, while the Demon Troopers blew chunks of cave out from the doorway and walls around him. Pistol Smoke decided to retract one of his pistols and use fragment grenades. He tossed two grenades into the room of Demon Troopers. They exploded the blast killing or maiming the remaining ten troopers. Without hesitation, Pistol Smoke emerged from the hallway with both 20mm pistols wide open and finished off the wounded. The guardhouse was now clear.

Pistol Smoke escaped without a scratch, but his actions caused his previous wounds to bleed again.

"Well done," said Gatlin. "Well done, dude."

"Hey I know; I learned from the best," said Pistol Smoke.

Nuke joined Gatlin and Smoke at what was now the room of death. "I sent the yetis back the way we came, just until we have this place cleared of Demon Troopers," he reported. "Then I'll go back for them and get them the hell out of here when we get out of here."

"What?" said Gatlin. "You can't come all the way back to get those creatures when we're done clearing this shithole. There won't be time."

"Yeah, well, I'm just gonna have to make time. Those so-called creatures saved my life, and given a chance, they would do the same for you. They didn't ask for this shit to happen. Hell, they had nothing to do with it. They're scared shitless of all the guns, especially yours, Gatlin. So yeah I will be coming back for them, with or without y'all," retorted Nuke.

"Hey, let's talk about it later guys," said Pistol Smoke. "We have company coming."

Gatlin and Nuke looked down the hallway. Coming toward the trio were better than forty Demon Troopers.

"Oh, man, that ain't shit. Look out," said Nuke as he aimed his custom-made bazooka. Nuke's bazooka was no bigger than and resembles a sawed off shotgun. He carried it in a holster on the side of his leg, and he could draw and fire it like one would a pistol.

"*No!*" yelled Gatlin.

Boom, boom. The Demon Troopers were separated from each other and some from their body parts.

"Hell yeah!" said Nuke.

"Oh shit!" said Gatlin as he opened his mighty cannons up once again on the oncoming crowd of Demon Troopers.

Pistol Smoke followed suit, and another battle began. Moments later, the threat of the Demon Troopers no longer existed.

"Damn, dudes, I don't think I got to kill any of them bastards," said Pistol Smoke. "Every time I went to pull the trigger, the son of a bitch would fall."

"Why did you freak out so bad, Gatlin?" asked Nuke.

"Because, you dumb shit, what if that damn cannon would have caused a cave-in and we got stuck in this underground maze? What would we do then? Huh?" asked Gatlin, right up in Nuke's face.

"Well it didn't, and they are dead, and we aren't, so calm down. Damn, take it easy, bro," said Nuke.

"Yeah, well you need to think before you just open fire. You are not the only one down here," said Gatlin.

"Oh what are you going to do? Tell on me," Nuke shot back.

"I don't have to tell on you, you dumb shit," said Gatlin as he pushed Nuke back several feet and looked his brother dead straight in the eyes.

"Okay, Gatlin, I got it. I'm sorry. I fucked up," said Nuke.

"Let's get the hell out of here," said Gatlin.

"There are two more cells down here," Nuke told them. "Then there's this long hallway that has real shitty lighting. It's the only place down here that really gives me the creeps. Then there are a couple more corners, followed by an opening that must be the front of the prison. There are a dozen and half or so guards there. After that, I think we'll be back out on the main path of the cave—a really wide path anyway."

"Then all we have to worry about is whether the path you're talking about is the same path that the Pumas are on," said Pistol smoke.

"We'll worry about that when we come to it. Look Out!" yelled Gatlin as he fires his weapon, killing four more Demon Troopers.

"What do you say we get a move on and get out of this place?" suggested Pistol Smoke.

"Yeah, let's get a move on. We're beginning to run a little short on time," Gatlin agreed.

The team work its way down through the underground tunnels of the cave prison.

"Hold up here," said Nuke. "Just down here are the last of the prison cells and then the long hallway. Let's get the prisoners first."

"Okay," agreed Gatlin, "but let's step it up. We need to get gone."

Nuke looked into the cells. He saw only dead yetis. The slain creatures were lying everywhere. "They have all been killed," said Nuke, anger rising within him. "Those fuckers slaughtered them all. They must have heard us coming and killed them. Son of a bitch."

"Let's make those bastards pay," said Pistol Smoke. "We'll hunt them down and return the favor in the name of the yetis."

* * *

Back out on the main pathway, second squad came to what appeared to be a large opening in the wall of the cave. As the squad approached the opening, they were fired on.

"They're shootin'," said Xtract. "It's Demon Troopers. Fire!" He opened fire out the window with his 20mm pistols.

Bolt-action began to mow the troopers down with the front-mounted 30mm cannons, after struggling momentarily to switch the Puma from automatic to standard. This allowed GrizzLee to also open up on the Demon Troopers with the awesome 80mm cannon atop the Puma. Second squad had reached the entrance of the cave prison.

* * *

"Do y'all hear that?" asked Pistol smoke.

"Yeah, those are Puma cannons," said Gatlin. "Bolt-action and second squad, are here."

"I have to go back and get the rest of the yetis," said Nuke.

"Ah shit," said Gatlin, turning to Pistol Smoke. "You go on ahead and try and meet up with Bolt-action and second squad. Help them clear the area of Demon Troopers. Nuke and I will backtrack and go free the rest of the yetis."

* * *

"Hold fire! Hold your fire! They're all down," called Xtract.

"Let's go in and clear this place out," said Bolt-action.

Second squad entered the prison, firing a few rounds into a couple of helpless Demon Troopers who had survived the assault at the entrance.

"Hey, Bolt-action, don't shoot. It's me, Pistol Smoke," yelled Pistol Smoke from down the dark, musky hallway.

"Hey, what's up, Smoke?" asked Xtract.

"Not much. You know, same ole shit, different place and time," responded Pistol smoke.

"Where are Gatlin and Nuke?" asked Bolt-action.

"Oh, they went back to get the yetis," Pistol Smoke told them. "They should be getting back pretty soon. There aren't any more Demon Troopers down here. We took care of that on the way up here. Man, I am glad that you guys made it. I damn sure didn't want to have to go back through this shithole again."

"So y'all encountered some resistance, huh?" said Xtract.

"Hell yeah, those bastards were all over the place down here. Nuke's estimation of how many we'd encounter was damn far off on the low end. I don't know about that boy sometimes," Pistol smoke added.

* * *

Approximately fifteen minutes later, Gatlin, Nuke, and the yetis all arrived at the front of the prison.

"Hey, guys have any problem finding the place?" asked Nuke.

"Not really. We kinda drove right to it. It was a hell of a lot easier than I thought it was going to be," said Bolt-action.

After a few minutes, the yetis began to walk out of the cave prison, some carrying their dead. As the yeti group reached the main path of the cave, they turned to the men and just looked at them, as if to thank the Allied Force team for all the team had done. Then the yeti family turned away and walked back along the main pathway, eventually disappearing into the darkness of the cave, their cave.

"Okay guys, listen up," said Gatlin. "We're about nine and a half hours until evac. We are about four to five hours away once we get out of this cave, if we leave the same way that we came in, and so far, it looks like the way we came in is the only way to get back outside. So let's get back on track. We still have to find Wrath, if it is indeed Wrath who's behind all this. We all know he aint gonna be guarded by just these stupid fuckin' Demon Troopers. So let's get what we can and get back on track. We are not only running a little low on ammo, but we are pushin' the fuel issue to the max as well. Remember, time is of the essence. Let's move out."

"Uh, guys, while we are all here together, without bullets flying all around our heads, I believe that it's time for everyone to get their wounds cleaned and redressed," said Xtract.

The team all bitched and moaned, but they followed Xtract's recommendations and sat quietly, except for an occasional outburst of profanities when the tape pulled a little too hard. Even for these big, strong warriors, pulling tape from the body hurt. The redressing of the team's wounds took about forty-five minutes.

"Okay, listen up, team," said Gatlin. "We have roughly eight hours and some change to sweep and clear the rest of this cave and apprehend Wrath. So let's get goin' and finish this thing. I really want to see some natural light and get out and away from this smelly-ass cave."

The two squads become one unit once again. In P-1, Xtract drove and Gatlin rode shotgun, with GrizzLee on the chair. Nuke drove P-2, with Pistol Smoke riding shotgun in the cab and Bolt-action up top in the howitzer chair. The team moved out on the regular heading—a heading whose destination none of the team members were sure of. But they pushed on because they had to.

*   *   *

The team had traveled another two hours deeper into the bowels of this seemingly never ending cave, without incident, when they reached a gigantic opening in the cave.

"Lights," ordered Gatlin.

Both Xtract and Nuke switched on their respective Puma's running lights and floodlights at once. The team found itself looking into enormous "room" the size of two Superdomes.

"What in the hell is this place all about?" asked Nuke.

"I'm not sure, but it appears to me that this is the end of the line," surmised Xtract. "There are no more paths to take. This is it."

In the floodlights, the team could see that the ceiling was at least two hundred feet high. The floor was clear of any debris or rocks.

"Let's check it out," said Gatlin.

"Damn, it's kinda like an old Roman coliseum where the gladiators fought the lions and each other back in the day," noted Pistol Smoke, as the unit moved into the enormous space.

"Yeah, no shit," agreed Bolt-action. "I don't like this one bit."

Finishing the drive around the "coliseum," the team had found nothing.

"Let's pack it in and get the hell out of here," concluded Gatlin. "If Wrath was here, he apparently heard us coming and bailed. Guys, I believe we missed him this time. Let's roll, X."

"I heard that. You don't have to tell me twice," said Nuke. "We're going home, people."

"I'm game. Let's get the hell out of here," Xtract agreed.

"Yeah, man," Bolt-action chimed in. "Get me the hell out of here, Nuke."

"I'm with you, sir," said GrizzLee. "I've had enough excitement for one operation."

The team headed toward the large opening in the side of the gigantic room. When they were within twenty yards of it, a gigantic iron door slammed down from the top of the opening to the floor of the room, blocking the team's exit and locking them inside this enormous room.

"What the fuck?" said Xtract.

"Shit," said Gatlin. "Get ready. This one isn't over yet. Take defensive positions."

P-2 followed P-1 as the two Pumas turned back toward the center of the room. P-2 pulled up beside P-1, leaving approximately twenty meters between them. The two vehicles shone their very powerful lights on the far wall of this gigantic cave room, opposite the iron door that had slammed shut in front of them. The two high-powered floodlights scanned the upper walls of the room.

When P-2's light bounced off the far wall, all the team members saw the same thing at the same time. Approximately fifty yards to the west of the team, a very large iron door, much like the one that had slammed down in front of them and locked them in the room, screeched slowly open. This door reached about forty feet up the side of the cave wall.

No more than a few seconds later, two more giant iron doors began to open. These two doors, some ten feet lower, flanked the first door. The three doors opened very slowly, and the team looked on in amazement of what was taking place right in front of them—of the technology in a remote cave in the middle of nowhere. The team had no idea what lay behind the three gigantic iron doors. But they all knew that they were about to find out.

"Arm up," ordered Gatlin.

GrizzLee and Bolt-action readied the powerful howitzers, while Pistol Smoke and Xtract manned the 30mm cannons from inside the cabs of P-1 and P-2.

"Nuke, grab all the ammo that you can carry," ordered Gatlin. "You and I are gonna take the 'rover' roles in this one. We will fight on foot and give them some mobile targets to try and keep them, whatever the hell they are, from just teeing off on the Pumas."

Nuke, with as many bazooka and RPG rounds as he could carry, readied himself for Gatlin's order. Gatlin armed himself with several clips for his MFG-25. His guns were ready, his left in mint condition and his right slightly damaged from the long fall from the back of the stone giant, which seemed to him and his team to have been a lifetime ago. The right gun was still working at about 60 percent efficiency. It would just have to do. That was as well as the team could prepare for what they were about to face from behind the three, large iron doors.

As the team gazed on, the three large doors continued their skyward journey.

"What in the hell is that fuckin' thing?" asked Pistol Smoke as something appeared behind the first door.

"I'm not sure, but there are two more just like him underneath him," said Bolt-action.

"You have got to be shittin' me," exclaimed Xtract. "Those are freakin' dragons. And they're a hell of a lot bigger than the one we fought earlier."

The three large dragons began to walk up closer to the open doors, preparing to take flight.

"Okay, let's put a fifty-meter distance between the two Pumas," said Gatlin. "Get ready to unload on these demon birds. Nuke, you take to the east, and I'll take to the west. We'll just have to kick some dragon ass on the run."

Moments later, just as the Pumas rolled into position, the largest of the three dragons that stood just behind the highest door let out a horrific scream. This particular dragon possessed a wingspan of a little better than forty feet, and it stood close to fifty feet tall. It was the leader, and as it took flight, it was soon followed by the two smaller dragons, each with wingspans of thirty feet in length and standing between thirty-five and forty feet tall. The team was now facing their toughest challenge to date, in a very hostile place, with very little cover.

After several nerve-racking moments of listening to what they had previously thought to be mythical creatures—the dragons flew at a very high altitude, screaming as they circled out of sight at the top of the cave—the team caught a glimpse of the first dragon. It was heading for P-1.

"Let's rock and roll!" ordered Gatlin.

The team opened up on the largest dragon. GrizzLee unleashed the unmatched firepower of P-1's 80mm cannon on the dragon, spraying hot, heavy lead all around the fast-moving creature.

"He's too fast," said GrizzLee. "My rounds can't hit him." He continued firing on the demon bird.

In response, the big dragon blew fire from its mouth, catching the cave floor on fire momentarily.

The entire team was firing on the biggest dragon. Not one of their hundreds of mighty rounds had even hit the dragon yet. Now the smaller two dragons joined in on the fray. They also began to blow fire all over the cave, catching the floor on fire, as well as the walls.

"Damn good thing that they can't shoot worth a shit either, or we'd be in some real deep shit right now," said Nuke.

"Do you not see what they're doing? These sons of bitches can shoot. They can hit whatever they aim at. They are catching everything on fire so that they can see us better and keep us separated for easier pickin's. We need to tighten up on our shooting and lead these bastards with our shots. Shit c'mon, man, they're freakin' animals for God's sake," yelled Xtract.

Nuke and Gatlin continued to maneuver about the cave floor, as the rest of the team continued to fire on the dragons from their stationary positions.

Then from the total darkness of the top of the cave, flying in low and fast, like a kamikaze pilot, one of the smaller dragons swooped down at P-2. Bolt-action was all over it with the firepower of the 80mm cannon. The dragon continued its dive directly toward P-2. The dragon's wing clipped the front of P-2, causing the Puma to rock.

Pistol Smoke, on the 30mm cannons in the cab, was firing on another dragon and didn't realize what was going on. "What in the hell was that?" he asked.

Bolt-action just continues his attack on the dragon, as it now began to regain altitude. This time, Bolt-action's rounds found their mark, ripping into the dragon's wing. The dragon screamed out in agony but didn't seem to slow its flight any.

"Don't worry, Smoke. It was just one of those damn birds getting a little too close and then paying for it. I nailed that bitch," said Bolt-action.

"Right on, B. A.," replied Pistol Smoke as he continued to fire on the other dragons.

Nuke, now approximately ninety feet from the rest of the team, spotted the big dragon swooping down toward GrizzLee on P-1, with its back to him. Nuke fired six, seven, eight bazooka rounds, missing with six, but scoring hits with two. The first struck the large dragon in the rib area. The second hit home in the back, upper part of its leg, blowing chunks of dragon from the sky.

The dragon stopped its descent toward P-1 and began to gain speed on its way up toward the darkness of the cave's ceiling.

GrizzLee turned the awesome 80mm cannon around and opened up on the big dragon. Gatlin, seeing the opportunity, also opened up on the larger dragon with his 30mm cannons. GrizzLee's rounds planted themselves in the same side of the body that Nuke's had. Even some of the nasty 80mm rounds ripped into the dragon's right wing. Gatlin scored hits to the dragon's midsection, as well as its heavily damaged right wing.

The large dragon was in obvious pain; its screams echoed throughout the hollow cave room. However, it was still in flight, and it again disappeared into the darkness.

The two smaller dragons were now flying in tandem. The twin dragons fired on Nuke and P-2, or more specifically, Bolt-action. Nuke ran from the dragons and waited until the evil birds' backs were to him. As they flew over him, Nuke noticed that they were flying at different heights. Nuke fired three RPG rounds, this time into the lower flying of the two dragons. Two rounds hit their targets, one nailing the dragon in its upper leg, the second burrowing into the middle of the mighty flying beast's chest. The hits knocked the dragon's flight plan out of whack, and it seemed to lose control, as it flew awkwardly for several seconds before regaining its composure.

The newly wounded dragon was licking its chest repeatedly as it flew toward P-2 and Bolt-action. Bolt-action once again unleashed his fury into the dragons. The higher flying of the two reached P-1 first, and Bolt-action inflicted the first wounds on this dragon, spraying rounds all across its underside.

Seconds later, the dragon Nuke had hit moments earlier was in sight. Again Bolt-action opened up, and this time, Pistol Smoke joining the attack. Both scored hits all over the dragon's body, using both P-2's 80mm and 30mm cannons. It's hard to say who hit it where, but the dragon now had wounds to its legs and wings, as well as its midsection and possibly its head. Blood fell from the sky like rain, painting P-2's hood and covering Bolt-action in dragon DNA, as the two dragons flew off into the darkness.

"Oh, man! We got 'em good that time, eh dude?" said Pistol smoke.

"Yeah, man, we got 'em," said Bolt-action, "but I got covered in demon bird blood."

"Hey, man, don't shower and let T. J. and X get some of that blood off of you so they can test it back home. You know what I mean?" said Pistol smoke.

"Hell I don't mind wearing this nasty, smelly shit if it means we can score hits like that every time," said Bolt-action. "That means we can get the hell out of here and get back home. Besides, where am I supposed to take a shower anyway? Damn, home; that sounds real good right . . . OH SHIT!"

The larger dragon, seemed to have appeared from nowhere, flamed the P-2, catching the hood and the sides, as well as the ground around the Puma, on fire. Bolt-action got a taste of the power that the dragon possessed, as he was forced to bail out of P-2's chair and onto the hard cave floor below, hurting his already badly broken leg.

From inside P-2, Pistol Smoke opened up on the dragon as it flew off. He wasn't worried about the fire on the hood of the Puma. He knew the armor was made to resist fire damage and that the flames would burn themselves out.

"How you doin', buddy?" Pistol Smoke asked Bolt-action.

He got no response.

"B. A., you okay, man?" Pistol Smoke asked. Again, he received no answer.

Suddenly, the P-2 was engulfed in flames. The flames were dangerously close to the ammunition hold aboard the vehicle.

From the darkness, Nuke emerged and grabbed Bolt-action under each arm, dragging his injured teammate out of harm's way.

Nuke returned to P-2, just as Pistol Smoke was climbing out of the cab. "GET THE FUCK OUT OF HERE. GET OVER THERE BY BOLT-ACTION AND COVER HIM. I'VE GOT TO GET THIS FIRE OUT!" yelled Nuke.

Pistol Smoke went to Bolt-action's side. He handed Bolt-action an M203 grenade launcher, holding onto the M249 SAW.

"Thanks, dude," said Bolt-action, "but I'd rather have my M24."

"Sorry, my friend, I just didn't have time to look for it, and these were right there in the cab with me," said Pistol Smoke. "Man, I'm sorry," he added as he looked in the direction of their abandoned vehicle. "I didn't even know the damn thing was on fire that badly. With the canopy on, I couldn't see you. I had no idea how bad that bitch got us."

"Smoke, don't worry 'bout it man. I'm cool, you're cool, and Nuke is tryin' like hell to get on top of that fire," said Bolt-action. I've got this. I'll cover you both. Go help Nuke."

"Are you sure that you're good, man?" asked Pistol Smoke.

"Go help Nuke, Smoke. That's an order," said Bolt-action.

"I'm on it, sir," said Pistol Smoke. He limped over to P-2 and began to help Nuke fight the fire that was getting way too close to the ammunition. If the ammo were to go, the explosion would not only kill Nuke and Pistol Smoke but possibly Bolt-action, as well as totally destroy nearly half of the team members' remaining ammunition supply, putting them not only short of men but also short on weapons and ammunition. That was just way to big of a price for the team to have to pay. So it was go time.

While Nuke and Pistol Smoke fought the fire on P-2, Bolt-action covered them with the M203.

Across from them, GrizzLee and Xtract fired on the large dragon, which had just reappeared, this time for an apparent attack on P-1. Xtract with the 30mm cannons and GrizzLee with the 80mm cannon ripped into the dragon, just as it blew fire and its napalm down onto the team of P-1.

Gatlin meanwhile was running around firing up into the darkness. As the tandem dragons flew by him, neither attacked. But Gatlin did, blowing the left wing completely off the lower flying of the two. The dragon screamed in agony as its one-winged body dove into the cave floor in an unprecedented display of lack of control. The other continued its flight around the gigantic cave room.

Gatlin and the team now had one of the dragons down. The downed dragon was about sixty yards from Gatlin. Gatlin slowly walked toward the downed creature, firing his 30mm arm cannons into the bleeding and struggling dragon and blowing scales and flesh out of it with every scoring shot. The dragon struggled to get back to its feet, but without both its wings, it just couldn't seem to gain its balance enough to take back to flight. Gatlin's relentless assault on it didn't help either. As Gatlin continued to walk toward the fallen dragon, he fired into the beast—using what he would later call his "walk and rip maneuver" in stories about this day.

From behind Gatlin, the large dragon spots its smaller partner on the ground and witnessed Gatlin blowing holes in its entire body. The large dragon swooped in undetected from behind Gatlin, hitting him in the back with its talons. The talon gashed across Gatlin's back and shoulders, knocking him hard to the floor of the cave.

Gatlin hit the floor about fifty feet from the fallen dragon. The downed dragon spotted Gatlin and blew fire at him. Seeing the action out of the corner of his eye, Gatlin rolled back out of the way and onto his back. But the flames caught him across the legs. Gatlin was able to extinguish the flames quickly by beating them out, using his hands, arms, and guns while he rolled around on the cold floor of the cave. Gatlin was burned but not badly; it could have very well been much worse.

As for the dragon that had inflicted Gatlin's newest wounds, Gatlin could now see its head, so he opened up both his cannons on the face of the dragon. The dragon's fighting days were over.

Gatlin got back to his feet and looked around for the big dragon and the other smaller one but doesn't see either of them. So he headed back toward the Pumas and the rest of the team.

Nuke and Pistol Smoke finally extinguished the flames that had engulfed the P-2, saving the team's ammunition and their own, as well as Bolt-action's life and a very valuable combination of weaponry and transportation.

"How ya doin', Bolt-action?" asked Nuke.

"I'm doing good, just help get me back up there before those damned things come back around," replied Bolt-action.

"Don't you think I should get on the 80 and you get inside on the 30s, just in case you have to bail again?" suggested Pistol smoke.

"Hell no, Smoke. You and Nuke just help get my ass back up in that chair," said Bolt-action. "We aint got time to talk about it like some old men sittin' around talkin' 'bout the fuckin' weather. Now get me up there. That's an order."

Nuke and Pistol Smoke boosted Bolt-action back into the howitzer chair. Pistol Smoke climbed inside the cab and got on the 30mm cannons.

"This time, the canopy is going to be open," said Pistol Smoke. "I have to know what's going on up there, man. I just can't let you do that again, B. A."

"That's up to you, Smoke. But you know that those hot-ass, spent shell casings are gonna land in the cab sometimes. They may even land on you, and like I said, they're hotter than shit," replied Bolt-action.

"That's okay. I'll live with it," said Pistol smoke.

Once the team was all back in position, Gatlin returned to the group. "How's everyone doin'? Are we still kickin' ass?" he asked.

"You know we are," said Pistol smoke.

"What in the hell happened to your back?" asked Nuke.

"Oh that," replied Gatlin. "That big-ass bastard got me from behind, but I got one of the smaller ones."

"You got one, as in dead?" asked Bolt-action.

"Yeah, it's lying over there, some hundred meters or so deader 'an a hammer," said Gatlin, pointing toward the heap of dragon flesh he'd left behind.

"One devil bird down two devil birds to go and they're both wounded," said Pistol Smoke. "Come to think of it, they sure as hell aren't doing much. It's quiet—too damn quiet."

"Yeah it's an eerie quiet, like the calm before the storm," agreed Nuke.

"Gatlin, you need to get over there to P-1 and let X take a look at that gash in your back," said Bolt-action. "It looks bad, dude."

"It's just a scratch," Gatlin protested, "granted, a very large scratch, but still just a scratch. I'll be fine."

"Yeah, but, bro, you're bleeding like a stuck hog," said Nuke.

"Let's not worry 'bout me and start worrying about the damn two dragons that are still out there somewhere, just waiting to attack—because I'm sure that they don't know what quit means—okay!" said Gatlin as he walked off toward P-1.

"I tell you what, man, if you look up the definition of *tough* in the dictionary, you'll find his picture," said Pistol Smoke.

"Really? That's funny," said Nuke, "because just the other day, I looked up the meaning for *asshole*, and I saw his picture there too."

"Oh, c'mon, Nuke, he's just as tough as he has to be. Don't take it personally. He just wants us to stay focused. He loves you, lil man," said Bolt-action.

"Yeah," said Nuke as he reloaded his hip bazooka.

When Gatlin reached P-1, he found the team discussing the whereabouts of the dragons.

"Hey, boss, where you think they disappeared to?" asked GrizzLee.

"Well, Lee, I'm not sure," Gatlin replied, "but they are probably doing, in a way, the same thing we are—regroupin'. What's up, X?"

"Just reloading," said Xtract. "I spent a lot rounds on that little battle man. Gearing up for round two and hoping that it's just a two-round fight. Anyway, how did you do out there afoot?"

"Well, we got one down, I finished him off over in that, I don't know, west northwest corner? He's dead."

"Oh, man, boss, what happened to your back?" asked GrizzLee. "You're bleeding badly."

"It's nothing to look into right now," said Gatlin. "We need to drop two more dragons first."

"Bullshit, Gatlin, that is a bad-looking gash," said Xtract. "Let me look at it or at least clean it up and get some dressing on it."

"Not right now," Gatlin insisted. "You can just as soon as we . . ."

"They are coming back, boss!" yelled GrizzLee.

The dragons were back on the attack, swooping down at the team and causing more chaos. This time, the two remaining dragons were more aggressive. Both blew flames nonstop at the team, catching everything on sight on fire. The roaring fires once again lit up the cave, with flames reaching as high as twenty feet up toward the ceiling, allowing the team once again to see the dragons in the glow.

"I'm tearing into them this time, boss," said GrizzLee. He opened up with the awesome accuracy and firepower of P-1's 80mm cannon, his rounds ripping into both flying fire-breathing creatures.

Blood continued to rain from the sky, onto the team, the floor, and the Pumas, some drops as big as dinner plates.

The dragons returned to the darkness at the top of the cave.

As the team was preparing for another attack, it came. This time, only the big dragon returned for more. Bolt-action and GrizzLee unleashed upon it with both 80mm cannons, as did Xtract and Pistol Smoke with the 30mm cannons. Gatlin and Nuke were still afoot. Nuke blew large holes in the beasts' with his much-faster RPG as soon as he found his range. Gatlin, as always, peppered the body of the dragon with his arm cannons.

The big dragon finished its flyby without inflicting any damage to anything or anyone. The team all realized that its flight had slowed considerably.

"HELL YEAH, WE KICKED ITS ASS THAT TIME!" yelled Nuke as he reloaded his RPG on the run. The custom-made RPG held five rounds at a time.

Just a few moments later, both dragons returned, the big one flying out in front.

"HERE HE COMES AGAIN. DROP HIS FUCKIN' ASS THIS TIME!" yelled Gatlin.

The team filled the dragon with so much hot lead it was sick. Dragon parts flew all over above the team, as the big dragon blew its last flame on its final dive. This dive was into the cave floor below. The dragon's body hit the floor of the cave and rolled several times before finally coming to a stop some thirty yards from P-2.

Just seconds later, dragon parts fell down all over the team. "Oh gross, I'm covered with dragon innards," said Bolt-action. "That's as fuckin' disgusting as you can get."

GrizzLee and the rest of the team got dragon on them as well, just not as much as Bolt-action had. The team all joked with Bolt-action for a couple of seconds. Then it was back to the business at hand—taking down the third and final dragon and putting an end to this battle.

Although the team could not see the third dragon, they could hear it as it disappeared into the darkness of the cave's ceiling. The third and final dragon simply screamed out its agony and anger but refused to stop or show itself to the team. Even though the team could hear the dragon still flying around up in the darkness, it was too high for any of the team to see or get a good shot on it.

"Damn, show yourself, so that we can drop you and put an end to your damn screaming, you big pussy," yelled Xtract.

"How would you feel if you were up against what he is up against and found yourself alone as your mother and brother lay on the floor dead and nobody in this place gave a damn about you?" said GrizzLee.

"I hear ya, Lee, but he's a bully," replied Xtract. "When things go their way, everything is good, but when it all goes to shit, like in this case, well this is what you get. You, Lee, probably don't know anything about being bullied with you size, but I was bullied, and this doesn't bother me one bit."

"Yeah, well it's still just an animal, and it just doesn't seem right to me," said GrizzLee.

"I'm sorry, Lee, nothing personal to the dragon. It's just time for us to go home," said Xtract. "Did I hear you say *damn*?"

GrizzLee didn't say another word.

After several minutes of the dragon flying around and screaming, Gatlin said, "Oh come on, shit. Someone find the cryin' bastard and end his ass. He's 'bout to drive me nuts, little cryin' bitch!"

Shortly after Gatlin had yelled out his thoughts on the matter, the walls again began to rumble and shake.

"What in the hell is that?" asked Pistol Smoke.

"Maybe its Wrath opening up his cage so that his little cryin' dragon can go back inside," said Bolt-action.

"X drive P-1 down toward that rumblin' and see what in the hell it is," Gatlin ordered.

Just as Xtract pulled forward, the walls opened once again. This time, two doors opened. These two doors were lower than the first three. From floor to top, they stood about twelve feet high.

"WHAT IN THE HELL IS GOIN' ON NOW?" Nuke yelled to Gatlin.

"I'm not sure, but we're about to find out," Gatlin replied. "It doesn't look like the doors are opening for that damn dragon to return. And I know damn good and well that they're not opening for us to leave. So tighten up and be on the ready. X, disregard my last and, everyone, man your positions this one aint over yet."

Once the two doors were open completely, the team couldn't believe what they were seeing right in front of their faces. Two very large figures emerged slowly from the two doors. As the figures cleared the door, the team could see what they were about to face—two beings, each standing close to ten feet tall, half man and half rhinoceros. The beings' upper halves were that of very strong men, each having not two but four extremely powerful-looking arms, and their lower halves were the powerful bodies of rhinoceroses. The shoulders, chest, torso, sides, and backs of these mutated beasts were almost completely covered in medieval-looking armor and chain mesh. Their heads were covered with iron helmets, with armor protruding from the front of the helmet down the nose bone, as well along either side of their jawlines. The two had very little flesh exposed.

Wrath's obsession with the medieval era, which everyone believes was where he came from, definitely showed itself in the beasts the team had encountered on this operation. In his four arms, one of the beasts wielded large swords, a couple of them as long as six feet. This one had some type of green hair coming from the top of his helmet. The other beast, the one that emerged second, carried an assortment of medieval weaponry. In his upper arms, he carried a crossbow with arrows that looked more like spears because of their size. In his lower right hand, he carried a gigantic, spiked ball and chain with unbelievable reach. In his lower left hand, he carries a large wooden mallet. He also had two large swords strapped to his enormous back. He, like the other beast, also had some hair poking from the top of his helmet. His hair was red.

"Well, Nuke, there's your damn answer. Are you happy?" said Gatlin.

"What in the name of all that is holy are those things?" asked Bolt-action.

"Aint no relatives of mine; I know that shit for sure," said Pistol Smoke.

"Those dudes look badass and pissed-off. This is gonna suck a lot," said Nuke, who was standing close to P-2 with Bolt-action and Pistol Smoke. All three of them looked in awe at what they were seeing. "Oh hell, we can kick their asses," decided Pistol Smoke. "Hell, they have swords and hammers. We have real weapons. No contest."

"I think you're wrong. This is going to be one hell of a brawl. I can feel it," said Bolt-action.

The green-haired rhino-man was the first of the two to step out and into the open cave. He let out a roar more powerful and horrifying than anything the team had heard before. Shortly after that, the red-haired rhino-man stepped out just behind the first. The enormous rhino-men, at first glance, did not appear to know why they had been released from their cave dwellings. The two just looked around the giant cave room. Green Hair begins to slowly walk away from the open doors behind them, followed shortly by Red Hair.

Then, from the darkness of the top of the cave, the dragon once again showed itself. It first flew over the two rhino-men. Then it flew by the team, screaming and blowing fire onto the cave floor surrounding the team.

It appeared to the team that the two rhino-men now realized why they had been released. In the glow of the burning flames, the rhino-men saw that they were not alone on the cave floor. Both walked toward the team, very methodically, looking at each other and then around at their surroundings and, finally, back at the team.

The team, still in total awe, didn't even fire a single shot at the passing dragon overhead.

"SNAP THE HELL OUT OF IT!" ordered Gatlin.

The team got their heads back in the game.

"Okay, listen up, guys. I want bazooka and RPG nonstop, along with 30s from both Pumas on the rhino dudes. I want Bolt-action and Lee to open them 80s on that fuckin' flyin' bitch. We have to get it down. There are just too many things to worry about that screaming asshole flyin' around up there. Let's do this," ordered Gatlin.

He and Nuke once again set out on foot to maneuver throughout the cave and look for open shots on their targets.

Bolt-action and GrizzLee spotted their assigned target at the same time, and they simultaneously opened fire with the fast action of the mighty 80mm cannons atop their respective Pumas. Spent 80mm shell casings soon littered the cave floor and small bursts of fire flew from the ends of the mighty cannons' barrels.

The loud noise of the awesome firepower momentarily frightened the two rhino-men. Their fright was very short-lived, as they picked up their pace from a walk to a trot. The apparent leader of the two rhino-men, the red one, made the first aggressive move toward the team. He raised and fired his giant crossbow.

"FIRE ON THOSE BITCHES!" yelled Gatlin.

The team opened up on the slowly approaching rhino-men with bazooka rounds and the combined 30mm cannon rounds from Gatlin and both vehicles' front-mounted cannons—an amount that could never be counted. Nuke switched to RPG for faster shooting and less loading. The team was hitting the rhino duo with just about every shot fired.

The two demon rhinos continued to approach without missing a step.

"What the fuck," said Xtract. "We have hit these assholes with everything we've shot, and the 30s are just bouncing off like freakin' ping-pong balls, and the RPG and bazooka rounds are just putting little dings in their armor and causing some various discolorations."

"So what in the hell do we do now?" asked Nuke.

"Stay on them," said Gatlin as he grabbed one of the bazookas off P-1. "I'll just have to find a weakness in their armor. Cover me."

"Boss, get back here," growled GrizzLee. "You don't stand a chance out there that far alone!"

As Gatlin disappeared into the darkness, the dragon reappeared. On its approach, Bolt-action and the 80mm cannon caught up and found their fast-flying target, filling its head and body with the large lead rounds. The dragon was now on a crash course.

"Bail out! Bail out!" yelled Pistol Smoke. "He's gonna hit y'all!"

The dragon, without a doubt, was on a collision course with P-1, GrizzLee, and Xtract. Blood poured from the giant scaled creature and splashed the floor of the cave like buckets of dark red paint. GrizzLee jumped from atop P-1 and rolled about twenty feet from the P-1. Xtract ran, reaching a good, safe distance just as the dragon did a death dive right into the cab of P-1 with a spectacular explosion. The team had ended one of the threats, but they'd paid a heavy price. They had lost some very valuable weapons and ammunition, as well as one of their only means of transportation.

Now the team was down to only one vehicle. Bolt-action was on the 80mm and Pistol Smoke was on the 30mm cannons from the cab of P-2. Nuke was on foot about thirty yards from the explosion of P-1. He continued his assault on the rhino-men with his RPG. GrizzLee ran over to P-2 and grabbed two M240Gs, one for each arm, along with several thousand rounds of ammunition, and covered the rear of P-2. Xtract strapped an RPG on his back and grabbed an M249 SAW and as much ammunition as he could carry and joined Nuke and Gatlin afoot.

Gatlin continued to run around in search of a vulnerable spot in the rhino duo's armor. The red rhino-man fired his crossbow at Gatlin, all the while swinging his mighty ball and chain furiously with his lower right arm. Gatlin was constantly dodging the mighty demon's every effort.

With the dragon down and out of action, the team's full efforts were now on the two rhino-men. To this point, their efforts were yet to even slowing the tandem rhino-man team down.

The green rhino-man focused on P-2, staring the vehicle down.

"HE'S CHARGIN'!" yelled Pistol Smoke.

"Okay, let's drop the motherfucker," said Bolt-action. "Open up on his four-legged ass."

Pistol Smoke fired the 30mm cannons wide open, and Bolt-action fired the 80mm cannon. From behind, GrizzLee unleashed a barrage with his awesome M240Gs on the oncoming beast. The P-2 team was scoring hits all over the charging rhino-man's body, hitting him everywhere imaginable.

"That son of a bitch ain't stoppin'. Shit, he isn't even slowin' down, dudes," yelled Pistol Smoke.

"Keep firing. This bastard has to have a weakness some damn where," called Bolt-action.

The team continued their unbelievable assault upon the ever-charging rhino-man. Moments later, the green rhino-man was within striking distance with his mighty swords. The beast swung his mighty swords. The first struck P-2's hood. The second slashed across Bolt-action's right arm, putting Bolt-action in even more pain than he was already in.

"Awe shit, he got me," said Bolt-action.

"You okay, dude?" asked Pistol Smoke.

"Yeah I'll live," Bolt-action replied. "But we need to hurry up and end this shit. I'm running out of body parts for these bitches in this cave to be fuckin' up on me."

As the rhino-man passed by the side of P-2, GrizzLee unloaded his assault on the beast at close range, with both M240Gs wide open. As GrizzLee watched the beast absorb all the punishment the team could dish out, it dawned on him that he should concentrate on the beast's arms.

The rhino-man swung his two right-hand swords at GrizzLee, missing with both. GrizzLee opened up on the beast's massive, sword-swinging arms. He tore into them with eerie precision, ripping deep into the rhino-man's arms as he slowed about twenty yards behind P-2 and turned for another attack.

"WE NEED TO TAKE OUT HIS ARMS! Concentrate on his arms!" yelled GrizzLee to the P-2 team. GrizzLee opened up on the charging beast. This time it would be the beast's left arms that would receive the majority of the punishment because they would be closest to the Puma.

GrizzLee noticed that the beast's lower right arm was just hanging on to the body by flesh; it flopped around as the rhino-man picked up his pace for his second pass. GrizzLee opened both M240Gs on the left arms of the charging beast. When the beast was approximately twenty-five feet from P-2, Bolt-action joined GrizzLee's assault, using the 80mm cannon on the arms of the massive beast.

GrizzLee was struck in the upper left shoulder with an arrow that the red-haired rhino-man had shot from across the dark cave room. The giant, five-foot arrow forced GrizzLee's body to twist and momentarily stopped his assault on the green rhino-man.

Bolt-action, however, continued his assault, and the tandem assault finally paid off, when the beast's lower left arm was amputated. The giant's arm lay just a few feet from GrizzLee. The rhino-man slowed ever so slightly and cried out in apparent pain.

Both Bolt-action and Pistol Smoke continued firing on the beast as Green Hair finished his ride-by attack. They focused on his remaining three arms, preventing the rhino-man from even swinging his mighty swords. All three of his remaining arms were badly damaged; large chunks of flesh and bone had been removed by hot, heavy lead. The green rhino-man disappeared into the darkness.

"Oh, yeah, baby, we ripped that son of a bitch a new one on that attack," said Pistol Smoke. "Great idea about the arms; truly outstanding work, Lee."

Nuke came over to P-2 to give them some support. He knew that both Xtract and Gatlin were staying on the move with the red rhino-man. The creature wasn't quick enough to keep up with them. The beast slipped a lot; the cave floor and his body style weren't compatible.

"I just came over to see how things were going on my way over to flank that red bastard over there," said Nuke. "Damn, Bolt-action, you all right?"

"I've been better, but I'll live," Bolt-action told him.

"Hey, Nuke, tell Gatlin and X that we figured out how to slow 'em down and maybe stop 'em," Pistol Smoke said. "We need to blow their arms off. That was Lee's great idea."

"Cool, I'll relay the message, Smoke. How are you, Lee?" asked Nuke.

From behind the P-2, GrizzLee gave Nuke a thumbs-up.

"Good work, Lee," said Nuke. "I'm outta here. Stay safe. We'll be done here in just a few. Later." Nuke took off in the direction of the area where Gatlin and Xtract were battling the red rhino-man.

Pistol Smoke reloaded the 30mm cannons, and Bolt-action reloaded the 80mm cannon.

Behind P-2 and out of sight of his team, GrizzLee applied pressure to his left shoulder and chest with his right hand. Blood just continued to pour out of the wound with every beat of his heart. GrizzLee slowly slid to the floor of the cave and sat with his back against the rear bumper, one M240G in his right hand and the other laying within arm's reach, cocked and ready for another attack. He knew that he was in bad shape, but there just wasn't time to do what needed to be done. He wouldn't put his teammates in harm's way while they worked on him, so he decided to just wait until this one was over. As GrizzLee waited for another attack, he just looked at the giant's arm lying in front of him, still slightly twitching and grasping onto the massive sword.

*   *   *

When Nuke reached Gatlin and Xtract, they were both in a battle with Red Hair. The men were giving it everything they had. Gatlin's guns began to overheat and slow considerably.

"GATLIN, WE HAVE TO BLOW THEIR DAMN ARMS OFF!" yelled Nuke.

From the darkness, Nuke was viciously struck from behind in the back, shoulder, and neck with one of the mighty swords of the already very badly wounded green rhino-man. The blow knocked Nuke to the hard floor of the dark cave. As blood leaked from Nuke's wound, his body lay motionless.

"No!" cried Gatlin. Gatlin witnessed the brutal and, to him, cowardly attack on his little brother. As the green rhino-man rode by Gatlin, Gatlin dodged the swings of his massive swords. It was clear that the beast's wounds were preventing him from controlling his weapons as well as he once had been able to.

The green rhino-man turned and came back to finish Nuke off. Xtract was keeping the red rhino-man at bay with

RPG rounds to the body and countless M249 SAW rounds to his multiple massive arms. As Green Hair approached Nuke, Gatlin's guns had just cooled enough to mount an attack of his own. So as the beast passed Gatlin's location, not even acknowledging Gatlin, Gatlin grabbed the giant's neck and threw himself up onto the creature's back. He jammed his cannon into the back of Green Hair's neck, just under his armor, and opened fire.

Gatlin rode the beast as if he'd done this before, all the while blowing holes into the raging beast's neck and shoulders. The rhino-man's blood was covering Gatlin and was beginning to puddle in the beast's back. Gatlin noticed that the arms and swords of Wrath's wicked creation were beginning to get a little too close, so he refocused his attack, firing into the rhino-man's remaining three arms.

In a matter of minutes, the beast was down to only one arm and was screaming, roaring, and bucking, in an attempt to get Gatlin off of his back. But nothing was working for him. He slowed very noticeably. Blood continued to puddle in his own back.

With the beast now unable to fight back, Gatlin went for the finishing attack. He shoved his awesome gun up and under the back of Green Hair's armor helmet and fired.

At first, some of the rounds were coming back and striking Gatlin's gun, but shortly, as Gatlin dug his gun in deeper, the rounds stopped coming back and started going in and staying in. Some even came out the sides and front of the beast's head. The green rhino-man slowed to a walk. Then the walk turned to a stumble, and the last sword just dragged along the floor to Green Hair's side. Black blood and very little gray matter spilled out from under the beast's helmet.

The green rhino-man stumbled more and more with every step, and then he began to fall. Gatlin jumped from the rhino-man's back, just as the beast fell to the floor, no longer moving.

Gatlin walked up to the beast. It was still breathing very heavily through its mouth. Gatlin shoved his MFG-25 handgun into Green Hair's mouth and unloaded the entire twenty-five-round clip into the mouth of the creature that had viscously and cowardly attacked his little brother.

"It's a family thing," said Gatlin to the beast as he kicked the rhino-man's face and popped in another clip. He turned and walked away.

"ONE DOWN, ONE MORE PUSSY TO GO!" yelled Gatlin as he made his way over to Nuke.

As the green rhino-man fell, the red one stopped his attack and retreated, disappearing into the darkness of the cave.

Gatlin reached Nuke just as Xtract did. "Son of a bitch, Gatlin, he's breathing, but he's out like a light. We have to get him back to P-2 before that asshole returns to finish him off," said Xtract.

"Help me get him over my shoulders. I'll carry him over, and you can cover us," said Gatlin.

Xtract and Gatlin managed to get Nuke back to P-2 without incident.

"Oh shit. No way. Not Nuke. Get him in here," said Pistol Smoke.

With help from Xtract and Pistol Smoke, Gatlin got Nuke into P-2's cab so that Xtract could work on him. As the dome light came on, the team could see the seriousness of Nuke's wounds. He was not only bleeding from the wicked slash from the sword, he was also bleeding from the nose and ears and even the right eye. He had a busted lip, probably from falling motionless, face-first to the floor of the cave. His nose was definitely broken.

The team was all once again together at P-2. They had one beast down and one to go. They have paid a very heavy price and all in the name of apprehending Wrath, who they had yet to even see. Gatlin and Pistol Smoke both had suffered burns on their legs. Only one of Gatlin's arm cannons was working at 100 percent, and he had too many holes in him to count. Bolt-action had the worst busted leg that any of them had ever seen, as well as a huge gash in his right arm. Xtract had various wounds and acid burns. GrizzLee had a giant gash across his back and an arrow wound to his shoulder and chest area that had produced a hole the size of a golf ball, the latter of which the rest of the team knew nothing about. Then there was Nuke and his extremely serious wound that the team was working on now. The team was down to one vehicle. They were running low on medical supplies and rations, lower on ammunition, and still lower on fuel. More importantly, they were running out of time.

But right now, those shortages were the least of their worries. They had to stabilize Nuke in a place where you wouldn't want to so much as change a Band-Aid. But they had no choice.

An eerie silence now filled the cave. Xtract stabilized Nuke and forced Gatlin to get his gash and dragon burns taken care of. Then he fixed Bolt-action's arm up. "How are you doing, Lee?" he asked.

"I got the rear covered; just fix them up," answered GrizzLee. He continued to listen to what seemed to him to be something else coming their way. He was quite sure that the rest of the team couldn't hear the noise, but he could. And he knew that something other than the red rhino-man was coming for them. He could feel the red rhino-man circling P-2 just out of the lights, in the darkness of the cave, waiting, looking, watching, and preparing for his next attack on the team. GrizzLee began to get a little cold, and he was becoming light-headed. But he remained at his post and covered the rear for the team.

After several minutes, Bolt-action said, "Hey, do y'all hear that? It's coming from behind us."

The walls were rumbling ever so slightly.

"Lee, can you tell where that noise is coming from?" asked Gatlin.

"Yes, sir," replied GrizzLee. "It's coming from the south of us."

"Well can you tell if it is getting closer or not?" asked Gatlin.

"Yes, sir, it is definitely getting closer. Whatever it is, it's coming in shortly," said GrizzLee.

"Well, shit, that's about right. Okay, listen up," ordered Gatlin. "Lee, you continue to cover the rear and keep us posted on that damn noise. Bolt-action, you get back on the 80. Smoke, you stay in the cab with Nuke and man the 30s. And *do not* let Nuke out of the cab if he does come to, no matter what you hear or what he says, even if you have to knock him back out. X and I are gonna have to go find that other rhino dude before whatever is on the other side of that wall comes in here with us.

"Take your posts and let's be sharp and end this thing, if it's ever gonna end."

Gatlin and Xtract went back out on foot to hunt down the red rhino-man.

The walls continued to rumble, and the rumbling grew louder and louder. Gatlin moved off to the west, and Xtract headed east.

The rest of the team members were all at their posts and ready to get it on once again. GrizzLee was still in a sitting position, but he was becoming very disoriented as he continued to try and slow the bleeding. The stop in the action had helped a lot, but the blood was still flowing.

* * *

Xtract spotted the red rhino-man. The creature was standing almost in the same spot where the men had first seen the beast, as if wanting back in.

I see you, Xtract said to himself.

The beast didn't see Xtract. But Red Hair did rear up and run in the opposite direction. Xtract realized that the rhino-man wasn't retreating; he was heading toward Gatlin. Xtract opened fire with his M249 SAW.

Gatlin, hearing the shots, noticed the rhino-man charging. He hunkered down behind a huge boulder that had fallen at some point during the battle and awaited the beast. As Red Hair approached, Gatlin readied his gun.

All the while, Xtract, giving chase, continued to fire on the creature.

When Red Hair was about eight feet away from him, Gatlin rose up from behind the boulder and yelled, "HIT THE DECK. I'M FIRING!"

Gatlin's onslaught against the raging beast hit Red Hair all across the front of his body armor, and just a few of his rounds hit their target—the beast's arms—as Red Hair passed at a rate of speed that neither Gatlin nor Xtract had seen the demon rhino possess until now. The red rhino-man didn't miss a step or pay any attention to Gatlin's attack as he passed him by, as if Gatlin wasn't even there.

At that point, Gatlin and Xtract realized that Red Hair wasn't charging Gatlin at all. The beast was heading for the P-2 crew. With no communications and no way of warning the rest of the team that an enraged demon rhino-man was on a collision course with them, the two could only hope that the team had completed first aid and returned to their posts, ready for what was heading for them at a very high rate of rage and speed.

Xtract and Gatlin had to take an indirect route back to the P-2 crew to prevent getting caught in the crossfire and getting hit with friendly fire.

"Okay lets double time it now!" ordered Gatlin.

The two raced toward the rest of the team.

*   *   *

The team was on alert. They all heard the unmistakable sound of Gatlin's guns. Now the P-2 crew could hear and even feel the ever-approaching red rhino-man.

"Ready yourselves," ordered Bolt-action.

They all pulled back the hammers on their weapons. Seconds later, emerging from the darkness like an out-of-control locomotive on a crash course with P-2, was the red rhino-man.

"FIRE, FIRE!" ordered Bolt-action.

Again, the P-2 crew launched a lethal assault on the charging rhino-man. The beast pulled back on his crossbow. He fired, hitting Bolt-action in the leg and actually pinning him to the chair of the 80mm cannon turnstile. Bolt-action yelled out in pain as Pistol Smoke continued to spray 30mm rounds into the arms of the enraged and out-of-control creature.

The beast passed P-2, swinging his mighty spiked ball and chain at Bolt-action. Bolt-action tried to get out of the way, but he was pinned to the chair, and the solid, steel, spiked ball landed in his ribs, breaking too many to count just then. Bolt-action simply bent over in pain. Quietly, he coughed up blood. Unable to as much as turn the 80mm cannon, he was unable to defend himself and, literally, stuck in a very bad way.

Xtract and Gatlin were still in pursuit of the enraged beast, but neither of them could keep up with the speed or the pace of the four-legged creature.

The rhino-man turned and came back for another attack, this time focusing on P-2's rear. GrizzLee, just about completely out of it, didn't even get off a shot.

This time, as the rhino-man passed the vehicle, he focused on the front-mounted 30mm cannons that Pistol Smoke had never stopped firing at him. Smoke's rounds had ripped deep into all four arms, but this demon was on a mission to kill and/or be killed. The rhino-man slammed his giant hammer down onto the ever-firing 30mm cannon, totally destroying the gun.

The red demon rhino-man turned once again for another attack. This time he charged the side of P-2. Bolt-action tried to regain his composure and fire, but the beast was much too fast. The beast swung on Bolt-action once again. Luckily for Bolt-action, the demon missed.

As the rhino-man passed P-2's rear, GrizzLee rose up and, with one swing of the mighty, five-foot sword from the amputated arm of the green rhino-man, connected with the throat of the beast. The beast's head flew nearly fifteen feet into the air before returning to the cave floor.

The headless body of the beast ran past P-2, blood shooting from its open neck. Moments later, the headless body dove into the cave floor and never moved again.

"Oh hell yeah, lee. Fuckin' good job. Did you see that fucker's head fly through the air? That was sick!" yelled Pistol Smoke from the cab.

Xtract and Gatlin finally made it back to P-2. "Good job, people," said Gatlin. "Damn good job."

"Hey, give me a hand with Bolt-action," said Pistol Smoke. "He's pinned to the chair, and he's all busted up inside."

Xtract and Pistol Smoke gently got Bolt-action unstuck and down from the chair, while Gatlin checked on Nuke. While Xtract was administering first aid to Bolt-action's new wounds, Pistol smoke stood by, looking at the south wall. He had momentarily forgotten about the rumbling, but the noise was definitely louder now and whatever was making it was closer.

GrizzLee emerges from the rear of P-2 with the demon's sword still in his hand and covered in blood. GrizzLee didn't say a word. His eyes just rolled back into his head, and he fell to one knee and then immediately to the floor.

The team rushed to GrizzLee's side. Gatlin emerged from the cab and helped Xtract and Pistol Smoke get the giant lifeless body of GrizzLee over to the side of P-2 so that they could fix the fallen warrior up, or at least try.

Xtract knelt beside his friend and did an initial examination. "Shit," he told the others, "this is his blood. Fuck, I thought it belonged to that fucker over there." He motioned toward the headless rhino-man. "My God he's been hit with an arrow, and it wasn't from this fight either. Why didn't y'all tell me how bad he was? Damn, he's lost a lot of blood."

"Damn, X, we didn't even know that he was hit," said Pistol Smoke. "You know Lee. He aint gonna tell you that he's hurt; unless you see it happen, you don't know."

"X, can you fix him?" asked a very concerned Gatlin.

"I'll do what I can, but shit, man, we lost most of our medical on P-1, damn near all the plasma," said Xtract.

"That aint no fuckin' answer, X," snapped Gatlin.

"I'll do my best, but Lee is going to have to help me.

"He's not going to be able to help us at all with whatever is on the other side of that damn wall," Xtract added. "But if y'all can keep whatever it is at bay for awhile, I can try and get him stabilized."

"That's better," said Gatlin. "Smoke, it looks like it's me and you, bud. You get up in the chair, and I'll cover the rear. We have to keep whatever it is off our wounded, so whatever it takes, bud.

"Here, Bolt-action," he added, handing Bolt-action one of the M240Gs that GrizzLee had been using and an ammo box. "Let's do it. If it gets real hot and you have Lee stabilized, feel free to join in, X. Bolt-action can cover Lee and Nuke."

"Oh you can count on me," Xtract assured him. "I'll be in this one until the very end. Our big friend is just exhausted. You know, he hasn't slept on this op at all. We all know that Lee needs to sleep every day. Plus, he's lost a lot of blood. If it comes to it, we'll all go down together."

The noise was louder than ever; whatever was coming was undeniably on the verge of finding them.

"What's the old saying," asked Pistol Smoke, "'we all survive or we all die.' Is that where we are now?"

"No," replied Gatlin adamantly. "Smoke, we are gonna win this one. I just know, so don't even ask me how. I just have a real good feeling about it."

"Yeah right. You're a very shitty liar also," replied Pistol smoke.

Nothing else was said as the two sat on either sides of P-2's rear bumper on the ready and looked at the now crumbling south wall.

Rocks and boulders shot from the cave walls and crashed to the floor.

"Here it comes," said Pistol Smoke.

"Yup," replied Gatlin. "On my mark."

The two took defensive positions on one knee and took aim on the crumbling south wall. Nuke awakened and walked out to be by Gatlin and Pistol Smoke. Nuke raised his RPG. The three just look at one another, not saying a word, and turned their attention back to the south wall.

The crashing boulders began to get larger, and some of the debris even managed to reach the team. Then a thin ray of sunlight—something that the team hadn't seen in a very long time—shot into the cave.

"Son of a bitch," cried Nuke. "This thing is coming in from outside."

As the wall fell to pieces, the once-dark cave was now filled with the light of the outdoors, of an apparently sunny day. The bright light completely blinded the entire team.

"Gatlin, come in. Can you hear me? Can you hear me? This is Stealth over the PA of The Crow."

"OH HELL YEAH!" Nuke raised his arms in a cheer, unable to contain his joy. "YOU HEAR THAT? THAT'S THE SWEET VOICE OF STEALTH. WE ARE GOING HOME. FUCKIN' A."

"Everyone, stay put. I'll go get her attention since there are no comms in this fuckin' cave," Gatlin ordered.

He made his way toward the south wall, which was now the team's exit. He had to get Stealth to land The Crow so they could get their wounded aboard.

As Gatlin stepped outside the cave, his headset began to work. "Hey, Stealth," he radioed, "you have no idea how glad we are to see you. Listen, we have wounded out the ass. Lee is bad. We don't know if he will last much longer. Bolt-action can't be moved. Nuke is in bad shape. I'm not sure how we are gonna get them out of here, but we have to get them some help pronto."

"I have Shadow, Blade, Crosshairs, and Nitro on board. Can they help move the wounded?" asked Stealth.

"No, they are literally gonna have to be carried out of there," Gatlin told her.

"Well okay," replied Stealth. "How big is that space in there?"

"It's fuckin' huge," Gatlin said.

"Spoken like a true hero." Stealth's tone was a mix of pride and teasing. "Keep your team clear. Crosshairs will blast a big enough hole and I'll put The Crow in there with you."

"Go for it," replied Gatlin. "Give me about five minutes to get back to P-2. Then do your thing."

"Copy that. Five minutes," said Stealth.

* * *

Eleven minutes later, The Crow had landed in the cave for evacuation. Stealth opened the rear bay door of The Crow, and Shadow, Blade, and Nitro rolled out three gurneys and rushed to P-2's side, where they found Xtract still working on GrizzLee, with a battered Bolt-action sitting by their sides.

"Oh, my gosh," gasped Shadow. "What happened here? What happened to all my big tough guys? My goodness, you all are a mess, every one of you."

"We'll tell you everything on the flight home," said Xtract. "Let's get Lee on The Crow ASAP and hooked up to some plasma."

Within three minutes, both GrizzLee and Bolt-action were loaded aboard The Crow. GrizzLee was immediately hooked to the onboard life support system, and Nitro and Shadow were taking care of him. Blade and Xtract worked on Bolt-action. Stealth helped Nuke to his bed and got his IV going. Crosshairs remained outside The Crow, keeping watch.

As Pistol Smoke and Gatlin finished loading P-2 onto The Crow, Crosshairs returned to the front and the bay door closed.

"Is that everything?" asked Stealth.

"No, not quite," said Gatlin. "See that north wall over there? Fire a half a dozen bunker buster missiles into that wall before we exit," he ordered.

"Copy that," said Stealth.

Stealth got The Crow up just outside the cave and turned toward the north wall. She gave the order to her gunner, Crosshairs, to fire. Four, five, six bunker buster missiles tore into the north wall, penetrating at least thirty feet into the side of the cave wall.

"Good?" asked Stealth.

"Well done. Let's go home now," said Gatlin.

Stealth turned The Crow around and gave her full throttle. She reached her flying altitude of thirty-five thousand feet in just seconds.

"We are going home, people," said Gatlin. "Operation Ice Cap is history."

"Amen," chorused those of Ice Cap's team who were conscious.

About halfway across the Atlantic Ocean, Blade asked Gatlin, "Did you get Wrath?"

"We didn't even see the bastard," Gatlin told her. "But I can tell you for sure that we put a hurt on his operation. He won't be goin' solo for awhile. He'll be back with Legion in no time—that is, if those half dozen bunker busters that Crosshairs sent into the north wall didn't take him out."

"Time will tell, my friend," said Xtract.

No one on The Crow asked about the mission. They all knew that the team would tell them all about it when they were ready. For now the operation Ice Cap team just wanted rest; they slept the rest of the way home. Stealth cued up some Bad Company on the stereo for them to listen to in their sleep.